COLLIDE INTO YOU

a touch of magic novel

Kelly Washington

Kelly Washington
P.O. Box 650092
Sterling, Virginia 20165-0092
www.kellywashington.com
kellywashwrites@gmail.com

Cover Design © 2015 Anita B. Carroll (race-point.com)
Edited by Susan Helene Gottfried (westofmars.com)
Proofread by Dayle Dermatis (soulsroadpress.com)

ISBN-13: 978-0-9906758-0-8 (Kelly Washington)
Collide Into You, Kelly Washington. -- 1st ed.

She's an army sergeant who sticks to the rules. He's a womanizer who loves breaking the rules. She hates him and he sorta can't stand her. By some freak accident (or was it?) they swap bodies, a la Freaky Friday. What can possibly go wrong?

When Army Sergeant Keira Holtslander, an orderly and rule-loving intelligence analyst, is reassigned to the Pentagon for a special assignment, she agrees to room with her brother's best friend, Dillan. But there's a problem. Several, in fact. He's sarcastic, egotistical, full of himself, extremely attractive, and a womanizer. Within a matter of days, her life is chaos. *She didn't like him when they met nine years ago, and her opinion isn't likely to change now.*

Businessman Dillan Pope has learned to use his looks, charm, and sexual skills to his advantage. Women easily tumble into his bed and business deals come about effortlessly. But when his best friend's little sister moves in, he knows he's in trouble. She's rather hostile toward him, which takes him by surprise. Not even his patented smile works on her. *But maybe that's why Keira, aka Sergeant Prim and Proper, has always been the one girl he hasn't been able to forget since their first meeting, nine years ago.*

When a meddling barista puts a charm on the roommates, causing them to swap bodies, they have less than one week to work together and undo the switch, or live forever in the others body.

But first, they must get along.

Maybe there's a reason they hated each other. And admitting the feelings that lay hidden may be the only way to undo the switch.

For my son -
who is my very own piece of magic.

CHAPTER ONE

Keira

"Wow," a masculine voice says from across the living room. Not *to* me. *At* me. And he says the word "wow" in two syllables. *Wow-wa.* It is my roommate, Dillan. Or, rather, I'm *his* new roommate. *Did he always have to talk so sarcastically?* I wait for his next comment. "Keira, whatever the opposite of amazing is, *that's* how you look today."

I look down at what I'm wearing, which is my Army Combat Uniform, or ACUs for short. My hair is pulled up in a low bun and, in the interest of time, I'm wearing pretty much zero makeup. I look exactly like what a twenty-seven-year-old staff sergeant in the Army is supposed to look like: like every other female staff sergeant in the Army.

I'm fairly close to being late for my first day at the Pentagon, and the last thing I need is for the man-slut I'm rooming with to harass me. I don't care that he's my brother's best friend, or that I've always had a secret *love-hate* crush on him, or that his abs are totally to die for and that looking at him is like looking directly at the sun. I'm rooming with him only because I need a place to crash before I find my own place.

Look away, Keira! Those abs will totally blind you.

My older brother, Jon, who's in the Navy and deployed to Bahrain, asked Dillan to let me stay here after the Army reassigned me to Washington, DC.

Dillan, shirtless and drying his hair, stands just outside his bedroom door. His wide-open bedroom door. Beyond him, I can see a naked female form sleeping on his bed. She's blond, leggy, and those are totally fake breasts.

Secret *love-hate* crush aside, in truth, after living here for only two days, I've come to the realization that I sort of don't like him. I'm glad that the living room separates our two bedrooms. Seriously, I don't want to hear sounds coming from his room at night. Not after what I heard yesterday.

I'm tired of trying to *not* look at Dillan, so I glance out the window. I still cannot believe that I'm living in a high-rise apartment with an amazing view of the Capitol, the Washington Monument, and the Lincoln Memorial. Too bad it came with a man-slut.

I try to figure out what Dillan's talking about when his lips curve in a victorious manner. I've been silent too long after the insult.

"What?" I ask, tilting my head. "Are you not used to women being clothed in front of you? Perhaps you're not exactly sure how buttons and all those crazy little fastening thingies work? Listen, can we insult each other later? I've got to catch the Metro."

He grins as he reaches for a shirt of his own, a blue, collared shirt, and purposefully buttons it up slowly, as if to illustrate that, yes, he knows how to dress himself. *What an accomplishment*, I think. *Whatever will he do next? Use his finger to pick his nose?*

I smile at the juvenile thought.

Dillan crosses the distance between us as he tucks the shirt into tailored trousers. He cleans up nicely. I know he isn't some bum. He works at a prestigious firm as some bigwig's senior executive assistant. Let me clarify: That bigwig boss is a woman. And if I've learned anything about Dillan Pope in the two days that I've been his roommate *and* from all the stories Jon has told me over the last few years, it's that he can charm anyone.

Myself excluded, of course. I find something unattractive about overly attractive men. Sort of.

My roommate clears his throat as if he has some big announcement. I roll my eyes and look at my watch. *Hint, hint, buddy.*

"I was just going to say that you looked much better this morning after you came in from your run," he says in a low voice. I study his chiseled jaw, his light green eyes, and his dark hair. Not that I was smelling him or anything, but he smells like sandalwood.

My run? That was two hours ago. "Can you please make sense, *Devon*?"

He chuckles. "It's Dillan, but you already knew that. Don't act like I don't affect you. I mean—" he shrugs "—I really don't care one way or the other. You're not my type." He slips on his shoes and folds his suit jacket over his arm and turns to go. "But, for the record, *Sergeant Holtslander*," he says with a smirk, "I certainly like the little running outfit a whole hell of a lot better than whatever that—" he motions up and down "—shapeless uniform is called."

He winks as he leaves the apartment.

I stare at the closed door and wonder, not for the first time in the last thirty-six hours, *what have I gotten myself into?*

Dillan

I leave the apartment with a little pep in my step and walk to one of my favorite places, Ellen's Corner Bakery, and wait in the usual long line. While not technically on a *corner*, Ellen's bakery feels like your grandmother's home. Your grandmother's home on steroids.

Mismatched, cushy chairs push up next to kitschy, antique tables. The walls are covered with famous faces, old newspaper clippings, artistic findings from all over the world, and, near the register, an older-looking wedding photo of a soldier and a young bride is on display. I love the place. So does everyone else, as evidenced by the long line.

While I wait my turn, I can't help but think about Jon's little sister.

Keira is cute, adorable, and, well, okay, she's freaking hot. I remember her little running outfit from this morning, which consisted of not much more than an orange sports bra and tiny—and I mean tiny—lime green running shorts. The outfit was bright enough to land planes.

It certainly landed *my* attention.

At six a.m., Keira returned from her workout. The lights were out. She didn't notice me at the fridge, drinking milk straight from the carton. But I sure as hell noticed her. God, those tan legs, her slim waist, and her dewy, sweaty skin. I wanted to bathe her right then and there.

With my tongue.

And when she bent over and began to stretch out...I nearly choked on the milk.

"You're deep in thought this morning, Dillan," the

cashier-slash-baker-slash-owner, Ellen, says.

She is a young fifty-year-old lady who I have seen every morning since moving to Washington, DC, seven years ago.

I add up the math... I've seen Ellen at least 2,555 times. Sometimes I am here *twice* a day. That's a lot of coffee. And muffins. And innocent flirting.

"You know I can't start my day without seeing you, Ellen," I tell her, grinning, and order the usual: a large black coffee. I can't help but flirt with her. "If I were thirty years older, sweetie, I'd romance you like it was no one's business."

"Careful what you wish for," she says in her sweet-as-pie voice. She stares at me in a manner that seems way too intense. "And I'm fairly certain that the thoughts running through that handsome head of yours would make Lucifer blush."

I get the feeling that in some other life, she might have been a witch. She gives off that vibe.

"Lucifer, yeah, but not you, Ellen."

"True," she says with a laugh as she makes coffee for another customer. Ellen points to a sign above her head that announces her bakery's thirtieth anniversary party next Tuesday. "Did you get the invite?"

"I wouldn't miss it for the world."

She smiles brightly. "And how's the new roommate? Jon's sister is renting your second bedroom, right?"

I wonder if Keira drank coffee. *Did it matter?*

"If you're asking me if she's cute, the answer is yes, but I can tell she's as boring as a snail. *Sergeant Prim and Proper.* She probably does twenty push-ups at every Metro stop."

Ellen arches an eyebrow. "You've told me all I need to know, Dillan," she says in a manner that suggests she believes just the opposite of what I said. Her eyes sparkle. "I can't wait to meet her."

"Oh, no you don't," I say. "I have no intention of bringing her here. You are mine, Ellen."

She laughs at my possessiveness.

"She's a soldier?" she asks. I nod yes. "Slim, five-foot-eight, with brown eyes and brown hair? Caramel skin? Is her last name Holtslander?"

I wonder if she has a magic crystal ball behind the counter.

"How on earth did you guess all that?"

"Because I'm standing right here, you idiot," Keira says with a biting tone. Without my realizing it, she was standing at the front of the line. "*Sergeant Prim and Proper* loves coffee, and the sign outside is big enough for a boring snail to see it."

"So you heard everything?" Even the *cute* part?

Ellen looks back and forth between us with a gleeful smile.

"Like I care," Keira says as she pours a pound of cream and sugar in her coffee and places a lid on top. She returns her attention to Ellen. "It was very nice to meet you. I'll see you again tomorrow."

I watch as Keira puts on her Army beret and leaves the store without acknowledging me at all.

"I like her already," Ellen says, and smiles so large that I can count all of her teeth. "You could use a challenge, Dillan Pope."

I nearly glare at Ellen, but then realize it wouldn't be respectful to glare at her.

"What's that supposed to mean? I could use a challenge?"

Ellen only laughs. "Aren't you going to be late for

work?"

I groan. "See you tomorrow."

I walk to work and take the elevator to the fourteenth floor of the Brookshire Mierkle Building in the Federal Triangle area in Washington, DC, and think, *what have I gotten myself into?*

CHAPTER TWO

Keira

I catch the blue line to the Pentagon Metro Station and get jostled around in the Metro car for two stops before I eagerly exit and practically run up the escalator. I exit the Metro station and, up top, a Pentagon security guard inspects my military ID and allows me to enter through the visitor's section.

Once inside, I turn immediately to the right, enter the Pentagon badging office, take a number, and wait for it to be called.

I'm supposed to meet my military sponsor at nine. The clock on the wall reads 8:55. Good, I have five minutes to bristle about my jerk-face roommate.

How could Dillan Pope be best friends with my brother? So they went to college together. Big deal. Jon's my hero. He's an amazing officer in the Navy, he's well read, and he has the most amazing boyfriend, Tanner.

Dillan's hot. I get that. He makes good money. But he's too sarcastic. He probably has sex with anyone who nods in his direction. And he looks at me as if I've got warts all over my face. There is no way on earth he could ever make it in the military. Of the nine years I've been enlisted, three have been in war zones. I've experienced things that would make his skin crawl.

I am not as boring as a snail, and I'm sure as hell not *Sergeant Prim and Proper*. I can be fun. I can be sexy. I like to hike and bike and run marathons. Those are definitely *un*boring things. I just can't do anything that will jeopardize my security clearance, like binge drinking, gambling, or stripping at parties.

Not that I would do those things even if I didn't need a security clearance.

An automated system calls my number and two minutes later, I walk out with my unsmiling face pasted on a white badge. I clip it to the pocket on the front of my uniform. Congratulations to me: the Pentagon has welcomed its newest member.

"Staff Sergeant Holtslander?"

I turn around to face the voice. If I'm not mistaken, it had a Texas twang to it.

A male staff sergeant shakes my hand. "I'm Justin Hauten. I am the junior enlisted advisor to the Chief of Staff of the Army and I'm your sponsor."

If anyone can give Dillan a run for his money in the looks department, it would be Staff Sergeant Justin Hauten. The way he said his last name, it sounded like Hot-In.

Yes you are, I think. I inspect him. He looks great in a uniform. I wouldn't call him classically handsome; I can tell he's had his nose broken a few times, but he's ruggedly good-looking with a lopsided smile that could easily melt hearts and land him on the cover of a few "most handsome" magazines.

I notice the black ring on his ring finger, which declares: Not available.

"Hi, yup, that's me, Keira Holtslander, Sergeant Prim and Proper."

"I'm sorry, what? Is that a nickname?" His thick eyebrows furrow briefly.

I laugh. "No, sorry. I was thinking of something else and it slipped out. Let me start over. I'm Keira Holtslander."

Sergeant Hauten nods. He seems friendly, but not overly

friendly.

"Let's walk and talk. I'll give you the quick tour since I know that this is your first time at the Pentagon. Then you'll meet the team. Your introductory office call with Colonel Benson is at thirteen hundred. He's a great guy and you'll like him a lot. He just returned from Kabul, Afghanistan. I read your file. You've been deployed a couple of times, right?"

I like that he didn't feel compelled to discuss the weather or other inane facts. Instantly, I can tell that he didn't see a *female* in front of him, he saw a *soldier*. From this point forward, I know that he'll be an ally.

He leads us through a turnstile. I swipe my new badge and we go up another set of escalators. When we get to the top, he halts in a large hallway that he calls "the concourse." It reminds me of an airport, but without the planes. The hallway is huge, and it appears you can buy anything from food to greeting cards. You can even open a bank account. Also, while I'm not entirely sure, I'm fairly certain I smell roasted nuts.

I tell him about my overseas deployments. "I had a tour in Baghdad in 2006 and two twelve-month tours in Afghanistan. One in 2009 and the other in 2012. Before my reassignment here, I was stationed at Fort Bragg and worked for the JSOC intelligence chief."

The sergeant cringes. "I have a feeling you are going to be a bit out of your element here." He leads us down the hallway and we walk up an inclined ramp.

"Why do you say that?" I ask. He's not good at hiding the fact that he doesn't think I'll enjoy my new assignment. Or maybe he doesn't think I'm qualified. I try not to bristle at the thought.

"The billet Colonel Benson has placed you in isn't an

intelligence billet."

I think about this for a second. It isn't unusual to work in a different field from what you are trained in, but it generally isn't too far from the norm. For example, the Army would never put me in an infantry position. I don't have the training.

"What will I be doing, then?" I ask.

He cringes again. I can tell that Sergeant Hauten is an intelligent soldier, but he's not an intelligence specialist. He comes across as an infantry soldier, which seems a little out of place in a place like the Pentagon. I wonder how he got his position.

"Colonel Benson will brief you on your job description at thirteen hundred today." He pauses as if he expects me to question him, but I don't, so he continues. "Anyway, let me orient you."

We stop at the top of the ramp. It's a junction of sorts. In front of us, there is a massive set of stairs as well as three different hallways. Also, from this vantage point, I can see outside into the inner courtyard. My brother told me that the Pentagon often holds concerts there in the summertime.

But I can already tell that I'm going to get lost. What I need is a map.

Sergeant Hauten starts pointing and explaining. "This is the innermost ring, the A Ring, and we're at the beginning of the 9th Corridor. Each office has a unique number that identifies where it is in the building. Think of it like a spoke of a bicycle wheel."

"Uh huh," I murmur. I can imagine a bicycle easily.

"There are five rings, A through E; five floors, one through five, but if you count the basement and the mezzanine levels, then it gets a bit complicated. I've been here a year, and I still get confused if I have to go downstairs. Anyway, for each corridor, one through ten—i.e. the bicycle's spokes, generally speaking—if you're walking from the inner ring to the outer ring and the office number ends in 0-50, go left at the office number's corresponding ring identifier. If it ends is 51-99, go right. If you're walking in the opposite direction, do the opposite. I'm sure you get the idea."

Okay. The Army has not trained me for this system. "Should I be taking notes? I feel like there's a test at the end of all this."

He laughs. I didn't think it was possible, but when he smiles, it makes him even *more* attractive.

"You'll get the hang of it. Everyone gets lost. All I want you to care about right now is how to find our office and how to find the Metro entrance. Our office is 2E801."

"Two echo eight oh one," I repeat.

"It's located on the second floor, the E Ring, in Corridor 8, room 01."

I process the sentence. "Oh, now it makes sense. That doesn't sound too hard."

He laughs again, like maybe he's convinced I'm mental. "I'm glad you feel that way because I'm going to make you lead me there."

Dillan

My boss, LouAnn Britton, calls me into her office as soon as I arrive, which she almost never does. LouAnn is an attractive woman in her fifties who has worked long and hard to earn a corner office and the title of senior vice president of Brookshire Mierkle Industries.

Seven years ago, she took a chance on me right out of college, and I've been her senior executive assistant ever since. Many within the company think I'm sleeping with her, or that I *have* slept with her, and that's how I earned the senior position.

While a somewhat accurate depiction of my womanizing ways—and seven years ago, I might have actually done something like that for a job—the rumors are, however, untrue. I've known the gossip for quite a while, and LouAnn only heard about it last year. I think she laughed for ten minutes straight after asking me if I knew what everyone was saying.

Another rumor surfaced last week. A rumor that I was LouAnn's biological son. Obviously, this is something my actual mother would object to hearing, but it's now out there and I assume that this is why LouAnn practically *ordered* me inside her office the second my feet landed on the fourteenth floor.

The receptionist, who hates my guts for some reason, didn't even have time to give me a curt greeting before telling me my boss wanted to see me.

"I have a job for you," LouAnn says after closing her office door. We are alone in her office, as usual, and I sit in my normal chair in front of her massive glass desk. Behind her, I can see the Old Post Office Pavilion, a building that's always nice to look at.

"Hit me with it," I say, referring to the job, not the building.

"It's a covert job. I'm loaning you out."

I smile. Sometimes LouAnn uses me to get the dirt on her rivals. Nothing illegal or even unethical. In LouAnn's world, she calls them, "integrated business partnerships" and "liaison exchanges" and uses them to build up the young crop of business officials and "cross-pollinate" the industry. So I'm not alarmed that she's decided to pimp me out again.

The last time she did this, I worked in Senator Murphy's office for four months, *assisting* in drafting the language for a small-business-friendly bill. Senator Murphy is, of course, a female, and her staff is composed mostly of the female gender. And, yes, other than the senator herself, I dated all of the ladies at some point or another during, or after, that liaison exchange.

In fact, Stacey, the woman probably still asleep in my bed, used to be an intern with Senator Murphy. We happened to bump into each other two nights ago at the 930 Club and didn't stop bumping into each other for forty-eight hours. We paused only when I had heard rustling out in the living room, which was when *Sergeant Prim and Proper* happened to move in.

I smile as I recall how red Keira's face had become when I opened the bedroom door to find out what was going on and she witnessed the full glory of my manliness. I'm shocked she could even look me in the eye this morning.

But, at the moment, I really don't want to be thinking about Keira Holtslander.

"Who am I being loaned out to this time?" I pull out a notepad, ready to take notes. Normally, I have a few weeks to prepare for such a role. LouAnn won't throw me in willy-nilly.

"Johnson Brookshire's office. I've heard a—"

This wasn't good. I stand up abruptly, interrupting LouAnn. "Wait a minute now. Johnson Brookshire hates my guts, LouAnn, and you know it."

"The president of Brookshire Mierkle has never verbalized his feelings for you one way or the other, Dillan. Admittedly, dating his daughter wasn't your brightest idea. If you'll remember, everyone, including the janitor, advised you against it."

I run a hand through my hair. "Are you trying to get me fired? Are you unhappy with me for any reason?"

LouAnn chuckles. "Stop acting like a girl, Dillan. This isn't about you, it's about me. Now sit down, because what I'm about to tell you is confidential."

I sit down. "I'll never break your confidence, LouAnn. I hope you know that."

"Why do you think you're still with me all these years later, kiddo? I've heard a rumor that Johnson is retiring this summer. The board of directors will take into account my seniority as well as my thirty-five-year tenure with the company, but I know deep in my gut that Johnson will not select a female. He'll go for one of the other vice presidents. Probably that asshole Terry Richmond from the New York office. I know I should have taken up golf in order to schmooze with the bosses, but the only balls I've ever wanted to hit were the ones between their legs."

I clear my throat and cross my legs. "You want me to go in and convince him you're the right person for the job?"

"That's the end state, yes, but first I need you to convince him that you're not such a douche bag for dating and then dumping his daughter. No offense, but you are sort of a liability right now, and I'd like you clean up your own mess."

"That's harsh, LouAnn."

"You'll get nothing but the truth from me, Dillan. Johnson doesn't know I know. He thinks you're coming in to help with a new client in our federal business sector. Apparently there's hostility with, or maybe *from*, this client, I'm not sure, but Johnson was pleased with your performance in Senator Murphy's office. Johnson thinks he's 'reassigned' you, but in reality, I put a tickle in the right ear and 'offered' you. Naturally, Johnson assumes he came up with the idea. I have no intention of disagreeing with this assessment."

"When do I infiltrate his office?"

"I like how you think." She hands over an accordion-style packet. "One week. Take that time to do research on the client and the Brookshire Mierkle team handling the account. If anyone can tame the beast, it will be my *son*, Dillan Pope." LouAnn did finger quotes around the word *son*.

I couldn't hold in a bark of laughter.

CHAPTER THREE

Keira

Thank goodness Staff Sergeant Justin Hauten is a patient man, because it takes me twenty-five minutes to find the office. I think about the things I can normally complete in that time. I could run three miles. I could cook a fairly decent dinner. I could take a nice bubble bath. I could have sex, twice.

I'm a little flush, and embarrassed, when Justin introduces me to the rest of Colonel Benson's team. Benson is *one* of the Chief of Staff of the Army's military assistants. General MacWilliams has five military assistants. One is a one-star general, two are colonels, one is a command sergeant major, and the last one is Justin. I've never heard of a *junior enlisted advisor* before, and Justin didn't really explain it to me when I asked, only to say that it was a new billet and that even he was mystified about the position.

I can tell that there's more to the story and maybe in time he'll spill the beans, but for now, I let it go. There's no reason to make my first day complicated, especially with a staff sergeant who is clearly unavailable.

At one o'clock, Justin shows me into Colonel Benson's office and then leaves.

The colonel shakes my hand. "Welcome to the Pentagon, Sergeant Holtslander. The Puzzle Palace can be a little daunting at first, so the first week, we give you a bit of latitude in finding your way around. After that, however, I'll expect you to be where you need to be ten minutes before the appointed time. First and foremost, you represent the U.S. Army, and secondly, you represent General MacWilliams at all times while you are in uniform."

"Yes, sir," I say automatically. I fully expected this and am rather used to such speeches and welcomes. I've done a few of them myself when Army privates arrived at my unit while I was stationed at Fort Bragg.

"How long have you been in the Army, Sergeant?"

"Nine years, sir."

"When are you up for reenlistment?"

"In three years."

The colonel doesn't answer right away. He appears to be thinking something over, and I wonder if it has anything to do with the billet I've been assigned to. I start to bite on a fingernail. After another moment, he pulls out a folder and lays it on his desk.

"I know your background, Sergeant," he begins. He's looking at my enlisted record brief, which is the report that details my entire Army career up to this point. "And I know that you are a 96B, an Intelligence Analyst, but that's not why I asked for you to fill this billet. It isn't an intel position. Well, I should clarify and say that the position isn't inherently intelligence related. You'll be reviewing documents for an internal review General MacWilliams is leading.

"Only four people know about the investigation, and you're that fourth person. I spoke with several Army commanders, looking for recommendations, and you quickly surfaced to the top of the list. You have a reputation for steady, professional work. You are not prone to jumping to conclusions and, if I've heard correctly, you somehow find reading Army manuals enjoyable. I'm happy to report that you'll be reading several more.

"I personally called every supervisor you have reported to and each has consistently praised you, your body of work, and the high nature of their trust in you. General MacWilliams reviewed the findings with me and wanted you right away.

"The next few weeks will be busy ones for you as you apprise yourself of the situation. You'll have quite a bit of reading to do that can only be done inside the general's secure office. In the initial stages of the investigation, all you'll do is read the documents. In the subsequent weeks, you'll have time to write up a formal report and brief it to General MacWilliams. At this point, the position isn't permanent. Once the report is done, it is highly probable the Army will send you back to Fort Bragg. However, if you impress the general, well..." He smiles, suggesting it is possible I'll stay on board. It isn't something he can actually say out loud. He isn't allowed to promise me anything. "Do you have any questions at this point?" Colonel Benson asks.

It's like he's dropped a bomb on me. Internal Review. So someone's done something wrong, and I have to read the raw material, analyze it, and present it in a coherent, unbiased manner. I do that every day. The material and subject matter might be different, but the methodology could cross over easily. *Maybe Dillan's title of Sergeant Prim and Proper wasn't all that far off.* Uh, I really don't want to think about Dillan at the moment.

Granted, if my job took me only a few weeks, then I'd be in and out of Washington, DC, sooner than I thought, and I wouldn't have to see Dillan's sarcastic face every day.

That was a plus.

I return my thoughts to the investigation.

"Is anyone else working this with me? Who can I

bounce ideas off of?"

"Obviously, General MacWilliams is not the optimal choice. You'll have your office call with him next week since he's on official travel overseas. You can come to me or Staff Sergeant Hauten. We are both cleared at the proper clearance level and understand the situation. Under no other circumstances are you to talk of this to anyone else, even if they claim to have a top secret clearance or the *need to know*."

"Roger, sir. I completely understand and know the rules of *need to know*."

"Let's get started. I'll show you to your office."

Dillan

When I get home, Keira isn't there yet and my weekend date has already left, but she wrote a naughty message with red lipstick on the bathroom mirror.

I think about removing it, but then like the idea of Keira discovering it. I want to find out what she'd do. Jon, who had become a bit more domesticated once he became serious with Tanner, would have laughed but said, "Dunno man, don't you think it's time you knocked it off and found a nice girl?"

Thinking about Jon makes me miss him more. He's been my best friend since college. I went the business route while Jon joined the Navy to fly fighter jets. The fighter jets never worked out due to his poor vision, but he was an outstanding staff officer who was recently promoted away from Washington, DC, to work for the Navy in Bahrain. Tanner, a professional baseball player with the Washington Nationals, had been showing a brave face for the last month.

While I certainly love Jon like a brother, it in no way compares to how Tanner feels about him. So if I'm missing Jon this much, I wonder how Tanner is taking it? I pick up the phone, ready to call him, when I remember that Jon put the entire Nationals' schedule on the fridge. I groan. Tanner is up in Pittsburgh, playing the Pirates for the next three days.

So there goes that thought.

The front door opens and slams shut as I mentally calculate when I can invite Tanner over.

Keira walks in. I didn't think it was possible, but her

uniform is more shapeless than it was this morning. Shapeless, but with wrinkles.

When she spots me, she scowls. You'd think she'd been battling an entire band of guerilla fighters all day long by the way she looks at me. It also occurs to me that I'm in the same position I was this morning when I spied on her as she stretched from her run. I wonder if she has figured that out yet.

"Rough day?" I ask. I look at the clock on the microwave. Seven p.m. Her features soften slightly. Maybe this is a good sign.

"You can say that," she says, looking at the fridge.

She moves toward me. Each step is some sort of wordless declaration of... something. Should I comfort her? Did she need a hug? I inhale when she's a foot a way. When Jon came home after a long day, I always got him a beer. God, I was totally the bitch of that relationship, wasn't I?

I swing the fridge open, lean in, and hit Keira with the door.

"What the hell?" she yells, backing up and grabbing at her shin. "You certainly know how to welcome a girl, jeez. I came over here to see if that was Tanner's schedule."

"Uh, sorry about that." I offer her the beer, but she gives me the evil eye, so I pop the top and take a large sip. "Tanner's up in Pittsburgh. I was thinking of inviting him over this weekend."

She sizes me up briefly, like maybe she thinks that's what I think *she* wants to hear after hitting her with the fridge door. I smile at her. There's no change, and normally there's a change in a girl's expression after I give The Grin.

Keira must be a robot.

"I doubt Tanner's going to be available since he's taking me to all the Nationals' games this weekend," she says, grabbing an apple from the counter. "I get to sit in the wives' box."

I must look crushed because her dry lips crack into a smile. I take another long gulp of the beer as I think of a good comeback. Damn, I've got nothing. Jon's shapeless little sister twists the knife just a little bit deeper in my back. Tanner and I were friends, right? He didn't just put up with me because I used to be Jon's roommate?

"That should be fun," I say. I look again to the fridge. I desperately want to change the subject. "Are you hungry?"

"What about sleeping beauty?" she asks, moving away from me.

I draw a blank. "What are you—*oh*, you must mean Stacey. No, she already left."

"Stacey, huh? I'm terribly impressed that you can remember their names. Thanks for the offer, but I have a lot of reading to do. I'll just have a protein bar and a glass of milk."

Right. *Sergeant Prim and Proper* probably doesn't eat anything with more than one gram of fat in it.

"Suit yourself." I finish the beer and place it in the recycle bin.

"I'm going to jump in the shower. Do you need anything in there first?"

I give her The Grin again. "Are you offering?"

Keira glares at me. "Are you always this much of a pig? Jon was so right."

"You and Jon talk about me? What about?" While I say it flippantly, something about the fact that she said, *Jon was so right* pierces doubt right through me. Like maybe Jon had serious concerns about me. I know he'd been joking for me to find the right girl, but when there are so many *right girls* out there, it certainly makes it difficult to choose just one.

Besides, what business does she have prying into my life? Just because she's Jon's little sister doesn't mean she has the right to judge me.

"You'll have to ask Jon," Keira says over her shoulder. She walks into the bathroom and locks the door. Seconds later, I hear her cuss rather loudly. She opens the door harshly. "I am not amused by sleeping beauty's message, Casanova."

I laugh as she slams the bathroom door shut again.

CHAPTER FOUR

Keira

Peeling off my uniform, I give the mirror—and its lipstick-written message—the darkest look I can muster. Who writes that kind of stuff? I mean, how cliche. *"Dillan - I can't wait to taste you again. I loved it when you put it there. xoxo Stacey."* The word *there* is underlined. The rest of the mirror is filled with red hearts, X's and O's. The *entire* mirror.

I can't even see my own reflection as I start the shower, just an entire tube of lipstick smeared across the glass. Which is fine. I don't need to see myself to disrobe. I also don't need to see how flush my face is. I can feel the heat emanating as I remember what happened two nights ago, when I walked in the front door and accidentally found Dillan standing there. In the nude.

I had had a suitcase in each hand and a green Army duffle bag strapped on my back, and I shuffled into the apartment with about as much noise as an ogre would make stomping through the woods. It was no wonder he flung his bedroom door open, turned on the lights, and spied me without shame. "Oh, it's you," he had said without a sense of urgency or embarrassment. It was almost as if he was glad he was showing me his goods. Like he got that part out of the way right away.

I didn't know he had a woman with him until the next day, not until I heard the *sounds.* Sounds that made me wonder just what exactly he could be doing to garner those particular moans. Admittedly, he had an amazing body and, uh, perfectly proportioned *equipment*, but I would never, ever say so out loud. Even if I had a gun to my head. Even if I had *two* guns to my head.

God, what a way to move into your brother's best friend's apartment. It wasn't as if I had never met Dillan before. I had, multiple times, in fact, but he was always wearing clothes and he wasn't having day-long sex one wall away from me.

I had to hand it to him: Dillan was consistent. He wasn't presenting a false front with me. He was being himself, and I could at least appreciate that, even if that meant he was a pig and a womanizer.

I cannot wait to summarize the last few days to Jon and Tanner in an e-mail.

Drying off and dressing in comfy clothes, I leave the bathroom. I'll let Dillan clean the mirror. I refuse to touch it.

As soon as I open the door, though, a delicious aroma and the sounds of sizzling ground me to the spot.

Dillan is cooking something. Something that smells appetizing.

Keep going, Keira. Nothing to see over there in the kitchen as your roommate cooks what smells like barbecue chicken. You have a mouthwatering protein bar waiting for you in your bedroom. Plus, you have a 108-page Army manual to read before tomorrow morning.

"I was going to tell you that I had thawed out chicken," Dillan says. His back is presented to me as he works a skillet. I can tell he's wearing an apron. Its strings are tied low on his back.

If I don't acknowledge him and keep moving, by the time he turns around, I'll already be in my bedroom. He won't know that I stopped dead in my tracks.

I make it only a few feet across the living room.

He turns around. "I made enough for you, Keira." He looks at me, my bedroom, and takes note of whatever weird expression I have plastered on my face, and says, "You can eat it in your bedroom, if you want."

Damn.

Why'd he have to be so accommodating right now? Why couldn't he have been a jerk? Now I feel bad about lying to him about Tanner's invitation. Yes, Tanner invited me to attend the games this weekend, but he also asked me to extend the invitation to Dillan. Both of our names will be at the will-call window.

"I, uh," I start, not knowing where to begin. Confess the lie or accept the food?

Dillan turns around and prepares one plate and then moves the skillet over the trash can.

"It's okay," he says neutrally. "I'm not good at remembering to eat leftovers, so I'll just throw out the extra."

"Wait," I say. I don't believe for one second that he'll actually throw it out, and I know what he's doing in order to get me to agree to eat his food. Guilt. He's guilting me into eating it. "Don't waste it," I say through clenched teeth. It kills me to compliment him. "It smells good. Let me put this stuff away—" I indicate my uniform "—and I'll be right out."

I hang up my ACUs in the closet and grab an old, thin, long-sleeved shirt to wear over my tank top. I retrieve the unclassified Army manual from my backpack.

I'll eat his chicken, but that doesn't mean I have to talk to him.

"Ah, I see that you're not the only one who has brought work home tonight," Dillan comments as I sit down beside him at the small kitchen table. I notice he has a stack of folders on the chair next to his. He peeks at my manual. "Army Regulation Twenty dash One. *Inspector General Activities and Procedures.* Sounds fascinating, Sergeant." He bites into the chicken.

"There's no need to be rude just because you've never met a female who relies on her brain, rather than her looks, to get ahead."

He smiles. "You are right, and I apologize. I'm sure that all the women I've dated with MBAs and PhDs would completely agree with you. Not to mention those who have interned with Senator Murphy or worked at the White House. Such bimbos, each and every one." Dillan takes a victorious bite.

So he dates beautiful, smart, educated women. Big deal. He moved through them fast. *That* is the issue. *But what's it to me?* I think. Oh, right, they write on bathroom mirrors.

"Perhaps you can clean Stacey's PhD lipstick diploma off the mirror tonight?" I take a bite of his chicken and very nearly moan. Wow, it's really good. Much better than a protein bar. *Don't let on how good his cooking is, Keira.*

He watches me as I eat. He's waiting for an indication if I like the food or not. His eyes narrow when I don't satisfy his inquisitive stare. I finish the chicken and pull out the Army manual.

"Yeah, I can do that," he says, standing. He takes my plate, stacks it on top of his, and puts both in the sink. I see him take something out from a lower cabinet. Dillan walks to the bathroom. Half a minute later, he returns. He shows me a red-stained paper towel. "All gone."

I nod and say "Thanks" before diving back into the manual on Inspections, Assistance, and Investigations. Earlier, during my office call with Colonel Benson, he tossed the regulation manual at me and said, "Memorize this before you arrive tomorrow morning." I spent the rest of the day, alone, in the general's secure office. When it was time to leave, it took thirty minutes to find my way to the Metro entrance.

Dillan sits down next to me and opens a folder. The room is silent for a while.

"Thanks for dinner," I say after reading and taking notes on the first three chapters. "The chicken wasn't completely terrible."

I feel him looking at me, so I glance up. A small smile forms on his lips. I'm blown away at its simplicity. I doubt he even knows he's doing it. That big, fake grin he likes to give everyone is just too over the top. But this—this boyish smile—*almost* makes me smile back at him. Almost.

"You're welcome." He goes back to his reading and I think that that's the end of the conversation until he says, nonchalantly, "Some of it is stuck in your teeth."

I give him a black look, but he refuses to look away from his folder, so I grab my stuff, head to my bedroom, tune the TV to Tanner's ball game, and finish reading the manual there.

Dillan

I watch Keira semi-storm away from the kitchen table. She isn't really mad. She's just not used to my personality. Which is fine. I'm not trying to impress her or flirt with her.

Not at all.

Not one bit. She's Jon's little sister. She's way too stuffy and boring and unlike anyone else I've ever met. *She is completely off-limits.*

I agreed to that weeks ago, after Jon called me up and asked for a favor. Asked if Keira could rent my second bedroom after her all-of-a-sudden reassignment to the Pentagon. After she settled in at her new job, if she didn't like the arrangement, she could find a new apartment.

"Dillan," Jon said over the long-distance phone call, "Keira is off limits. You know what I mean." I knew what he meant, but if I remembered correctly, Keira was twenty-seven years old. A grown woman who could decide for herself if I was worth her time or not.

"Is your sister easy, Jon?" I had asked him. In hindsight, I realize it was the wrong question to ask.

"Let me be clear," Jon said without any hesitation in his Navy Commander voice. "If I find out you've tried to, or successfully, seduce my sister, our friendship is over. She's not your type. Do you understand?"

It irritated me to no end that Jon would mistrust me like that. Was the sentiment earned? Yeah, probably, but I thought Jon had known me long enough to know that I would never jeopardize our friendship over a quick hookup.

"Wow, ease up, buddy," I said to my best friend. "I was

only kidding. Sorry. I've met Keira before, remember? She's totally not my type. If I recall correctly, she's a by-the-book type, right? Besides, she's a staff sergeant in the Army. She'll totally kick my ass if I try anything with her."

After that, the conversation took on a friendlier tone.

But now, as I think back on that phone call and how I've been acting toward Keira, I realize that if she tells Jon everything, then I might be in the market for a new friend. However, Keira didn't seem like the type to complain to anyone. In fact, she was as sarcastic toward me as I was to her. I wasn't used to that. *You could use a challenge.* That's what Ellen said.

I sigh. The first challenge I want at the moment is the one with Johnson Brookshire and this new federal client. The second challenge I want is for LouAnn to succeed Johnson and for me to move up in rank with her.

Ignoring Keira is not a challenge. And ignoring her from here on out is what I plan to do. There. A plan. I'm good with those. Before I return to LouAnn's documents on the federal client, I send a quick e-mail to Jon and Tanner.

I type: "Keira moved in this weekend, and she seems to have survived her first day at the Pentagon. All good here. I'd like to tell you that she sends her love, but she's not one for conversation, and she'd probably accuse me of putting words in her mouth. So I'm sending my love, instead. Stay safe. Dillan."

I check for missed calls or e-mails. I see one from Stacey and another one from a girl I met several weeks ago. I don't click on either of them.

Returning to LouAnn's documents, I immerse myself in her quirky sidebar notes. My boss comments on everyone and everything in such a non-politically correct manner that I can't help but laugh out loud.

Everyone once in a while, I look at Keira's closed door, as if by my looking at it, it will open up. But it stays closed. I can hear a slight murmur from the TV in her bedroom.

Once the light goes out from under the door, I stop looking altogether.

CHAPTER FIVE

Keira

It's dark when I slip outside. The cool air feels refreshing on my skin as I jog toward The Mall. I pass the Natural History Museum, cross the street, and hit the wide, gravelly running path that, at this point, is somewhat deserted.

Yesterday, I ran toward the Capitol and circled back, intending to run the full two-mile course, but with my move and all over the weekend, I was exhausted, and I didn't run as far as I wanted to.

I didn't feel any more rested this morning, not after reading all night and taking page after page of notes, but the idea of running—alone with my thoughts—invigorates me.

I pause long enough to pop in my white earbuds and press play on my playlist. Today, I head toward the Lincoln Memorial. When I run, I let everything go. Worry. Stress. Sometimes I think about work, or improving my run time, and sometimes I'll do mundane tasks, like count the number of cars that drive opposite me or I'll calculate the running ratio of women to men.

This morning, I'm trying not to think about two things: Dillan and the Army manual I read last night.

Something about sparring with Dillan was fun, and it shouldn't be. I shouldn't look forward to insulting him and I definitely shouldn't look forward to seeing him in various stages of undress. But I did, and it didn't help matters any when, this morning, as I'm tiptoeing through the living room, I noticed that his bedroom door was open.

He was alone. I had expected the leggy blonde to be tangled up in his limbs. What I found, instead, was a thin sheet *barely* covering his groin and thighs. The picturesque moonlight shafting through his large windows told me everything else I needed to know. He wasn't wearing any clothes.

I swear it was as if he'd carefully arranged for it to be that way. It wasn't like he knew I'd be up at five this morning to go for a run. So that thought was stupid.

The other stupid thought that I had was that instead of walking out the front door, I should walk into his bedroom, climb in next to him, and get a different sort of workout on.

Stupid, right? Idiotic.

He'd probably laugh me right out of his bed.

After thinking that thought, and the others, this morning, I huffed out of the living room, no longer trying to be quiet about my activities.

A smug smile of satisfaction grows on my lips at the idea that I disturbed his sleep as much as he disturbed me.

I pick up my pace as a song on my playlist is a faster beat, and race against an imaginary opponent.

I see every color imaginable on those jogging around me. Hot pinks. Flaming purples. Bright oranges. While running isn't necessarily a dangerous sport, it is always a good idea to be visible in dim lighting.

After I've circled The Mall twice, the number of runners increases, and the sun makes an appearance. I strip off my T-shirt and tie it at my waist. The baby blue sports bra glows against my tan skin, and the color clashes with the electric green workout pants I'm sporting today.

There's something about me, as a runner, that likes the idea of not matching whatsoever. Like it's a way to be different *and* disobedient. I rarely coordinate my running outfits. I just grab a top, a bottom, socks, and shoes each morning, in the dark, and dress. Sometimes even the socks don't match. Of course, if I'm running with an Army unit, I'm pretty much locked into wearing my physical fitness gear. Nothing exciting, different, or disobedient about Army attire.

With thoughts of Dillan long gone—okay, maybe I'm still thinking about those abs—I focus on the possibilities of what I may be investigating over the next few weeks.

If the documents were classified, then maybe it was a security leak, or maybe a special operation failed and the general needed an independent review of the concept of operations. But I didn't have experience on those fronts. Not really. And I would have remembered hearing about any special forces' loss of life.

Maybe the general himself was under some sort of investigation and I had been brought in to clear him of wrongdoing before it was made public.

That seemed more plausible. More and more generals these days are getting into trouble for stupid mistakes that they knew they shouldn't have gotten involved in. Affairs. Sexual harassment. Travel fraud. Conduct unbecoming.

But those sorts of documents weren't highly classified. In order for something to be classified top secret, or higher, it had to have grave consequences against our nation's security if released to the public. However, until Colonel Benson allowed me to read all of the documents in the general's secure office, I could only speculate.

Until then, I could only guess at what I'd be researching while avoiding all thoughts of Dillan and his abs and that carefully arranged sheet this morning.

Before I know it, my six miles are up, and I walk my

way back to Dillan's apartment. When I walk through the door, his bedroom door is still open, and without appearing too obvious as I thread through the living room furniture, I notice that his bed is empty and I hear the shower running.

Not wanting to question my disappointment, I slip into my own room, close the door, and stretch out.

Dillan

The smack of the front door wakes me. Groggily, I peer at the red numbers on the clock beside my bed. It's just after five in the morning.

Either someone else is moving in, or Keira left the apartment to go for a run.

I toss off the sheet, step into the living room, and find it empty. Something that suspiciously feels like disappointment washes through me. *What the hell?* I think, running my hand through my hair. Did I hope to find Keira out here? What was it about a woman who *didn't* want me that made me want her more?

Even though I'm naked, I knock softly at Keira's door. I already know she won't be inside, but just in case, I want to make sure she didn't fall out of bed or something.

Here, let a naked man help you up, you poor thing. Beds are such dangerous things. I'll climb in with you to make sure the coast is clear.

The door isn't closed all the way, and it squeaks a little when I push it open further.

The room is plain with white walls, a double-size bed, a nightstand, and a flat screen TV mounted on the wall. After Jon moved out last year and moved in with Tanner, I converted his room into a guest bedroom. The only other people to sleep in this room were my mom, my sister and her useless boyfriend, and now, Keira.

Devoid of personality, it still looked like a guest bedroom. Keira hadn't done anything to personalize the room, which gave me the impression she only planned to stay long enough to get her feet on the ground and find her own apartment.

Which was the original arrangement, wasn't it?

I never imagined she would stay longer than a few weeks. Oh, I knew I'd flirt with her mercilessly, maybe even show her the ropes of DC, but it wasn't anything more than that. I knew it. She knew it.

Besides, Keira had only been in town for what, three days? It wasn't like she'd have a boyfriend in less than a week. She didn't seem the type. In fact, the more I thought about it, the more I realized I had no idea of what type of woman she really was.

As Jon's sister, I knew enough about her to know she was funny and sarcastic, and cute as hell. I also knew she was an avid runner and had won a few marathons. She had spent some time overseas. Jon mentioned once that Keira was a little quieter after the last deployment, a little more reserved than usual. But Jon chalked it up to the harsh realities of serving in a war zone and said she'd get back to being herself in no time.

As I survey the room, I notice that half a dozen uniforms hang in the closet. I shouldn't go inside, but I do. For the most part, the uniforms are the same type that she wore yesterday. That shapeless, computerized-camouflaged uniform. Beside those, I see a black, formal-looking jacket with gold buttons down the front. It's the type of jacket she'd wear to a ceremony or a military ball.

On the left side, in capital letters, her last name, HOLTSLANDER, sits below two colorful ribbons. On the right, I take note of several rows of ribbons, each different from the other, but no less impressive. Lower on the jacket, I spot other items that either represent her branch of service, combat service, or are awards she has received.

Instantly, I know that Keira is a good soldier. Her

uniform proves it. It's spotless and those ribbons—which I suspect are awards and accomplishments—mean she's done a lot of good things in her career. She is respected and admired. Jon has always spoken highly of his sister and her success in the Army.

Taking a deep breath, I leave her room and return the door the exact same way I found it. I've been in here too long already. God knows what Keira would think if she came back and discovered me, naked of all things, staring into her closet. I'd be a first-class creep, for sure.

She'd kick my ass first and ask questions later.

But the thing that hits me the hardest is the fact that Jon's little sister—no matter how cute—is really off-limits. She seems to like rules and manuals and standard operating procedures. I like to break the rules and I'm still not sure what a *standard operating procedure* is supposed to be, but I'm sure I'd do the exact opposite of whatever it instructed me to do.

We are incompatible and, now that I've had a peek behind the curtain, so to speak, I find that I could easily turn off my *flirt* switch. Keira won't be here long anyway, so it doesn't matter.

I can deal with her for a few more weeks.

Let me amend that.

I can *ignore* her for a few more weeks.

Smiling, I head back into my bedroom and put on boxers and a pair of shorts. I sit down in front of my laptop and see that Tanner's replied to my e-mail.

Tanner's a short, but-sweet-type of communicator, and he's funny as hell. It's easy to understand why Jon fell hard for the ball player. After reading a few lines, I realize that Keira lied to me about Tanner's invitation for this weekend.

Tanner writes, "Did Keira tell you that I got tix for the both of you this weekend? Bring a date. See you at the Nationals Park, Friday, 7:05 pm. If you're late, I'll tell all of your lady friends that you've suddenly developed a craving for packaged meat. I don't have time to send out five hundred e-mails, but I will if I have to. I'd ask you to give Keira a hug for me, but I'm fairly certain she'd punch you in the face, so I'll have to wait to do it myself. Don't say anything, but I have a big surprise waiting for Keira. If it goes well, it will benefit you, too. Xoxo Tanner."

I reply back to Tanner and then send an e-mail to Stacey, asking if she wants to go to the game with me. Whistling, I jump in the shower to get ready for work. Keira will be back any minute now.

Tanner might have a surprise for *Sergeant Prim and Proper*, but after that little lie of hers, I'll have to come up with my own surprise as well.

CHAPTER SIX

Keira

Dillan's out the door before I exit the shower, so I don't have to feign ignoring him, but the fact that I didn't get the opportunity to give him the cold shoulder certainly was a little annoying. Damn him for being efficient and quick this morning.

It doesn't take me long to dress and leave the apartment as well, and I already know that I'll be making Ellen's Corner Bakery a normal part of my mornings from here on out. When I step inside her door, the delicious smell of pastries does dangerous things to me. I want to consume every single thing in her bakery. I chuckle. The Army would have a thing or two to say about that when I no longer fit in my uniform.

I know that the extraordinarily long line will also become a normal part of my mornings. Yesterday, when I popped in the place, it didn't take me long to spot Dillan near the front of the line, and I quickly took notice that, when he ordered his coffee, he didn't leave right away. He stayed and talked with the owner. He showered her with compliments and he spoke with her as if he actually cared for her.

This went against everything I had ever thought about Dillan. *Nice?* No way. Not in a million years. And yet, there he was, yesterday morning, ruining my day even more.

I tried to ignore him as I moved up in the line, but when I heard, "If you're asking me if she's cute, the answer is yes, but I can tell she's as boring as a snail. *Sergeant*

Prim and Proper. She probably does twenty push-ups at every Metro stop."

It wasn't even that serious of an insult. It was more juvenile in nature. Something an eighth grader might say to one of his buddies.

No, Dillan, I thought. *I do not do twenty push-ups at every Metro stop.* There isn't enough room.

The line moves fast as I think about yesterday and it isn't long before Ellen's cheerful face smiles brightly at me.

"Good morning, Staff Sergeant Holtslander," she says. "Same order as yesterday?"

I smile back at her while asking her to call me Keira, not Staff Sergeant Holtslander. It shouldn't surprise me that she would remember my order. It is in her best interest to keep me as a customer. But there is something about her keen eye and the way she studies me that gives me the impression she is doing more than sizing me up for my coffee order.

"Surprise me instead," I say, wondering how she might react.

Ellen grins as she goes to work on brewing me a perfect cup of...something.

She hands it over and I take a little sip. *Heaven in a cup*, I think.

"It's amazing," I say without preamble. I can't place what it is. It's not chocolatey or any other normal coffee additive. "This is delicious, Ellen."

"Thank you, Keira. Here." She hands me something else. It was a flyer for the bakery's thirtieth anniversary. "I hope you can make it."

Her celebration is next week. I don't see a reason as to why I can't make it. It isn't like I have a social life. Other than Tanner and Dillan, I have no other friends, and I don't exactly consider Dillan a friend.

I fold up the flyer and place it inside my Army notebook.

"I'd love to come. Thank you."

"How are you holding up, living with Dillan?" Ellen asks. She asks it in a way to suggest that she's sort of apologize-asking the question, like maybe she's commiserating along with me. But the old woman didn't fool me. She loved every second Dillan flirted with her.

I snort. "I wouldn't classify my arrangement as *living with Dillan.* I'm renting his guest bedroom. There's no reason for me to be *holding up*, Ellen, unless you mean to ask, is he insufferable, egotistical, and does he like to push everyone's buttons? Then, yeah, I seem to be holding up okay, since none of it bothers me because the man doesn't mean anything to me."

Ellen smiles at me as she works another customer's order.

"You could do with a bit of disorder, Keira," Ellen says.

"Disorder is the exact opposite of what I could do with," I say, laughing. The old woman certainly has charm. She easily disarmed me with one quick smile and a generous spirit. But I don't exactly enjoy the fact that she seems to know what might, or what might not, do me good.

Dillan is in the *what might not do me good* category. Is Ellen trying to do a bit of matchmaking? I narrow my eyes and glance down at my coffee. What is in the coffee?

I shake my head. That is a stupid thought. The coffee is delicious because one, it's coffee, and two, it's coffee. I return my attention to Ellen.

"If you say so, Keira," she says. "Don't be late for work now."

Ellen walks away to attend her ever-growing line, and I head to the Metro, sipping a delicious cup of coffee.

I could do with a bit of disorder, huh? I think. I wear crazy-color running clothes and I just asked her to surprise me with coffee. That's about as much disorder as I would ever want.

Dillan

After rushing out the door and grabbing coffee from Ellen's, I spend the rest of the day researching Brookshire Mierkle's federal client, Joy Fromm Acquisitions.

Joy and *Fromm* were two different people—half-siblings, apparently—who did not get along after their father died, and one or both of the brother-sister team staged a coup with little success. Most of their smaller contractors left them as a result.

Brookshire Mierkle would go in, seal the cracks, fill their ranks with highly qualified employees, endorse the team behind Joy Fromm Acquisitions, pat them on the back, and send them on their way.

According to one of LouAnn's notes, that wasn't likely to happen. She writes, "They'll just go back to bickering. It isn't about the company, it's about them. They hate each other. Amanda Joy hates Ken Fromm because her father left her mother for Ken's mom."

A little sibling rivalry never killed anyone, but LouAnn didn't put it past Joy and Fromm.

"You can't fix a typical *Cain and Abel.* They'll kill each other," she quipped on one of the pages. "No pressure, kiddo."

I sit back at my desk, wondering why Johnson Brookshire would be taking a chance on a company that probably wouldn't make it in the end. LouAnn didn't have a problem sending me to the wolves. She seemed to get a kick out of me struggling like a drowning puppy for the first few days of an assignment. Johnson Brookshire would probably enjoy it if I did drown.

Dating his daughter, Abigail, a college intern last summer, really wasn't the smartest thing I could have done. At first, I didn't even know who she was. Kissing her in the janitor's closet seemed like a good idea in the moment, and her skirt provided easy access. In my defense, she seemed just as caught up in the workplace romance as I was, and innocent kissing and petting turned into something else.

A full-fledged relationship.

Once I learned Abigail's last name—courtesy of the head janitor who caught us multiple times in her closet—I couldn't back out after that. Even Abigail, who confided in me that she was dared to flirt with me, didn't want a relationship, but she was scared enough of her father to act the wounded bird and for several weeks, we were a pair of humping bunnies.

But even the whirlwind of an office romance dwindles into a weak breeze after being caught. We no longer seemed to appeal to each other, and one of us had to end it. Granted, I wish now that Abigail had taken that lead, but she let me do the "breaking up," and Johnson Brookshire, already angry that his daughter had been taken advantage of—*I entirely disagreed with that assessment*—had it out for me ever since.

Perhaps attaching me to Joy Fromm Acquisitions was a way to fire me. Knowing what I know—that the company probably won't survive—if I'm on the team to restore the troubled company, Brookshire could use it against LouAnn and her bid to replace him. Or he could just be a vindictive son of a bitch and will enjoy watching me fail. It's not as if Abigail is around anymore. After the internship, she and her adorable ass returned to her Ivy League university, and I haven't seen her since.

Sighing, I take a look at the roster of Brookshire Mierkle employees working the case. Something is wrong here. I squint my eyes, but it doesn't change that my name is the *only* name on the list. I lift the paper, hoping another list is behind it.

Nope.

So LouAnn pimped me out on an impossible task that Johnson Brookshire probably wanted me to fail on. Talk about a challenge. The thought reminds me of Ellen's statement, which makes me think of Keira. I still have to think of a good surprise for her lying to me.

I look at the clock. It is late afternoon, and I can take work home with me.

I wonder if she'd be interested in going out tonight. Not like a date. I'd be showing her some of DC's highlights, and a good restaurant served a useful purpose. Everyone had to eat at some point.

Knowing what I know about Keira and her intelligence background, I doubt she can leave early and bring anything back to the apartment to work on, and I don't have her work number. It's not like I can call her up or even visit her office. No doubt the Pentagon is guarded like a fortress.

Not that I would force my way in just to ask a girl if she wanted to eat at a restaurant with me. Romantic, yes. Legal, no.

I pack up my work, tell LouAnn that I'm leaving to write up my last will and testament, and head home.

CHAPTER SEVEN

Keira

My head swims in overly worded personal letters. General MacWilliams' windowless, secure office, while well-appointed with gorgeous, dark wood furniture, is on the small side. It's made smaller by the two large boxes stacked against a wall.

Boxes that I have to go through in this office. Nowhere else.

I suddenly feel like I need more coffee from Ellen's. Too bad the Pentagon doesn't have a satellite office for Ellen's Corner Bakery.

I stare at the boxes and I can see the future for the next seven days: me reading every single document contained therein. Sometimes I wish secrets would remain secret.

After the plane hit the Pentagon in 2001, a renovation team came together to revamp the entire Pentagon, one wedge at a time. As the story goes, unbeknownst to anyone but a select few within the Department of Defense, during the last stage of renovation, a construction worker found an unassuming trunk hidden inside the walls along one of the corridors.

Why no one seemed to question why someone hid a trunk in a wall was beyond me. However, the trunk was locked, and the renovation team, who happened to have a tight deadline, stored it in the nearest secure storage room —the Chief of Staff of the Army's storage room.

And there the trunk lay dormant for several years. Someone would see it, wonder about it, but never take action. Everyone was busy in those days and no one had time for a trunk that probably contained nothing but old manuals.

Two months ago, a renovation official remembered the trunk just before his retirement and informed the general, who told Staff Sergeant Justin Hauten to find a pair of bolt cutters and open the "darned thing."

Inside, it contained letters between an Army officer and a woman, whom I could only describe as a young German woman. Years of letters, dated between 1955 and 1957, that, at this point, appear to be more or less pen pal style. But I'm only at the beginning.

My job, according to Colonel Benson, is to read the letters in chronological order and determine if any classified information had been passed along in them.

This morning, after the colonel gave me the assignment, my first response was that most classified material over fifty years old, minus a few exceptions, was automatically declassified. Colonel Benson, with a chagrined expression, wasn't interested in my immediate answer and said I was getting ahead of myself.

Well, you called me in for a reason, right? But I shut my mouth from saying more.

General MacWilliams wanted three questions answered: One, did the Army officer reveal classified information in his letters? Two, who the hell hid the trunks in the wall? Three, why were both sets of letters together?

Of all the questions, the last one, for some reason, gives my heart a pang. *Why* were both sets of letters together? I'm not necessarily a romantic person, but for some reason, it feels tragic.

However, personal feelings aside, one thing is clear to me: I will know the answers in a few weeks, but I wonder if I'll be happy with my conclusion.

Now, as I sit at the desk reading the letters from 1955, the door to the general's office buzzes, interrupting my thoughts. Someone swipes their badge against the reader, and Justin appears. He doesn't open the door all the way. I can tell he doesn't plan to come in. His body language is fairly easy to read.

"It's time to lock up the SCIF, Sergeant Holtslander, so I'm afraid that I have to ask you to stop for the day."

I rub my eyes. I have been reading since eight this morning. Justin doesn't have to be afraid to tell me to pack up at all.

"I was at a natural stopping point, anyway," I tell him.

The way he glances at the boxes, I can tell he's glad it isn't him working the case. Then his face softens when he says, "Letters have a way of bringing people together, don't you think?"

I find his question odd, but also a little revealing. Letters must have a special meaning to him. I know Justin has combat experience and I wonder if it was letters from a loved one that kept him sane. I know that the emails I received from my brother during my last deployment got me through some pretty tough days.

"I think letters, and communication in general, help us remember what's important to us, Sergeant Hauten," I say, standing up.

He nods. "I'd prefer it if you called me Justin. You must hate being locked away in here all day," he adds after I put everything away and grab my notebook. Colonel Benson made it clear that while, yes, this was my workspace, General MacWilliams oftentimes had need of the secure room, and that I should keep it clean. Justin looks down at my notebook and makes a face. "If your notebook has work-related notes in it, you'll have to leave it here."

I crack a sudden smile. I love it when other people follow the rules, too.

"It's not my first time in a secure office, Justin. I know the rules by heart. In fact, I wrote a couple of the manuals on this very subject. My notes are on the table. This is my personal organizer."

He opens the door wider for me, and I pass through. He spins the cipher lock and annotates the date and time on the log taped to the door. I have a meeting with the security team tomorrow to gain permissions as well as the code to the door. I can't keep asking Justin to open it for me each day, now can I?

We say our good-nights to Colonel Benson and I follow Justin out of the suite.

"How are you liking DC so far?" Justin asks.

"I've been here a couple of times when I visited my brother. He's in the Navy, but is now stationed in Bahrain. I guess you could say I'm getting used to it. Other than my roommate and my brother's boyfriend, I can't say that I know many people here."

"Your brother's *boyfriend*?"

The expression on his face doesn't escape me. He's curious about this fact, but not in that *tell me all the details so I can judge you* way. He seems genuinely curious.

"Tanner's amazing. I love him to death. Jon and Tanner better get married soon or I swear to God I will strangle one or both of them for being stupid."

"That's pretty cool," he says. I can tell he wants to say more on the subject, like maybe I've hit a topic he's interested in, but he stays quiet. I glance at his ring finger and observe the black band. I shouldn't speculate, but I do. I wonder if Justin is gay. If he is, at least he knows I'm a fan of gay marriage and that I won't judge him.

As we move through the corridors, I notice that we aren't headed in the direction of the Metro entrance. We go up two floors and into a reception area.

I'm about to ask him where we are going when he clears his throat and says, "Some friends and I do this thing every Tuesday. We call it *Tuesday Night Trouble.* Dinner, hiking, a movie, that type of thing. If you're not doing anything, you're more than welcome to join us tonight. It's Nebraska's turn to pick the venue, so it may not be the best night to join the group, but if you do, you'll get to know my friends and family. We can be a little..." He trails off, but a humorous voice from inside the reception area finishes the statement for him.

"Fun, crazy, insane, and extremely good looking. Take your pick," the owner of the voice says. He's a tall man with red hair, and if you exchanged his uniform for a plaid shirt, he'd be a dead ringer for the Brawny Paper Towels man. "Though my bet's on *extremely good looking.*"

"Sergeant Holtslander, this is Sergeant Sean Walker," Justin says, introducing me to his friend.

Or maybe this is his boyfriend.

"Call me Nebraska," Sergeant Walker says easily. He's over six feet tall, built like a machine, and handsome in a goofy way. If anything, the twinkling, *I don't take anything seriously* look in his eyes makes me like him all the more. I can also tell that Nebraska and Justin are just friends, maybe even best friends, and when Nebraska winks at me, it solidifies my impression. The freckles on his face are just too cute to ignore.

"Nice to meet you, Nebraska." I shake his thick hand. I could easily fit two hands in one of his. He holds my hand for a second longer than necessary. *Is he flirting with me?* The idea is almost laughable. Almost. Other than Dillan, who is way over the top with his antics, men do not often flirt with me. "I'm Keira."

"Are you going to join us?" Nebraska asks.

"That depends," I say. "What's the plan?"

"It will dazzle and inspire you like nothing you've ever experienced. Let me ask you two simple questions," Nebraska says. The way he says it, it reminds me of an announcer for one of those late-night infomercials.

"Oh...kay..." I answer haltingly. I'm not sure what to make of him. He's funny and goofy, but I also get the impression that he'd jump in the middle of a fight just for the hell of it.

"How good are you at bowling?"

I let out a laugh. I suppose I was expecting something else, like *breaking and entering* or playing a game of double-dare across a four-lane interstate.

"Oh dear," Justin mutters.

I look between the two friends. The taller of the two, Nebraska, is grinning like he's high on excitement, and Justin, with his dark hair and dark expression, appears ready to enter a dungeon, never to see the light of day again. How could one suggestion garner such two opposite reactions?

"I guess I'm all right at it," I say. "What's the second question?"

"We need another person to even out the teams," Nebraska says. "Got anyone in mind that might want to go?"

"My roommate might be interested. Sounds like fun."

Justin shakes his head.

"You've never been bowling with Nebraska before. By the end of the night, you'll have a completely different definition of *fun*."

Dillan

After I get home and change into casual clothes, I wonder about how to ask Keira out to dinner. Should I make it more of a challenge, like maybe I'm daring her to hang out with me, or should I be nonchalant about it all?

Doubt creeps in.

Maybe I shouldn't have made reservations.

Normally, I'm much more confident than this. I smile, and the girl says yes. Or, the girl *asks* me, I smile, which makes her smile, and then *I* say yes. None of that will work on Keira. In fact, it stands to reason that no matter what I say or how I say it, it will have the opposite effect on her.

Then do the opposite.

Act like you don't care if she goes or not, Dillan.

In fact, I plan on *barely* mentioning it to her. I'll make it more of an afterthought, *If you're not busy, Keira, feel free to swing by. But I'm sure you're too busy for going out tonight.*

Of course, the opposite of opposite could occur, meaning she'll agree with me that she is too busy to go out. Then I'll find myself sitting alone at a restaurant that I really didn't want to eat at anyway.

Be honest, Dillan. You want to impress Keira while, at the same time, you want to piss her off, too. You can't have her, and you want *her* to want *you*.

So much for my oath of ignoring her. She's not even here and I cannot *not* think about her. In a matter of days, the woman has me unbalanced. She's strong, smart, highly functioning, independent, sarcastic, cute, and, worst of all, she's immune to me.

It's no wonder that I'm thinking about her. What I should be thinking about is how to get back at her for lying to me.

"You look deep in thought," Keira says from the door.

I'm standing in the middle of the living room, gazing idiotically at the damn wall. I didn't even hear her come in.

"How long have you been standing there?" I ask.

"Long enough to realize you've had some sort of conversation in your head." She gives me a once-over, like maybe she's trying to figure out why I'm dressed casually. Or maybe she's picturing me naked. I like the last thought better. "Is that Jon's shirt?" Keira asks.

Ah, so she was inspecting my beat-up *VonSault Summer Rock Fest* T-shirt. Jon, Tanner, and I flew to Germany two years ago to attend the five-day-long fest. Sadly, I don't remember much of it. Too much Dunkelweizen. Though I do remember that that's when Jon and Tanner revealed their feelings for each other.

In a way, that summer rock fest was the start of my life changing.

Jon and Tanner quickly turned serious and I turned into the welcomed third wheel. I wasn't bitter about it. Not in the least. I couldn't be more happy for them, and they make a great couple. In a way, wearing the shirt made me feel a bit closer to them, to the way it used to be.

It dawned on me that maybe I want what they had. That maybe I'm not complete, either.

You could use a challenge. Was that challenge standing in front of me, giving me an odd look?

"Dillan?" Keira had a bored, yet amused, look on her face.

"Jon and Tanner have the same shirt. I was just

remembering the fest, the beer, and the pretty German girls. Good times."

Her eyes narrow at me, which was the point. I don't want her to know what I am really thinking.

"Do you speak German?"

"No, but I'm fluent in a woman's body language."

"Right," she says, and walks away from me. When she reaches her door, she turns around. "What's my body language saying right now?"

I put my finger to my temple, as if to illustrate that she's a puzzle. I study her unguardedly. Her dark hair is pulled up in a bun, but it's a little disheveled, and wisps of hair frame her heart-shaped face.

I would call her charming, but I would never admit to using the word *charming*.

She's still wearing her Army uniform, but it isn't difficult to imagine her in her running outfit. Keira, at five-eight or five-nine, is on the slim side, and I wonder what she looks like naked.

Reading Keira is simple. I don't need a dictionary or a translator to know that she's annoyed at me and probably with the discussion, too.

"It says that you're hungry," I say.

When she laughs, I know I caught her off guard, and in a good way. Maybe she isn't a robot.

"Do you want to go out tonight?" Keira asks.

She says it so fast that I get the impression she blurted it out before she could change her mind. Victorious lightning strikes shoot up and down my body. *Why yes, I am an agreeable gentleman*, I think.

But I should haven't felt smug so soon. She wasn't finished.

"The sergeant I work with asked me to join his group

tonight. They need even numbers for the two bowling teams, and with me added, it makes the numbers odd. So I volunteered you."

"Wait," I say. I keep the jealousy out of my voice. "Let me get this straight. You were asked out tonight, but because the group now needs another person—any poor schmuck will do—you signed *me* up?"

"Calm down, Dillan. It's not like I put you on a black market donor list for organ harvesting. It's just bowling. I talked to Jon about it and he said you can—"

I cut her off, suddenly upset that she consulted Jon before asking me.

"That I can *go*?" I scoff. "I don't need Jon's permission to go out with his sister."

Keira's mouth turns into an O. Instantly, I know I've said the wrong thing. I let the idea of her going out on a date affect me. I've turned a simple conversation into something else entirely.

Into something *awkward.*

"To spare yourself any future embarrassment, let me finish what I'm saying before you jump in with the first stupid thought that materializes in that brain of yours," she says. "Jon said you can *bowl really well.*" Keira clears her throat. "Did you and Jon argue before I moved in? I mean, you two are still friends, right?"

Should I fib or tell the truth?

"He's still my best friend and will be for the rest of my life. Jon's like a brother to me. He cares about you, that's all."

"You sounded like an automaton just then. I'm not in elementary school, Dillan. Obviously something was said. Spill it."

I can't tell if she's upset or if this is just everyday

business with her brother.

"You're off limits." I take a few steps toward her. I see her working her jaw, like she's trying to keep her anger in check. I like how hot she looks right now. "I'm not allowed to touch you." A few more steps. I lower my voice. Maybe by telling her she isn't allowed to have me, I can work this in my favor. *But am I willing to endanger my friendship with Jon just to get a rise out of Keira?* Yes. Yes, I am. "I'm not allowed to flirt with you." I'm a few inches away. She smells like cherry Chap Stick and dusty books. "I shouldn't fix your hair." I tuck a wisp behind her ear. She shudders under my fingers. "I'm not supposed to tell you that you're beautiful or that I want to know how your lips will taste." I trail a finger down her chin and move in slightly. "And guess what?" I ask now that my lips are scant seconds away from being able to kiss her delectable lips.

"What?" she asks in a husky whisper.

She swallows quickly, and her intake of breath and the fluttering of her eyelids burns my insides like something fierce.

I can't believe I'm about to do what I'm about to do.

I take a step back. Then another, and another, until I'm several feet away. Her eyes shoot daggers at me, but other than that, she looks just like she did earlier. Inconvenienced. Annoyed. Then bored.

"I won't be doing any of those things, Keira," I say seriously. I feel the lie deep in my stomach, but there's no way I can let Keira know that she truly affects me. If I kissed her, she wouldn't have stopped me. Not right away, at least. She was caught up, just like I was. But there would have been regret on both sides, and I didn't want to live like that with her. "I promised Jon that I'd keep my distance. And I keep my promises. Plus," I say, raising a hand as if to illustrate the point further. She lifts an eyebrow like she just can't wait to hear the wisdom. "I spoke to Tanner this morning." Both eyebrows go up now. "I know that you lied about this weekend. Not nice, Keira."

There. I got her back, but if the anger coming off her had a heat signature, I'd have first degree burns all over my body.

It was totally worth it.

CHAPTER EIGHT

Keira

I can't believe I almost let him kiss me. I can't believe that I kinda-sorta-maybe wanted him to kiss me. Dillan! My brother's best friend. The man whore I'm rooming with. The man who's sexier than just about any other man I've ever seen. And he played me. Oh, he played me good.

I take a deep breath and curb my anger. I've got no one but myself to be angry with. Dillan was being Dillan. I expect him to act that way, and I shouldn't have succumbed.

But I did, dammit!

"Is that all Jon said to you on the subject?" I ask as if it's no big deal, as if I wasn't upset that my brother decided to treat me like a child. Granted, this is Dillan Pope we're talking about. But still. I certainly wasn't desperate enough to jump in the sack with my roommate after living with him for all of three days. I know enough about his reputation that Jon shouldn't have to worry about it. Furthermore, who cares what I or Dillan do? It isn't Jon's business who I date. "Because he said a whole hell of a lot more to me."

Dillan folds his arms across his chest. "Yeah, like what?"

"Jon rattled off all the STDs you've had, how many sexual partners you've been with, and how you have a penchant for blondes. Needless to say, Jon is rather happy that I'm a brunette."

My roommate doesn't look pleased. His face has turned red and his eyes narrow. I glance at the clock. He follows my gaze.

"Am I keeping you from your bowling orgy?" he asks roughly. His voice is equal parts sandpaper and quiet displeasure. All I can think about is how this is a lot like foreplay. I sort of like it.

"Why does everything have to be about sex with you?" I ask. "This," I motion between the two of us, "shouldn't be complicated. We're roommates, not lovers. Once you get past the fact that we can be friends without having to have sex or flirt or whatever, the quicker we can over whatever hostility you hold toward me."

Dillan grits his teeth. "I do not feel any hostility toward you, Keira."

"Is that so? Then how come you went as far as pretending to try and kiss me to prove a point? That's not just hostility, that's playing with someone's emotions. *My* emotions, Dillan. It isn't fair. It isn't nice. It's sexist. I get it. You're good looking. You can have almost any girl you want just by blinking at her. I'm not some doxy or a girl you can pick up for a one-night stand. Look at me," I say. I tug at my uniform, illustrating my next point. "I'm a soldier, Dillan. I've been deployed three times. I've seen things no one should have to see, and I've got to live with that. I'm proud to serve our country. I love it, in fact. You may think I'm stiff and stuffy, and that's fine. It doesn't bother me. Well, maybe it does a little bit, but those things aren't all that define me, so I can let the insults slide off my back. Besides, I know you really don't mean them. Listen," I pause. "I'm sorry for lying to you about Tanner's invitation. I promise that I was going to tell you."

My roommate lets out a long breath and shoves his hands in his jeans pockets. "I guess I never thought of it that way. I'm sorry for treating you with anything less than respect, Keira. Can I call a cease-fire? How about a treaty? The Dillan-Keira Peace Treaty?"

I stare at him for a moment. He truly looks sorry. Penitent, actually. For some stupid reason, I also notice that his hair is a bit lopsided, and lopsided is exactly how I'd describe the boyish grin tugging at his lips right now.

"Okay. I prefer that it be called The Keira-Dillan Peace Treaty. So..." I hesitate, wondering if I should bring the bowling subject back up. "Did you want to go bowling or not? I agreed to meet them at six."

He looks at the clock and sees what I do. Fifteen minutes from now.

"You do realize that if I go, the peace treaty doesn't apply to bowling, right?"

"I'm not worried," I say with a grin. I'm glad we settled our differences. I have a feeling things will be different from here on out. I turn to go inside my bedroom to change. "I'll be out in a minute."

"Two, eight, and twelve," Dillan says suddenly.

"What?"

"I've had two *curable*, sexually transmitted diseases, eight one-night stands, and," he pauses, obviously counting, "Twelve serious-ish relationships."

"Oh," I say for lack of a prepared response. How does one respond that something like that? I can't just say *thank you* or *that's awesome* or *congratulations*.

Truth is, that's not nearly as bad as I thought it would have been. As for the first number, well, zero would have been better. Two wasn't terrible. As for the second, I'll honestly admit that I assumed it would be in the higher double-digits. Eight one-night stands? That isn't a deal breaker, not for a man in his thirties.

Twelve relationships? That's a lot of ex-girlfriends.

What about just regular hookups that weren't one-night-stands or relationships? That number must be pretty high and, if I'm being honest with myself, I don't want to know it.

"Your turn," he says. Dillan is grinning like he's trapped me in a manner I could never get myself out of. "Out with it. I told you mine, now tell me yours, or I'll force you to tell me."

"Why on earth would I tell you that information?"

"Well, just by saying that, you've already confirmed for me that the answer isn't zero for any of them. Tell you what, Sergeant Brunette," he laughs. "Whoever has the higher bowling score tonight wins."

"Meaning that if you have the higher score, I'll owe you an answer?"

"You're a quick one!"

I roll my eyes. "What do I get if *I* have the higher score?"

He cocks an eyebrow. I feel like there's a world to discover inside those eyes. "What do you want to know?" he asks.

I think about this and realize that there isn't much I want to know. Well, maybe I should rephrase it by saying *I don't know where to begin* with what to know about him. Secretly, I want to know everything.

Then I have an idea. It's stupid, but playful, and I actually want to know the answer.

"You know what Stacey wrote on the bathroom mirror?" I ask, and Dillan nods. "I want to know what she meant when she wrote, *I loved it when you put it there.*"

I have a feeling he'd like to do more than *tell* me about it. If given the chance, he'd *show* me.

"Seriously?" he asks with a short, disbelieving laugh,

like maybe I'm punking him. "It's not what you think it is, Keira."

"Then you shouldn't be afraid to tell me in, oh," I check my wristwatch, "four hours from now."

He shakes his head. "Ditto. You've got a deal."

Dillan

Keira exits her bedroom wearing a colorful quarter-sleeve T-shirt, jeans, and blue canvas shoes. Her hair is not quite up and it's not quite down. More of a slap-together, messy ball at the nape of her neck that looks adorable as hell. I can tell that she doesn't give a crap about what she looks like tonight.

It's on the tip of my tongue to ask her, *Is that what you're wearing?* But I hold back. She's comfortable and I completely respect that.

I mean, it's just bowling.

Also, whoever's asked her out, I can tell she doesn't view it as a date. Otherwise, I imagine she would have put more than five minutes into getting ready. Hell, she spent more time arguing with me than getting dressed.

In short, Keira is the exact opposite of what I've come to expect women to look like when going out. This isn't necessarily a good or bad thing, just an observation. Strange how it took just one conversation with Keira to make me realize this.

She gives me a quizzical look that says, *Stop dallying, we need to go.*

And my response is, "I'm sort of expecting you to lead the way. I have no idea of where we are meeting your coworkers at."

"Yeah," she starts in a way that gives me the impression I won't be happy to hear where we're going. "About that. I'm supposed to tell you not to discuss, with anyone, living or dead, where we end up tonight."

"That makes no sense whatsoever."

"Just go with it, Dillan. I know. It's apparently a *secret* bowling location. I couldn't quite get all the details from Nebraska—that's his nickname, his real name is Sean Walker—about the bowling alley's real location."

"Are they going to blindfold us or something? Are they intelligence analysts, too? Is this some sort of intel game?"

"One question at a time, please. I feel fairly certain that I can speak for all intelligence analysts out there and state that no, this is not some sort of intel game. These guys are not intel types. Their backgrounds are in infantry and armor—guns, weapons, stuff like that."

I give her a crazy look as I lock up the apartment.

"And this is supposed to reassure me?"

She laughs.

"I'll admit it sounds...unorthodox, but the way they described it, it should be a lot of fun."

"So, once we get there, I cannot tell anyone where this amazing, secret bowling alley is? Because whoever owns the bowling alley isn't interested in new customers or making money?" I hope she's getting the sardonic tone in my voice. "Are you sure this isn't a black market for organ harvesting?"

"I've told you everything I know," Keira says, laughing as I throw her own joke back at her.

"Not *everything*," I quip.

A small blush spreads across her cheeks. I know she isn't exactly an innocent. At twenty-seven, she would have had a boyfriend or two. I don't recall Jon ever talking about Keira having a boyfriend, but that didn't mean she didn't have one. Just meant she probably didn't discuss it with her brother.

Did I want to know her numbers? *Honestly, Dillan.* There's no way she could come close to my total number of sexual partners, and I'm not such a pig that I'd disapprove whatever her number happened to be.

I've always hated how guys' sexual conquests were celebrated whereas those of the opposite sex were generally frowned upon, or they were downright called sluts or whores. It's not like women were having sex by themselves. Still, I wasn't completely honest with her a few minutes ago.

She'd freak out if I told her my actual number was closer to the forty or fifty range.

As we make our way outside the apartment building and walk to the corner of Constitution and 9th, which is where her friends are picking us up, I find that as I walk in silence beside Keira, it's a nice feeling. I don't feel compelled to fill the space with idle chitchat or unimportant conversation, but I do want to know who I'd be meeting tonight.

Once we hit Constitution, I watch as Keira's eyes follow everyone who runs by us, and I wonder if she'd rather be running right now instead hanging out with me. On the other hand, it was her choice to ask me to tag along. Maybe she's wondering if *I'd* rather be doing something else instead of spending the night beating her at bowling.

"Who's picking us up?" I ask.

"Yeah, about that..." She trails off again. I get the feeling this is going to be a pattern tonight. "Nebraska mentioned other names, but I don't remember them. And Sergeant Hauten's significant other might be there. I'm not sure if his S.O. is a man or woman."

"That won't bother us," I add.

"Exactly. In fact, I only got the invitation after I talked a little bit about Jon and Tanner. Gives me the impression that Hauten—Justin—knows I'd be cool if he happened to be gay. Plus, he's very attractive, but he's obviously taken, so it doesn't really matter to me one way or the other."

Sergeant Justin Hauten, I pray to God that you're gay.

I didn't like the idea of Keira finding another man attractive if said man was straight. Good lord, Dillan. *Get. Over. Yourself.* I find Keira attractive, but that doesn't mean I don't find other women attractive, too.

"What kind of car should we be on the lookout for?"

Keira laughs. "Nebraska said it would be a gray minivan. The guy's a big guy, but unless one of them has kids, a minivan seemed a bit on the domesticated side. Actually, I'm very curious about tonight. Nebraska had me laughing so much that my side hurt after a few minutes."

"Sounds like you're going to be working with a fun group." I think about how I'll be working solo on the Joy Fromm case. Not much to get excited about.

"I think I see them," Keira announces, then waves at a gray minivan.

It pulls up to the curb and a beefy man with red hair jumps out. He's at least four or five inches taller than me.

"Keira!" he booms before folding her into a hug. It startles her as much as it surprises me. *Is this Sergeant Hauten?* Is this the type of guy she's attracted to? He releases her quickly and then reaches for me, an arm outstretched. Instead of shaking my hand, he pulls me into a hug as well. "You must me Keira's boyfriend," he says, pushing away, his hands still on my shoulders, assessing them. "Solid. Well built." He turns me around, inspecting me. Introducing himself appears to be an afterthought. "I'm Nebraska. Nice arms. You're on my team."

"Ah," I stammer.

Perhaps I could start by correcting him on the *Keira's boyfriend* part, but there's just too much to choose from and I'm all topsy-turvy after his man-assessment. I would also be lying if I didn't admit that I liked the fact that he complimented my arms. It's always nice to be appreciated, even by men I've never met before.

Keira's already inside the minivan talking to someone else as Nebraska gestures to the sliding door. "Got to get going, buddy" he says. "Cops don't exactly like curb hopping around here. Plus, I'm pretty sure they've tagged the car. We'll have to ditch it soon for another one."

"Tonight?" I ask.

Jesus, who the hell is this man? Ditching cars. Assessing men for bowling teams.

"Naw," he says as I step into the minivan. "I'd say we've got a few more days with this piece of shit."

He slides in next to me, effectively moving me down the bench seat with zero effort on my part. My left side is crushed up against a car seat. And there's a baby in it.

"Let's go, Julia," Nebraska says, thumping his hand against the roof of the car. The minivan pulls out into traffic as Nebraska makes the introductions. "Julia's driving, you already know Keira in the passenger seat, you lucky dog, Justin and Aaron are in the back row, and this precious little girl," he reaches over and gently pets the baby's golden hair, "is Ruby. She's my Ruby-Doll."

Ruby, who happens to be asleep, can't be more than a few months old.

I turn around to acknowledge the men, who sit close together, and the man on the left has his arm outstretched on the seat behind the other. *Definitely a couple.*

And gorgeous as hell.

Not that I notice those kinds of things, but damn, they gave Jon and Tanner a run for the money in the looks department.

"I'm Justin," the man on the left says, leaning forward slightly. "Nice to meet you."

"Aaron," the other says. We shake hands. Aaron is clean shaven while Justin sports a five-o'clock shadow. "Hope you don't get car sick."

"Normally, no. But..." I laugh as my stomach does a tiny somersault after the minivan makes a sharp turn.

Facing forward, I try to get a good look at Julia. I can't see much, except that she has blonde hair.

There's nothing for me to do but ask the most obvious question possible. "So, whose team is Ruby on?" I ask.

Nebraska, who's still leaning over me and cooing at the baby, straightens up and slaps me on the back, as if I just earned a kudos point from him.

"I like your boyfriend, Keira," he says.

CHAPTER NINE

Keira

Julia turns the minivan onto Virginia Avenue, and after a few minutes, she turns west on Canal Road and drives along the Potomac River for a few miles. She's a quiet driver, and other than a few words and questions about my liking Washington, DC, and learning that she's Ruby's mom, I mostly listen to the men in the back.

When I first turned around to say hi to Justin and Aaron, I found it difficult not to gape at them. Justin, with a gruff, five-o'clock shadow and brooding eyes, is an attractive specimen, but he is nothing compared to Aaron.

Holy crap that man, with his jet black hair, clean, chiseled jaw, and lean build, could have me panting if I didn't know instantly he and Justin are a couple. They weren't overt about it, but I could tell from their body language. And if that isn't proof enough, the matching black bands on their ring fingers certainly gave it away.

I let Dillan deal with the *Keira's boyfriend* flap. I found that it didn't irk me when he didn't correct Nebraska after he said it a second time. Truth is, I really don't care what others think of me. Not really. I'm not seeking their approval. After tonight, if they never want to see me again, I'll be okay with it.

Probably.

Okay, maybe not. I always found it difficult to make fast and steady friends. It isn't that I'm not lovable.

I've had several boyfriends over the years. None that I wanted to spend the rest of my life with. They were tolerable for a while. Until the next move or deployment or some other Army-related reason to move on. I rarely date military men.

When I come home at night, I don't want to talk about the Army or the war in Afghanistan or the latest Presidential policy that affected the troops.

I want to go to ball games and watch reality TV and talk about books. I want someone to run with me, and not only that, but to *keep up* with me when we run. It almost doesn't matter what he looks like.

I never expected to find myself in a minivan filled with a motley crew headed to a secret location to go bowling.

A motley crew and a baby named Ruby-Doll.

You could do with a bit of disorder, Keira.

If this isn't disorder, I don't know what is.

Julia pulls the minivan over on the side of the road, parks, and flashes her hazards.

"Is something wrong with the car?" I ask.

"I thought you said we weren't ditching the car tonight, Nebraska." Dillan says.

Is there panic in his voice?

Nebraska laughs. "Just waiting for traffic to clear before we turn down the road."

There's plenty of daylight left and I can see traffic going both east and west. I don't see any other roads to turn down.

I hear Justin sigh in the back of the car. As I remember it, he wasn't overjoyed at the prospect of Nebraska's choice tonight. Other than the huge secrecy of it all, I'm beginning to see how Nebraska could be something of a liability, both legally and in terms of someone's sanity.

"Once we stayed parked here for an hour before traffic cleared," Aaron says. His statement doesn't help matters.

"How many times have you come here?" I ask.

"Just the once," Justin answers dryly.

"I was still pregnant then," Julia adds. "I peed on the side of the road at least four times. I wasn't happy about that and felt the urge to shoot anyone who looked my way. Let's hope it doesn't come to that this time."

Shoot? It's on the tip of my tongue to ask what her profession is, but Nebraska claps his hands as loud as a male cheerleader.

"Eastbound is clear," he says eagerly. I swear he sounds like a ten year old as he says it.

"Westbound has two cars," I say. "If that holds, I suspect you can turn down this mysterious non-visible road."

Julia throws me a grin that tells me she's both amused and annoyed with the situation. I assume that this is why she's the driver. At least she has a little bit of control.

"I guess I don't understand why we have to wait," Dillan says. "I mean, who notices it when someone turns down a side road?"

"People notice it when the road isn't supposed to exist," Nebraska says.

"The cars have passed, Julia," Aaron says.

Without warning, Julia flings the car into drive. My head spins. Gravel spits out from the back of the minivan as she completes a U-turn, heads eastbound for a split second, and then immediately turns right.

Into the trees.

In the direction of the Potomac River.

"Um... I don't see a road," I start, but other than letting out a scream, I'm somewhat mute as she drives at the trees. I'm taking my cues from the others.

Chancing a glance at Dillan, I almost laugh at how big his eyes are, but I'm sure mine are just as alert. When I face forward, the trees loom straight ahead and I throw my hands onto the dash.

Just before the first tree, Julia shifts the car at an angle and drives between two tall trees, barely missing each one on either side of the minivan. She never once hit the brakes.

Who *are* these people? I've been working in the intelligence community for almost a decade and I have never encountered anything like this before now.

Daylight fades as we enter the canopy of the woods. The tires crunch on gravel, so there's some sort of man-made road here. Any second now, we're going to plunge into the Potomac River.

Dear Jon, I internalize my farewell note to my brother, *Sorry for getting into a minivan full of strangers just as they were about to commit vehicle-borne suicide. Love, your baby sister, Keira, aka, Sergeant Stupid.*

After a tense minute of rewording "my last goodbyes," I see a gray building rise up between the tall pine trees. Okay, so maybe we aren't about to take a bath in the Potomac.

The building is institutional-looking and it gives me the creeps. I imagine ghosts loitering inside its walls. As we pull up in front of it, I see a dozen other cars parked there as well. Perhaps this place is a secret, but others certainly know about it.

Before Julia jumps out, in a low voice, she says, "Welcome to the gang. You and me," she motions with her hands, "are the sane ones. Word of warning: don't accept any of Nebraska's bets tonight."

"Okay," I say, but mostly to myself since Julia's already out of the car before I can respond. I unfasten my seat belt.

"At least it was quicker this time," Aaron says to Justin.

I turn around to say something, but Aaron leans over and kisses Justin briefly on the lips. A tingle stirs in my belly.

There's something exciting and sexy watching two men kiss. Justin's eyes meet mine. There's a challenge there. *Say something*, his gaze orders. *I dare you to say something negative.*

"You have an interesting family, Justin," I say. I see a smile form on his lips as I exit the car.

What I don't say is, *I wish I had what you had.*

Though, perhaps without the crazy field trips.

Dillan

It isn't long before I come to the conclusion that Nebraska must have some sort of death wish. He also had a propensity for the carefully—or not so carefully—crafted double negative sentence.

Within a few minutes of entering the minivan, I learn everything that I need to know—that I *want* to know—about the man.

His semi-professional boxing career was cut short by his enlisting in the military. Some sort of court-ordered mandate. "I'll get back into boxing once I'm out," he says enthusiastically, as if he's giving a pep talk to a group of teenagers. "I'm still pretty fit. I might even get into mixed martial arts fighting. I'd ask you to punch my stomach. It's as solid as a rock, but I'm a little gassy tonight. Should've said no to that sixth corn dog."

I'm the only one listening, and it's because Nebraska continuously leans over me to talk to Ruby-Doll.

I learn that he was once featured on the cover of *People* magazine after a national news anchor said *yes*, and then *no*, to his marriage proposal, and that he still gets fan mail from all over the country.

"Elderly ladies are the best pen pals, ever, man!" he quips.

Then there was something about a former company commander shooting Justin, or as Nebraska calls him, *Hotten*, in Afghanistan; several Federal detainments; a seedy bar called The Itchy Nail; and how he solved—single-handedly, apparently—one of the biggest military conspiracies ever to exist that the public never knew about.

"Can't say much about it, of course," Nebraska starts, "but if you get a few beers in me, I can't promise not to *not* tell you all about it, Dillan. I feel like I can trust you. Any friend of Keira is a friend of mine. I mean, I just met her today. But I like you, man. You have a confident-looking face. So..." He hesitates after the car is parked in front of the big, gray building. My fingers are practically embedded into the passenger seat's headrest. "Are you two dating or what?"

"The appropriate answer is, none of the above."

I rub my jaw. *A confident-looking face?* I've never heard that particular compliment before.

"Ah, I see," he says, nodding. "Sometimes you shoot and you *don't* score."

He then *helps* me out of the minivan. To my left, Julia removes Ruby's car seat, rolls her eyes at us, and carries the whole thing with her.

"It's not like that. We're roommates," I say.

One of Nebraska's red eyebrows raises.

"Excellent. So Keira is fair game?" He claps his hands together.

"What?" I choke out. *Fair game?*

Hell no. Everyone else is already in the building. The sign in front says *Potomac Hospital for the Criminally Insane — Juvenile Ward. 601 Canal Road. Washington, DC.*

Nebraska elbows me.

"Thought so, buddy." He eyes me knowingly. "Don't worry. I've never messed with another man's girl before, even if she isn't his girl yet. Man code."

"Do you—do you think she likes me?" I ask quietly.

Why do I sound so insecure? I'm Dillan freaking Pope. Ladies man.

Charmer.

A sexy devil.

The man laughs like he's never laughed before.

"Not really. I don't think she looked at you once, pal." He puts a hand on my shoulder in a reassuring manner. Then he squeezes it. "I meant what I said earlier. Great arms. Amazing shoulders. I'm really glad you're on my team. Justin and Julia, who are both highly competitive, always kick my and Aaron's asses. Hope you're good at bowling. I've got a bet brewing for tonight that I can't wait to tell you about. Come on, let's go in."

Once inside, and after a security check-in counter where we have to leave either a hundred bucks or our drivers license, I fork over two fifties and meet the rest of the gang at lanes eleven and twelve.

The area is bright and atmospheric. The walls are white and contain bowling slogans and high scores. The smell of popcorn hits me so strongly that I remember I haven't had dinner. Which reminds me: I forgot to cancel the reservations.

The overhead speakers play rock music from the 1980s. Half of the lanes are full, and the rolling and crashing of pins completes an authentic picture.

If I didn't know the building once was a criminally insane ward for teenagers, I would have called someone a liar for even suggesting it. And this is just the first floor. What were the other three floors converted into? I ask Nebraska if he knows.

"I hear the second floor might become a gym, the third floor a restaurant and conference center, and the fourth floor is apparently reserved for several penthouse-style suites."

"Seems like the type of place well-paying corporate

owners could rent by the week to do some team building. Secret conferences off the grid, you know." I tuck the knowledge away just in case I need it for the Joy Fromm case. "How'd you find out about this place?"

I find an eighteen-pound ball. It's orange, blue, and purple, all swirled together.

"I won a bet against General MacWilliams a few months ago."

I'm not sure who General MacWilliams is, but I think he might be Keira's new boss.

"What kind of bet?"

"I bet that I knew exactly how much he weighed. If I was right, he had to tell me a Washingtonian secret. If I was wrong, I had to do two thousand push-ups. The way I see it, either way I was going to be a winner. The man's a sucker for harmless bets."

"That's not true," Justin says as he ties on his bowling shoes. "The man's a sucker for *any* bet, especially the kind he thinks he doesn't stand a chance of losing."

"So how did you win?" Keira asks. She asks it behind me.

I didn't realize she had been listening. The timing is interesting since we've got our own little bet going. I wonder if each of us thinks we won't lose. Probably.

"I've heard this before," Julia says, shaking her head, but not in an irritating way. I thought, at first, that she and Nebraska were a couple, but apparently I was wrong. "I'm going to order a few pizzas and then feed Ruby. Does anyone want anything from the snack bar?"

Everyone gives her their orders—which is mostly beer. I hand over a twenty, hoping it will cover what I owe. It's the last of my cash and I don't feel comfortable using my credit card here. I notice everyone else hands her cash, too.

"I'll take my niece," Aaron says, and Julia hands a sleeping Ruby into Aaron's arms.

Niece? Other than Ruby's white-blonde hair, I can see a bit of resemblance. But I won't ask. None of my business.

"I wonder if she's wearing her gun," Nebraska says nonchalantly, but there's a gleam in his eye as he watches Julia walk away.

The ball nearly drops from my hands.

"What?" I ask.

"Julia's a field agent with the FBI's Washington Bureau. Since I've known her, I think she's arrested me at least twice. Maybe three times. But the warrants don't stick. Counting on the fourth happening tonight. Anyway, you don't want to know about that." *Actually, I do*, I think. "So," he says louder, reminding the group of his center-of-attention status, "how'd I win the bet? Simple. I'm a former semi-pro boxer. Knowing what people weigh comes with the territory. I followed him to the men's locker room. I took my guess and then he stood on the scale, clothes and all. I won, he lost, and he told me about this jewel of a place."

As he's talking, I notice that Justin and Aaron both mouthed, *"I'm a former semi-pro boxer"* at the same time Nebraska says it, and I have to wonder if this statement is Nebraska's typical answer for the many questions asked of him.

All of them—Julia, Ruby, Nebraska, Justin, and Aaron —feel like one big family. With the exception of Ruby also being Aaron's niece, no one is related, but I can tell they experienced something big enough to keep them together.

I know that Justin, Nebraska, and Aaron served together overseas, that Justin and Aaron are a couple, and now the three of them work together at the Pentagon. How did Julia go from arresting Nebraska to becoming part of their family?

It was all cute *and* chaotic, if something could be both.

Sometimes, a family is more than blood relation. It's who understands you, who accepts you, who loves you.

I look sideways at Keira. This is why *her* brother is a brother to me.

"Lanes have been turned on," Julia says as she puts three big pizza boxes on the round tables behind the swivel chairs. Someone from the snack bar follows her and places four pitchers of beer on the other table. "Me, Justin, and Keira against Nebraska, Aaron, and Dillan. Team who loses has to pay the exit fee for the entire group."

"Exit fee?" both Keira and I ask at the same time.

"I told you it would be an interesting night, Keira," Justin says with a smirk on his face. "This is the kind of establishment where you pay the privilege to enter *and* exit. Trust me when I say we found out the hard way last time. Polishing fifty bowling lanes is not fun. We brought enough cash to cover you two since you didn't know."

I stand next to Keira as Julia throws a strike in lane eleven. Nebraska, after two goes, knocks down only seven pins. Everyone gets a turn. I knock down eight and pick up the last two, and Keira gets a strike with her twelve-pound, bubblegum-pink ball. I scowl at her and she sticks her tongue out at me. Justin throws strike after strike while Aaron, after he puts Ruby back in her car seat, never manages to knock all the pins down.

Other than Julia, who's the designated driver, whenever someone gets a strike, everyone takes a gulp of beer.

The competition seems to be between Julia and Nebraska, and after seven rounds, they are somewhat even.

"I've got to beat Julia tonight, buddy," Nebraska

confides in me after he throws two strikes in a row.

They must have some sort of bet going, and I wonder if this is what he said he'd tell me about later.

I've already had two beers and my aim is either getting better or it's getting worse, but I just can't tell. What I can tell is that Keira has barely finished her first beer, so she's on her game and isn't as buzzed as I am.

I watch as she steadies herself, takes aim, and moves forward. Her slim hips sway left, right, left, right, and it mesmerizes me.

"Strike!" Julia announces even though none of us need a verbal announcement. Amazingly, Ruby barely makes a noise, even while awake. "She's got my stubbornness," Julia says to me as I look down at her. "Plus, she's used to loud noises and these guys' loud voices. They're softies around Ruby."

"Seems like a great, loving family to me," I say. I didn't mean it as a loaded statement, like, *explain it to me why you're such a loving family*, but Julia stares at me for a long second, then nods.

Finally, she says, "Yeah, I don't know what I'd do without my guys."

Nebraska, for a tall man, runs gracefully up to Julia, nudges her side, and proclaims, "Guess who beat your score, Agent Fenske?" Julia looks up at monitor, and her face darkens. She must have lost the bet and I have to wonder what exactly Nebraska will extract from her with his win. "Your turn, Dillan," Nebraska says, nudging me. "Last round for you and Keira."

I look at the scoreboard in the ceiling. I'm at 231 and Keira's score is 207.

The first roll, I knock down six. Stupid nerves! I pick up the last four on the second throw. With the extra, third turn, I demolish all but one pin. My final score is 256.

"Beat that, Sergeant Brunette," I whisper in her ear as she passes me to get her ball.

She picks up her pink ball and crushes out two strikes in a row. I cringe as I see the score.

If she gets five pins with her third bonus roll, we're even. If she knocks six or more down, she wins. She retrieves her ball from the holder, steadies herself, and my eyes lock on her hips. The ball rolls and seven pins bite the dust.

Final score: 258. I sigh into my hands.

On the way out, Nebraska and Aaron hand over three hundred dollars for our exit fee of fifty dollars per person. Julia, Justin, and Keira's total score obliterated ours.

Keira saunters up to me and places her hands on her hips.

"When we get home, I'm getting that answer, Dillan."

I almost laugh out loud. I didn't mind telling her, bet or no bet.

But she is going to be *so* mad when she realizes what she *won.*

CHAPTER TEN

Keira

For the entire ride back, I couldn't get the word *home* off my mind. I can't believe I said it.

Home.

Dillan's apartment wasn't home. I would barely classify it as a place to crash, but never a home.

Now he is going to think that I like living there and that I want to stay. Granted, I haven't even begun to look for an alternate living situation. And it isn't like Dillan has hinted that I should stay. He hasn't said anything about me moving out, either.

What I can't figure out is why it even matters to me what he thinks. And why do I want to know what the lipstick message means? Dillan's attractive. So what? I've been down this thought-road before.

You are attracted to him, Keira.

No, I'm not.

It's not lost on me that I'm talking to myself *and* that I just won a bowling game in a refurbished juvenile mental ward. I don't see how it can get worse.

"Thanks for joining us tonight," Julia says. She sounds genuine. It takes me a second to realize we're just outside Dillan's apartment building. It is almost eleven. Time to go. "Before you go, I need you to look directly into this pen-like object so we can wipe your memories." She holds up a regular pen and laughs.

It actually wouldn't surprise me if she had something like that. I don't work much with the FBI since their focus is mostly centered on domestic issues while my specialty is in security intelligence. But the government has cool toys.

"I had a great time," I tell her, yawning.

She hands me a business card. Julia Fenske, Field Agent.

"Me, too," Dillan says, leaning forward.

We say our good-nights, leave the minivan while no one really listens as Nebraska talks about ideas for *next time*, and enter the apartment building.

"I have a feeling that whatever the *next time* event is, it might be highly illegal," Dillan jokes. We're the only ones in the elevator going up. I look straight ahead, but I smile at his statement. "You're quiet," he says. "What, no gloating over your win?"

"For the record, I never gloat. Plus, there really wasn't much at stake, was there? I don't see the need to gloat over winning a trivial bet."

He turns his entire body to face me.

I automatically look at him. One eyebrow is raised in a questioning *I totally don't believe you* manner. His jaw is dark with stubble. His light green eyes search mine for a quick moment.

"Okay, then. If it was so trivial, I suppose you don't want to know what Stacey meant."

The elevator dings and we get out.

"I already know what it means," I say.

The lipstick message said: *I loved it when you put it there.* I mean, there's only so many places a man can put *it*. And putting it *there* is never going to happen with me. Dillan unlocks the door and secures it after we enter the apartment.

His keys jingle as he places them in the ceramic bowl on top of the narrow half-moon table near the door.

Standing there and staring at him will never do, so I

move to the fridge to take out a bottle of water. I do a double take after looking again at the fridge's contents. It's full of food. And not just bachelor condiments and the obligatory lonely onion.

"So tell me what her message means," he says as I inspect the fridge.

Chicken thaws in a bottom shelf, three types of peppers decorate an internal drawer, and some sort of marinara with chunky herbs and spices sits on a higher self, next to eggs, yogurt, cubed cheese, and a pale yellow ball of dough.

Granted, one of the shelves is full of uniquely labeled beer. Even I appreciate a good beer.

For an intelligence analyst, I am a bit slow on figuring out Dillan enjoys cooking. I suppose I didn't put two and two together until now.

Dillan — I can't wait to taste you again. I loved it when you put it there. xoxo Stacey

She wasn't referring to sex at all. Stacey was talking about his cooking.

His food.

"The bet was that you had to tell me, not that I would tell you what I think it means," I clarify, closing the fridge.

I finish the bottle of water and place it in the small recycling bin under the sink.

I lean against the island that separates the kitchen from the living and dining areas. He leans opposite me. Dillan's eyes are a bit bloodshot. He drank at least twice as much beer as I did.

"A bet is a bet." His voice is husky and I imagine that this is how he sounds when he wakes up in the morning.

His bedroom voice.

I clear my throat to dislodge the stupid, betraying thought. It was doing things to me, like allowing me to imagine myself lying next to him, hearing him talk like that to me.

It felt too...intimate. Remember, Keira, you really, really, *really* don't like this guy. Beer and victory made a silly goose out of me.

A couple of minutes go by.

"I don't have all day." My words are laced with impatience. Good, let him see that I find him irritating. But my impatience doesn't appear to have an effect on him.

"Before you moved in Saturday night, I spent a good portion of the day making tiramisu. Stacey enjoyed it Saturday night."

That is way too easy of an answer. I know there is more.

"But she wrote *tasted you* and *when you put it there.* I don't see the connection."

My cheeks flush after repeating her red-hued words. I'm not a prude, but I suppose I'm not above asking embarrassing questions to get an answer.

Dillan grins. "I had hopes that you might say those exact parts."

"Don't be a dick. Just answer the question so I can go to bed."

"Retract the fangs, Sergeant," he says with a highly false chuckle. He didn't like being called a dick. "Stacey enjoyed it because we ate the tiramisu off of each other." He leans in closer. The grin is gone. It's replaced with something else. Hunger. Just because another woman found him sexy enough to eat food off him didn't mean I would, too. "It got pretty messy and...sticky. I spent at least an hour licking sweetness off of her." He pauses. "Including *there*. Especially *there*."

There is nothing logical to say to that. It's...crazy.

It's...doing funny things to my stomach. *Lustful* things to my brain.

Snap out of it, Keira. He's talking about things he's done with another woman. There is no earthly reason why you should want him to do the same thing to you.

"Look at the time," I blurt out. "I don't want to make you late for your STD appointment in the morning."

I stop at my bedroom doorway.

"Don't be like that."

"Like what?" I turn around fast.

"Judgmental," he says with a sigh. "I would never judge you, Keira. I happen to like sex with women who also like to have sex. It's not a big deal. I don't cheat. I'm safe. And I worship the ground they walk on when I'm with them. No one gets hurt. None of the women I date are interested in long-term relationships. I'm not out there breaking hearts. But here's a question." He pauses again. "Why does any of this matter to you?"

His face changes expression. From defiance to concern. He thinks someone like him broke my heart.

But he's dead wrong.

I never let them get close enough to break my heart. I've never been in love and I certainly don't plan on falling head over heels for him or anyone else.

Before he can question me about broken hearts and past boyfriends, I say, "You're right. It doesn't matter to me. I'm just tired." He looks at me like he doesn't believe me. I nearly close the bedroom door, ready for the conversation to be over, when I add, "I didn't mean to seem judgmental, but..."

But you challenge what I know and make me want to come out of my own skin. Like maybe there's a part of you that only needs to bring it out in me.

"But what?" he asks when I don't say more.

"Use a tarp next time. The cleanup will be easier."

He continues to laugh long after I close the bedroom door.

Dillan

For the amount of time Keira inspected the inside of my fridge—grabbing a bottle of water takes, what, five milliseconds?—I knew she figured out what Stacey meant. Well, she figured out that the gist of it involved food.

Keira's face went from pale to pink to blushing red. But not the type of blushing I would have liked, which is the *you turn me on, please rip my clothes off*, blushing red.

Nope.

Her blush was the *I can't believe I just repeated those words* and, as orderly as Keira was, the tarp suggestion was funny. And valid.

All that licking made my taste buds numb for two days straight. I'll never look at, or eat, tiramisu in the same away again.

Originally, I wanted to leave the answer vague, plain, and utterly boring. I made food. We ate it. There. End of story. But, no. She had to have an exact answer to Stacey's lipstick statement.

It's her own fault for getting angry.

There's a bit of rustling inside Keira's bedroom and I wonder if she's throwing her stuff back inside that hideous duffle bag, ready to leave.

Doubtful. Keira isn't the spiteful type.

What she is, is stuffy, professional, and very proper. Besides, it's nearly midnight and she has nowhere to go. In the morning, she'll go back to ignoring me. I should do the same. I should stop egging her on.

I tidy the kitchen and go into my room.

As I strip down to my boxers, I forget that my bedroom

door is open—I'm not fully used to the idea of having a female roommate—and spot Keira standing in the dark living room, staring at me.

Her hair is pulled up in a high ponytail and her caramel-colored skin practically glows against a white tank top and billowy white shorts that may or may not be underwear. I'm hoping for underwear, but Keira would never leave her bedroom unless fully attired.

"I was heading to the bathroom," she mutters.

I can totally hear the horror in her voice. She wants to make sure I know that she didn't come out here to watch a peep show.

I let out a short laugh.

"You saw worse when you moved in." I was fully naked when she moved in. "Well," I clarify. "I wouldn't call it *worse*."

"No, you were right the first time," she says. Ouch. Miss Bee has a stinger. Her mouth is grim. "While I'm out here," she continues, "I might as well tell you that our living arrangement isn't going to work. Give me a few days to figure something out. Thanks for allowing me to stay here. I know you agreed to it because Jon asked for a favor. But our personalities don't mix and I don't need the added stress of wondering if I'm going to find my roommate in various stages of nudity or tangled up with another woman. Bedrooms have doors for a reason."

I go from being amused and high on life to feeling about two feet tall.

She doesn't let me respond. Immediately, she goes into the bathroom, does her thing, and quickly retreats back into her bedroom. I hear the soft click of the latch, and when I hear her push in the lock on the doorknob, I fume a bit.

Does she honestly think that I'm going to barge into her room without her permission?

Okay, this morning when I looked at her uniforms doesn't count. She wasn't in there and my first motive was to make sure she was okay if she was. Curiosity, naturally, was my second motive.

Reaching out, I close my bedroom door—I lock it to spite her—and flick on the television. I barely register what's on the channel. But it's noise. I kick the boxers into my dirty clothes pile, turn off the light, and get into bed.

I lay there for a while, trying to figure out exactly where I went wrong in my approach with Keira.

Truth is, it started out wrong. From the exact moment she entered the door Saturday night, to tonight, when, as I was trying to be truthful with her, it all backfired in my face.

Face it, Dillan, Keira isn't your type, and you two are not compatible.

She's in a completely different world than me. Other than an Air Force captain I dated a couple of years ago, I know next to nothing about women in the military. There's no reason to start now. Obviously, Keira built up her own set of roadblocks and there is nothing I can do about it.

It still stung that she'd rather move out than deal with me. I'm not exactly a monster. I've never heard of a case where someone flirted with someone to death. But what a way to go. *Cause of death, doctor? A sudden case of Overflirtacitius, nurse.*

It takes me a while before I fall asleep because, deep in my gut, I have a feeling things with Keira are going to go from bad to worse.

CHAPTER ELEVEN

Keira

The next time I see Dillan for more than ten seconds is at Tanner's baseball game on Friday night. For the last three days, he has avoided me like the plague. And I don't blame him. I told him to back off, and he backed off.

There is zero reason for my disappointment. He did exactly as I asked. He even went as far as leaving *The Washington Post's* Apartments for Rent section out for me yesterday.

Part of me wanted a fight. No, that's not right.

I want someone to fight *for* me. It sounds lame even to my own ears. Wanting Dillan to fight for me is like asking the ocean to completely evaporate. Impossible. Dillan won't change his stripes for anyone.

Wednesday, Thursday, and Friday, I immerse myself in General MacWilliams' office. I read the letters and take notes. Wash, rinse, repeat.

The first hundred letters or so—the original letter and its subsequent response—from 1955 and 1956 are nothing special. They read perfunctory.

Topics included the weather, current events, and books. At first, I wondered if the letters were really about something else. Weather meant war. Current events of the day described classified information. Books might have been something about politics. But I never found a pattern. They weren't like lyrics, where the words by themselves could be interpreted innocently or, as intended by the songwriter, not so innocently.

For the most part, these two individuals seemed to truly

only want to discuss surface topics—polite pen pal letters that no one would think twice about.

And, as 1956's letters came to a close, I felt that the woman, Greta Weber, was warming up toward the Army Officer, Major William Hall. She had begun signing her letters, *Warmly Yours, Greta.*

The only thing that made this odd, in my opinion, was that it involved an Army officer and a foreign national.

I decide to ask Colonel Benson about it.

"Sir," I say after the secretary lets me in his office with a stern two-minute-max warning, "are you aware of any military letter-writing programs from the 1950s that encouraged Department of Defense officers to communicate with foreigners? From what I've read so far, these two individuals do not seem naturally inclined to write to each other. I've found nothing in common between them. I'd like to think that some sort of code is involved, but I've yet to come across anything that raises my suspicions."

Colonel Benson barely looks up from the e-mail on his monitor. I have no doubt that he has more important items on his plate right now.

"We have a U.S. pen pal program in place for deployed troops," he says. "But I'm not aware of a foreign government version. I recommend you talk to the Pentagon Historian's office. They would know. Sergeant Hauten can show you were they are located."

He logs off his computer and walks me out of his office. His secretary gives me an *I told you so* look.

I hang back in the reception area after Colonel Benson departs for his fourteen hundred meeting.

"Mrs. Atkins, do you know the office number for the Pentagon Historian?"

The secretary, who sits behind an L-shaped desk, flips

through a massive rolodex. She must have three decades' worth of numbers stored in that thing. That's about how long I think she's worked at the Pentagon. She's a fixture.

The reception area is part waiting room, part common room, and part detention center. The vibe is somewhere between *welcoming* and *forbidden.* Mrs. Atkins manages General MacWilliams' day-to-day schedule, as well as that of all of his military assistants, the same way a MLB coach handles his players: with grit, determination, and a bit of well-placed praise.

The bowl of candy on her desk probably helps, too.

Piss off the secretary and your life is hell from that point forward. She's your entry point to the highest ranking Army General in the Department of Defense.

So when she smiles at me, I feel like I've won a prize.

"Here you are, Sergeant Holtslander." Her voice is filled with sugar as she hands me a small slip of white paper with the information on it. "Word to the wise, Sergeant, they are called The Historical Office of the Office of the Secretary of Defense. *Not* the Pentagon Historian."

"Thanks, Mrs. Atkins," I say, pocketing the paper.

I leave the reception area, head to the D Ring, enter the top secret facility that the general's secure office is located in, and return to my task at hand: reading letters, taking notes. Greta seems friendlier, though the Army major is still reserved.

I repeat this process Thursday and Friday.

I call the historian's office, but they can't see me until next week.

By the end of the week, I'm ready for a break, and Tanner's game against the Orioles tonight cannot come at a better time. I change at work and hop on the yellow line, transfer to the green line at L'Enfant Plaza, and exit at the Navy Yard.

I'm an hour and a half early, but fans of both the Nationals and the Orioles are already arriving at the stadium. The way Tanner once explained it to me, when these two particular teams face off, the stands are packed due to the fact that the Nationals and the Orioles are regionally so close to one another. Fans from both sides have relatively easy access to the stadium.

At the will-call window, I pick up my ticket and make my way to the diamond seats section. I wonder if Dillan's seat is right next to mine. Probably.

When I find my seat, only a few others are in that section, but a woman comes up to me rather suddenly.

"You must be Alec's *new* girlfriend." It's a statement, not a question, and very passive aggressive. She must be referring to Alec Huffman, the Nats pitcher and reigning playboy.

The woman, who looks to be in her early twenties, is brunette, tall, slim, but with ample cleavage that she amply displays. Her sleeveless arms are full of tattoos. The only thing that makes me think she isn't just an airhead is the fact that she wears thick, purple glasses.

She reminds me of a hip librarian who could spout Shakespeare in three different languages.

However, her rudeness certainly wipes away whatever nice thoughts I might have had.

"You must be making assumptions," I say, turning away from her to observe the field.

Someone rakes the infield dirt while someone else traces the bold lines of the diamond. Typical pre-game stuff.

Ignoring the woman doesn't work. She moves down two aisles and sits next to me.

"Sorry about before. It's just that we've heard Alec has

a new girl. I'm Zoe, Randy's fiancé." Randy "Big H" Hernandez is the Nationals' catcher.

I take a calming breath before responding. "Well, when you do meet Alec's new girlfriend, one thing is certain: your friendly welcome will knock her off her feet."

Zoe scoffs as if she's never been told off before.

Then, after a pregnant pause, she asks, "Aren't you going to tell me who you are?"

"Hadn't considered it."

Zoe, *the committee chair for the welcoming party*, stands abruptly. "What a bitch!"

I've been called worse. Out of the corner of my eye, I see Dillan.

And right behind him, his date. I'd rather deal with them than Zoe. *That* must be why I'm somewhat pleased to see him.

Dillan

I make the introductions. “Stacey, this is my new roommate, Keira, my best friend’s little sister. Keira, this is my date, Stacey.”

Our two seats are right next to Keira’s, so I place Stacey next to her, and I sit on the other side of Stacey. I’m not trying to avoid Keira, but I figure it’s best for everyone if the ladies sit next to each other. That way, neither thinks I’m doing anything fishy, like having sex with both. Not that Keira doesn’t already know I’m with Stacey, but I don’t want Stacey thinking the same.

But as wishes come true, both end up ignoring me and talking to each other all night.

After the initial *hi-how-are-you-I’m-great-thanks-for-asking-how-are-you-doing* is done and out of the way, Stacey gets right down to the very thing she wants to know.

“Tanner is your brother’s boyfriend, right?”

“Yeah,” Keira answers proudly. I know that she loves Tanner. “They’ve officially been together for two years, but it’s been longer than that.” Keira does finger quotes around the word *officially.*

Wait, what? No, she’s got it wrong. Tanner and Jon got together at the *VonSault Rock Fest* two summers ago. What else don’t I know about?

“That’s so sexy,” Stacey says. “I mean, I know Jon’s your brother, so *you* don’t think it’s sexy. But a man in love is something to behold. A man in love has his act together and he doesn’t have to prove himself to anyone around him.”

Keira has an odd look on her face, like maybe she can't believe she's enjoying her conversation with Stacey. Or maybe it's Stacey's profound view on the state of men in love.

"All I know is that Jon's never been happier than when he's with Tanner. It's not lost on either that they'll have a tough road ahead of them."

I lean forward. "Because of their sexual orientation?"

Both women glare at me as if they suddenly realized I was a Yeti wearing a kid's party hat.

"No," Keira says. "Because Jon's in the military and away from home a lot, and with Tanner in the majors, he's gone half the year with training and away games."

"I've seen it work," Stacey adds. "My dad met my mom before he was drafted during the Vietnam War. He proposed, Mom said yes, and he went off to war, she enrolled in college and then a foreign exchange program. They were separated for seven years before they saw one another again. Since that date, they've never been apart for more than a day."

"That's an amazing example of devotion," Keira says.

"Well," Stacey says with a small chuckle, "they hate each other now. After fifty years, they pretty much can't stand the sight of one another, but they don't know how to operate without the other. My folks are highly co-dependent. It's a fascinating case study. In fact, my brother went into psychology in order to study my parents and couples like them, and to learn why they usually stay together. Some of his papers for the Veterans Affairs have been published in *Psychology Now*. Perhaps you've heard of him; his name is Dr. Bergdorf Stacey."

Keira shakes her head, but I already know what her next question is.

"So Stacey is your *last* name? What's your first name?"

"Don't laugh, okay?" Stacey says. She pulls her long blonde hair to one side and runs her fingers through the bottom half in a brushing manner. "It's Bernadine. Berg is my twin. I think, to overcome the horrible *joint* nickname of BernaDorfy in our youth, we excelled at everything we tried. Sports, academics, public speaking, foreign languages, everything. I was a member of every club possible in high school and college. So was Berg."

A few minutes later, the game starts.

We cheer as loud as possible when Tanner runs out of the dugout. Stacey and Keira talk throughout the game, but I only catch parts and pieces of the conversation.

For some stupid reason, I'm miffed that they haven't talked *about* me or *to* me. Isn't that what they are supposed to do? The rational part of my brain knows that this thought is a fallacy. I suppose I didn't expect the two of them to hit it off so quickly. Or at all. I thought there'd be claws and terse words exchanged.

But neither woman was threatened by the other. I've never experienced this before. I've never experienced a situation where the one woman I *am* dating is becoming friends with the one woman who doesn't *want* to date me.

Could there be two such women on the planet as there are right now? And both within arm's reach?

Improbable.

After a couple innings, Stacey announces she's starving. "I could eat about five cheeseburgers." She leaves to go to the snack bar.

I look over at Keira. She's watching the game so fiercely that she doesn't blink.

Obviously she's trying to avoid a conversation with me.

"Enjoying the game, Keira?" I ask, leaning over Stacey's

empty seat.

"I *was*," she says, inching further away from me. "Stacey's very nice. I like her. I take back everything I said about her before I got to know her better."

This isn't going the way I pictured it. I didn't want to talk about Stacey.

I wanted to talk about *us*.

"Have you found an apartment yet?"

Her mouth sets. So that must be a *no*, then.

"I'm still looking—GREAT CATCH, TANNER!—did you see that, Dillan? Nats are up by two going into the eighth."

I missed the play, but I catch it on the Jumbotron. The Orioles' batter hit a straight shot right at the short stop and without blinking, Tanner caught what must have been a fast-flying, hard-as-hell ball.

As the team runs off the field, Tanner takes off his glove and shakes out his hand at his hip. I knew how important the majors were to Tanner. Injuries are taken seriously. Hopefully, it isn't bad. The last thing he'd want was to be sent back down to the minors team.

At the top of the ninth, Stacey returns. It's a good thing neither Keira or I wanted anything from her trip because she was empty handed and late.

"Can you believe that the guy behind me in line knew my brother?" Stacey asks.

"Huh?" I ask.

"I know," she agrees with whatever she thinks my 'huh' means. "What are the odds that *he* would say that *I* resembled someone he previously worked with?"

"I'd say pretty high considering that it's a regular pick-up line for guys," I say.

Stacey's angrily arched eyebrows practically wrestle me

to the ground. I notice Keira's amused expression.

She's enjoying the show. So now they're both interested in paying attention to me?

Great. I can't win.

"You don't think I know that?" Stacey asks.

Right, I think, coming to my senses. The blonde Amazon knows how to handle guys. She must have to beat us away with sticks.

"He knew Berg and everything. His papers, his current research. Oh, look." She points. "The game's over. Nats won. Dillan?"

"Hmm?" I rub tired eyes.

"Didn't you say we needed to stay put after the game? Something about Tanner meeting us?"

Keira answers before I do. "We're meeting him right outside the locker room. Then, if he feels up to it, we'll head out for drinks."

Then I remember what Tanner said in his e-mail. *I'd ask you to give Keira a hug for me, but I'm fairly certain she'd punch you in the face*—an accurate prediction, my friend—*so I'll have to wait to do it myself. Don't say anything, but I have a big surprise waiting for Keira. If it goes well, it will benefit you, too.*

What could be both a surprise to Keira and a benefit to me? Maybe he plans to let her stay at his rarely used house in Maryland. Did he think I eagerly wanted her out of my apartment?

We line up with everyone else as they leave, but instead of exiting the stadium, we make our way to the locker rooms.

While we wait, Stacey peppers Keira with a hundred questions about the Army. I figured Keira would be uncomfortable talking about her military career, but other than her recent deployment, she answers Stacey without hesitation. Keira probably didn't realize I could tell she omitted talking about her time in Afghanistan.

While I've been in Keira's company in the past, I have to admit that she usually comes across as reserved and somewhat ill at ease. Now, however, her demeanor is anything but. I watch Keira, waiting for her to turn and observe me observing her, but she never takes her eyes off Stacey as they talk.

Twenty minutes later, Tanner emerges and scoops up Keira in the biggest hug possible. His bronze skin matches hers as he twirls her around. His left hand is taped up.

So the catch *was* hard enough that the team's medical officer must have been worried enough to immobilize it. Not that that stopped Tanner from lifting his future sister-in-law off the ground.

After I introduce Tanner to Stacey, I look at him expectantly. Where's this surprise at? I wonder.

The surprise came in the form of a five-foot-eleven-inch-tall baseball player named Alec Huffman, Nationals pitcher as well as arguably the franchise's most famous player.

Alec's smile is perfect—damn him—as he assesses Keira confidently. The man figures he's already got this one in the bag.

"Keira, I want you to meet Alec. As soon as he knew you were coming, he demanded an introduction to the woman I cannot stop raving about. Even if that woman is a sister to me."

I can't read Keira's expression. She's turned away from me. So I can't tell if she's surprised or not, but I'm sure as hell not *benefitting* from this whatsoever.

CHAPTER TWELVE

Keira

Tanner introduces me to Alec. He's a tall, athletically built man with unruly reddish-blond hair, dark blue eyes, a smattering of freckles, and a perfect smile that could easily melt a solid bar of gold. His hands are thick and calloused as he shakes my hand.

Last year, the tabloids linked the Irish-American ballplayer with at least three young starlets as well as a former Playmate of the Year. *People* magazine put him in their Fifty Most Beautiful issue while also highlighting his charity work with a local breast cancer research foundation.

I couldn't decide whether to hate or admire him.

"Tanner has told me so much about you, Keira," Alec says after releasing my hand. "In fact, we can't get him to shut up. I feel like I already know you. But his description did not do you justice."

I hear Tanner laugh while Dillan tries, and fails, to suppress a groan. Stacey stabs Dillan in the side with her elbow. Dillan groans again.

Alec ignores them as he shoves his hands in his jeans pockets. It's an unguarded type of action, like maybe he's actually shy and not the playboy the press has made him out to be. "My dad was in the Army and if I hadn't been recruited by the pros in my sophomore year in college, my plan was to enlist as well."

"Ah, so that's where I went wrong," I say, smiling. "Uncle Sam recruited me long before MLB could come calling. Didn't have enough time to perfect my fastball."

Alec laughs at my silly joke. He must really want to impress me if he found it funny. Or maybe he's used to meaningless chitchat.

"How long have you been a ball fan?" he asks.

I take a peek at Tanner to see if he's listening.

He is.

"The second I met Tanner. So, about three years."

When I first met Tanner, he was still in the minors trying his damnedest to make it into the majors. Like Alec, Tanner was recruited out of college, but he'd spent two years working his ass off in the minors, whereas Alec, from what I knew about him, which isn't much, landed in the majors almost right away.

Alec has one of the best fastballs in the league. And pitchers, like home run hitters and quarterbacks, are some of the most sought-after players in professional sports.

In the same vein, Alec is one of the most sought after players *off* the field, too. Endorsements. Romances. Talk show appearances. He is worth millions.

What on earth does a staff sergeant in the Army have in common with a professional baseball player?

Not a single thing, I think.

"Tanner's one of the best shortstops I've ever played with," Alec says with a nod in Tanner's direction. "And..." He lowers his voice and takes a step closer. My heart speeds up. "He's also one of the nicest guys around. Professional. He takes the game seriously. Tanner practices hard. He is respected on and off the field. He also happens to have the coolest future sister-in-law ever. By the way, that's a direct quote from him."

This time, I shove my hands in my pockets.

I've never been good with compliments. It always feels like I should give a compliment in return. Maybe I should imitate Nebraska here: feel Alec's shoulders and then order him to bowl on my team.

But I have a feeling that might not go over too well. Or it might be the perfect compliment for a ball player.

No matter what, I'm certainly out of my element here.

"Thanks," I say at last. "I'm very fond of Tanner. Every time we're together, I want to handcuff him to me so I can spend a little more time with him." *Like I said, I'm awkward with compliments.* "Okay, that came out way too psycho-like. I guess what I'm saying is that I wish I could spend more time with him and my brother, Jon."

"The military and the majors," Alec says with an understanding tone. "Individually, neither is ideally suited for long-distance relationships. Put the two professions together, like Tanner and Jon, and they might not see each other for a year."

"Yeah—" I start, but someone brushes past me.

It's Zoe, the girl I met before the game started. "Excuse me," she says over her shoulder. Her arm made the briefest contact with my elbow. Might have been intentional. Maybe not. But my guess was on the first thought. If not for the smug-like expression, she'd be an attractive woman.

I notice that Alec tenses up as she walks past him. If she said something to him, I couldn't hear it, but Alec's reaction was one of pain or humiliation.

For a man with a playboy reputation, my first impression of him was anything but that. Whatever his relationship to Zoe was, it wasn't any of my business. For all I knew, this conversation—*this friendly meet and greet*—was a one-time deal. I'd probably never see the mega-rich ball player again. Not like this, at least.

No doubt I'd see him if Tanner had a get-together, or at other ball games. But that'd be it. I had no illusions of starting a relationship with the famous player.

Or starting a relationship with anyone, for that matter.

My eyes follow Zoe as she goes inside the locker room and then comes out with her fiancé, Randy "Big H" Hernandez. His hair is wet from the showers and the young catcher reminds me more of a high school kid rather than a professional player. Young, lanky. He couldn't be more than twenty-one or twenty-two.

Zoe passes us on the walkway while Big H stops. Alec's mouth works as if he's clenching his jaw when Big H says, "Got a sec, bro?"

By the way Zoe interacted with me earlier, I doubt that Big H wants to talk about tonight's game or the accuracy of Alec's last few pitches, which were less than stellar. Nope.

There's some sort of history here between the two of them.

When I glance over at Zoe at the top of the walkway, I see a Latina bombshell standing next to her. Big H's sister? Alec's former girlfriend? It might explain why Zoe was rather hostile to me.

"Excuse me a moment, Keira," Alec says politely even though I can tell his insides are on a low boil.

"Of course," I say automatically.

What could I say? *No, I'm sorry Mr. Millionaire Ball Player, but I will not excuse you for a moment. I have a beer waiting for me. I haven't a moment to spare.* He and Big H head up toward Zoe and the Latina Bombshell.

Tanner comes to my side.

"That was odd," I tell Tanner.

"That's Maria, Randy's sister," Tanner says.

And that's all he needs to say. I understand completely when Big H and Zoe leave Alec and Maria alone. She's talking with her hands while his hands talk to his pockets.

"I'm guessing the tabloids have had it all wrong?"

Tanner nods.

"I can spot a *player* a mile away," Stacey says.

She's slightly behind me, but I hear her softly spoken words perfectly. Dillan remains silent. I wonder if Stacey places Dillan in the player list. He's taken the silent, brooding type to a new level tonight.

Normally, I can't get him to shut up.

Stacey continues, "Alec Huffman is no playboy. Everyone loves a bad boy, though, and however false, it's a reputation he has yet to refute publicly. I can't help but feel a tiny bit sad for him."

"What the hell for?" Dillan asks. "The guy's a millionaire, he can date whoever he wants, and he's living his dream by playing ball."

Stacey shakes her head at him as if he doesn't have a clue.

"Think about it, Dillan. Just like Tanner here, Alec's probably played baseball since the moment he could grasp something in his hand. Every day. Every weekend. After school. Coaches. Practices. Games. Tournaments. Championships. You name it. Years and years and years of hard work. Years and years of sacrifices and not just for him. His entire family. Imagine how much it costs to be as good as Tanner and Alec and any other major ball player? Your definition of his success—money, women, dreams—are the by-products of hard work. Yes, he's living a dream, but it took twenty years of work to get there. He has to stay in top shape because there are hundreds of young hopefuls ready to take his place. Yes, he's a millionaire, and that's because others are willing to pay him because of his hard work. He can date anyone he wants because he's good-looking, successful, and wealthy. But I'd bet all the money *in your wallet* that that's not how Tanner or Alec view themselves. The sporting franchises expect certain traits in their players, and thus our famous friends here create public personas. So, yeah, I feel a tiny bit sad for Alec because no matter what he does, not many will know the real him. It's unfortunate."

As Stacey dissects Alec in front of our eyes, I watch as Maria storms off. Alec stays at the top of the ramp for a moment, his back still turned to us. It must have been a tough breakup by the way his shoulders sag slightly. I do know that Maria wasn't in the stands with us.

Did Zoe call her when she saw me?

Did Maria show up to learn the truth?

All I know is that there is too much drama around Alec Huffman. True or not true, drama is drama, no matter how it's shaded. *I don't do drama.*

As Stacey finishes her analysis, her subject matter turns around, signs a few autographs for fans, and walks back to us.

"Sorry about that," he says in a tone that suggests he's trying to appear more optimistic than he really is. "Anyway, Tanner promised we'd all get a beer. Is that still the plan?"

Tanner glances at me. He wants to know if I'm still interested. *How sweet.* I smile and nod.

"Sure is," Tanner says. "Preston's Pub on First is within walking distance, and while their beer can't match Dillan's home brew, it has a great selection. Their wood-fired pizza isn't bad, either."

"You brew?" Alec asks Dillan.

Alec wedges himself between me and Dillan as we walk out of the stadium.

I remember the shelf full of beers in his fridge. Did he brew those? I had no idea Dillan was into that. Jon never mentioned it before.

As we walk, Dillan talks about his beer label, *Nine Year Crush*, and how it took nine years to get it just the way he wanted.

For some reason, his eyes shift to mine when he says that.

I tilt my head.

Interesting trivia: I met Dillan for the first time nine years ago.

Dillan

To my relief, Keira actually doesn't seem to be all that interested in Alec Huffman. But then again, when have I ever been known to accurately predict Keira? Right, never.

The first time I ever met her, Jon invited me to his parents' house for a barbecue celebrating Keira's high school graduation. I was twenty-one—so was Jon—and I remember being extremely curious about meeting my best friend's little sister. Jon, naturally, admired her, which was the exact opposite of how I felt about my own sister. In my mind, Keira must be perfect and I wanted to find out if it was true.

I had recently discovered that college girls, for some reason, adored me more than I deserved, and it was pretty much zero effort on my part to woo them with one or two well-placed smiles. Jon made me promise never to *use* women, and I didn't, but they sure as hell used me.

My first time was actually the summer I graduated high school, and it was with the newly divorced Ms. Grace, my thirty-nine-year-old calculus teacher. I've been a student of higher learning ever since. At least I can claim I had received an A in her class long before she seduced me.

But when I met Keira, it wasn't like she fell all over me. Her friends did. Her neighbors did. Her friends' moms did. Not Keira. And that made me take notice of her. Her skin tone was somewhere between almond and bronze, a combination of a backyard swimming pool and her being an avid runner.

On top of that, she was utterly gorgeous in a yellow summer dress that I prayed would be see-through. That prayer didn't come true, and she ignored the crap out of me. Refused to even acknowledge my presence. That made me want to impress her, which, for whatever idiotic reason, made me come up with the idea of jumping off her parents' two-story roof and into the deep end of the in-ground swimming pool.

Not one of my best ideas.

Luckily, Jon stopped me from doing it, and to this day, Keira has no idea of how close I came to immortalizing her graduation party. I snuck away, instead, and drank an entire six-pack of beer at a convenience store. Well, five beers. I shared one with the homeless man who sat with me on the curb. It was the worst beer I had ever tasted before or since.

I wanted Keira to notice me. I wanted her to throw herself at me. Later, Jon told me that she said I was a disgusting man whore-pig who shouldn't be let loose on the general population. Keira. She has a way with words.

She wasn't right. She wasn't wrong.

She started off as a little crush. A tiny, whispery one. The type of crush you know you'll never, ever fulfill, but it fills your dreams on the nights you're lonely and especially on the nights where you might have been with someone, someone you shouldn't be with, but you still felt alone. In here. In your heart.

Nine years.

When I finally found the exact right ingredients in the exact right doses to make my own beer to get the taste of that day out of my head, I felt like I had regained some of my dignity. It took nine years. Keira might never know what prompted me to start my own home brewery in my spare time. But *I* did.

By ignoring me that day, she inspired me to become a

better version of myself. Even now, Keira still doesn't like me. Joke's on me, I suppose.

Nine Year Crush.

Now, however, after the game, as we walk to grab a beer and as Alec asks about my brewing path and how I came up with the name, I don't tell this story. I tell another one.

"Tell me if I'm wrong, but I feel confident that there's a woman involved," Alec says with a small laugh.

"With Dillan," Tanner chimes in, "there's always bound to be a woman involved."

For some reason, Keira glances at Stacey after these two statements, and Stacey also notices.

"Oh, none of this bothers me," Stacey says with a wave of her hand as she checks her e-mail on her smartphone. "God forgot to add the jealous bone when he created me."

What she doesn't say is, *I have nothing to be jealous of. Look at me. Goddess Bernadine Stacey can have any man she wants.* Keira, on the other side of Stacey, smirks. I wonder if she's thinking the same as me.

"Watch it, Nguyen," I say to Tanner in my easy-going voice. "I want you all to picture a twenty-one-year-old college student. Sure, he's easy on the eyes, but is he smart? Is he tenacious? Is he hell-bent on winning every single bet given to him? Absolutely."

Everyone laughs. Tanner opens the door to Preston's Pub. The place is packed and we shift, dodge, and wiggle our way to a back corner with a stand-up table and no chairs.

The smell of pizza punches me in the gut. I'm so hungry, I want two to myself, like right now.

"So," I continue my story. "This great-looking, smart, ambitious kid enters a small beer competition. And loses big time. It crushes him. It deflates his soul. It makes him question his purpose in life. But mostly, it embarrasses him." Keira watches me seriously. Can she tell I'm lying? "And avoiding embarrassing moments are what motivates the kid to keep trying. And he does. For nine years. When it came time to name the beer, *Nine Year Crush* seemed rather appropriate."

"That's a great journey," Alec says and then orders a round of beers for our table. All the waitstaff and the owner stop by to say hi to Alec and Tanner. "Ever thought about expanding? Selling it to local pubs?" Alec asks me.

"Not really." I laugh him off, but he asks the questions that I've been asking myself. I made the beer. It's good. *Really* good. Everyone who has had it loves it. Now what? That's the question. I can't stop brewing it. Not now. And I can't reveal the truth to anyone, not even Jon. Certainly not Keira. "I mean," I say. "I only just got it right. I should probably make a few more batches before I self-congratulate."

"Dillan's a great cook, too," Keira blurts out.

I'm nearly too stunned to respond.

It might be the first compliment she's ever paid me. And she said it in front of *other* people. I should ask Stacey to check Keira for signs of a fever. I stare at my roommate for half a second.

"Thank you," I say. I wonder if this is her way of apologizing for the other night.

"I concur," Stacey says, leaning into me. She's not one for a public display of affection, but she kisses my ear, whispering, "And a fine baker." She leans back, saying loudly, "I'd call him a complete package."

Tanner laughs, Alec grins into his longneck bottle before looking over to Keira, and Keira, after finding a few pair of eyes on her, shifts uncomfortably.

"I can neither confirm nor deny Stacey's statement," she says in a rush, her cheeks flushing.

Alec clears his throat. He looks ready to go.

"Let me know if you change your mind, Dillan. About selling your beer. I'd need to grab a few samples from you, but Nationals Park likes to carry locally brewed beer. Tanner," he adds, turning to his teammate. "Sorry, bro, but I can only stay for one beer tonight." They shake hands. "It was really nice meeting you, Dillan and Stacey." He shakes our hands as well. He pauses at Keira and this is where my stomach pulls. "I was wondering..." He hesitates.

"Yes?" Keira asks.

At some point in the evening, her hair has come partially undone. She looks a little tired, like maybe she's had a rough week. But the flush at her cheeks gives her a healthy, lovely glow.

"Can I offer you a ride home?" Alec asks.

Keira's mouth makes an O, Stacey gives the pair a dazzling smile, and Tanner Nguyen, my best friend's boyfriend, my good friend, the guy who's setting Keira up with someone I cannot possibly compete with, decides to be helpful by adding, "I trust Alec with my life, Keira."

Damn you, Tanner, and your awesomely amazing matchmaking skills to the stars. With friends like these, who needs enemies?

Where was a two-story building and a swimming pool when you needed one?

"Okay," Keira finally answers Alec. "That'd be nice. Goodnight everyone."

She hugs Tanner and Stacey. Keira just nods at me and says something about seeing me back at the apartment. I'm back to being that twenty-one-year-old college guy trying to impress an eighteen-year-old girl who refuses to see him at all.

"Night, Keira," I mumble at her passing figure.

I watch as Alec takes her hand in his and walks her to the door. Everyone greets him on the way out, slapping his back and congratulating him on a great game. They make way for him, for her, and it just now dawns on me that there's nothing I can actually do to get Keira to notice me. I'll call it *The Nine Year Lesson.*

CHAPTER THIRTEEN

Keira

I let go of his hand as soon as we exit the pub. The air is thick with pre-summer heat, even at eleven at night, and the buzzing of bugs fills the gaps in my conversation with Alec. His car is at the stadium, so we have to retrace our steps.

"How long have you been in the Army?" he asks. It's usually everyone's first question. Men will go on to ask about my training, how well I handle weapons, my deployments, and wonder how long I plan to stay in.

Women sometimes ask the same questions, but add other touches. Am I ever sexually harassed? Are all men in uniform hot? And how do I manage to resist all of them? Have I ever been discriminated against? They wonder if I'll ever have children and if I'll stay in the military if I do. I have stock answers for most, but I keep the real answers deep inside.

"Nine years," I answer easily. Some of the real answers: Have I been sexually harassed? *Yes.* Are all men in uniform hot? *Not normally.*

I have been discriminated against a couple of times due to being a woman. During my last deployment, my former brigade commander told me that he didn't think I could do as good a job as my predecessor—a male staff sergeant. His statement implied it was because I was a female, even though my work ethic and solid reputation preceded me.

I don't know if I'll have children. I don't know if I *want* children, so this means I don't have to worry about my military career ending. As if children somehow derail a woman's career in the military. I can name at least four women Army generals who actively raised their children *and* served their country *and* were deployed multiple times. Not to mention plenty of other active-duty single parents who actively serve.

"How old are you? Twenty-seven?" he asks, and I nod. We're now walking through cars in the lot. He stops at a svelte Corvette. It's red, curvy, and gorgeous all over. "Do you plan to stay in until retirement?"

Please let this be his car. I love it already.

"I have no reason not to, to be honest. I love what I do. It's extremely fulfilling. It certainly isn't glamorous like Major League Baseball." My insides rejoice when he unlocks the driver's side door, leans in, and then opens the passenger side door.

"Hate to break it to you, Keira," he says over the roof, staring at me as I stare at his beautiful car. "Pro ball isn't as glamorous as you might think. Half the season, we're on the road. Wrecks the hell out of families. Other half is here or in training or, in some cases, physical therapy and benched."

I slide into the bucket seat. I haven't kept a close watch on Alec's career, but he must have recently finished physical therapy. Then I remember one of the tabloids reported he had been in rehab and the cover suggested it was for drug or alcohol addiction. Tucked in there was a story about a wild night with a Nats fan. Who knows what's truth or not?

"You're certainly painting a lovely picture for me, Alec."

He turns the ignition. "I like how you say my name. Alec. Just Alec."

"Oh," I say for lack of a prepared response. "Do you go by another name? I have to admit that I only follow

Tanner's career. So you might have to cut me some slack on my not knowing your facts and figures."

Alec turns to me, briefly, as we pull out of the parking lot.

"Ditto, Keira. With you, I only want to be Alec. Not a superstar, not a famous person, and not this perfect person fans have built me up to be."

I return his smile. "So you're not claiming to be an infamous player *and* playboy?" Hopefully he can tell I'm only kidding.

"Well, that depends on which Alec you want to meet tonight. Choice A is the real me. Choice B is the celebrity persona that fits the lifestyle of a MLB pitcher."

The Corvette glides down mostly empty roads. It won't take long to reach Dillan's apartment.

"Do I have to choose? I think I'd rather enjoy my few moments with you, say good night, and have bragging rights by claiming that I not only met you but I had one beer *and* a ride in your Corvette."

We pass Ellen's Corner Bakery. A figure locks up and I can only assume it's Ellen, but whoever it is is taller and thinner than Ellen. When I turn back, whoever it is is gone.

"I don't know what to make of you," Alec says with a chuckle. "Most girls would be climbing on me by now—not that that's what I hoped would happen," he quickly amends when I shoot him a dark look. "I don't know how else to say this, so I'll say it like this: you're sort of straight-laced, but I don't mean that in a bad way. You're like a police officer."

Dillan's apartment rises before us and Alec parks in a spot half a block down from the main entrance.

"I'm a soldier," I say. "There's a distinction."

"I would agree, but I've never met a soldier like you. In fact, most get a little crazy. Not all the time, of course. But you..." He hesitates. "Do you ever get crazy? Like, is the craziest thing you've done is sleep on mismatched sheets? I mean, do you even put sugar in your coffee?" I can tell he joking by the huge smile plastered on his face.

Keira Holtslander, you could do with a bit of disorder. It's only because we passed Ellen's bakery that her voice has jumped into my head.

"The craziest thing I've done is jump out of thirty-three perfectly good airplanes."

"That's definitely crazy."

"I should be going." I reach for the handle. "Thanks for the ride."

"I want to see you again."

My heart stops. Why does this happen? The man is gorgeous. Nice. And by all accounts, a really decent guy. Spending time with him for a few weeks wouldn't be so bad, would it? He isn't a soldier, so that's a plus in his favor.

"I don't know, Alec." I keep my hand on the handle. "I might only be here for a few weeks before I go back to Fort Bragg. It's probably not a good idea for me to get involved." Sometimes, even *I'm* too rational to myself.

"Whatever you've read about me is wrong. I'm not like that."

I search his eyes. Even in the dark, I can tell he's being truthful. I sort of thought so the entire time. Besides, Tanner indicated as much, and I trust him a whole lot more than I trust my instincts when it comes to men.

"I believe you," I say.

"Then say *yes*. Or, rather, don't say *no*."

"Normally, if I can't say *yes*, then I say *no*. However, I can't say *no*, but that doesn't mean *yes*."

"Okay, I'm sort of confused now. I don't know if you're saying yes, no, or a maybe so. Let's put it this way. I'm up to bat and you're pitching me the ball. By the way, it's a perfect, gorgeous curve ball. Have I struck out or do I get a base run?"

Smiling, I ask, "You really want to use *bases* for your analogy? Because it normally means something else entirely."

Alec laughs, and I like how it sounds. Normal. He probably likes me for the same reason I like him. We're just different enough from the other to keep it interesting.

"I know, I know," he pleads with his hands. "Sorry. Been hit too many times in the head."

My own hands itch at the door. *Disorder. Disorder. Disorder.*

"Yes," I say, finally. "I'll see you again, but under one condition."

On a scrap piece of paper, I write down my cell phone number, but I do not hand it over yet.

"Okay, what's the condition?" Laughter coats his words. He's happy. I smile stupidly in the dark and hope to God that he can't see it.

"Would you visit our wounded soldiers at Walter Reed Medical Center in Bethesda? I think the soldiers would love to meet you, take pictures, and have you sign autographs. I can put you in contact with the right people."

For a split second, I wonder if I've asked the wrong thing. No doubt Alec Huffman is inundated with these types of requests. If it wasn't soldiers, it would be other charities or foundations or schools wanting his presence to elevate their cause.

"Normally," he says, slowly, "if I can't say no, I must say yes."

"So it's a yes?"

"I think we're both saying yes."

"Here." I hand him my number, smile, and climb out of the car. "I had a fun time. Good night."

"Me, too." Alec calls a good night, waves from the car as he drives off, and I stand there longer than necessary. Footsteps click behind me. Turning, I find Dillan watching me with a guarded expression. Sometimes I just can't seem to understand him. One minute he's carefree Dillan, the next he's thoughtful and considerate.

I don't do drama. Stacey's nowhere in sight. Just Dillan. He holds two cups of iced coffee. I recognize the logo on the sleeve. Ellen's. Lucky him got coffee before she closed. Silently, he moves in step with me, hands me one of the cold cups, and we head to the apartment together. Silently. It feels off. *He* feels off. Normally, I would welcome his silence.

Glancing at him sideways, I take a sip of the delicious brew. I taste a hint of something. Cinnamon, maybe, combined with thick whipped cream.

"Something on your mind?" I ask.

He glares at me and I nearly drop my coffee. What had I ever done to deserve *that* type of look from him?

"Yes," he says quietly, but his words are laced with venom. "Yes there is."

Dillan

After Stacey drops me off, I discover I'm in the mood for coffee. I doubt Ellen's Corner Bakery will even be open, but I jog over there anyway. I need to expend some energy after finding myself thinking long and hard about Alec Huffman giving Keira a ride home.

Alec Huffman. Famous. Rich. And, actually, nice. He was, after all, interested in my beer. It wasn't one of those *"I'm just trying to be nice and make conversation"* talks. He actually meant it.

Trying Ellen's door, it's locked, but the lights are still on. I see a figure move in the back. Knocking loudly, the figure—Ellen—turns around, a broom in her hands. When she opens the door, her grin couldn't have been bigger. The scent of fresh chocolate chip cookies makes my mouth water.

"I thought I might be seeing you tonight, Dillan," she says softly, letting me inside. "I have something for you."

I follow her to the back—I've never been beyond the counter before—and the area is just as cozy as the front of the bakery. Yellow walls. Purple wainscoting. Various sized frames showcasing old pictures, drawings, and crayon-colored thank-you notes written, no doubt, by children. Against a back wall, she opens the door to a silver fridge and hands me two ice-cold iced coffees.

"Two?" I ask her. Okay, I'm not *that* thirsty. I'd be up all night with this much caffeine. The cold seeps into my hands. How long had these been in her fridge?

"One is for Keira, you handsome blockhead," she says with a laugh. She places the broom against the wall, unties her apron, and hangs it upon a hook near what looks to be the door to her office.

I inspect the plastic cups. Other than the whipped cream on top, I can't tell what flavor they might be. "Are they the same type of coffee?"

"Nope."

My eyes narrow at her suspiciously. What kind of game is she playing tonight? Ellen smiles mischievously.

"Which one is mine?" *Does it even matter? Just take a drink from one, Dillan.*

"Oh, only you can decide that." She leads me back to the front of the bakery, turning off lights as we pass through. "Tell Keira I said hello. Now, off with you," she says as she all but shoves me out the front door.

"How much do I owe you? For the coffee?" I hold up my hands as if I need to remind her of what she gave me. By now, my hands are numb.

For some reason, Ellen laughs, and I find the entire situation to be odd. Is the old gal drunk?

"Consider it already paid for," she says. Ellen's light blue eyes twinkle at me. Whatever the secret is, she keeps it to herself. "Don't forget about my anniversary celebration on Tuesday."

She pats my back, closes the door in my face—all the while smiling—and locks up the bakery. She switches off the main lights, which includes the OPEN sign, and I watch her figure recede deeper into the bakery and then disappear into a door that leads to her apartment above the storefront.

What an interesting woman, I think. Strange. Odd. Confusing, but interesting.

As I walk the quiet streets, I see a red Corvette parked on the curb in front of my apartment building. Instantly, I know it's Alec's car. I don't know how I know. I just do. I shouldn't dislike the man. In fact, the ballplayer really wasn't that bad of a guy. But then I wait for Keira to exit the car. And she doesn't. Not for a while.

I wait there like an idiot.

When she steps out, she watches Alec's car disappear like a love-struck girl. My footsteps announce my arrival, and she turns. I hand her a cup of coffee.

I want to tell her that she's beautiful.

She smells wonderful and the little smile playing on her lips, while I know it isn't for me, is bewitching. I want to warn her away from Alec Huffman. Say that he isn't any good for her. That she should keep her distance. But that'd make me a hypocrite. Didn't Jon say the exact same things about *me* to her?

So I stay silent, even as she looks sideways at me.

I get mad at myself. I get so angry that I want to squeeze the coffee cup in my hand and throw it to the ground.

Keira affects me. She affects me more than she should, more than I should let her.

"Something on your mind?" she asks.

I wanted her to ask me that and then I *didn't* want her to ask me.

When I answer her, it comes out wrong. It comes out mean, spiteful, hurtful, and almost every emotion I could possibly feel is embedded in my words. No doubt my expression conveys the exact same emotion.

"Yes. Yes there is."

Keira blanches and nearly drops her coffee. Damn. I didn't mean to alarm her. Well, I did, but not in *that* way. Now she probably thinks I've heard from Jon, that maybe there's something wrong. I want to ease her mind.

Her brown eyes are large and mixed with worry and something else. Confusion. Rage. Probably more confusion.

It might surprise her to realize that the same emotions are punching me in the head, too. Actually, I doubt Keira would care what I might be feeling at the moment. Or any moment, for that matter. Apparently she snagged a Major League Baseball player tonight. Without trying.

Me? I'm just her roommate. Her *temporary* roommate.

What did I want to be to her? Obviously something more than a roommate. I can't say that I've ever considered a serious relationship with anyone before. Not really.

But Keira... She deserves someone better than me. Then again, I can't seem to get over the fact that I don't even exist to her in the first place.

I can't have her. But it's more than that. She doesn't want me.

Is that why I'm angry right now? Is that why I've opened the apartment door and slammed it shut behind us? I turn on the foyer lamp, but the rest of the apartment is dark.

Keira reacts to my slamming the door. She spins around, her eyes blazing.

"I swear to God," she starts. "You must be bipolar or something because you're acting like a complete jackass right now. Either tell me what's wrong or go to hell." She pauses. "Or better yet, go to hell anyway. In the morning, I'm out of here. This has got to be one of the worst weeks of my life. And trust me when I say this, Dillan Pope, I've experienced some pretty messed-up shit before."

I have to hand it to her, she holds her own very well. She's no cowering fool, but I wish she'd lighten up a bit. Show some skin, so to speak. But she's so bottled up that I feel like that any moment, she's going to burst into a million glass fragments, and I certainly don't want to be in her trajectory path.

A cut from Keira would be like getting sliced with tiny, sharp razorblades. You don't feel the pain until it's too late.

So I do what I always do in uncomfortable situations: I turn into a smart-ass.

"Is this the part where you lecture me on what it means to be a soldier and how you're this special snowflake in a sea of snow? If you move out tomorrow, Alec *playboy* Huffman won't know where to pick you up."

Her eyebrows rise.

"Jealous much?" She crosses into the kitchen and tosses the empty coffee cup in the sink. I figure she'll talk more about Alec Huffman, but she doesn't. "Furthermore, your analogies are stupid." Her words have a sting to them. "You don't know the first thing about what it means to be a soldier or how serve your country, so I don't expect you to understand honor, pride, and integrity. I certainly don't expect you to know what it's like to be in my shoes: a woman serving her country. So the jealous thorn burrowed up your ass tonight doesn't mean crap to me."

I am *not* jealous of Alec Huffman. I adjust my stance at the doorway—I haven't moved since we entered the apartment—and confirm that, no, there's nothing *burrowed up my ass.* Not that I really needed to check.

Her speech done, Keira leans back against the counter, her arms over her chest.

Your turn, her body language declares. She has a bored look on her face, but I suspect it's just a mask. Is this what she does when she faces tough situations? Shuts down and pretends it doesn't affect her?

Does this mean she's pretending *I* don't affect her?

Don't get your hopes up, Dillan. For all you know, she's lulling you into a false sense of security before she makes you cry.

No doubt she's seen and experienced things I could only dream of, and not all of them good. But it's not like she was forced to enlist in the Army. No one coerced her into becoming a soldier, and no one made her stay in the Army for nine years. Her experiences, her troubles, her hardships came with the job.

I never felt sorry for her before and I wasn't about to start now.

"So what?" I say. "Am I supposed to worship the ground you walk on because you are a woman who *also* happens to be a soldier? Big freaking deal, Keira. I bet every time you feel the least bit threatened by someone, you throw out the *I'm a soldier* bit in order to win an argument. If you want my honest opinion, it's a *below the belt* type of statement, as if you're claiming no one can understand where you come from and how you're just so special and above us mere mortals. I admire your selflessness and your service to our country, but you don't have to throw it in everyone's face all the time. Other people have difficult jobs, too, sweetheart, myself included. I happen to work in a political minefield, but you don't see me waxing poetically about it everyday. So here's a bit of advice: get over yourself."

As an encore, I finish my iced coffee, slurping rather loudly to get up the last of the whipped cream. I'm not even sure what Ellen put in the coffee before she closed her bakery tonight, but I swear I tasted chocolate laced with cayenne pepper. It's on the tip of my tongue to ask her if she also tasted cayenne pepper in her coffee, but I figure it's the wrong time to change the subject.

"Ditto," Keira says. "After tomorrow, none of this matters because I have no intention of ever spending more than ten seconds in your company again. Have a nice life."

I think I hear her mumble something about me being a *man whore* under her breath.

She's in her room before I can respond to this man whore comment. The door closes without hesitation, and she locks it, too. This time, I am certain that she's packing. Keira won't have a problem finding an apartment. It might take her a few days, but she can stay in a hotel or, as much as I hate to admit it, Alec might let her stay over. Then again, maybe not. Who lets someone they just met crash at their million-dollar house?

As Keira said, it doesn't matter. When I wake up in the morning, I won't have to worry about seeing Keira.

Or thinking about her.

Or wondering about her.

After tonight, she is nothing to me.

CHAPTER FOURTEEN

Keira

My mouth tastes like crap. Good lord, what did I eat before I fell asleep? Sunlight pours in from the wrong side of the room and, for some reason, it feels like I'm naked under the sheets. Naked? That's a stupid thought. Turning slightly, I crack my eyes—why do my eyes feel so heavy?—and find that everything is wrong.

The walls are painted light gray, with dark blue trim. The images on the wall—canvas-style abstract artwork—certainly aren't mine. The television is on the opposite side of the room. The smell is all wrong. It smells like sandalwood. Like Dillan. I don't want to be smelling like Dillan right now.

I'm in the *wrong* room.

Not only that, I'm in the *wrong* bed.

What? The? Hell? There is no way on earth that I climbed into Dillan's massive, king-size bed last night. Not after *that* hellacious argument. Glancing over, I confirm that I'm alone in the bed. Thank God. Yes, there was that one time I did think about climbing into bed with him, but that was just a passing thought. A heat-of-the-moment thought. I was probably dehydrated that day.

Staring out the window, I try to figure out what time it is, but I'm momentarily distracted by the fact that the blinds and the curtains are wide open. I can see into the building next door. What on earth does Dillan do when he needs to change? Display his goods to the world? Apparently. He's good at doing that.

I still haven't figured out why I'm in his room, or where

the owner is. His clock reads eight in the morning. Good. I can still go for a run before it gets too warm. Rubbing my eyes, my hands feel *weird* against my face. My face feels *weird* against my hands. I push my hands away from me and suck in my breath.

Manly hands.

Hairy and rough-cuticled, manly hands.

Ohmigod. Ohmigod. Ohmigod. Okay, there must be a logical reason for this. Don't hyperventilate. I eye the white sheet as if it might decide to strangle me. It's up to my neck. My chest looks surprisingly flat. Ohmigod. Ohmigod. Ohmigod. I jerk the sheet down. Flat chest. A man's chest. A scream bubbles in the back of my throat.

It's a dream. This has to be a dream. Surely I'm still asleep.

I pull the sheet lower and nearly pass out. There's male *junk* between my legs. For some reason, taking inventory makes me feel better.

Hairy pubic mound. Check.

One penis. Check.

Two testicles. Check.

Ohmigod. Ohmigod. Ohmigod. Holy shit...the penis...it's *erect.* I poke it. It moves. It bounces. It's freaking real.

That scream? It's still in the back of my throat. I swallow hard. I throw a manly hand over my mouth to keep from yelling. The same finger that just poked the alien penis feels the front of my neck. I swallow again. An Adam's apple. My mouth instantly dries up. I don't think I can open my eyes any wider than they are at the moment.

This cannot be real. Please, dear God, if you're listening, stop whatever this madness is. Wake me up, please. Ohmigod. Ohmigod. Ohmigod. Wait. If this is a dream, if I pinch myself, I'll wake up. Relieved, I decide to pinch the part of me that would hurt the most. The testicles. But I don't really want to touch them. I've never really found testicles attractive.

Reaching down, I take the veiny, paper-thin skin in between two fingers and pinch hard.

I am *so* not asleep. My stomach rolls and I feel like I'm about to vomit. Any second, my intestines are going to rip through my groin. I ball up, waiting for the pain to pass, but it feels like I'm dying. Don't breathe. Don't move.

What the hell is going on?

A sheen of sweat dampens my body. No wonder men collapse after they've been kicked in the balls.

Once the pain subsides to a dull ache, I shove the sheets off me. My feet are huge, wide, and I swear to God I must be the size of a giant. *Get out of bed, Keira. Make sense of this.*

I don't seem to be capable of operating whosever body this is. My feet crash into things. Clothes. Shoes. Books. DVDs. None of which are *my* things. Dillan has a mirror on the wall. A full-length one. I step just shy of it. If I step into view, I'll see what I am. Who I am. See what this utter madness is, and I'll be able to get help. Call a doctor or something. *Yeah, um, hi, I am a woman but stuck in a hairy, unfemale-like body. No, I'm not transgender. I was a woman yesterday. Today, there's manly junk hanging between my legs. Don't hang up on me.*

I close my eyes and step to the left. I crack one eye open. Then the other. Maybe if I breathe deeply, things will seem better. Or maybe I'm suddenly insane.

Keira Holtslander is *not* standing in front of me.

I'm tall. I have Dillan's brown hair, his light green eyes, his shit-eating grin, his *I haven't shaved in two days* jaw, his smooth, touchable chest, his *I can make any woman happy* penis, his finely sculpted arms, shoulders, thighs, calves, and, if that wasn't the worst of it, I own his cocky stance. God, I want to punch his—my—handsome face.

Take a deep breath. Now take another one. Well, shit, that doesn't help. I can't contain the scream any longer. When it comes out, I sound just like Dillan. But I'm not the only one screaming. Next door, I hear my own voice cursing up a storm.

Dillan

My first thought is I wonder if Keira has moved out. My next is to wonder why I'm sweating profusely. When did I put on all these clothes? Who wears sweats to bed during the summertime?

Reaching over, I grab at empty air, intending to shift my alarm clock to see what time it is. But my arm keeps on going, and I hit the side of the bed instead of finding a side table with a clock.

Okay, that's weird. Did I move the blasted thing in a heat of anger last night? It's possible. Once, I rearranged my entire bedroom and forgot about it. I blindly jumped over the spot my bed used to be and hit the arm chair, instead. So, yeah, it's possible that after my argument with Keira last night, and after two or three or six beers, I might have shifted things around.

The room is rather dark, and while I never close my blinds, maybe I did that, too.

What a strange morning.

I feel like I need to brush my teeth for an hour straight to get this odd taste out of my mouth. Hopefully my beer doesn't leave that type of aftertaste. If so, I'll quickly be out of business if I agree with Alec and allow his offer of getting my beer sold in Nationals Park.

Uh, I think.

Alec and Keira. Keira and Alec.

Wait. Didn't I tell myself last night that I wasn't going to think about her anymore? That after last night, I didn't have to look at her, talk to her, or think about her?

Right. *Dillan, you're such a blockhead. You're thinking*

about her right now. Well, I'm thinking about her because for some reason, it seems like I can smell her all around me.

Cinnamon buns. It smells like cinnamon buns right now. Is she baking in the kitchen? That'd be the first. If she was, she wouldn't share any of it with me. That's for sure.

I rub my eyes and stop. I flex fingers. I turn my hands around. Light as air. Soft. I feel over my face and find smoothness. Arch eyebrows. Soft lips. Tiny ears. Long hair.

Huh?

I grip up and down my arms. I *do not* find the type of muscle definition I had expected. My arms are slimmer, but still strong, like that of a woman. Or maybe someone who's been wasting away in some dark cellar for years. The room is dark, but I'm fairly certain I'm not someone's captive.

There must be two blankets on top of me right now. No wonder I'm sweating to death. I don't even recognize the blankets. I mean, did I leave my apartment last night and buy blankets? That would have been some night—*uh oh.*

I do remember. These are Keira's blankets. I remember them from the other day when I inspected her room.

Holy shit.

I'm in Keira's room.

That's problem number *one.* Problem number *two* is that I don't feel like myself. Normally I have to take a huge piss when I wake up. At the moment, other than the sweating, I wouldn't mind snuggling in deeper into these blankets and then, later, going for a run.

My leg muscles tingle and ache, like maybe I need to stretch them out. I kick off the offending blankets that I shouldn't be under in the first place and grab my thighs.

My first impression is that my thighs are smaller, but

very chiseled, like some sculptor had taken a year to perfect every inch of muscle.

While that wasn't my first thought about something being very wrong, it sort of cemented it for me.

I can admit that there's something wrong.

I'm in the *wrong* room.

I'm definitely in the *wrong* bed.

If Keira catches me in here, I'm dead. But that's only if she hasn't moved out already. If she's gone, then I'm just an idiot for mooning over her and sleeping in her bed.

But wait. If she had moved out, she would have taken her blankets with her.

She hasn't moved out.

That means that at any minute, I'm chopped liver.

I jump out of the bed, find the window in her room, and shove the curtains aside and pull the blinds up. Sunlight flows in. The morning is well advanced. I'd say it's eight or nine in the morning.

Then I notice I'm not as tall as I should be. Looking down, I inspect my *light as air* hands.

They are *not* my hands.

They are dainty.

Small.

Feminine.

There's barely any hair on them.

I don't know why I'm not screaming.

I don't know why I'm not hopping around and acting like a lunatic.

Okay, I know. It's because I'm dreaming. I convinced myself that I didn't like Keira and I'm now dreaming about *being* her.

Dreams can be clever bitches. Until Keira is out of my life, I vow not to sleep or dream.

Ever.

That should take care of the problem.

All I have to do now is wake up. But first, I cannot wear all of this clothing. I swear to God it's like a sauna in here. I rip off the clothes and catch a glance at my lower half.

There's stuff missing.

Notably my penis.

This is the worst dream ever. But something tells me that I'm not actually dreaming. All of this feels very real.

Instead of what I expect to see, I find a neat triangle above glorious lady-parts.

Holy shit. *Why am I looking down at a vagina?* I don't think I've seen one quite from *this* angle.

I should not own a vagina. Nor a perfectly formed pubic hair triangle.

My thighs are spectacular and I've seen them before. *On Keira.* I've ogled Keira's legs enough to recognize them instantly.

I take a slow breath and move my hands up over a smooth, flat stomach, and over small but exquisitely formed breasts.

I don't need a mirror to realize I'm in Keira's body. If I'm in *her* body, does this mean she's in *my* body?

For a fleeting second, I'm deliriously worried about what will happen when she finds out. I have a feeling hell is about to descend upon earth.

The scream that comes out of my mouth confirms it. It's Keira's voice. I shout every curse word I know.

When I hear my own voice from the other side of the apartment, I know that the worst day of my life has just begun.

CHAPTER FIFTEEN

Keira

I don't care about clothes. Clothes are the least of my problems. I throw open Dillan's bedroom door, screaming at him to come out of *my* room. When I see him—*when I see my body*—walk out of my bedroom, I'm stark naked.

Well, except for the socks. Dillan kept my socks on.

"Were you checking me out?" I scream at him, in Dillan's voice. This is going to scar me for life. "Why are my clothes off of my body?" Dillan doesn't seem to be capable of words, so I slap him. I slap my own face. This is going to scar me for life. I can't help thinking it repeatedly. "Why did you take my clothes off, Dillan?"

He—I—*oh, I don't know anymore*—flinches.

"I didn't know I was in *your* body at first, Keira," I hear my own voice yell at me. This is too weird. "When I woke up, I had about seventeen layers of clothing on. Cut me some slack. It's not like I have experience with body swapping. I just found out—jeez, I don't understand what's going on." Dillan moves in a circle, deep in thought. "I'm you. You're me. I sound like you, but I can't wrap my brain around the fact that I'm staring at myself from over here." He stops short, shaking his head quickly, staring at my—*his*—midsection. "I have really great abs, don't I?"

I smack my own face again. "Focus, please," I say in as authoritative a voice as I can muster at the moment. I'm close to breaking down. "Obviously, we *both* cannot be experiencing the same dream. This is for real. Holy Christ. I'm in man whore's body."

"No need to be insulting, sweetheart," Dillan says

snidely, hands on hips. Wow. *I really sound like a bitch sometimes*, I think.

"Let's get dressed. I can't think when I'm looking at myself naked. Then we can figure this out." *With alcohol. With electric shock therapy. With a psychiatrist willing to prescribe drugs. Lots of drugs.*

"Good idea," he agrees.

We move to our respective bedrooms only to figure out —too late—that we need to head into each other's bedrooms for clothing. *Does my butt actually look like that when I walk?* So straight and proper, like I have a stick up my rear.

No wonder Dillan thinks I'm Sergeant Prim and Proper.

I rummage through Dillan's drawers and find very little in the way of underwear. Most of it is on the floor. Sighing, I pick up what I hope is a clean pair—I'm certainly not going to smell them to check—and slide my legs into them. Well, I try to, at least.

Dillan's legs feel like a ton of bricks. How does he lift these legs day in and day out? Thankfully, the bed catches me when I stumble as I try to put on the boxer briefs. I throw on a T-shirt and a pair of jeans.

The button is on the wrong side of the jeans, but I manage.

Just barely.

Dillan

I'm very familiar with women's underwear. The shape, the size, the sexy factor. I've pulled underwear off many a woman over the years. What I've not done is put them *on* a woman. And not put them on *as a woman* myself. But, how hard can it be?

Keira's underwear are tiny, orange with zebra stripes on them, and I wish I was observing them in any other situation other than this one. I would have rather been taking these animal-striped panties from her body and then dive into her using my own wild moves. No such luck today. Or ever, probably.

I hold open the waist of her panties and slip one leg in, then the other, and shimmy—yes, shimmy—them up my legs, over my hips, but I pull them up *too* far and I give myself a wedgie. Okay, that's not very comfortable. Why do women wear thongs? I'm actually shocked Keira owns a pair. Reaching around, I adjust the thong part of the underwear and pull the strip of fabric out of my derrière as best I can.

Probably best if I don't tell her about this.

I snag a tank top from a drawer, and, because I can't find anything that resembles pants, I slip on what I think is a pair of her running shorts. They are way too short, but they sure as hell make my legs—her legs—look fantastic.

Probably shouldn't tell her that, either.

When I look up, she's glaring at me from the doorway.

Keira

"This is entirely your fault," I yell at him. Yelling won't get us anywhere, but it makes me feel better. What makes it worse is that it isn't my voice yelling at him. It's his voice yelling at him. This is way too confusing. Also, I don't know how this might be entirely his fault. But accusing him also makes me feel better.

"Listen," Dillan says, lifting an arm. "I'm not a good yeller. My tone just isn't right for it. So, please, stop yelling, Keira. I don't want my own voice to become irritating to me. Once we figure this out and switch back, we can yell at the other in our own bodies again. We can yell at each other for the rest of our lives. But, until then, let's call some sort of truce."

I sigh. He might have a point, but that doesn't mean I have to agree with him.

"Let's start with the obvious," I say.

"Okay."

"I'm you. You're me. Do you agree with this?"

"Sort of," he says.

"What's *sort of* about this?"

"Metaphysically, everything about me—Dillan Pope—is the same. My thoughts, my ideas, my likes and dislikes are all mine, and I acknowledge that in this body—your body—I am Dillan Pope. I just happen to be Dillan Pope residing in Keira Holtslander's body. It's a body switch, but not a complete switch. Otherwise, we wouldn't know we switched."

I listen to his words carefully. Makes sense. Doesn't help us out, but he's correct. I know that I'm me, but in his body. That means that because I still own my own mind, I have the desire to do the things that I like to do: run, date men, watch baseball on mute, and read technical manuals. But that also means Dillan will want to do what he likes to do, but in *my* body: date women, act like a jerk, prance around naked for the world to see, cook, and brew beer.

"All right," I say in response. "I understand what you mean. Now that we've figured out that our minds are intact, I'm still not entirely convinced we aren't insane. How did this happen? People just don't wake up in other people's bodies."

"It's certainly never happened to me before. But we must acknowledge that it must happen, otherwise how do you account for this?" He waves a hand between us.

"We have to run into each other," I say. "I'll collide into you and you'll collide into me."

"What?"

"Like the movie. They run into each other to see if they can switch bodies."

"Wait, there's a movie about this?" Dillan asks.

"Well," I say. "It wasn't a documentary. It was a movie."

"Did it work? I mean, is that how they switched bodies?"

I shake my head *no*. "But I'm willing to try it."

Dillan nods. "Okay, me, too."

Dillan

I move to the other side of the living room, ready to charge at my own body, but Keira has another idea. Seriously, it is so odd to see myself outside of looking into a mirror. My mannerisms are being enacted right in front of me, and it's a bit disconcerting.

"No, we'll run at each other from the bedrooms. If we move the couch and the coffee table, it will be a straight line," Keira says. "And it doubles the distance."

"Will that make a difference?" I ask.

"Don't know, but whoever made this happen will see that we're very serious about changing back."

"Maybe we should try to figure out who made this happen before we start injuring each other. I can hurt you. And I don't mean me, in your body. I mean my body can hurt your body. I've got at least fifty pounds on you, Keira."

"Good," Keira murmurs absently, moving the furniture. "You'll feel the pain right now. Not me."

"You'll care when it's your face with two black eyes and a broken nose."

Keira stops pushing the coffee table and looks up. "Maybe you have a point."

"I thought you'd see it my way," I say boastfully. Finally, she concedes a point to me. But the victory is short-lived. I'm still stuck in Keira's cute body. I don't want to be stuck doing girl things, and Alec Huffman better not try to kiss me before we can change back. "Has Alec Huffman kissed you yet?" I blurt out.

"What?" I hear my voice all but yell at me. Keira

stands up straighter than an arrow and places her hands on her hips. It isn't a good look on my body. "How is that any of your business, and what does it have to do with *right now*?"

"I was just thinking about what happens if we don't change back. Like, if we have to live each other's lives until we figure it out."

"That is not going to happen," Keira says with so much determination that I believe her. She sits down on the couch she just moved. I sit on the coffee table. Her body is small enough that I'm not worried about breaking it. "So let's figure out who did this to us," Keira says.

CHAPTER SIXTEEN

Keira

"Who knows that we are bickering?" I ask. "Or, who hates us enough to ruin our lives?"

Dillan cringes. "I've got a boss who wouldn't mind seeing me in less than favorable circumstances. But I don't see Johnson Brookshire doing something like this. I suspect that whoever did this knows the both of us and wants to teach us a lesson."

I nod, thinking. "In the movies, the two main characters have to learn a lesson. Then they change back. Okay. I'll go first."

"Huh?"

Dillan doesn't catch on very fast, I think.

"I, Keira Holtslander, no longer think Dillan Pope is a dirtbag, a man whore, or a jerk. He's a very nice guy." I stand and nudge him on the elbow. "Your turn." I observe my own body. I should probably gain a few pounds. Looking at myself from this angle, I think I might be a little too slim.

"Oh, right," Dillan says. "Really? A man whore? That's harsh, Keira. I'm telling you right now, this isn't going to work." He clears his—my—throat. "I, Dillan Pope, still think Keira is annoying, bossy, and Sergeant Prim and Proper, but she isn't as bad as most other people on the planet."

I roll my eyes. "You're supposed to say it like you like me."

"But that would be a lie, Keira," Dillan says without hesitation. The fact that it's my own voice saying that to me cuts me to the bone. "Look, I need a break. I'm feeling this sensation like maybe I need to go to the bathroom."

This jolts me. Oh, crap. "Leave the door open when you go."

"What?" Dillan says. "You're insane."

"In case you haven't noticed, this entire situation is insane. Besides, you might need help."

"I am a grown man. I do not need assistance in going *potty*."

I shut my mouth. Fine. "When you come out, we need to discuss some rules."

Dillan

Keira, in my voice, yaps at me about rules and not doing *this* and not doing *that.* Like I need assistance. I lift the seat, pull down the running shorts and the thong, and stand there, ready for release.

My hand reaches down to do its normal thing and comes away empty.

Oh, right. No *external* equipment.

Nothing to aim with.

Nothing to hold on to.

With a groan, I reset the seat and sit down on the toilet. I actually don't know if this is going to work. I release the muscles slowly. I'm not exactly worried about some massive waterfall gushing from my lady-parts, but will it *flow* down? To the side? Down my thigh? I mean, I have zero control here.

After a few seconds, I have successfully mastered allowing Keira's body to eliminate urine into a toilet. Seriously, I want a trophy right now. Maybe two trophies, if I can get the thong back up without giving myself a wedgie.

Then I realize I need to wipe.

Crap.

I sit back down, grab what I hope is the right amount of toilet paper—fifty squares?—and reach into the danger zone.

Does one dab?

Rub?

Scrape?

Do I move my hand front to back, or back to front?

How far *up* into the folds do I go? Since when did a simple process turn into a theoretical question?

I wonder if there is an emergency hotline for this type of thing.

Keira is so not going to like any of this, so I'll keep all of this to myself. I hardly see how it will come up anyway.

I go with *dabbing.* It seems the quickest and the *least* intrusive method. I maneuver the thong without killing the heinie and pull up the running shorts.

There. Easy as pie. Being a girl is totally easy.

Keira

I shift uncomfortably. I can't seem to stand or sit down. There's just too much going on in these jeans and I have no idea of how to situate Dillan's frank and beans. I mean, I don't think there's enough space in there for them to fit.

While Dillan's in the bathroom allowing my body to pee, I'm out here waiting.

Waiting for him to scream bloody murder.

Waiting for him to faint.

He's been in there for eleven minutes. What the hell can he possibly be doing?

Then it hits me. He's a guy. He's probably touching everything.

My everything.

He's a guy in a girl's body. A dream come true. Okay, maybe not. But my heart speeds up at the thought of him touching me in certain places. *Be honest, Keira. You don't like the idea of him touching you anywhere. The only touching you've ever wanted him to do is when you were in your own body.*

I shake my head. Giving up control isn't easy. I want to be in there with him. Watching. Ensuring that my personal privacy isn't abused or misused. While Dillan isn't that bad of a guy, I didn't want to afford him the opportunity to explore.

Dear Lord, how is this going to work? Who would want to do this to us? And why?

The bathroom door opens and I—Dillan—step out. I look at him expectantly.

He grins sheepishly. "I didn't realize women pass gas

when they pee. It isn't loud. It's more of a *poof*."

"Don't be crass," I say. I'm trying to stay cool, but I can feel the heat on my face. I can't believe we are having this conversation. But certain things must be said. "There are rules. No touching my parts except for legitimate reasons. No looking at my parts. No kissing anyone. There is absolutely no sex being done upon my body."

"*No sex being done upon your body*? That's about the least romantic way I've ever heard it said," Dillan says.

"Swear to it."

"Fine, fine," Dillan says. "Miss Prude can have it her way. Can I venture to guess that I don't need you to swear the same? Looking at my body probably disgusts you, so I'm not worried about what you might do. If this lasts more than a day, I suspect my body will get a case of blue balls. I'll let you figure out how to relieve the discomfort." He looks at me. "Why are you shifting nervously?"

"No reason," I say.

"You have to pee, don't you?"

I cross my legs again. "Nope. I'm fine. Thank you."

Dillan moves around me and begins to push me into the bathroom.

"It's best if you figure it out now. Just be careful of the zipper."

He closes the bathroom door on me and I'm alone with Dillan's body. I don't want to be alone. Dillan's image greets me in the mirror and it, fleetingly, alarms me. *Get a grip, Keira.* I unbutton the pants, and slide the zipper down.

Dillan's privates bulge the area. I pull down the pants and the boxer briefs and his penis springs free.

I hear Dillan outside the door. "You're going to have to grab it, Keira. Pretend it's a pistol."

He practically laughs at me. Why does he get to enjoy this and I don't?

"I will do no such thing," I say through the door. My teeth are clenched as I say it.

I agree, internally, that I *have* to grab it, but I do not intend to pretend it is a pistol. Dillan's private parts hang there. Soft. Somewhat wrinkled.

For some reason, I think of a wrinkled dog, the Shar-Pei, and I laugh. But then hearing me laugh in Dillan's voice ruins it. I gently take Dillan's organ in two fingers and go. And I feel relief. Immense relief. I've had to go since I woke up this morning, but I didn't want to admit it.

I clean up, wipe the seat—I'm apparently not that good of an aim—and open the door. Dillan greets me with a shit-eating grin that looks stupid on my face.

He asks, "Was it as good for you as it was for me?"

I grin back. "You have a small dick."

Dillan

"Now who's lying?" I say as she insults my manhood. "But I'll let that one slide. I probably deserved it. I feel like we're making strides here. Hungry?" I move toward the kitchen and take out breakfast items.

Keira glares at me as if I've sprouted two heads. She must not like that I've changed the subject. Or maybe she wanted a longer argument.

While we are no closer to figuring this out, I have an idea. Sometimes, when I cook, ideas come to me easier.

"I think it was Ellen," I say as I scramble eggs. Keira's behind me, brewing up a pot of coffee.

"You mean Ellen, from the bakery? You think she did this?" Keira looks at me skeptically after taking down two coffee cups. I don't blame her for not really believing me. Sweet Ellen wouldn't hurt a fly, but I've seen something more in the old lady.

"I know you've just met her, but don't you get the feeling that she knows a bit too much about you?"

"I always thought it was just a keen business eye. Though I do know what you mean. The first time I met her, I got a sense of foreshadowing, like she was preparing me for something ahead of time."

"Exactly," I say, excited. Yes. This feels good. Collaborating. Fixing. Not screaming at each other. "After breakfast, we'll march down there and order her to change us back. We should be ourselves before lunch."

Keira smiles. "I wonder if it was in the coffee."

"When I visited her last night, she just so happened to have two pre-made iced coffees for us. One for me, one for you. She was very specific that one was for you. I wonder what might have happened if Stacey was with me, and if she drank one."

"Probably nothing. If the drinks were specific to us, then I doubt you and Stacey would have swapped. Granted, I wish you *were* with Stacey last night. We would have avoided this whole thing to begin with. At this very moment, I would have been looking for an apartment. You and Stacey could have been...eating dessert without my bothering you."

I bristle slightly, but Keira isn't looking at me. That's the problem. She does bother me. I wonder if Keira wishes she had spent more time with Alec. I don't want to think about him, but I just can't seem to help it. I'm a man—currently in a woman's body—and competition doesn't sit well with me. Survival of the fittest and all that.

Keira places plates on the counter and I scoop eggs onto each. She loads a piece of toast onto each plate and pours herself a cup of coffee. Black with sugar. I don't have any cream.

"You seem," I start, but then hesitate, wondering if I should say anything. "You seem chipper this morning. I think this might be the most social you've been with me, Keira."

She takes a big bite. "I'm just glad we figured it out. Once we see Ellen, we can fix this and go our separate ways. I don't know if you noticed it this morning, but I packed up last night. All I have to do is get my own body back and walk out that front door."

CHAPTER SEVENTEEN

Keira

While I look okay in Dillan's body—T-shirt, jeans, tennis shoes, I force Dillan to change out of the clothes he picked for my body this morning. He's next to me as I pick out a quarter-sleeve, green jersey knit top and a pair of black capris. I point out a pair of black slip-on Keds, and he slides a foot into each.

"Lovely," he says sarcastically. "I look like a grandmother now. Thanks."

"I don't exactly have a designer wardrobe, Dillan."

"I'm telling you now, if Ellen doesn't change us back, I'm going shopping at the Pentagon City Mall. I refuse to wear what's in your closet. I've been a woman for a hour, and I have more fashion sense than you do."

"Whatever you buy, I get to keep."

He scoffs. "As if any of it would fit my body after the change, and Stacey's pretty much an Amazon compared to you."

"Right," I mutter. "Now it's my turn to say *thanks.* Jerk," I say under my breath.

Dillan laughs. "You get riled up too easily, Keira. Loosen up. You might have more fun if you do."

"Are you having fun, Dillan?"

"You're missing the point, and I'm not talking about this situation exclusively. I'm talking in general."

We leave the apartment.

"So you're the expert now?" I ask accusingly. With Dillan's legs, my stride is longer than normal, and I have to rein in my step. Dillan isn't that much taller than me, maybe three or four inches, but it makes a world of difference in looking around. "Being tall is awesome," I say.

"Yeah, well, being short isn't all that it's cracked up to be," Dillan says beside me.

"Just wait until they whistle."

"Really? Do guys still do that?"

I just laugh. Once outside, it isn't long before we're standing outside of Ellen's Corner Bakery.

When I read the sign on the door, the urge to murder someone is overwhelming.

Namely, one Dillan Pope. But if I did this now, it wouldn't be murder. It would be suicide.

"Closed for renovation. Ellen's Corner Bakery will reopen on Tuesday for our 30th Annual Celebration. We hope you'll join us then."

"Ellen didn't say anything about this last night," Dillan says. His tone is dejected and pitiful.

"Does she live upstairs?" I ask.

He looks up at me quickly. "Yes! Maybe there's a door around back."

We aren't messing around anymore. We literally sprint around the block and head straight down the delivery road that serves the business.

What gets me is that Dillan, in my body, gets there much faster than I do, in Dillan's body. The man's in shape, but compared to my runner's body, he's a bit of a clunker.

Dillan stops at a door labeled 34.

"Are you sure this isn't just a delivery door?" I ask.

"I'm not sure of anything, Keira," he whisper-yells at me.

He knocks on the door.

Then he starts to pound on it as if his very life

depended on it.

And, in a way, it does.

I join him, and after several moments, we hear movement behind the door. It opens with a metallic creaking, but it's Ellen, all right.

"Dillan, Keira," she exclaims in delight. The telling part is that when she says our names, she looks at the true person, not the gender. At first, I wasn't sure Ellen was at fault, but now I know for certain. Ellen swapped our bodies. She smiles, then says, "I wondered when I might be seeing the both of you. Come in, come in. Pardon the dust, please."

Dillan

It's a dark hallway and in any other circumstance, I wouldn't follow someone I barely knew down a darkened hallway. But this wasn't just any other circumstance. This was me getting my body back. My genitalia back. My dignity back.

If Ellen could do something like this—make people switch bodies—what else could she do? Should we be worried? Should we be scared?

It's just Ellen, I keep telling myself. Then the other part of me keeps saying, *Yeah, the same Ellen that gave you a vagina this morning. So keep moving, buddy, figure this out, and get on with your life.*

Keira's close on my heels when Ellen opens another door that leads into her bakery. We pass a huge electric mixer as well as boxes of ingredients: flour, sugar, stacks of coffee, stuff like that. Last night, it smelled like chocolate chip cookies. Today, it smells like cinnamon buns.

"Have you had breakfast yet?" Ellen asks.

"Eggs and toast," Keira answers. "Normally that would satisfy me, but..." She trails off.

"You're still hungry, I imagine. Different appetite with that body, I'm afraid," Ellen says. "I've made a few things. I knew you'd come by sooner or later, and I've got some sticky buns straight out of the oven that need icing. If one of you will do the honors, the other can help me make a pot of coffee."

I stop short. "Ellen, you know what we are here for. Let's not play games. Frankly, I'm not sure if I ever want a cup of coffee from here again."

"Really, Dillan," Keira says. "If you're not careful, she will turn you into a toad."

Ellen laughs. "This isn't fairy tale magic, Keira. Besides, I don't do toads. Messy creatures."

"So it's magic?" I ask.

"Not really," Ellen answers. And that's all she says on the topic. She pulls out the sticky buns and thrusts a jar of white icing in my hands. "Apply liberally," she orders. We sit down at a small bistro-styled table that, with dozens of deep scratches, has seen better days.

"But there's fifty buns here," I protest. Ellen gives me the evil eye, but that doesn't deter me. "You're closed until Tuesday, Ellen. What are you going to do with fifty icing-topped sticky buns?"

"It's for my granddaughter's Sunday School bake sale."

"Oh," I say.

"So, you are probably wondering why all of this is happening?" Ellen says conversationally, as if we just happened to stop by for some *other* reason.

"I'd say that's an understatement," Keira says. "We'd like you to change us back."

I watch for Ellen's reaction. Or lack of one. Other than taking a sip of her coffee, she barely moves a muscle. "I can't," she says at last.

"So you admit that you did this?" I say. "But you can't change us back? That doesn't make sense."

"Only the two of you can change yourselves back."

"Dillan," Keira says, "I told you that we had to learn a lesson. We just have to find out what it is first."

"Very good," Ellen says, praising Keira. "Last week, I gave each of you a task. A task you didn't fulfill. So, I had to take matters into my own hands."

"A task?" I nearly yell at her. Trust me, I'm not proud

of myself. "What are you talking about? I don't remember any tasks."

Ellen takes another sip of her coffee. I smear icing all over sticky buns with a little too much force. Some are flattened now. Keira eats a plain bun, and watches us both wearily. Just because she's in my body, it doesn't mean she can eat whatever junk she wants to.

"Dillan," Ellen starts, oblivious to my selfish thoughts. "I said you could use a *challenge.* Keira, I said you could do with a bit of *disorder.* You may think you know what I meant, but obviously you did not, because as of two o'clock this morning, you swapped bodies, and will remain so until you fulfill the tasks."

She inspects my work and *tsks.* I'm almost done with spreading the icing on the smashed buns. I have a feeling that once I'm finished, our time limit is up.

"What about a clue?" Keira pleads.

Ellen smiles understandingly. "Think about who you've swapped into and go from there. Thank you for your help today, Dillan. These should sell like, well, like hot cakes." Ellen chuckles at the smashed buns. She looks at the old-style watch pinned to her apron. "You two have until the celebration to figure it out."

"But that's days away," I say. There's no way I can be Keira for several days.

Keira stands. She looks as hopeless as I feel. "What happens if we don't solve it?"

"Then the switch will be permanent." My stomach falls. "Worry not," Ellen says with cheer. "I've yet to have a couple fail."

So she's done this before? I think. *How comforting.*

Keira

The walk back to the apartment is a quiet one. Each in our own thoughts. A task. A lesson. *You could do with a bit of disorder, Keira.* Well, this certainly qualified as disorder, but I'm fairly confident that this isn't what Ellen meant.

Disorder is the exact opposite of what I need or what I want. As a soldier, my life is a series of rules, regulations, and order. A big stress on the *order* part. It's what I liked about being in the military. I always knew what was expected of me.

I don't know if I can do the unexpected. I don't know if I can be Dillan. I'd go crazy. Insane. We're talking about the man who wanted to jump from the top of my parents' house into our swimming pool at my high school graduation party. To impress me, of all things.

Oh, I knew about that. Jon told me a week after it happened and I pinky-swear-promised never to let Dillan know. Sort of a secret within a secret. It was an easy promise to make, since, at eighteen, I had no intention of ever talking to Dillan again.

Now that I *am* him, for all intents and purposes, I feel certain that I am about to get to know him even better. Way better. I am not prepared for this.

I'll never be prepared for this.

Take, for instance, the way he smells. It should be virtually impossible to be attracted to oneself, but here I am, in Dillan's body, loving the way he smells. God, I'm so disgusted with myself right now that I want to vomit up the cinnamon bun I just ate.

And don't get me started on all the sly looks I've been

getting from the women we've passed on the sidewalk.

Not just sly looks. *Invitational* looks. Even at ten in the morning, Dillan's a stud. I'm not denying that. What I want to deny is the fact that I'm now suddenly experiencing the feeling firsthand. How tiring it must be to be Dillan Pope. He's probably used to it, like how I work out a muscle group until I plateau. You have to change things up in order to see results.

Well, Ellen certainly did that. Changed things up. And this is the result.

The head on my shoulders is like twice the size of my own.

I swear, my hands are huge paws. I feel like I'll crush everything I try to touch.

Everything about the essence of me is trapped to a clunky, muscled male body that could never run a mile in under six minutes.

Don't forget the junk, Keira. Oh, I'm not. With every step, I can feel Dillan's *package.*

His impressive package. Walking is tough enough. Running? Dear God, let's not think about what happens to the stuff downstairs when men run.

Okay, I'm sort of grossed out now.

Thankfully my phone rings and I pick it up without thinking.

Dillan

I glance a couple of times at Keira. She plods along in my body as if I'm just too heavy for her to operate my legs. In a sense, I can understand. In her body, it feels like I'm floating on thin air.

She's just so light and tiny compared to me and, as an experiment, I want to sprint the rest of the way back to the apartment. Even up the stairs. Of course, I do no such thing. Not after seeing how women are looking at my body, and noticing Keira's reaction.

She sort of looks ticked off.

For all I know, she's internally calling me a man whore and every other negative adjective she can think of. It's disappointing that she thinks of me as a man whore. Granted, I don't begrudge her the thought. Fair game is fair game, and women who do the same thing are often called worse. Much worse.

So while I don't think that I deserve the title—it's not like I go out and randomly have sex just because someone has given me the *come hither* look—it comes across as disheartening that she of all people would think of me in that way.

I guess what I mean is that since she's a soldier, her job, in a sense, is to protect our freedoms and equal the playing field between our genders. At least, that's how *I* see her job. Doesn't mean that she sees it in the same light.

Keira's phone rings just as a man on the sidewalk lifts his head slightly and gives me the "What's up?" line.

He just hit on me.

Oh, wait. Strange as it may sound, for a second there, I

actually forgot I was in her body.

"Hello?" Keira answers her phone. It dawns on me that whoever is calling her will not expect *my* voice on the other end of the line. And, by the expression on her face—my face—I can tell she didn't think of that, either. Shit! "Uh..." my masculine voice says slowly into the phone, then, "Our phones look the same. I must have picked up the wrong one." Pause. I wonder who's calling her. "Yeah, h—she's...uh...right here. Hold on."

Keira cups the mic on her smartphone. Sweat beads her forehead.

"It's Alec," she mutters. "I don't care what you have to say, just find a reason to end the call."

Her eyes—my eyes—shoot laser daggers at me. I look at the phone rather stupidly. I could really mess things up for her with Alec. But she'd never forgive me, even if she didn't like him. Keira would not appreciate me taking control of her life.

But she may not have a choice.

Both of us may not have a choice.

You could use a challenge, Dillan Pope. Ellen's sweet voice pops into my head.

Pretending to be Keira will be a challenge. And I have to start being her, oh, right about...now.

I take the phone from Keira's outstretched arm. We're still outside and about ten feet from the apartment's entrance. Actually, it was at about this spot that I gave her the coffee last night.

Somehow it seemed fitting.

"Hello," I say in a shaky voice. I'm not sure if I've mastered Keira's voice mannerisms. I doubt I'll ever master anything about her. Including wearing women's underwear.

"Keira?" a man's voice says on the other end. He almost sounds confused. "This is Alec. We met last night..." His voice trails off.

Wow, I think. It's telling that someone like Alec Huffman would be uncertain if a girl remembered him or not. While it may be a mean thought, other than Jon and Tanner, how many men call for Keira?

"Hi." I clear my throat. What would Keira say in this situation? I mean, other than *hi*?

It's not exactly easy being a girl when said girl is staring at you like she wants to murder you.

"Hi," I say again, but louder. *The man's not deaf, Dillan.*

If I just keep saying hi, maybe *he* will end the call. God, when did I become a pansy? Probably the second I was transported into someone else's body.

Keira continues to glare at me, all the while motioning at the watch on her wrist. *Hurry it up*, her expression declares. *Or I will shove you down the drainage pipe.*

"Hi," Alec says with a touch of humor. He must think I'm nervous. Seriously, he has no clue. "So..." Alec says. "I was wondering...if you don't already have plans for tonight, would you like to go out on a date with me?"

I'm speechless. Keira's looking at me like, *you better tell me what he's saying,* and all I can think of is that a Major League Baseball player just asked me out.

There's something giddy-feeling about being asked out on a date.

Even if I am living it through Keira's eyes.

It feels like I'm smiling.

The muscles around my mouth are stretched out as I say, "Yeah, I'd like that. Pick me up at eight."

CHAPTER EIGHTEEN

Keira

Calmly, I take my phone out of Dillan's hands and walk into the apartment's lobby entrance. Dillan's on my heels, trying to explain how and why he just agreed to go on a date with Alec Huffman.

"He was extremely persuasive," Dillan says with a little bit too much glee. He's proud of himself. He thinks he's got the best of me. "Alec never gave me the opportunity to say no."

I jam my thumb on the elevator's up button. When it doesn't come down in the five seconds I've allotted for it to do my bidding, I pivot left, open the door to the stairwell, and run up.

Dillan follows. Which is what I expected. What I don't expect is to be winded after about two flights of stairs, but I keep running.

Even if it kills me.

"No one can be that persuasive in a one-minute phone call," I say in between breaths. I feel like I'm a car that's been rearranged to walk on two legs. "You really need to work on your aerobics, Dillan."

"Don't you want to know what he said about you?" Dillan asks. I stop suddenly and he smacks into me. I have to catch onto my own body to keep Dillan from flying backward down the stairs. "Thanks," I hear my own voice tell me.

"No," I say. We've stopped at the fifth floor. I need a break.

"No...what?"

"No, I don't want to know what he said about me."

Dillan gives me a puzzled look.

"I don't believe you're being honest with me. And...with yourself. How can you *not* want to know what he said?"

This stops me in my tracks even though I'm not moving.

I can't...I just can't.

Love is unpredictable.

It's unstable.

And looking at *myself* and hearing *my own voice* ask me that question makes this entire situation highly unfair.

It's like a slap in the face.

But I have to ask myself: Am I interested in Alec Huffman?

No. Not really. Well. Maybe I am. I don't know. I'm flattered. There. I can admit that.

"I don't want to know because I'm not vain," I finally answer. "Also, you weren't on the phone long enough to discuss me."

I had been inspecting Dillan's watch like a hawk when he was on the phone with Alec, so I know that in the seventy-one seconds he was on the phone, forty were devoted to saying *hi* like an idiot.

The rest, well, the rest was Dillan agreeing to a date.

There wasn't much room left to compliment me considering that I had taken the phone out of Dillan's hands after hearing the words, *"Yeah, I'd like that. Pick me up at eight."* I hung the phone up without a second's hesitation.

A group of teenage boys holding skateboards come down the stairs and around us. Dillan moves and begins to take the stairs two at a time. He shouts down, "You are no fun. Arguably, the most famous player for the Washington

Nationals wants to date you and what do you do? You hang up the phone on Alec Huffman."

Dillan keeps going up as the teenagers gasp while looking me—inspecting Dillan's body—over.

"Dude," one of the boys says. "I didn't know that Alec Huffman was gay."

I'm not surprised that they have mistaken the situation entirely. It certainly doesn't help that my idiot roommate had to shout down a statement that made it sound like Alec Huffman had asked out another man.

"My sister is going to snap," another one says. They keep talking, but after two floors, their conversation is too low for me to hear.

His sister isn't the only one who's going to snap.

Dillan

For the majority of the day, Keira hibernates in her room—her real room—and keeps the door closed. At times, I hear sounds from the television from her room waft into the living room, but she keeps to herself.

I'd prefer it if we could work this situation out together. Keira must feel otherwise.

Other than the challenge of being a woman for the next few days, the only other challenge I can think of is the Joy Fromm case.

I plop on the couch—it's still on the other side of the room; we never moved the furniture back after that silly plan of running into each other—and busy myself with reading the case file on the company.

Tucked in a folder is a picture of Amanda Joy. Sixty-five with a short, silver bob, her professional head shot isn't unlike anyone else in her position: CEO of a business. Powerful. Smart. Diabolical. She looks the part. She also looks like she could eat children for dinner, but even I have to admit that in order for women to break through the glass ceiling, they have to take on strong, competitive personas that, while these personas could rival that of their male counterparts, often landed them the labels of bitches or backstabbers.

My experience with LouAnn Britton taught me that this isn't the norm and that women bosses are the best kind out there. Tough, but effective. Kind, but aggressive. Caring, but not emotional.

LouAnn, for all her redeeming qualities, is someone I highly respect.

Even when she loans me out to the wolves.

Speaking of wolves, I pull out a picture of Ken Fromm.

He is in his late thirties; a product of his father's second marriage after a disastrous divorce to Amanda's mother, and handsome enough to charm his way through any obstacle. Ken's Ivy League upbringing contrasts with Amanda's. Her father wasn't yet successful during her early years, and by the time Ken was born—the elder Mr. Fromm had married his mistress—Amanda was already running a good portion of her father's business.

One might argue that it was *because* of Amanda Joy, then Amanda Fromm, that her father's business took off. Savvy marketing, wise mergers, a solid business plan, and the fact that Amanda was a military veteran elevated Joy Fromm Acquisitions within the ranks of defense contractors.

Ken came on board and took everything apart—the integration between all departments; the single-layer leadership that allowed for seamless transparency—and, in its place, installed an antiquated hierarchy that never matched what Amanda Joy had built up over the years. Stovepipes were created, meaning departments stopped communicating. The left hand never knew what the right hand was doing.

The company hemorrhaged. It lost contracts. Employees fled. And, for the final nail in the coffin, the elder Mr. Fromm died, leaving his company—and his family, one might argue—to pick up the pieces.

A company can have but one captain. But who was it going to be? Amanda Joy or Ken Fromm?

That's what LouAnn, and Johnson Brookshire, need me to figure out and implement. Not only that, I have to get both Amanda Joy and Ken Fromm to agree.

It will be a challenge. A *huge* challenge.

This must be what Ellen meant when she said I could use a challenge.

If not, then we're screwed.

When I look up from Ken Fromm's picture, Stacey, who somehow entered the apartment as quietly as a ninja, is staring at me.

Keira

I forgot about Stacey. It's only after the front door opens and closes and hearing voices that I realize she's in the living room. How could I forget that Dillan has a girlfriend?

I don't want to have to deal with a *girlfriend* while I'm trying to figure this whole thing out.

"This is just weird," I hear Stacey say. "Keira, why are you reading Dillan's work files?"

I put down an Army manual on written-materials-slash-official-correspondence and quietly inch my bedroom door open, just enough to see and hear how Dillan responds.

Stacey's back is to me. I don't have time to admire her linen shorts, her crazy long legs, or her long blonde hair. I'm focused on the scene before me.

My body sits on the couch. Folders and pictures are scattered around Dillan.

He's a little like me: when we get into a project, we really immerse ourselves wholly. That's why, even after feeling hopeless for the last few hours, I have every confidence that between the two of us, we'll figure this out.

I don't blame Stacey for questioning me, er, my body.

By all outward appearances, it looks odd that Keira would be studying Dillan's materials.

I see Dillan turn toward Stacey. Thankfully, he doesn't look scared or excited or shocked. I have to remember that Dillan is a smooth guy.

He can charm the venom out of a snake if he has to.

"Hi Stacey," I hear my voice say from the living room. From my bedroom door, still barely cracked open, I'm holding my breath. "You just missed Dillan's boss," Dillan says.

Stacey scrunches her nose. "LouAnn was here?"

Was there a challenge in her voice? Okay, maybe I'm just being paranoid.

Regardless, I start ticking off reasons to break up with her.

Thumb: I'm not ready for a commitment.

Index finger: I don't deserve you.

Middle finger: I'm interested in someone else.

Ring finger: My life is a little too complicated at the moment for a relationship and I don't want to hurt you.

Pinky finger: I'm moving to another country.

Dillan and I haven't come up with a reason for, well, about anything if we encountered someone who knows us. I probably shouldn't have shut myself in my bedroom the moment we came back from Ellen's Corner Bakery, but I do my best thinking when my own body isn't looking at me or questioning me.

Granted, this is a brand new problem for me, but, still... I should be afforded an opportunity to decompress.

On second thought, maybe avoiding Stacey altogether might be the best plan. I mean, this is Dillan we're talking about. How long would the relationship have lasted in the first place? Exactly.

Dillan responds, "Yeah. I like LouAnn a lot. She reminds me of an Army general, but, you know, more fashionable. Anyway, she had a great idea. Dillan is, uh, stumped on his current project, so she suggested I take a look at everything and offer an opinion. I just love, love, love regulations and stuff. Plus, it turns out this company has Department of Defense contracts and connections. That's really what she wanted me to look at."

I just love, love, love regulations and stuff?

My God, does he have to lay it on so thick? I mean, I *do* love regulations, but I would never say it like *that.*

However, Stacey seems to buy it, and as far as explanations go, it isn't a bad one. Not great, but it was fairly adequate in the moment.

"Did he leave with LouAnn?" Stacey asks.

She looks around the room and cranes her neck to look into Dillan's room. The door is wide open. As usual. Other than the pigsty contained therein, there isn't much to see.

"Yeah, I guess so," Dillan says, and I watch as he shrugs my shoulders to make it appear as if it is something that Keira couldn't care less about. Twenty-four hours ago, that statement would have been one hundred percent true. Now, not so much. "All I know is that LouAnn left a few moments ago. It's possible that Dillan went with her. I wasn't paying attention."

Stacey moves and I lose my visual advantage. All I know is I cannot leave this room looking like Dillan unless Stacey either leaves the apartment or goes into the bathroom. God, I've never wished for someone to have to pee as much as I want Stacey to right now. I'd even welcome her writing another lipstick note on the mirror.

"What happened to the living room?" Stacey asks from the other side of the room.

I still can't see her.

"I think Dillan got bored last night or this morning. It was like this when I woke up."

Stacey laughs. "He does like to rearrange furniture for some reason. Now, why he would put everything into one corner is somewhat mystifying. Speaking of mystifying, I think I'll wait in his bedroom and surprise him when he gets back. Don't say anything, okay?"

A grin spreads on Dillan's face. He can't wait to see what happens when his body finally makes an appearance.

"I wouldn't dream of ruining your surprise, Stacey," my voice says back to her.

Dillan's bedroom door closes behind Stacey. I give it a few minutes before I leave my bedroom.

It takes everything within me not to pummel Dillan. The shit-eating grin on my feminine face irritates the hell out of me.

"I wouldn't go in there if I were you," Dillan says.

He doesn't have to worry.

I don't plan to.

Dillan

Part of me wants nothing more than for Stacey to drag Keira—my body—back to my room and ravish her. Oh, Keira wouldn't have a problem stopping whatever Stacey had planned. And knowing Keira, she has no interest in having *sex done upon her body*—whether it's her in my body, or me in hers.

Furthermore, knowing Stacey the way I know Stacey, Keira's eyes would be opened way more than she would have ever wanted when it came to what the tall, blonde Amazon liked to do in the bedroom.

I prefer to keep that information to myself, thank you very much.

I watch as Keira stands outside of her bedroom. Her eyes are guarded and I can tell she has no interest in sticking around to find out what Stacey plans. I don't blame her. I'm only glad that I came up with enough of an explanation of LouAnn suggesting Keira help out with my case. Stacey's smart. Very smart.

If I hadn't brought LouAnn into the equation, I doubt she would have believed me. Believed Keira, I should say.

My stomach grumbles and I realize it's dinnertime. I have two hours before Alec Huffman is picking me up for our date.

Strangely, my stomach somersaults. I still can't believe I agreed to the date on Keira's behalf. I suppose it's because I don't want to seem like I'm ruining her life.

Her chances *at* happiness.

Even if it isn't with me.

I shake my head. Keira watches me and sometimes I

have a feeling that she knows what I'm thinking about. If she only knew.

But then again, that would scare her off even more.

And that's the last thing I want to do. Scare Keira Holtslander away.

She was already a skittish doe to begin with. Never mind her knowing that all I wanted to do was lick her entire body, head to toe, and recite poetry in her ears, and bring her to the brink of ecstasy over and over before allowing a climax to crash over her.

But, then again, I happen to be looking at *myself* as I think these thoughts, and it makes me somewhat queasy.

Oh, who am I kidding? I can't help but think about Keira in that way.

Well, I probably could if I tried hard enough, but that'd be too much work.

Keira whispers something that I cannot hear, but I can certainly understand her movements. She's headed toward the front door.

Keira is leaving.

I don't want to be here—in Keira's form—while Stacey waits for Dillan to show up.

Quickly, and quietly, I pack up the Joy Fromm files and rush over to her. In fact, it feels like I do a little skip, which is something I never want to do again. Especially once I'm back in my own body.

"I'm going with you," I say to her.

She only nods. I doubt she cares what I do as long as I don't impede her progress. She'd probably trip me if she had to. However, that isn't necessary.

Together, we slip out the front door and silently lock it behind us.

CHAPTER NINETEEN

Keira

Something about sneaking out of Dillan's apartment, and away from Stacey, feels clandestine. As if we are spies slinking away from a dangerous plot before something goes *boom.* We run down the stairs and out onto the pavement. The sky is clear, the air warm, and, strangely enough, I'm sort of getting used to Dillan's body.

Not the chunkiness of it all, but it feels like I'm experiencing life anew and through fresh eyes. Sounds are different, like lower pitched. I seem to be more in tune with sounds I never used to pay attention to: cars going by, kids talking, the way my feet hit the sidewalk, which is harder... heavier.

Colors are muted. Blue is blue, and red is red, but there's a tint of gray to it all, as if, to Dillan's vision, vibrancy isn't as important as it is in my own eyes. So the blue sky, while clear and bright, just isn't something to behold. It's just the sky.

And I love that. I love that my senses are on overdrive.

I'm starving and I want to eat stuff that I generally don't care for. Fatty, greasy food.

"Do you know what I want more than anything else right now?" I ask Dillan.

"What's that?" He laughs as I look down on him.

Even my own laugh seems pleasant to me.

To Dillan's ears.

My hair, naturally brown and wavy in parts and ruler-straight in others, glimmers in the sunshine. Dillan has no idea of how to put my hair up in a ponytail, so my strands are scattered all over the place.

I spin my body around, not caring who sees since it seems like I'm manhandling my roommate, and fix the ponytail. Dillan appears happy to comply, though he does say something to the effect of not damaging the china. *You break it, you buy it.*

"I'm dying for a hot dog with sauerkraut and thick-cut french fries doused in ketchup," I announce as if it is the most scandalous thing I've ever said.

Dillan looks down over my own body—he's still wearing the *grandma* clothes I made him wear—and says, "Will you let *me* have some, or are you training for some marathon you haven't told me about?"

It occurs to me that maybe the only thing Dillan truly knows about me is that I'm Jon's sister, that I'm in the military, and that I'm an avid runner. Then I wonder if that's all that I really am.

Those three things can, and often do, define me.

Sergeant Holtslander is the fastest runner in the unit. Or, *Keira's an intelligence analyst in the military*, and, *have you met Jon's little sister, Keira?*

There's nothing in there about boyfriends or kids or amazing facts, such as Keira *always gets the answers right when she watches* Jeopardy. I don't, of course, but something like that might be pretty cool.

Maybe dating a MLB pitcher will shake things up. Well, let me amend that. Dillan dating a MLB pitcher *for me* might shake things up.

It dawns on me somewhere between the transformation and the fact that I want a hot dog that I was—*I am*—a boring, uninteresting person.

You could do with a bit of disorder, Keira Holtslander.

"Are you crying?" Dillan asks me.

He puts his hands out, palms up, as if to catch imaginary rain. As if he is trying to find a logical reason for the wetness on my cheeks.

I swipe a hand over my face. The stubble on my jaw jolts me and I try to dismiss the sinking feeling of being stuck like this forever.

"No, of course not," I say. "But, on the off chance that I am, it's really you that's crying. You should stop being so emotional."

Dillan looks at me seriously. "Trust me. I'm trying."

Then he smiles. Wait, no, *I'm* smiling at me.

Oh, stop trying to figure it out, Keira.

Dillan says, "We've got two hours until the big date. I know a great place for dogs if you're willing to travel for it."

Dillan

Grown men should not cry. Women transformed into grown men might want to cry when they realize how hairy, gross, and smelly we are.

When I notice Keira crying—it was a little cry and nothing to be ashamed of—I immediately felt for her. It's been a crazy day for both of us, but more so for her.

She moved up here last Saturday, was thrown—apparently—into the deep end when she arrived at her job in the Pentagon, and, within seven days, she's been transported into the one man's body she can't stand.

Waves hand...that's me.

It's no big secret that Keira doesn't like me.

Jon has casually mentioned it here and there over the years. Something about how she thinks I'll never grow up. But over the last few years I've made great strides at maturing.

I'm serious at my job, I pay all of my bills on time—there was a period in my life when I didn't do that at all, and I had the bad credit to show for it—and, even if I have to turn in my man-card, I've hardly looked at another woman since Keira, with a duffle bag and two suitcases, walked, no, *barged*, into my life a week ago.

But have I really ever looked at another woman, seriously, after seeing her nine years ago?

I could answer *yes*.

I could answer *no*.

Depends on what your definition of *looking at* means. I suppose what it really means is that yes, I've looked at other women, but I don't keep thinking about them after they are out of my life.

Not like how I've often thought about Keira over the years.

Does that make me a sap?

If it does, I don't care.

I look at Keira—at myself—and hear that if she wants a hot dog and ketchup-drenched french fries, I will go out of my way to make that happen.

She grins at me, letting me know she's up for the challenge of getting the perfect dog, and we half-run, half-walk to the Metro station. After a transfer onto the Silver Line, we exit at the Reston West station, and we walk the rest of the way to the Reston Town Center in Virginia.

"This is kind of a cute place," she tells me once we enter the town center.

The place is comprised of stores, boutiques, restaurants, hotels, and a movie theater.

In the fall, the town center celebrates Oktoberfest, complete with polka bands and multiple beer venues. I might see about renting a booth this year, but I guess we'll see what happens.

The same arena, in the wintertime, transforms into an outdoor ice skating rink that's brimming with kids and adults of all shapes and sizes. During the rest of the year, I hear it's a great place for after-work happy hours, but I live a bit too far from here to make it a regular event.

We slip into a booth in the back of Hoolin's Dog Shack.

"Well, *cute* is subjective. I'd say it's a useful place for just about anything," I say as I chew a small bite of my hot dog. With Keira's baby-doll-sized mouth, I can barely fit anything more than a tiny portion of food at one time. When I eat a dog, I want to take man-size bites. Not these little, puny, infant-sized nibbles. "It must take you a full hour to eat *anything*," I say, rolling my eyes at her.

Okay, maybe her mouth isn't *that* small, but it's smaller than what I'm used to, and if I don't watch it, I'm going to end up choking.

Keira, on the other hand, has eaten her sauerkraut-laden hot dog in two bites.

Two freaking bites. I shouldn't be jealous, but I am.

When she orders a second hot dog with double the sauerkraut while I'm only halfway done my dog, I feel insignificant as a human being. I mean, I haven't even touched the french fries yet.

"God," she says with delight. Granted, I'm hearing her talk in my voice, so "delight" may or may not be her intended emotion. "God," she repeats, taking another bite as if she hasn't eaten anything this good in years. "I love your mouth."

Did she just say that? I love your mouth.

Keira appears to realize her mistake and I stay silent. How will she talk her way out of that one?

"Uh, that came out wrong," she explains, wiping her mouth.

A spot of ketchup dots her upper lip.

In a movie, the guy—that's me, sort of—would lean over and kiss it off. Movie-guy would be smooth, suave, and, if it wasn't a kiss, he'd make it seem like a kiss was about to happen, but would instead use a napkin to wipe the condiment from her lips.

Movie-guy is a complete tease.

But, alas, this isn't a movie.

"So, it came out wrong?" I prompt her to keep talking as I pop a fry in my mouth. Perhaps it's mean of me not to mention the food on her upper lip, but I feel confident that with her next gargantuan bite, the ketchup will get caught up in it and take care of itself. “Are you saying you *don’t* love my mouth?”

“You know what I meant, Dillan,” she whisper-yells at me.

My thick eyebrows are furrowed at me.

“Oh, I’m sorry,” I say. “I don’t read minds. Care to explain?”

My smile must be a little too bright because she growls at me and throws a french fry at my face.

Then, all of a sudden, she bursts out laughing.

Keira

For a few minutes there, I let it slip my mind that I wasn't in my own body and all I can do is laugh. Yeah, looking at my own face is still a bit disconcerting, but Dillan has his own mannerisms so that it kind of, sort of, seems like I'm talking to someone who happens to look *like* me, but *isn't* me.

I suppose the logical part of my brain hasn't accepted the transformation.

Who would?

But, deep inside, the part of me that realizes life isn't fair and that the world can be strange and full of mysteries has come to grips with the information. I don't accept it. I don't understand it. But I realize I can't change anything unless I work with Dillan.

Ellen's clue was to look at the person we swapped into and go from there.

So, I'm trying.

I'm trying to get to know Dillan.

The real Dillan and not just the five-minute abridged version that I currently know about. If this was a regular meeting-slash-date-slash-*let's-run-away-from-our-problems* dinner, I'd concentrate on his face or his eyes or how amazing his arms are. But I can't do any of that, or I'd be admiring my own physical traits on him and that would be a tad weird.

More than weird. It would be demented.

And I can't get out of this situation without discovering more about Dillan. Not exactly altruistic of me, but it's not selfish, either, since he would benefit from it, too.

If it works.

So, while I'm genuinely enjoying myself in this moment, I'm not good at recognizing a double entendre before it comes out of my mouth, and Dillan, the ever astute sexual being that he is, is having too much fun at my expense because of it.

I ignore him in favor of eating a third hot dog, and he says something to the effect that I'll have gas later on. I know one thing for certain: I won't be running back to the Metro after this meal. I might even top everything off with a root beer float. Haven't had one of those since I was in high school.

"So, you were saying?" Dillan prompts me again.

He's obviously done eating after just one hot dog and four french fries and a couple of sips of lemonade. Can't help it if my body has a small stomach and is used to petite portions.

"It's nice to eat a big meal for once," I say.

"Can I translate that into meaning you like big things in your mouth from time to time?"

"You—you," I stammer. He baited me and I fell for it. Hook, line, and sinker. "You, Dillan Pope, are *bad*."

"You're not just now coming into this realization, are you? If so, you're not a very bright intelligence analyst."

He says it with good humor, but I still steal another fry from his plate and throw it at him.

He tries to catch it in his mouth, but misses.

Alec wouldn't miss.

Alec.

Sighing, I say, "We should get back. Alec's going to pick you up in forty-five minutes."

"You know, I can cancel the date."

"No, no. I don't want you to miss out on your big-time

date with Alec Huffman. When you get back, we'll stay up all night, gabbing like girls, and discuss every second of the date in ad nauseam details. Plus, his car is awesome."

"I wonder if he's a good kisser," Dillan murmurs in a fake-serious tone.

"He probably is, Dillan, but you—we—are not going to be finding out tonight."

I pay for the food on the way out since Dillan took care of the Metro fare, and we walk back to the Metro station.

"Do you remember the first time we met?" Dillan asks.

I wonder where he's going with this. I do, in fact, remember.

It was my high school graduation party. I was eighteen and I thought I knew everything there was to know about life and boys. At the time, Jon, who I already idolized, said he was bringing his college friend, Dillan Pope. But not to meet me. To meet our parents.

We knew already that Jon was gay and, at first, we thought Dillan was his boyfriend. Jon quickly disabused us of that thought, and informed us that Dillan was not only straight, but a straight-up player, and, coincidently, his best friend.

"Dillan's the love 'em and leave 'em type," Jon told me the day before my party over the phone. Jon, to my knowledge, never sugarcoated his words. He was real. Honest. And, sometimes, brutally so. *"He sounds horrible,"* Miss Expert me had replied, and Jon said, *"Naw, Keira, he isn't that bad. How bad can he be if he's my best friend?"*

From outward appearances, they had absolutely nothing in common, but I've had that one statement in my head for nine years: How bad can Dillan be if he's my brother's best friend?

Dillan came to the party dressed to impress. Dark slacks

and an open-collared, white polo shirt, a clean shave, and swoon-worthy looks. Intense, light green eyes below thick, brown eyebrows, a straight nose, chiseled cheekbones, and kissable-looking lips. He was tan from being a part-time lifeguard. It didn't hurt that he wore a smile.

What sealed the bad vibe deal, for me, was the fact that everyone within a one-mile radius reacted to him like catnip.

Well, if everyone else wanted him, I sure as hell didn't.

That didn't stop me from stealing sly glances at him from the corner of my eye when he wasn't looking at me. And he always seemed to be looking at me. It was, after all, my graduation party. It took effort on my part, but I completely avoided Dillan Pope the entire day, and when he disappeared, Jon made up some story about how Dillan had made other plans.

Of course, a week later, Jon told me the real story, and a part of me has felt guilty about it ever since. Well, slightly guilty. I can't be held accountable for Dillan's method of dealing with rejection.

"Do you mean my graduation party? You were there, right?" I ask this nonchalantly, as if I can't be bothered to remember if he was there or not.

Dillan glances at me in surprise, but there's something else there in the expression.

Doubt?

Like maybe he knows I'm lying.

Dillan

During my freshmen year at college, a girl named Maritsa told me she could tell when I was lying. That my face did this *thing*, this shifty-eyed, looking at something else—like her nose—*thing*.

I spent a month studying my face in the mirror. I checked for obvious expressions. Shock. Anger. Everything. But how could I tell I was lying to someone? It wasn't something I could practice alone. I had no intention of asking anyone to help me master the problem, and whipping out a handheld mirror before every conversation was a nonstarter.

Not to mention vain. My attempt to combat an expression that I couldn't control came in the form of always trying to be honest. I wasn't always successful, but I can say that I tried.

So when Keira finally answers my question about the first time we met, I find out, firsthand, exactly what this *thing* is.

I watch as my face does a shifty-eyed, looking at something else—my ear—*thing* and I nearly want to thank Maritsa verbally, and loudly, for clueing me in. Granted, it's several years late, but I have almost no doubt in my mind that Keira just lied to me.

Lied right to my face about the first time we met.

Now, why would she lie about it?

It wasn't like she fawned all over me at her graduation and was now trying to make it seem like no big deal. I don't think she looked at me once. However, if she's lying about it...if she wants me to think she doesn't really remember, then she's hiding something.

What that something is now captures my attention.

Big time.

Like, I want to claw and dig and explore until I receive a favorable answer.

Forcing Keira to do my bidding is never going to happen, and for obvious reasons: I have no sway over her. And...I find that I don't want to force her into anything she wouldn't naturally want to do in the first place.

Honestly, I like her the way she already is.

Ornery.

Sarcastic.

Stand-offish.

Okay, maybe that last bullet doesn't encourage me, or anyone, to get close. Perhaps that's how she likes it. But... maybe all I ever needed to do was chisel away at her outer layer, like water over a stone, and, over time, to discover the inner workings of what made Keira *Keira.*

"Why do you ask?" she says.

We step into the waiting Metro car and sit on an empty two-seater bench. Keira is careful to keep her thighs—my thighs—from touching me. She looks like she wants to cross her legs, but she doesn't. Probably worried about pinching a certain part of her anatomy.

"No reason," I say. "I was thinking, though, it's almost nine years to the day since then. If I recall, your graduation party was in early June."

"June fourteenth," she clarifies for me. Oh, okay.

What is today? June eleventh.

"That's next Tuesday. The day we have to figure *this* out or, you know, forever doom and gloom in these bodies."

"Do you think it's a coincidence? That on the anniversary of our meeting, we have to solve a riddle that transforms us back into our own bodies?" Keira shakes her head like it's too much to believe, like something so trivial could dictate something so momentous. "It's not like our riddles are the same. It's a different task for each of us."

"Mine is *I could use a challenge.* Yours is *you could do with a little disorder.*"

"Similar, but not the same. I'm of the opinion that just by changing us into the other, she's fulfilled both tasks herself. How much more of a *challenge* or *disorder* can two people take when you switch their bodies? It is inherently challenging *and* full of disorder."

She whispers the *switch their bodies* part of her sentence. While we aren't loud, there are other people in the Metro car.

"Not to quibble," I say. "Ellen did say that because we didn't figure out the tasks early enough, she caused this to happen. I think we need to figure out what her original riddle meant for each of us. Once we do that, we might have a solution."

Keira turns to face me now, and our knees touch. It doesn't appear to bother her. Or maybe she's angry enough to not care.

"I knew Ellen for less than forty-eight hours when she said that to me. How the hell am I, a reasonable woman with a modicum amount of intelligence swimming her brain, supposed to know what a baker, who also happens to be a witch, meant when she mentioned that I could do with a bit of disorder? Honestly, I thought she meant I should choose a soy latte versus a non-fat, no-whip mocha next time."

My own light green eyes search my face intently. "You know her better. What did you think she meant when she said it to you?"

I thought Ellen meant that Keira was my challenge, but I would never admit to it out loud. Keira would only laugh at me.

Ellen said it right after meeting my roommate for the first time, after saying how much she liked Keira.

Should I admit this to Keira?

What if I'm *her* disorder, and she's *my* challenge?

My God, if that's the case, we're doomed.

How can I get the one girl I've always liked, who's never liked me, to like me in three days?

"Here's what I think, Keira," I say confidently, which belies how I really feel, which is gloomy. "I think Ellen's trying to be a matchmaker."

CHAPTER TWENTY

Keira

Matchmaking? Yes, I sort of had that same hunch, but I didn't want to admit it to myself. I can't undo nine years' worth of half-negative, half-positive thoughts about Dillan.

He's always been that unattainable yet unfixable guy in the back of my mind.

You want him, but you know he's not good for you, so you keep him at a distance.

You keep your dreams about him at bay.

You date safe guys who are more boring than you are and somehow, Keira, you consider that to be an accomplishment: that you haven't risked anything.

Your heart.

Your dreams.

Your aspirations.

Your *life.*

What if I had let Dillan sweep me off my feet back then? I probably would have just been a *tumble and run* to him. Another notch in his belt.

But people change.

I've changed over the last nine years from an insecure know-it-all into an even more insecure know-it-all. I've just kept those insecurities to myself, in imaginary—and orderly—plastic bins with labels on them.

On the other hand, I'm not some silly girl who requires a man to make her feel complete or worthwhile or confident or secure in her own abilities. In fact, I behave the exact opposite.

And I can't undo all of that in three days. Three days

to the year, nine years ago, that I first met Dillan Pope.

Ellen has a wicked sense of humor, that's for sure.

I gaze out the window as we pass through Tysons Corner. Clouds form overhead, and it isn't much longer before the large plexiglass window has streaks of rain marring the scenery. I wonder what Alec has planned for the date. He didn't seem like the dinner-and-a-movie type.

I don't think it's necessary to drill the rules into Dillan's head again, so I refrain from lecturing him how there's no kissing or fondling or *any* sexual interaction allowed.

I doubt Dillan wants to kiss another man.

The most they'll do is high-five each other.

Dillan

Observing Keira on the Metro ride back, I notice a pattern: she retreats when presented with a personal problem. Now, I have every confidence that if she encountered a professional or military problem, she'd fix it in less than fifteen seconds...or at least she'd have some sort of solution.

But when it's personal, she keeps her thoughts and feelings to herself.

Jon used to be that way when we first met.

He was reserved, quiet, and shy. Once he got to know me, and once he realized I wasn't a threat, he loosened up. Jon wasn't exactly obnoxious, but he had zero qualms about letting someone know when they were being an ass. Hell, he gave me an earful from time to time—and more recently when he told me that Keira was off-limits.

Jon didn't have anything to worry about on that front. I was already in her off-limits list.

Did I have hope?

Yes.

The way she lied about the graduation party...something inside of me lit up when I suspected that maybe, just maybe, she felt some sort of spark for me. I've been around enough women to know that if they didn't care about you, they wouldn't spar with you over anything.

Keira spars with me.

She *allows* herself to get agitated by me.

And if she didn't care about me—in some fashion—she wouldn't argue with me. At least, not in the same manner she does. She didn't automatically discount the matchmaking idea I mentioned a few moments ago. But then again, she didn't say anything at all.

Wordlessly, we transfer onto the Orange line and exit at Federal Triangle. As we walk to the apartment, Keira's phone beeps and she pulls it out.

"It's a text from Alec," she says.

It seems to take her forever to read it out loud.

"Did he cancel?" I ask when she doesn't say anything after a few minutes.

Doubtful, I think. She wouldn't have that scowl on her face if so.

"Not exactly," Keira answers.

I open the front door to the apartment and say, "Well, that's certainly helpful, thanks. I'll just go into your room and get ready."

I look down at what I'm wearing.

Uh.

Grandma clothes.

I wasn't thrilled at her other options, which weren't much. Not unless I wanted to wear her Army uniform. On second thought...if I wore her uniform, I might get free drinks all night.

God, to be a woman in uniform must be like winning the lottery. The alcoholic-drink lottery.

"He wants me to wear workout clothes for the—" Keira stops. I look at her and see where her eyes are focused.

My bedroom.

Stacey.

Oh no. How could I forget about the Amazonian beauty waiting in my bedroom?

Stacey is standing outside my bedroom. But wait, there's more.

She's wearing a see-through bra and panties. Her blonde

hair is pulled up and she leans ever so slightly against the doorframe.

And she looks pissed. We've been gone for an hour and a half.

"Inside," Stacey bites off. "Now."

I take a step forward, but luckily I remember it isn't me she's glaring at. It's at my body. Keira.

"See ya," I call over my shoulder. I am more than happy to let Keira handle this without me. I make my escape into Keira's bedroom before either woman can stop me.

One wouldn't give me a second glance.

The other, well, she was probably shooting daggers at her bedroom door.

Keira

Now, I normally would never check out a woman. But damn, Stacey is incredibly beautiful. Thick, glorious blonde hair, ice-blue eyes, perfect bone structure, and flawless skin to compliment those high cheekbones, a bountiful chest, a tiny waist, and just-wide-enough, flared-out hips.

I try, and fail, to remember those reasons I came up to break up with her. Something of Dillan must still be in there—*there*—because my lower-half tingles. Like, tingles and itches and my hand is dying to adjust the area.

I clear my throat. I must not, at any cost, go into that bedroom. My stomach gurgles. I think I'm going to be sick. I don't know if it's the hot dogs or what, but my hand flies to my stomach.

"You know," I tell Dillan's girlfriend, who's now moving toward me. I feel like one of those victims tied to a railroad. Stacey's the train. "I don't feel all that well."

She starts pushing me into the bedroom.

I have never been in this particular situation before and my brain literally flies the coop.

"I have the exact prescription waiting for you in your bedroom, Dillan. I've had more than an hour to come up with how to punish you. I hope you don't have plans tonight."

In addition to being incredibly beautiful, Stacey is incredibly strong. My manly body obeys her and she throws me into the room and then shoves me onto the bed. She doesn't even bother with the door. I try to get up, but she easily thwarts my movements.

Like some sort of ninja, she removes my shirt well before

I even know she's done it. She throws it across the room. Great. There goes the first article of clothing.

I grasp at the edge of the sheets, pulling it, and only manage to bring it over a few inches. Not enough to cover Dillan's chest. I'm not willing to think about what the man-junk between my legs is doing at the moment.

It's intense.

It's heat.

It's confusing me.

Stacey laughs. "This is new. Playing the virgin tonight?"

I keep my eyes plastered to her determined face and not her sheer lingerie as she crawls on top of me and begins to fumble with the button to my jeans. I say *fumble* because my hands are actively blocking hers.

Her eyes narrow.

"Really, I don't feel well," I say. I stress each word as I sit up.

Unfortunately, I have bad timing. Stacey re-situates herself and I end up head-butting her.

Dammit! Now I'm a girlfriend beater. Dillan must have a thick skull because I barely felt it.

"Ouch," she mutters, rubbing her forehead. The skin is a little red around her hairline. "I swear, it's like you've never done this before. You really must not feel well, Dillan."

"Sorry."

My stomach gurgles loudly. Stacey, still sitting on me, jumps a little and tilts her head questioningly.

It's totally the hot dogs.

I feel the pressure move lower into my belly. Normally I am in full control of my own body. My *regulated* body.

Normally I can make it to a restroom in time. But I'm

not in tune with Dillan's body. This might actually be normal for him.

I'll never forget Stacey's expression right then. It's a cross between surprise and disgust. Like she can't believe what's happening.

My ass vibrates when I fart.

It's more or less an explosion. It's loud enough to wake the dead. It's loud enough to tear Dillan from my bedroom.

It's loud enough, and stinky enough, for Stacey to scramble off me, dress in a hurry, and rush out of the apartment.

"I told you those hot dogs were going to get you," Dillan says from the open doorway.

His arms are crossed as he looks down at me.

I suppose I traded one embarrassment—Stacey seducing me—for another—passing gas in front of other human beings.

"I think I just broke up with your girlfriend," I say.

Dillan

"Oh my God," I say without thinking. "That smells terrible." I back away from the door, waving a hand in front of my face.

I need a gas mask for that one.

I'm not worried about Stacey. Either she'll be back or she won't.

"The way she was sitting on me didn't help," Keira says meekly.

As far as excuses go, it was on the weak side, but now is not the time to challenge her.

Keira isn't wearing a shirt. Stacey must have taken it off before Keira could stop her. I'm actually impressed that she was able to keep Stacey's experienced hands off her for as long as she did.

"Here." I find the shirt on the other side of the bedroom and hand it to her. Her face is red as she puts it back on. "I should have warned you. Stacey can be a bit..."

She avoids looking at me.

"Aggressive?" Keira suggests, before stalking out of my bedroom. She takes a few hard strides to the fridge, grabs a beer, and downs it in a few gulps. She's been a man for less than a day, but she's already mastered the *I'm upset so I'm going to drink a beer* method of coping with something. "My goal was to avoid her at all costs. I wasn't exactly successful there, was I?"

"I'd say you were entirely successful. I don't think I've been this entertained in years."

Her nostrils flare.

"I'm so glad I can amuse you, Dillan. Is there anything

else you'd like to see? I'm taking requests."

"Whoa, put the fangs away, Sergeant."

Keira finally looks at me and stops cold.

"What the hell are you wearing? Alec will be here in five minutes."

I conduct what I presume is a fashion model's pose. I twirl around and place a closed hand under my chin. All that's missing is glaring lights, heavy makeup, and a purple feather boa.

Make that a dozen purple feather boas.

"You don't like? Before Stacey erotically pushed you into my bedroom, you mentioned Alec said to wear workout clothes. Ta-da!"

"I swear to God," she mutters under her breath. "So you chose a sports bra and my competition shorts? Why not meet him wearing my underwear?" For some reason, she suddenly squats down and looks up my legs. "Jesus," she hisses. "You have to wear athletic underwear under those shorts. Unless you want the world to see my labia."

Keira thumps my forehead.

Ow!

"Your la—" I sputter. "I got dressed with my eyes closed, Keira. As much as I wanted to look at your amazing body in the mirror, I didn't. I respected your wishes. I grabbed stuff and put it on."

"Oh," she says. She looks at me without blinking for several long seconds. It's like she's never seen me before. "I, uh, well..." She hesitates instead of apologizing. "Let's pick out another outfit, okay?" She walks to her bedroom door. "By the way, your beer is really good."

I can feel the smile tugging at my lips.

"Thank you. I accept your apology."

She stares at me like she's debating whether to cut me

down or compliment me further.

Finally, in a soft tone, she says, "Thank you for getting dressed with your eyes closed. It's actually kind of sweet."

The smile on my face grows as she slips into her bedroom and comes out with a pair of dark brown yoga pants and a pale pink T-shirt.

"I'm kind of a sweet guy."

"Don't push it." Keira shakes her head, laughs, and then throws the clothes at my head.

"Wouldn't dream of it," I say as I dress.

I'm such a liar.

CHAPTER TWENTY-ONE

Keira

I feel a little better about the situation. Okay, not really. I'd rather not be in this predicament in the first place, but at least I can tell that Dillan is trying to be respectful toward me and his temporary ownership of my body.

Yeah, he's sarcastic, but maybe he isn't so bad.

And maybe I shouldn't be so hard on Dillan. He is, after all, my brother's best friend. My thoughts are diverted by a knock at the door. Dillan answers it. Alec and Tanner step inside. Alec looks casual but adorable. His red-blond hair and blue eyes stand out against a faded baseball jersey and long athletic shorts.

He turns to Dillan. "I thought we might take a turn or two at the batting cages."

"Sounds like fun," Dillan says. He uses a chipper voice that I wouldn't be caught dead using. "I'll see you two later," he calls to us, waving a dainty arm. I do not wave that way.

Tanner shifts around as Dillan and Alec leave. I try not to stare as the door closes. I want to call out something about curfews and serial killers and the importance of safe sex. I don't, of course.

Tanner nudges me in the ribs. "Hey, bro."

After a mini-panic I just say, "Hey, bro," back. Do they hug, or shake hands, each time Dillan and Tanner see each other? In the end, I go with a back-slap greeting. "Want a beer? How was the game this afternoon?" The white tape is still around his wrist. I wonder how many innings he played.

"I'm crushed you didn't watch it on TV," he says with a laugh. "I'll take that beer, though. The Orioles got the best of us today." Tanner moves into the living room and asks, "What happened to the living room?"

I hand over a beer. I keep one for myself and we survey the room together. It was like someone lifted the entire apartment, tilted it sideways, and all the furniture slid to the far end of the room.

"I was thinking of rearranging the furniture. Change isn't bad, right?"

Tanner gives me an odd look. "Is this the final configuration?"

"I think I was going for an abstract look. Furniture as art. Or something like that."

"Oh, I see how it is." He gives me a look that I can only understand as a *knowing look.* Like he understands a deeper meaning attached to my words. Hopefully he will enlighten me because I have no idea of what his look might mean.

"How is it?" I ask. To hide my confusion, I take another sip of beer.

"You're trying to impress Keira."

I nearly cough up my beer. "Come again?"

"Come on, Dillan. This is *me* you're talking to. Jon and I both know that you've had the hots for her for years."

Dillan

There's a small part of me, as I slide into Alec's Corvette, that wants to stay in Keira's body as long as possible. This car is a *love at first sight* car. Buttery-soft seats. Sexy red exterior. And when the engine revs, I can only describe the sound as a woman's version of a wet dream.

The core part of me—of Keira's body—purrs and I seriously consider making out with Alec Huffman.

If he tries.

I'm not opposed to enjoying new experiences. Once, long before Jon met Tanner, Jon kissed me. We were a few beers in and he wanted to know why every woman I met wanted to kiss me.

We were twenty-one, full of college textbooks, legally allowed to drink, and Jon had a lot of pent-up sexual frustration. I remember wondering at the time why it took him so long to kiss me. It wasn't that I wanted him to. I figured he'd try one day and, when he realized I didn't think of him that way, that he'd get over his infatuation. Because when he first met me, he always looked like he wanted to devour me.

After being dorm buddies for a few years, he asked me if I wanted to go to his sister's graduation party and meet his parents.

It was late at night and we were sitting in our dorm room, on the couch, watching old movies. When I said yes, he leaned over and kissed me.

Briefly.

I don't think our lips touched for more than a few seconds. When Jon pulled back, I read his expression. He knew. He knew I'd never think of him that way. But he also knew I wasn't offended.

"Just wanted to see what all the fuss was about," Jon said after a few minutes.

"What's the consensus?" I asked in return, smiling. I felt euphoric as well as buzzed.

"I don't see what the big deal is," Jon said, laughing into a beer.

And I agreed. I still do. Years later, when he met Tanner, I turned the tables on him and asked him what the consensus was.

He grinned and answered, "I understand now what all the fuss is about."

Now, as I sit in Alec Huffman's car, I'm reminded of that conversation as he looks over at me—at Keira—smiling like he genuinely likes her, and I can't help but admire the MLB pitcher's taste in women.

Once we are back in our respective bodies, will Keira want to experience, firsthand, what all the fuss is about with regards to Alec? Or with me?

It's only then that I realize it's not my decision to make.

Keira

I stare at my brother's boyfriend, a man who is like a brother to me, and I try to keep the shock off my face. Apparently it doesn't work.

"Don't act like we haven't been down this road, Dillan. I know that Jon feels differently about you liking his sister, but in the end, you know he'll be cool with it."

"I don't like Keira," I say. How can Tanner stand there and claim this? Like *I* don't have a say in the matter. *If Dillan decides it's okay, then who cares what I think?* "And I'm sure she doesn't like me. I'm in the mood to go for a run. Want to go?"

He feels my forehead. "Run? What are you talking about? And you don't like Keira? Since when?"

I let the running comment go. I can't begin to explain the itch in my legs that make me desirous to go running. Like right now.

"Since she moved in," I say. "She's a real pain in the ass."

"In what way?" Tanner asks with an arched eyebrow. Clearly, he isn't believing a word I say.

"She's..." What would Dillan say about me? "She's too quiet."

"Uh huh. Because a quiet person is often accused of being a pain in the ass. What else?" Tanner puts his beer down and starts to move the furniture back to their proper places. "You just going to stand there, or what?"

I move the coffee table to where I think it goes. I can't seem to recall how the living room was previously arranged. How fastidious is Dillan?

"I suppose I should turn topic and tell you why *she* doesn't like *me*. I'm egotistical. I date a lot of women and she thinks I have no regard for their feelings. On at least two occasions, she's called me a man whore. I'm sarcastic. I don't take anything seriously. I also believe she thinks I'm too good-looking."

"It's almost as if she wrote down the list for you," Tanner says faux-seriously. He finds a remote, changes the input on the TV, and magically finds a set of game controllers I never knew existed. "If you ask me, bro, if Keira really said that to you, then flip it. She means the exact opposite. I've seen the way she looks at you. And," he says, pointing a finger at me, which then points to the couch, as in *sit down now*, "anytime any of us talk about you, if she's around, she hangs onto every word."

How do I look at Dillan? I thought I was pretty good at the *he disgusts me* look.

I do *not* say the exact opposite of how I feel about Dillan. And if his name *is* mentioned, which it hardly ever is, I feel like vomiting.

The TV blares to life. Tanner hands me a game controller. It has like fifty buttons. *Oh no.*

On the TV, the *NFL Pro* seal spins around until Tanner touches a button. It flies out of view and a roster of teams lines up. Dillan's name is in the upper right whereas Tanner's is in the upper left.

"Anyway," Tanner says, finishing his beer. "As much as I love her, I'm not here to talk about Keira. I don't want to do that to you, especially when she's out on a date with someone else. I'm feeling lucky about tonight."

"Why's that?" I'm inspecting the controller as if it has an engraved set of instructions on the side of it. No such luck. I knew I should have played video games with Jon growing up.

"You seem out of sorts tonight. So, being the good friend I am, I plan on taking advantage of the situation and kicking your ass in *NFL Pro*."

I find it a little bit ironic that a MLB shortstop plays NFL video games.

Dillan

Thankfully, the batting cages are indoors. Not long after we arrive, it begins to pour heavily outside. Alec explains how the cages work, and it isn't long until balls are flying at me.

While I'm not anywhere near professional level, I've played ball for a good portion of my life, and with Keira's athletic build, I'm hitting more balls than not.

Honestly, I'm having a ton of fun just goofing off and hanging out with Alec. It feels less like a date and more like an activity gathering. I'm surprised no one has bothered Alec for autographs and such. Other than the clerk behind the desk when we entered, no one has so much as looked at us.

"You have a powerful swing, Keira," Alec says from the cage next to mine. "Even though you are a runner, your upper body strength is impressive."

"Thanks," I say, as if I can take all the credit.

"I'm going to increase the pitch speed for you." He makes a few changes on the electrical box in my cage. "It may be tough to see the ball at first, so be careful. I want to see what you can do." Alec moves back to his cage and watches.

The ball flies and I see it, and swing, too late. As the ball whizzed by, the *whoosh* tone was higher. Another comes. Then another.

On the seventh or eighth ball, I finally connect. It's harder on my hands and the vibration from the bat flows up my arms and into my shoulders. I get a few more hits in before the pitches run out.

"Wow," I say once the sequence is done. "That was intense. How fast were those pitches?"

"Sixty miles per hour."

That didn't seem like much.

"How fast are your pitches?" I ask.

"Well," he says, looking up as if to check an invisible scorecard. "My fastballs are anywhere between eighty and eighty-five. I've had a few over ninety, but that's an exception. Curveballs are slower, and I think I clock in around seventy-eight miles per hour on those. Knuckleballs are trickier to calculate. If I had to guess, and if a pretty lady just so happened to ask me that question, then I might be forced to say I'm in the mid-sixty range for a knuckleball."

I'm man-crushing right now.

First the car.

Now this.

"Impressive," I say, though I keep my tone neutral. I don't want to gush like a schoolgirl.

Alec just smiles.

We return the equipment to an attendant and head back to Alec's car.

"I had a good time," he says once we are both buckled in.

"Me too. I haven't played baseball in a while." I realize the slip too late.

"When did you play baseball, Keira?"

"Uh..." *Think quick, Dillan.* "The Army will sometimes put together those corny confidence-building activities. We've played baseball a time or two."

"I can see that. Sounds cool that you get to do that from time to time. It's just nice to spend time with you, Keira. I feel like you're someone I can talk to. Travel and hardships and people thinking they know you based on the uniform you wear."

"Like how you can't be someone *other* than an MLB pitcher?"

"Yes, exactly. You must be able to relate. When people see you in your military uniform, they only see one facet of you and yet, somehow, it defines you. Doesn't it feel so suffocating?"

"Yes," I say slowly. Am I guilty of the same thing when I look at Keira, or, for that matter, Alec Huffman? I see a rich ball player who has every privilege at his fingertips. "The uniform..." I hesitate. *How can I possibly speak for Keira on this subject?* "The uniform is tradition, it's honor, and, whether I like it or not, it's symbolic. Symbolic of war. Of freedom. Of hardships. But it's more than that. It's the colors of a brother- and sisterhood, of teammates who have your back in any given situation. Yes, it gives someone a quick snapshot of who you are. Your name, your rank, and what branch of the military you serve in. But the uniform and the items pinned onto it are not exclusive to just me. It's a part of who I am, but not *every* part of who I am."

While I spoke, it felt like a part of Keira was talking through me. Like I somehow knew the right things to say just now, and I cannot explain it whatsoever.

When I finally look to see where we are on the road, I find that we are parked outside my apartment building.

"That was beautiful, Keira," Alec says. He turns off the car's ignition. "I understand. When people—fans, journalists—see me, all they see is the jersey. The team logo. Who I'm dating. How much my contract is worth. What my statistics are for the year. For the last five years. Am I a good bet. I'm a business machine *within* the business machine, and I'll only be included in that machine for as long as I'm successful within it. No one ever says it, but the minute you enter the MLB, or even the minors, someone puts an expiration date on you. Most of the time it's a self-inflicted expiration date. Some days, Keira, I'm telling you, it feels like there's a tourniquet somewhere on my body tightening just as another one loosens. Give. Take. Win. Lose. Somewhere along the way, I lost what I loved about playing ball. I know that being in the military is not the same thing as playing for the majors. For one thing, the pay scale is completely out of whack. But when I asked you to go out with me, and you gave me the one condition of visiting the wounded soldiers, I knew that you would understand how I felt. You didn't ask for anything flippant or frivolous. You asked for something selfless and heartfelt. I've been doing a lot of thinking since last night. I want you to know that this year, this season, I'm playing in honor of wounded warriors everywhere and I plan to pledge my entire salary, minus adequate living expenses, to them."

I open my mouth to say something, to thank him. But *I* had nothing to do with it. I could never take credit for that. I just happen to temporarily own the face of the woman who should be sitting here right now, hearing this.

With just one meeting with the rich ball player, she somehow got him to realize that there was something bigger than him out there and he planned to put his money where his mouth was.

My insides pinch and tighten.

When do I get to see this side of her? Oh, right, I think.

This is Ellen's way of allowing me to see it.

Of allowing me to see what I missed the first time around.

CHAPTER TWENTY-TWO

Keira

Tanner glares at me from time to time. Actually, he seems to be looking at me a lot more than he does at the game. It certainly doesn't help that I keep pushing every button possible on the game controller while giving him sideways glances in the off chance that he isn't noticing.

He does.

After a few minutes, my fingers begin to go numb. My stupid quarterback keeps throwing the ball into the stands and I've managed to hit one of the digital cheerleaders.

I'm pretty sure Dillan wouldn't do that.

"You've restarted the game four times, Dillan," Tanner says finally with a loud sigh. "It didn't think it was possible, but you have succeeded in deleting a year's worth of game data." He puts the controller on the coffee table, stands up, and gets another beer. "And I had an effin' brilliant roster, too," he says, and downs most of the beer. "You are not yourself tonight, Dillan."

I look up sharply.

There's no way he could possibly guess the true reason for my look, but it almost seems like he can tell I'm not Dillan.

Oh, he'd never suspect I'm Keira. Why would he? But I can't act like Keira, and I have no idea of how to act like Dillan.

"So let's talk about it," Tanner says, and sits back down. He turns to me carefully, as if he plans to crush my depressed spirit, as if it's for my own good. "I can tell you're mad at me."

"What?" I didn't expect Tanner to say that.

Why would Dillan be mad at Tanner?

Oh, right.

He set Keira up with Alec. Dillan is, supposedly, in love with Keira.

I feel like rolling my eyes at that one.

"I know that the last month has been tough on you," Tanner says softly. "With Jon gone, I know you miss him, and having Keira here probably doesn't help."

I almost feel like crying. I—the real Keira—miss my brother more than anything.

Dillan, on the other hand, was just a roommate.

Just a friend. Why should I care how Dillan feels about my brother being deployed?

And why is Tanner apologizing?

Tanner keeps talking. "And I know you think I stole him from you."

I study his handsome Asian-American face and then the white medical tape on his wrist. He's had a tough road.

If anyone could possibly understand what Dillan and I are going through, I have a feeling Tanner wouldn't even blink an eye.

"Stole him? From me? I don't think that," I say, louder than I probably needed to. "Jon's my brother." I amend the statement when Tanner gives me an odd look. "Jon is *like* a brother to me. I only want him to be happy. And the two of you...well, you're soul mates. Anyone with half a brain can see that."

"It wasn't always that way," Tanner says simply. "He was in love with you for a long time, Dillan." I sit back, stunned. I finish the beer as I think about that. *My brother...in love with Dillan?* "I know this isn't news to you, but you didn't know that I knew. Strange," Tanner says, shaking his head. "For some reason, I feel like I can open up to you tonight. He hated that you never wanted him. Jon thought that if he was patient enough, if he loved you enough, if you realized that the women you slept with didn't mean anything to you, that you'd see him—the real him—and fall madly in love."

Dillan

There's a pause, a breath, and it takes me a second to realize Alec is coming in for a kiss.

I turn sideways in just enough time, and his lips gently land on my cheek.

"Sorry," he mutters, his face red. But not nearly as red as my face. *If Keira finds out...* "I shouldn't have done that," Alec says. His tone is still apologetic.

He must not be used to being rejected.

That goes for both of us. I find it nearly hysterical that the two men who can probably get any woman they want both want the one woman they can't actually have.

Keira.

Well, I knew my fate. Alec, on the other hand, might have a chance.

If he goes through with visiting the wounded soldiers, she'll see the side of him that I got to see tonight. As much as I would love to sabotage that, it would probably be the worst thing I could ever do.

To her.

To Alec.

To the wounded soldiers.

I'm a dick, but I'm not *that* much of a dick.

"It's okay," I tell Alec once he moves back to his side of the car. The car is small and we aren't that far from each other. Our shoulders almost nearly touch. "It's just that I don't...ah..." I trail off.

"Kiss on the first date?"

"Correct."

Keira doesn't let me kiss boys on the first date. It's so

absurd that I nearly laugh out loud, but Alec would never understand and I have no interest in wounding his pride.

Alec smiles. I ignore the dimples in his cheek. I should never notice such things. Keira would notice. Not me.

"I know that most people go out on dates on the weekend," Alec says. "But I have an away series coming up Thursday. Can we get together Monday night?"

I try to think of something fast. What would Keira agree to?

Would she say yes, or no? And not just that, what would Keira want me to say in her place?

I want to say no, because that's what I would want her to say, but I can't say no because I'm then controlling her life.

And that's a big no-no with Keira.

I can't say yes because the longer Alec is interested in Keira, the crazier this whole thing is going to get.

Plus, by saying yes, I'm still controlling her life. I can't win.

I, on the other hand, actually want to hang out with this really cool MLB pitcher.

"Yes," I say without too much eagerness. I don't want to seem desperate. "If you want to come over, I can cook us a meal. And..." I wonder if he likes video games. "And we can play video games. I—uh—Dillan has a huge TV. I haven't played in a while. Are you interested?"

This way, it's low key, he can drink my beer, and we can hang out like guys.

There's totally nothing romantic about any of that.

"I'd love to, Keira," Alec says.

Keira

"I had no idea," I say. I'm speaking for both myself *and* Dillan in this statement.

Tanner nods understandingly. I can't believe my brother was in love with Dillan. Is that why he declared Dillan couldn't be so bad if they were best friends?

Was he just waiting for Dillan to change his mind? To, what, realize that he was gay? Or to realize that he'd never find someone who loved him more than Jon Holtslander?

"I was jealous of you, Dillan. I worried that one day, you'd take a look at Jon, realize you wanted him for yourself, and that he'd run back to you. It wasn't until he finally moved in with me that I knew you would never love him in that way. To be honest, it was a huge relief to me, Dillan. But to be even more honest, if you're such a blockhead that you can't see what's in front of you, that you're willing to waste your time chasing skirts the rest of your life, then I knew you didn't deserve Jon."

"Tanner," I say, sitting up. I feel like vomiting. Any minute now, I'm going to throw up a hot dog or two. I don't know if he's chastising me or what. I just don't know where he's going with this conversation. "Why are you telling me this? I love Jon, as a brother. I love you, as a brother. I never led him on. Ever. I promise."

While I wasn't sure if this was true or not, I'm confident that Dillan would never string my brother along just to keep him single.

"This isn't about Jon," he clarifies. "Not really."

"I'm lost, Tanner."

I have no clue.

I'm a girl in a guy's body, trying to figure this out. I can tell, however, that Dillan and Tanner have never had a heart-to-heart before.

This feels raw...intense...blistering. It almost feels like an intervention.

But for what?

"In the three years I've known you, I've waited for you to tell Keira how you feel. But you've never acted. You always chicken out and, instead, chase some other girl who will never make you happy. That's why I set her up with Alec Huffman: to open your eyes. Stop thinking with your dick, Dillan, and start thinking with your brain. Again, I don't know what's different about tonight. You seem off. I feel off. Maybe I'm missing Jon too much. I don't think you have much time to fix things."

I sit stock-still.

It's interesting that this information will never get to Dillan unless I choose to tell him. Sure, Tanner's opened up to me, and I love that he has, but it won't do any of us any good, and I don't see him repeating this when he's finally in the company of the real Dillan.

"What am I supposed to fix?" I ask.

If Dillan is truly in love with me—maybe *love* is too strong of a word—why hasn't he said anything about it?

My true self answers back: *It's because you've closed yourself off, Keira. You never let anyone close enough to get to know you. You'd rather be alone than have a broken heart. You'd rather be in control, and being in love means losing control.*

"If I have to answer that, Dillan, then you're far worse than I suspected. Fight for her. But more than that...fight for yourself. Don't be afraid of the disorder that love causes. It crashes around you. It blinds you. It heals you.

But, more than anything else, Dillan, when you find the right one, it no longer feels like chaos. It's like a series of falling dominos that pierces your heart. It elevates you into another plane of existence. All at once, you realize you've never breathed real life until you truly experience love. Breathe, Dillan. Just...breathe."

Tanner may think he's talking to Dillan, but I tell myself that I'm the one who was supposed to hear this.

Don't be afraid of the disorder that love causes.

How?

Dillan

When I slip inside the apartment, Tanner shoots up quickly and acts guilty. Why would Tanner need to feel guilty about something?

"Hey guys," I say. Keira's voice sounds way too happy right now, but I can't control it. The real Keira shoots me a dark look.

"How was the date?" both Keira and Tanner ask at the same time. Tanner seems to be back to himself, whereas Keira, with my brooding face seems to, well, *brood.*

"It was fun. It was tough hitting those fastballs. Don't know how you do it, Tanner," I say. "I think my arms are still vibrating."

Tanner laughs. "I won't be hitting anything for a while, actually."

"What do you mean?"

"The wrist. Coach wants me to lay off of it for a week. I have an MRI scheduled on Monday."

"So you're not playing in the Nationals-Diamondbacks series in Arizona this week?" I ask.

"Yeah. Just a precaution," he says, but I can tell he's extremely disappointed. He fought for so long to make it to the majors. *If the injury is serious...* I dislodge the thought. Doesn't do any good to think about the negative side of the equation. "I'll be there, just not playing. Anyway, Alec texted me before you came in, Keira. He's my ride home." Tanner folds me into a hug, as if by hugging Jon's sister, he is, by extension, hugging Jon. He slaps my body on the back. I see Keira wince. "I'll let you know how the MRI goes."

"Thanks, Tanner. Hopefully it isn't anything serious," Keira says, slapping Tanner on the back as well.

How much of my beer did they drink? And why do they seem to be acting so distant toward each other right now?

After Tanner leaves, I say, "That was weird. What did you two talk about? Did Tanner figure out something was up?"

She gives me a sheepish grin. "Sort of. He talked about Jon and their relationship. Stuff like that. He misses Jon. Tanner said something to the effect that he felt like he could confide in me—in you—tonight. I took that to mean that you two normally do not have searing, confidential conversations."

Oh shit, I think. Tanner knows my true feelings for Keira. Well... I suspect *he* suspects my true feelings for her. But would he actually talk about it? That's the question.

She looks at me as if she's debating what to tell me. It must be bad.

"I might as well tell you..." she says nonchalantly, but I can tell that whatever it is, it is important. She doesn't want me to know that it is important to her. "Tanner says he knows that Jon was in love with you. For years. I—" She pauses. "I had no idea Jon ever felt that way about you, Dillan." She says it in a way to suggest that Jon liking me *in that way* was ludicrous. "I take that back. When Jon invited you to my graduation party, I thought you were his boyfriend. Jon was very clear that you were his best friend and that you like women a whole hell of a lot more than any other man he knew."

"Keira—"

"And that one sentence, the way he described your womanizing ways, has colored my opinion of you ever since."

"Keira—"

"That was wrong of me. I shouldn't have put so much stock into what Jon said. But he must have been bitter that you didn't return his feelings. Naturally he wouldn't want you to transfer those feelings onto me. Not because he would have been jealous. Jon only wanted to protect me from falling for you when you had no interest in any one girl for more than a couple of weeks. It's what brothers do to protect their baby sisters."

"Keira—"

"Tanner confided that he was jealous of you. Funny, right? He was worried that Jon would always pine after you. I think a part of him still believes this, and I don't know why. I suppose distance has a way of casting doubt upon any relationship. I screwed up the football game, and he could tell something was wrong. I'm not very good at being you."

She stops talking.

I had no idea that Tanner was ever jealous of me. Granted, at the beginning of our friendship, I knew that Jon had a thing for me. I didn't know it was love. I didn't know he was in love with me. Never, in a million years, would I hurt Jon in such a deliberate way. He is my best friend.

Jon will never forgive me if he knows how I feel about his sister. He will always think of me as a womanizer, as someone unworthy of Keira's affection.

And he would be right.

"Keira?"

"Yes," she answers.

"Thanks for telling me," I say. "You didn't have to do that."

She takes a few measured breaths, and I wonder why. Is

she upset about this information? I wouldn't be surprised if she is, but surely she must realize all of this happened long before Jon met Tanner.

Keira stands in front of me. In fact, she's less than a foot away. I have to look up at her. At my face. She appears to be searching my eyes for something. She turns toward her bedroom, her *real* bedroom.

"I suppose I'll unpack," she says quietly. Dishearteningly. "If we're lucky, we'll be ourselves in the morning. But..." She trails off and I have no problem guessing her thoughts.

I doubt we'll be that lucky.

CHAPTER TWENTY-THREE

Keira

There's very little to unpack. My uniforms. My running gear. And... that's about it. I have nothing else to call my own. No books. No DVDs. Not even a picture frame of me and my family. It's all in storage.

Looking at it, I know that unless Dillan and I break this...this...curse or whatever it is, we'll be doomed to spend our lives as the other person.

And if I'm Dillan, then *I* won't be wearing these uniforms ever again.

He will.

Monday he'll go into the Pentagon and act as me because there's no calling in sick. I have a job to do. I have a job to do even if I'm not the one actually doing it.

This is problematic. How can Dillan, a person with zero security clearance, waltz into the Pentagon with my credentials and do my work? It goes against everything I stand for. It goes against my having a security clearance and allowing an uncleared person access to classified information.

My heart nearly stops.

This is bad.

This is very bad.

I am going to fail General MacWilliams' assignment.

This investigation.

Everything.

My entire career is now on the line. It's on the line because some lady decided it would be, what, funny...or exciting...to alter the rest of my life.

At first, I wasn't pissed. Well, I was, but not like this.

I thought we'd be back to ourselves after lunch, that we'd be laughing about this as I moved out of Dillan's apartment.

I'd say something like, "So long, schmuck," as I walked out the door. Now, well, now everything feels bleak and dark and unhealthy. Unhealthy because I want to hurt Ellen.

I want to hurt Dillan.

I want some control back and now, that will never happen.

On top of all this, now I feel like I have to worry about Jon and Tanner, and about their relationship. Something happened. That much is clear. I don't know what, and while I don't understand why Tanner decided to confide in me—in Dillan—tonight, I sort of realize that I'm at a precipice in my life. I don't know what I want. I don't know what I need.

And I have no way of figuring it out while I reside in my roommate's clunky, hunky, gorgeous body.

Dillan

There's a knock on my door. I'm sitting on the bed. My real bed. And wondering what the hell I'm going to do now. Keira knocks again and enters without me saying anything.

"I saw the light," she says as she peeks through the cracked door. My clock reads one in the morning.

"I guess neither of us can sleep, huh?" I say. I'm a genius in times like this by saying the most obvious thing that comes to mind. The one thing that no one actually needs to hear. That's me. Mr. Helpful.

"I'm worried about Monday," Keira says. I've been worried about the same thing. "How are we going to do this, Dillan? I can't be you and you—you cannot be me. It goes against everything I stand for, as an intelligence professional, to allow an uncleared person access to classified information. If this came out...if anyone found out...Dillan..." She hesitates, and I can see the turmoil on her face. "I will lose everything I've worked so hard for. Not to mention it could land me in military prison."

"Who could possibly find out? And if they did, who would believe it?"

"True," she agrees. "But integrity and truth are only important when they are needed the most. When things go well, everyone is truthful. Everyone can claim to have integrity. However, when the shit hits the fan, that's when those two components are high in demand."

"I see what you mean," I say, nodding. I pat the bed next to me. She sits down and her weight—my weight—dips the bed's edge lower, and I sort of lean into her.

"Sorry." Keira doesn't appear to notice. Her mind is on heavier topics. "So what do we do? We can't call in sick for the rest of our lives."

Keira laughs a hard, bitter laugh, and I can tell she's thought about that very thing. Then she turns serious and clears her throat.

"I know how you feel about me, Dillan." I whip my head around, staring at her like a dumbstruck fool. Tanner. That son of a bitch. "I think I've always known, but Tanner confirmed it tonight. Love is my *disorder.* I've never...I haven't ever..."

She can't seem to finish her statement.

"You've never been in love?"

Part of me feels pity for her. The other part rejoices. If she's never been in love, then I am not competing with anyone for her affection.

Then I amend that thought. I'm competing with the Army. With her career. With her future.

That's worse than a never-broken heart.

"No," she answers. "Never. And I don't plan to ever fall in love, Dillan. Is love worth it? I don't know. That's why you need to know this. We'll never change back. Ellen swapped us for a reason. Disorder. Challenge. I have to learn to fall in love."

"I think I understand," I say slowly. I'm amazed she's opening up to me.

Maybe she doesn't have a choice. Neither of us does.

"No you don't," she says as she looks into my eyes. I wonder what she sees when she looks back into her own face. "If my task is to fall in love—*to do with a bit of disorder*—what do you think your challenge is?" I shake my head. I know what she is going to say. I've sort of known this the whole time. "Your challenge is to make me fall in love with you."

"Not an easy task, Keira."

My heart stops.

It thumps.

It crashes against my chest like a prisoner trying to escape a terrible fate: death row.

"It's an impossible task." Her voice is sad. "But I know how we can start."

I lift an eyebrow. Okay. There's something hopeful in that, right?

Keira

"I really don't see how this is going to help, Keira," Dillan says.

We're outside. The air is hot and muggy and it's pitch black. Well, other than the streetlights, which hum with life. And bugs.

He stretches out beside me. He wears my hot pink top and neon green shorts. I'm wearing a pair of his long gym shorts, socks, and shoes. And no shirt.

If we're going to do this, we're going to do it right.

Plus, I've always wanted to run without a shirt on. Call me crazy, I suppose.

"I don't expect you to understand, Dillan," I say and I lean forward, stretching my hamstrings. Dillan has the tightest hamstrings in the damn world. "Running allows me freedom. It allows me to be a little disobedient."

What I don't say is that if I'm going to be stuck in his body, that I need to get this heavy frame used to running. Because I'm not giving *that* up.

"Yeah," he says. "But in the middle of the night? Someone might mug us."

"Of what? Our dignity? We have nothing of value. The worst that can possibly happen is that a politician will convince us to switch political parties."

Dillan snickers. Yeah, sometimes I am funny. Not often, though.

"Congress isn't in session, Keira."

Of course he'd know a Washingtonian tidbit like that. He's dated every female Congressional intern over the last seven years. Naturally he'd pick up on that type of information.

I try to keep my jealousy in check. He's being a good sport about running with me tonight. That's something.

Dillan has no idea of how to stretch out, so I say, "My calves get a bit tight after the third mile, so make sure you stretch them out good now."

"Three miles? Seriously?"

I give him a dark look. "*You* won't have a problem, Dillan. My body, which is a running machine, has completed eight marathons. This old thing," I say, moving my arm up and down Dillan's body—my God, he has a great chest, "will probably die after the first mile. In your body, I feel like one of those junkyard junkers that doesn't even have a steering wheel, whereas you are a sleek new Mercedes."

"So what you're saying is that I'm going to kick your ass tonight?" Dillan asks.

"That's exactly what I'm saying." I smile. I can't help myself. I'm shocked that I even suggested running tonight. Since I'm in Dillan's body, I know I'll suffer the consequences tomorrow. "You don't even have to go easy on me, Dillan. One of the cool things of you being me, I can watch you and study my stride. See if I need improvements or tweaking."

"That makes absolutely no sense to me, Keira. But I'll go along with it just to please you." He gives me what I can only consider The Grin, but on my face it doesn't have the cheesy affect that it would have had it come from his real face. I try to do The Grin, but he only laughs at me. "Not nearly good enough, Keira. I've perfected that smile over the years. One cannot master it in a day."

"If you say so, creep." He looks hurt, but only briefly. "Okay, so we'll walk to The Mall and run around it at least once, if not twice."

"I swear you're trying to kill me," Dillan says.

"Like I said, you'll be—"

He shushes me, placing a finger over my lips playfully.

"*My* body, Keira. You're trying to kill *my* body."

It's like his finger sears my lips. A small shock goes through me.

Dillan

Keira huffs and puffs behind me and I swear to God that running is some sort of sacred sport that I never knew existed. Granted, I'm in Keira's amazing runner's body. So I'm sure that this has something to do with it.

I'm ahead of her as we pass the Washington Monument. I've never been out this late at The Mall before.

People look at us as if we are insane.

And we are.

It's a Saturday night and we choose to *run* The Mall.

We are not normal people.

Normal people hit up bars or clubs or hang out at friend's houses. We...run.

"Slow down!" Keira demands. I speed up instead, ignoring her. "I am going to kill you, Dillan."

She really is a wonderful runner. No wonder she's won a few marathons. Her legs are sleek, chiseled, and I have fleeting thoughts of them wrapped around me.

I know how you feel about me, Dillan.

My heart thumps again and I slow down to keep from gasping for air.

She knows.

She knew.

She thinks she's always known.

Love is my disorder. I've never been in love.

All of these things run though my head as she catches up to me. I wish I knew how to make her fall in love with me. I've never actually had to try. I don't even know if anyone has fallen in love with me.

What if I'm not "love" material?

What if I'm only "lust" material?

That's why it's a challenge, Dillan, you dumbo.

Ellen. You are a sly woman.

Keira sucks in air, leans over, and tries to say something, but words fail her. She just can't breathe right now. It's been only a mile.

She wasn't kidding when she said I needed to work on my aerobics. I feel like I could run all night, into the day, and then into the next night. There's something so earthy about running that I never knew about. I wonder if—when—we change back, if she'll let me run with her.

That might be fun.

"Sorry I didn't slow down," I say. "You told me not to go easy on you."

"I didn't think your body would be this...bad," she sputters out in between heavy breathing. "I honestly thought I'd make it at least to the two-mile mark before expiring." She points to her crotch. "How on earth do you run with these *things* dangling between your legs? If they aren't jarring with each step, they're flapping or flopping or, worse," she seethes, "they get pinched between your gigantic, monstrous thighs. I need duct tape or something..."

I laugh and snort at the same time. *Duct tape?*

"It's called a jock strap. I guess it's something men get used—"

Instantly my mouth goes dry. She rubs her hands down her chest in an unassuming manner. I doubt she even knows she's doing it.

She's feeling *my* chest and I imagine her hands going lower.

Exploring.

Then I shake my head. She'd never do something like

that.

Keira tilts her head. I'd love to know what she's thinking right now. Probably something about Army manuals or the best way to torture people who inadvertently see classified information. Then I think about how she might torture me, and my head is pretty much lost from that point forward.

Because I have a feeling I'd *love* for her to torture me.

"What are you thinking about?" she asks me suddenly. My mouth is still an O. "I know that face..."

She trails off. Her face is flush, but I can't tell if it is from the run or something else.

Something more.

Like arousal.

"Nothing!" I answer just as quickly as I can.

Her lips tighten. "Don't lie to me, Dillan Pope."

"You want the truth?" She nods wearily after narrowing her eyes. Keira knows I won't answer how she expects me to answer her. "I was thinking about how I want to kiss you right now."

CHAPTER TWENTY-FOUR

Keira

I back up a little, as if he'll suddenly kiss me. Right now.

Like, right now. But that's just silly. Dillan's just being...Dillan.

Smooth.

Suave.

Sexy.

He's all those things, all the time. Even when he's in my body. Strange how when I look at him—*at Dillan in my body*—I no longer see my face. I see him. He's in there, regardless of the external package.

I look past him, down to the glowing Lincoln Memorial. It stands out much like a lighthouse does on a rocky cliff, alerting those on the sea of oncoming land mass. I need some sort of warning system for when Dillan gets too close to me.

Now might be a good time for one.

When I turn my gaze back to Dillan, he's closer.

Warning: Danger Zone.

He's way too close and I back up.

Again.

"You said you wanted the truth, Keira," Dillan says, his voice an octave deeper than my own normal voice. He's turned on. Aroused. "I've noticed that you turn inward when confronting personal problems. From this point forward, I'll always be honest with you. Trust is the opposite of disorder, right?"

Trust. Truth. Honesty. All of those things are the opposite of disorder.

But all of those things are inherently separated from disorder. Right?

Can't have both. Trust *and* disorder.

"I'd say that in most circumstances, yes, trust is the opposite of disorder. But in our circumstance..."

"Let's forget logic for a moment. Logic didn't swap our bodies. An old lady did. Let's even forget our circumstances, too. If you trust someone or something, then that something isn't completely out of order. It's not in a state of disorder."

"So you're saying I should trust you?" I ask sarcastically.

He gives me an exasperated look and places his hands on his hips.

"No, that's not what I'm saying at all, Keira." His lips bunch up and turn white. "Part of my challenge is to be honest with you from this point forward and hopefully earn your trust in the process." He smiles as if he's figured everything out.

It's not a bad idea, actually. Will it work, though?

"So, when you look at me right now, in your body, you want to kiss me?" I ask.

"Is it weird? Yes," he answers with a small laugh. "Do I want to kiss myself? Hell no. But I'm not talking to myself. I'm talking to you. You're Keira Holtslander, regardless of what you look like on the outside. I've wanted to kiss you since your graduation party. You wore a yellow dress and your hair was shorter and your smile..." He pauses while I hold my breath. *He remembers what I wore?* "You smiled a lot easier back then. Now, not so much. I don't know what you've seen, what you've experienced over the last nine years since you were that eighteen-year-old girl, but every time I look at you, I always have the same thought: that whoever you fall in love with will be the luckiest damn son of a bitch on the planet. Am I going to kiss you right now?" he asks. I'm still holding my breath and feeling a bit dizzy. My insides are melting and betraying me. *Kiss me!* I scream internally. "No. *I* won't be the one to kiss *you*, Keira."

"What?" I breathe the question out.

A small wind comes by to cool me off.

As sweaty as I am, I feel a bit cold at the moment.

"You will have to be the one to kiss me. No matter what, it will be your decision."

Dillan

The look on her face is priceless: it practically says, "In your dreams, buddy." But then there's something else, a different look. Concession? Agreement? Or maybe it is one of defeat.

"I—" she starts, then stops from saying whatever she planned. She looks conflicted. "Okay," she says, finally.

"Just *okay*?"

Did she sort of, kind of, maybe just agree with me? My legs tingle and the urge to sprint around her, around The Mall, around the whole world kicks in right then. I jump up and down a few times, flexing my leg muscles.

"Yeah," she answers. "Just okay."

"I'll take it. Now..." I trail off, taking a few steps away from her. "Chase me."

"What?"

I might as well have told her to build an ancient pyramid. I take a few more steps.

"It's two-thirty in the morning. We have nothing else to do." Well, nothing that *she'd* agree to, namely allowing me to ravage her silly. "If we're going to run, let's do this right! By me kicking your ass."

With that, I sprint away from her. Her groan, though, is loud enough for me to hear. But she runs after me and after a few minutes, I can hear her laughing like a lunatic.

She'll never catch up to me. So she doesn't have to worry about me thinking she'll catch me and then kiss me.

That's what movie-guy would want.

Or maybe that's what movie-girl would do.

However, I don't think one kiss will swap us back. A

kiss is just a kiss. Well, a kiss from Keira would be something a lot more than just a kiss, but still. I doubt Ellen would undo her little magic spell if our lips happened to accidentally-on-purpose touch.

It would still be wonderful, though.

A whole hell of a lot of wonderfuls.

I pass in front of the Lincoln Memorial and notice that Keira doesn't stick to the path.

She's running at a diagonal now, across the lawn, and right for me. My God, she's determined, and in about three seconds, she collides into me and takes me down with her.

Her hands cradle my head and I know that while she did what she could to lessen my impact, she skinned her elbows on the gravel.

"You may be faster than me," she huffs out. Keira's the first to talk, but only because I can't breathe with her on top of me. "In this form, I'm stronger than you."

I sputter a laugh. It's a weak one.

"You couldn't stop, could you?"

Keira groans.

She's still on top of me and it doesn't seem like she's going to remedy that any time soon.

"No. Once I started sprinting at you, it was like I was a bulldozer without a brake pedal. Plus, I think every muscle in this body is cramped up right now."

Ah, so that's why she isn't moving.

"Is your mouth cramped?" I stare at her lips.

She tightens them into a thin line.

Nope.

Not cramped.

She arches an eyebrow. In truth, she's only a few inches away from me. I can feel her heavy breaths on my jaw.

She's also very, very sweaty, and it's sort of gross.

I bet that if I pushed a little bit, she'd slide right off me.

Instead of getting up, which is what I expected, she leans down. Her eyes flutter shut, briefly, like a butterfly's wings, and her lips lock with mine.

It's a tiny, whispery kiss, and after a few seconds, she lifts her head back up.

My heart has literally exploded.

Everything tingles.

My breasts, my stomach.

There.

Instantly, I want more.

A lot more.

One kiss is not enough. I want everything. Of her. Of us.

I want to breathe her in, consume her, worship her.

"Nothing?" she asks.

Huh?

"What's nothing?" I'm not thinking straight.

Keira has, effectively, scrambled my brain. Honestly, I don't want to be thinking straight right now.

When she doesn't answer right away, I pull her down and kiss her.

With hunger, passion.

Every ounce of feeling I possess goes into that kiss.

Keira

When his lips crash on mine, I think I'm going to die. I thought a small, chaste kiss would do the trick.

I thought that when I lifted my head up a few seconds ago, that I'd be me.

That Dillan would be Dillan, and we'd be back to ourselves lickety-split.

All I succeeded in doing was igniting the fire in his eyes. In myself.

My God.

I want to erase the space between us.

I want to get as close as possible and do nothing but kiss Dillan all day, all night.

His arms pull me in and I snuggle in. His legs open and I find that I nestle perfectly in his embrace.

And when his tongue touches my lips, I want to embed myself as far into him as possible.

My hands are on his face, possessing him, owning him.

This.

This is what I've wanted for so long.

But doubt has a way of creeping into tiny, insecure cracks.

But...I'm in the military.

But...I'll get deployed.

But...it will never work out.

But...will you be faithful to me?

But...will I be enough for you?

But...can you keep up with me?

But right here, right now, he wants me and I want him. What's to stop us? Why can't we do this? We are obviously attracted to one another. Even in the opposite form.

Which is...weird.

Strange things start happening to me. My body warms up. I'm flushed. Overheated. I feel a buzzing. My ears ring.

Is it working? Are we changing?

God, say yes. Please. I can't do this again. I can't be Dillan for another day.

He grinds up into me, and an intense heat spreads into my lower region.

Dillan's penis.

It's...it's...hard.

It feels like pure energy, like I'm engorged with sexual prowess, and all I can think about is this: touch it, use it, massage it, feel it.

In me.

When it begins to throb, I panic.

Dillan

Things move. I want her to consume me. We shift to get comfortable. My legs. Her legs. My hands. Her hands. Her penis.

Wait, what?

I suck in a breath, I hear the catch in her throat, and she scrambles away from me. Her eyes, at first, are unfocused. But it isn't long until a shadow passes over her face, a dark shadow, and I know she's upset.

The dark sky has nothing on the anger deep in Keira's expression.

"*It* moved," I say, sitting up.

Okay. I feel extremely weird right now. My own penis was erect against my—Keira's—most intimate parts. How to process this...is...is...very difficult. Does this mean she is turned on? That if she's aroused, it stimulates an erection?

If yes, then I'm worried about my own mental state right now. If no, then I'm worried that my rock star genitalia has turned traitor.

"*It* did not move," she says with as much grit and determination as humanly possible. She stands, but it isn't pretty.

Keira wasn't lying when she said she was cramped up. She's sort of hunched over like an old man. She stares at her crotch. The area is tented.

"I think it's a good sign," I say, standing up. I try to help her, but she won't let me. "I mean, that *it's* erect. That's a good sign."

It means you like me, Keira.

A small victory parade goes by in my head right now.

With fireworks, marching bands, and those twirling baton things. On fire.

Lots and lots of fire in this parade. Granted, I sort of feel like a thirteen-year-old boy for referring to my penis as *it*.

"I don't want to talk about it, Dillan."

I don't blame her for being confused. It reminds me of the time my dad explained *the birds and the bees* to me. I was seventeen when that happened—probably a few years too late for such a talk—but useful all the same since I didn't lose my virginity until after high school.

"Right, Keira, I'm sorry," I mutter. "It will, uh, subside. The erec—"

"I know what you're referring to!" She rubs her face and scratches at the beard growing there. The last time I shaved was Friday morning. The idea of Keira using a razor against my jaw scares the shit out of me. She'll slice my throat instead. "Can we just go back to your apartment?"

"Yeah, sure," I say.

One step forward. Two steps back.

CHAPTER TWENTY-FIVE

Keira

I stare at the toilet, the seat is up, and I'm in the ready position. No, I don't need to throw up. That would be too easy. I've tried to pee for the last five minutes, but this damn erection will *not* go away.

Dillan, trying to be helpful, only succeeds in being annoying on the other side of the door.

"Sometimes it takes a few minutes," he says without prompting. Thankfully, he isn't in here with me. Not that he didn't try. I have a feeling that if he asked again, I might succumb, let him inside, and order him to tell me what I'm doing wrong. "There is another way, of course," Dillan says after another minute passes.

"Yeah, and what's that?"

Do I really want to know the answer?

"Masturbation."

My stomach drops. Yes, of course that would be his answer. I've avoided looking at the male junk between my legs, but I can no longer avert my eyes. It isn't unlike my previous lovers' nether regions, though his is somewhat more...*impressive.*

He's cut and it's thick, long, red, and it throbs under my fingertips. I don't even know why I'm still touching it. It isn't like I'm aiming it or anything. I'm aroused *and* I have to pee.

What a stupid conundrum.

I'm also a little hungry.

Dillan owns a perfect specimen. Part of me would love to experiment by touching him and just seeing what happens. I mean, I have the opportunity to experience what it feels like to be a man.

To have sex...as a man.

To masturbate...as a man. Would it feel like a rush? A thrill?

Yes. All of those things. But would it be right? No. I don't want him doing any of that while he's in *my* body. Plus, I have no doubt that I'd do it all wrong anyway.

I'd probably rub the skin off or something.

"Not. Going. To. Happen," I say to Dillan through the door.

He just laughs.

"All right, calm your horses, sweetheart," he says. I wonder if he's actually sitting against the door as he talks to me. "Since we may be here a while, I might as well tell you that Alec asked you out again."

My head tilts and I resist the urge to groan.

"What did you say?"

"I invited him over Monday night. I'm cooking him dinner. Afterward, we'll conduct a bit of a romantic, *NFL Pro* video game foreplay. If we have time, we might even mud wrestle. At any rate, he seemed receptive to the idea. You do own a bikini, right?"

Part of me wants to be angry at Dillan. The other part is confused as to why I'm not angry. I guess I'm just too confused to think straight. I could probably sort everything out if I wasn't in his body. As I listen to him and mull out my emotions, the erection subsides.

Finally, I pee. Hooray! Now where's my gold star?

"I assume everything after the video game piece is a spot of fiction, right?" I ask, opening the door.

He falls over.

He was, indeed, sitting down and leaning against the

door. We both look like shit.

I'm splotchy after the run. Dried sweat clings everywhere. I wonder if he can see the confusion and frustration on my face.

Dillan, who still hasn't figured out how to make a simple ponytail, seems, I don't know, oblivious? *No*, I think. *He's more than clued in.* Dillan is an expert at all of this.

Granted, not the body-swapping part, but everything else. Foreplay. Lovemaking. Flirting.

He stands up in the doorway, a silly grin on his face.

"Depends on your definition of *fiction*," he says.

Shaking my head, I reach around him and fix the ponytail. It's not like I need to see what I'm doing since I've been pulling my hair up my whole life. Besides, I don't want to get too close to Dillan.

Might have a repeat of Operation Erection, and deflating said Operation Erection isn't exactly easy.

I suspect he can read my mind. He doesn't even move a muscle.

"Monday night, huh?" I ask. "Because of the away game series in Arizona?"

"Yup," he says casually.

Dinner. That isn't so bad. And I can hang out in the bedroom to make sure Dillan behaves. Satisfied, I smile at the thought. I look at Dillan expectantly.

He doesn't move.

Clearing my throat, I say, "Dillan?"

"Yes?"

"I'd like to leave the bathroom now."

Dillan

We settle for our own bedrooms again, and this time neither of us leaves the room to talk to the other. Not that I wouldn't mind it if she came back in. Just being close to her does amazing things to me.

I'm tired as hell, though I'm kept awake because my body sings.

It hums.

It wants her.

I want her. I want to feel her on top of me again. I want to feel her lust—her desire—pulse against me again.

I want. *I* need.

This isn't about me, is it? It's about Keira. It's about getting her to trust me. And if I keep trying to hump her every time I'm within a foot of her, then she'll never, ever, come to trust me.

Earlier, as we stood in the bathroom, and I spied the shower behind her, all I wanted to do was grab her by the shoulders and direct her into the tub. I'd clean her. Slowly. Precisely. To the point of no return.

It sounds strange given the fact that she's in my body, but I have a feeling that once it started, I wouldn't know where she began and I ended. I want to be the same with her. One with her.

When that happens, then we'll swap. I'm sure of it.

Well, I'm not one hundred percent sure. But, close enough.

Eventually, as the sun starts to rise, I fall into a deep, undisturbed sleep, and several hours later, Keira wakes me up by punching one of my shoulders.

"Wake up," she orders. "Make me some damn breakfast, Dillan." She holds a cup of coffee and it's enough to lure me right out of bed and into a sitting position. I take it from her and look over at the clock. Three in the afternoon. "What's the plan for today?" she asks.

Sunlight pours into my bedroom. Keira's wearing a pair of my black boxers and a black T-shirt. I really need a shave, too.

"Plan?" I croak out.

The coffee burns my tongue. Needs a bit of sugar. That must be remnants of Keira saying that. I like my coffee black.

"We did what I wanted last night. You know: running. Now, it's your turn. I must warn you, though. I can hardly walk. All of your muscles have atrophied." She shrugs as if it's no big deal. But even the shrugging appears to hurt. I stifle a laugh. She adds, "You are getting old, after all."

"Old? My ass. I'm thirty. I'm in the prime of my life, thank you very much." I stand up and wish to God that I hadn't.

Everything hurts. Badly. My legs are like solid bricks.

"You may have been born thirty years ago, but your muscles are at least a hundred."

"I think I overdid it last night," I say.

"Which part of last night are you referring to?"

I give her an unenthusiastic, flat grin.

"Ha-ha. Funny. How about *all* of last night?"

Liar! You do not regret a single thing and you know it.

Now it's her turn to look at me in a perturbed fashion, like she knows what I'm thinking but refuses to acknowledge it out loud.

"You may have a point."

"What would *you* like to do today?" I ask after taking

another sip of coffee. "I mean, what will make you understand me better?"

"I'm curious to learn the history—the real history—behind your *Nine Year Crush*." There's something behind her back. She swings her arm around. Swimming trunks. She tosses a tiny bathing suit at me. "I hear your building has a swimming pool."

I am going to kill Jon.

Keira

A couple of minutes later, Dillan shouts, "Um, Keira! I need help. Like, tons and tons of help here." I'm nearly shocked when he enters the living room naked. I'm not used to seeing myself in the nude like this. Like, ever, I suppose. In his hands he holds the bikini like it's a writhing snake. "How on earth do you put this on? It's nothing but a bunch of strings."

Chuckling, I manage to get it on him and snug enough so that it doesn't fall off the second he moves.

"There," I say. The green-and-yellow paisley bathing suit looks good on my frame.

Dillan, however, is standing like a spaz and looks just plain awkward while wearing it.

"I'm shocked you actually own a bikini. I just figured you swam in a scuba diving outfit."

"Didn't have enough room in the duffle bag when I moved up here."

Dillan shakes his head. "She's got jokes. I like it."

"Come on. Let's go."

The pool in Dillan's apartment is on the roof. The heat of the sun glares down and the place is packed. Luckily, we're able to find at least one unoccupied chair. We'll share. I put our towels down and look around.

The roof is more than just the pool. There's a small bar area for social gatherings and, on the other end, a presentation stage. The type where someone might put on a play. Or sing karaoke. My bet's on the latter thought.

The Capitol and the rest of The Mall are somewhat visible from the edge. This will be a great place to watch

Fourth of July fireworks. I'll have to remember to ask Dillan about that later on.

I'm not immune to the looks we receive the moment we step out onto the roof.

Everyone stares at us.

The women ogle me and my bronze chest, whereas the men, and some boys, stare at Dillan. I'm not sure if it's because they think he's good-looking or if it has anything to do with the fact that he shuffles like an old man.

An old man in a little bikini.

It dawns on me that maybe Dillan's had a relationship or two with some of the women in his building. Great.

One more thing to worry about. I view everyone with distrust. I know I shouldn't, but I do.

Then I realize it's because *both of us* are shuffling like senior citizens.

I'd love to jump into the deep end, but my hip flexors, and every muscle attached, won't let me do more than slowly walk into the pool.

A second later someone grabs my hand.

Dillan. He walks down with me.

"Steps. Hurt," he mutters. "Ouch."

"You just want me to break your fall if you slip," I say, pretending to sound insulted.

He looks down at our still-clasped hands and says, "Something like that."

I shake free from his hand, dive under, and, with protesting limbs, I swim to the opposite end of the pool and back again. I don't care how much it hurts. He might have been a lifeguard in college, but I can tell he isn't a natural swimmer like I am. I practically grew up in the pool in our backyard.

So while he doesn't have the muscle memory, I have the

knowledge of how to swim. I surface in front of Dillan.

"So... I'm guessing that Jon told you?" he asks without preamble. I see the worry—no, the terror—in his eyes.

By the end of all this, once we've swapped back into our respective bodies, we are going to know so much about the other that we'll either be sick to death or madly in love with each other.

I'm not sure which ending terrifies me more.

"You're free to correct the record, Dillan. That is if you didn't actually plan to jump off the roof of my parents' house and into our pool." He grunts and his nose flares. "I'll make a deal with you," I say. "Tell me what *you* planned to do and I'll tell you what *I* planned to do that day, too."

He gives me a look. An *I-hope-you-planned-something-naughty* look. He won't be disappointed.

"Deal," he agrees. "But you go first."

Dillan

She presses her mouth together like it's something she's used to doing on a regular basis. It looks odd on my face, but it's all Keira in that expression. I ignore everyone around us. The men, the women, none of whom I even know, and concentrate on Keira.

On the woman I'm in love with.

I cannot deny it any longer.

Every woman I've been with has been to get *her* out of my head.

Unsuccessfully, I might add.

I wasn't a virgin when I first met Keira, but I wish to God that I was. I wish that she had looked at me that day at her party, called me over, and wanted to explore her sexuality with me.

In my dreams, I think. I would have been happy just talking about the weather with her.

"Okay," she says slowly. She directs me to the deep end and we sort of huddle and dog paddle in an empty corner of the pool.

I have to repeatedly adjust the bathing suit. It continuously rides up my butt and I'm paranoid enough to assume that, at some point, the top will float away, as if it has its own agenda. *In a world, where bikinis rule the nation, one man will stop at nothing to save the world from President Bikini's evil plot to overthrow the government...*

I shake my head. Sometimes my mind goes in a juvenile direction.

Keira's about to tell me something important and I'm

worried—okay, *worried* is too strong a word—that her bathing suit has nefarious plans.

"I only pretended to ignore you at my party," she says in a hushed tone. "I was very, very aware of you."

"Uh, Keira, you didn't just pretend. You *did* ignore me. Trust me. I know when a beautiful woman is ignoring me."

"I can prove it to you. You wore dark slacks, a white polo shirt, and you had a black backpack slung over one shoulder. You were clean-shaven, tan, and your hair was much shorter than it is right now. Everyone was drawn to you. I was, too. And that was the problem."

I take a deep breath and ask, "That you were drawn to me?"

I'm shocked that she remembers what I wore. The only reason I remember is because I've spent the last nine years trying to forget that day. Even small things stay in your memory.

Keira moves in closer and our feet occasionally touch.

"No, because everyone *else* was drawn to you. Jon told me that you were some sort of woman magnet and, at first, I didn't believe him. Not until I saw you. Dillan, I swear to God that I wanted to find any reason possible to give you a tour of our house and have that tour end in my bedroom. It was my high school graduation party. I was a grown up. In theory, at least. I wanted to do grown-up things...with you. But when everyone else practically adored you from the start, it sort of disgusted me. Obviously, you wouldn't be interested in some eighteen-year-old virgin who had designs of *losing it* to you."

I'm having trouble breathing.

Suddenly I'm back to being that twenty-one-year-old kid trying to impress Keira.

So I tell her everything.

About my plan of jumping off the house and into the pool.

The beer with the homeless guy.

About how I worked harder on making my own beer, harder than I've ever worked on anything else before, and that I did it all because of that day.

That defining, momentous, crashing day nine years ago.

"Nine Year Crush," she says at the end of my speech. *She's not making fun of me. This is a good thing.* "It has a good ring to it. Promise me one thing, Dillan. If you ever make it with this beer. If you actually sell it, because I don't know what your plans are, I want you to tell the real story behind the brand. It's a powerful story. Without it, without that failure, so to speak, you wouldn't have been motivated enough to build it. We failed nine years ago, Dillan. We should learn from that."

CHAPTER TWENTY-SIX

Keira

After dinner and after it becomes apparent, to me at least, that we aren't going to swap back before the morning, I come to the realization that I need to instruct Dillan on how to act like me tomorrow at work.

The do's and don'ts of military life.

He sits down with me at the dining room table. Seems a bit formal after he confessed a defining moment in his life. A moment that shaped him over the last nine years.

It's not like I'm prepared to snuggle in bed with him to discuss these things. I'm not ready for that. Yes, I like Dillan. I more than *like* him. It's funny that once he swapped into my body, I'm able to see the *real* him.

If I think about that thought for too long, I'll confuse myself, so I leave it at that.

What would have happened if we both acted on our initial thoughts all those years ago? Would we be here now? Would we still be together? Probably not. I needed to make my own mistakes. To grow up. To learn how to be a strong, independent woman who wasn't defined by a man's love.

Because the greatest love a woman can have is the love she has for herself.

Do I love myself? Do I respect myself? Have I made all the right choices for me, thus far?

I don't know. Maybe Dillan will help me realize this. Maybe, for some reason, I can't discover this in my own skin. It's one thing to think about something objectively, but this body swapping thing takes the premise to a whole new level. I suppose I have a few more days to figure this out. Otherwise, there's no point of learning a lesson if we won't change back.

I write something on a piece of paper as Dillan watches. After I give it to him, to which he gives me a "huh?" look, I turn on my laptop and find a diagram of the Pentagon.

"That," I point to the paper, "is where my office is located in the Pentagon."

I then proceed to explain how to enter the building, how to find the office, and the names of the individuals he'll encounter. I write that down, too.

He nods as if he's getting everything up to this point, but I can see a question forming.

"Yeah," he says, "That's all good information, but what am I supposed to do when I get there? I mean, am I supposed to be deciphering cryptic code or something?"

"My background is in security intelligence. Basically, on how to protect classified information, the proper way to classify a document, and when, where, and how to declassify it. There are four main classification codes for the United States Government. Top Secret. Secret. Confidential. And Unclassified. Now, without getting too specific, there are compartments *within* each of those classifications that restrict who can see it. Just because someone has a Top Secret clearance doesn't necessarily mean they can see everything and anything marked Top Secret. There's something called *need-to-know,* meaning an individual, in the course of their official duties, has a valid *need-to-know* for the information. Only if they are properly read-on, or briefed, to that level, then they can see it."

"What level do you have?"

"I possess a Top Secret and several sensitive compartments within the Top Secret domain. All you need to know, for the next few days, is that you are cleared to enter the room number I wrote down for you, as well as General MacWilliams' secure office. I don't have the codes for it yet. You'll have to get Sergeant Justin Hauten—you met him at the bowling game—to open it for you."

"Okay," he says. "I can tell that this is important to you. But you never really answered my question. What am I supposed to be doing all day long tomorrow?"

"This is where things get somewhat interesting."

Dillan

"I'd call that the understatement of the year," I tell Keira. "Things got interesting yesterday when we woke up. If we can deal with this, we can deal with anything."

Keira smiles at me. "The reason General MacWilliams brought me to the Pentagon is to perform a special duty. I doubt I'll be here longer than a few weeks." My heart constricts with this knowledge. *Did Jon tell me this information in the beginning or not?* "General MacWilliams is the Chief of Staff of the Army. He's the highest ranking Army general in the country. Don't fuck up around him, okay? In fact, if you see him, keep your head down."

"Yikes, Sergeant Brunette," I say as I put my hands up in a surrendering manner. "I'll solve everything by walking backwards. Will that work for you?"

She scoffs. "Only for those that are walking *opposite* you. Now, the folks walking behind you...you'll be face to face."

"Stop being so logical, Keira," I say. "I was only joking." As if she didn't already know that.

"My job—your job—is to read several hundred letters from the 1950s and determine if classified information was passed along in the passages."

"Yeah, I doubt I'll be successful at that."

"I don't blame you. It isn't exciting work, and everything I've read to this point leads me to believe that the letters are benign. However, I get the feeling it may go in a romantic direction. When you get home tomorrow night, we can discuss it."

I nod. "I think I can survive one day as you. If I get lost or seem confused, I can always blame it on the fact that I'm new there. Plus, you are pretty. People like helping pretty people."

"Do not, under any circumstance, act like some wounded bird that needs constant assistance." She says this through clenched teeth.

I recoil slightly. God forbid that I compliment her.

"Lighten up. Seriously. You'd think I just signed you up for a filmed gang-bang. I have one more question."

"What?" She looks ill at ease.

Her face is white, her mouth grim. I already know she won't sleep a wink tonight due to worry.

"Do I get to wear a gun?"

I duck easily when Keira throws her pen at me.

Keira

I spend the night tossing and turning. I chat with Jon on instant messenger, but he won't discuss what's wrong between him and Tanner.

Jon only wants to know one thing: Has Dillan hit on me?

I roll my eyes.

Big brothers.

"No, of course not," I type. "You're being too hard on him, Jon. Don't forget that several years ago, you told me that Dillan couldn't be that bad if he was your best friend. Besides, he and I have compared notes. I know what you told him and he knows what you told me."

The screen blinks as I wait for his response.

"You remember that? Okay. This is worse than I thought. Who are you and where is the real Keira?" he types back.

Then he does a quick smiley face in the next line.

I'll admit that my tune is drastically different from what it used to be when it came to Dillan.

Usually I have no qualms with making fun of him, calling him a man whore, stuff like that. I find that I can't bring myself to do so right now.

I'm not surprised that Jon is suspicious.

"Just tired is all, I suppose," I type back. "Plus, I'm worried about Tanner. I think he hurt his wrist pretty bad on Friday's game."

"He didn't tell me that..." Jon writes. "Did he seem okay when you saw him last?"

"I can tell something's wrong, if that says anything. You

didn't break up, did you?"

Because I will strangle you if you did. Tanner is the best thing that's ever happened to you, Jon.

"No," he types back, and for a few minutes, that's all he writes. Then, "We had an argument." Pause, then, "About you."

"That's...odd." Tanner, who wants Dillan to *go after me*, mentioned that Jon didn't agree with him.

"Keira, how do you feel about Dillan? Truthfully."

He had to bring in the *truthfully* caveat, didn't he?

He only does that on special occasions or when he thinks I will lie to him. Which means he suspects something.

I think about what to type. I can't be too fast or too slow about it.

Obviously, I'm not over-thinking any of this...

"He isn't all that bad," I finally write back.

"*He isn't all that bad, Keira?* That's like you saying he's wonderful. You've never said that about anyone before. Ever."

"I know." I can't think of more than that right now. "What was the argument about, Jon?"

Silence.

I'm about to write another message when he finally replies. "Tanner has this idea that Dillan really likes you. I happen to disagree."

"That's it? That doesn't sound like an argument to me. So what if Dillan likes me? I thought he was like a brother to you. Would you be so—" I pause typing, wondering if I should finish my question, but I press on. It's too late now to stop. "—opposed to the match if it were true?"

I hold my breath. I didn't know until I wrote it that it would mean a lot to me if Jon was okay with the arrangement.

Not because I want him to rule my life or make decisions for me.

It's because I love and trust my brother and his opinion means the world to me.

But he never answers.

My stomach drops.

A dozen minutes go by.

Slowly.

I stare at the screen with watery eyes. The question hangs there, but he hasn't left the conversation. I can tell he's still logged in.

It is official: Jon does not like the idea of me and Dillan together.

I step away from my laptop.

I try to lie in bed and fall asleep. I roll over. I turn on the TV. I read Dillan's case files.

Nothing helps.

But I must have dozed off because two hours later, at four in the morning, I hear the telltale ding of an instant message.

I jerk up fast and rush to my laptop.

"Sorry for the delay in my answer, Keira. I broke my keyboard. I won't bore you with how or why it broke. Suffice to say it took me time to find a new keyboard. There is a lot about Dillan I don't like. But there's a lot that I do like. In fact, I love him (as a brother) and there isn't much I wouldn't do for him. Here's the deal: he doesn't deserve you, Keira. Not in a million years. Then I thought about that. In my mind—in any brother's mind—no one deserves his little sister. So this isn't against Dillan. Now, if we were talking about Alec Huffman, I might have a different tune. That man is, pardon the honesty, a fucking hottie. Around the time I met Tanner, I had this delirious wish that Alec was gay. (He isn't, by the way. If wishes were pennies, I'd have zero pennies.) Anyway, too much information. Here's the thing, Keira: it's your life. You get to decide who gets the privilege of making you crazy each and every day. If that person is Dillan, then you have my blessing. Not that you needed it, or even wanted it. I've been telling Dillan that he needed to find the right girl and settle down. I never considered *you.* I wonder why? You're probably laughing at all of this. You were probably pulling my leg back there. So I'll shut up. I have to go on shift as it is, so I can't stay long. I love you."

"Love you, too."

After that, sleep comes easily.

Dillan

In the morning, I tell Keira everything I can about my job, LouAnn Britton, Johnson Brookshire, and the Joy Fromm case.

"And you have a meeting with all of them today. So, you know, good luck."

I'm wearing her frumpy uniform. It really is rather shapeless, but comfortable. So that's something. She's still in my boxers and a T-shirt. I wonder if she had a boner this morning, but I can tell she isn't in the mood for flirty banter.

"Good luck?" she mimics as she fixes her uniform on me. She isn't gentle about it, either. The dark circles under her eyes are about as big as the wheels on a monster truck. LouAnn is going to eat her for lunch. I feel sorry for Keira, but I can't wait to hear all about it later on. *Voyeuristic-pity-curiosity?* Sure. I'll go with that. "Do I need to be worried about anyone wanting a hookup?" she asks once she's determined I'm presentable.

"Like an office fling?" I ask.

"I mean, is anyone going to try and assault me today?"

"Well, when you put it *that* way, the answer is no." I shift my head and give her a dead-on, wide-eyed stare. "Do *you*?"

She huffs. "No, of course not. It really isn't attractive when you're flippant."

I look at the clock. It's still early. I woke up three hours earlier than necessary so that I could get ready, eat breakfast, and help Keira shave my face.

She doesn't know that last part yet.

"Does that mean you find me attractive the rest of the time?" I ask. She throws me a dark look and I laugh. I knew she wouldn't answer the question. "Before I go, Keira..." I walk into the bathroom and come out with a razor. Her face is one of pure panic. "You're beginning to look shaggy. I have a reputation to uphold, you know."

I take off the uniform top to keep it from getting wet. I'm not sure why I'm worried about getting drenched, but I am. Luckily her uniform includes a tan T-shirt, so it's not like I'm walking around in the purple bra I managed to put on this morning.

Keira has colorful underwear. I love it.

She rubs her jaw and closes her eyes in defeat.

"I'll do it," she says, and takes the razor away from me.

I just laugh at her. *Oh no you're not.* Turning on the faucet, I fill the sink with hot water and soak a washcloth in the water, then I hand her the washcloth.

"Put this on your face. It will soften the skin."

Keira covers the lower half of her face. I pull out a bottle of drugstore conditioner from the shower and place it on the counter; I don't use shaving cream. I take the washcloth away and gently smooth conditioner over her jaw.

"This is going to feel weird," I say in a tone that suggests I often shave other men. *Just a normal occurrence. Nothing to worry about here.*

"You don't say," she deadpans.

I move the razor with the grain and then against, pulling skin taut here and there. Above the lip is the hardest. I've given her a few nicks, but nothing bad. During the entire ordeal, Keira didn't move a muscle.

She didn't even blink.

I'm not sure if it's because she's terrified I'll hurt her or if it's because she has complete faith in my shaving capabilities.

"There." I remove the excess conditioner with a dry towel.

Keira swipes a hand over her jaw and nods appreciatively.

"Not bad."

"I've got mad skills, Keira. This is just the beginning."

"Mad skills?" She shakes her head as if she believes me, but not for the reason of shaving. Naturally, I wasn't referring to shaving in the first place. "You don't have to keep reminding me that you've slept with a hundred women."

I deserve that. Sort of.

"You rounded *really* high, Keira. If you take that weekend-long, fifty-person orgy out of the equation, I'd say the number is in the forty-to-fifty range."

I swallow hard, waiting for her reaction. In most circumstances, it isn't difficult to admit my number. But I've never admitted this information to a woman, much less the one I'm in love with.

Am I trying to push her away? No, I think. *You're being honest with her. Above all, Keira admires honesty in others.* But what if that honesty solidifies my slut status in her mind? A status she cannot—and will not—dislodge? I suppose I'll have to take my chances.

Like I said earlier, I'll only be honest with her from here on out, even if that honesty drives a wedge between us. A *bigger* wedge, I should say, since one has existed since I met her.

"Do you keep track of them on some sort of spreadsheet, or is that number a guess?" she asks. Her eyes are dark, cold. "Maybe via alphabetical sorting?"

"Judgmental much?" I ask. "I told you that I would be honest with you. It's the only way you'll get to know the real me." I curb the anger and the string of profanities on the tip of my tongue. If this were in reverse, if Keira had slept with fifty men, I wouldn't exactly be a happy camper, either. I might hate her. I might say things I regret. I can't be that person. Taking a deep breath, I say, "No, I do not keep a list or a little black book or anything like that. My number of partners is a guess, at best. It may be higher, or, hell, it may be lower."

"Doubtful," she mutters under her breath.

"I won't apologize for experimenting in college or for spending time with women I found alluring and amazing and willing to spend time with me. The problem is yours, not mine. You'll have to find a way to deal with it while you're in my body and as we try to return to our own bodies. Now..." I pause, and button up her Army uniform top. "If you'll excuse me, I have a nation to save, one classified letter at a time."

I let the door slam when I leave.

CHAPTER TWENTY-SEVEN

Keira

The problem is yours, not mine. I handled that really well, didn't I?

I dress carefully. Well, okay, not carefully. I should say I dress with care. Dillan has an amazing closet filled with designer suits. He must make a lot of money. Not that I care about that sort of thing. I find a clean pair of boxers, an undershirt, and I select a Ralph Lauren suit.

While the undergarments are plain and white—which isn't exactly my normal taste—the suit is gorgeous. The shirt is thick, light blue in color, and made of an extremely soft cotton twill fabric. I tuck the tails into dark gray slacks. The jacket is royal-blue, doubled-buttoned, cashmere, and it feels like clouds against my skin. Holy crap, he has great clothes.

I inspect three rows of ties. There must be fifty of them. But what's in a number?

Everything. If that number means his number of sexual conquests, then yes, it's an important number. Forty or fifty women? Really? *At least it isn't a hundred, like you suspected, Keira. Well, what did you expect?* I knew going into this that my number would be way lower.

A grand total of four men.

Four men who never once knocked my socks off. Never made me moan with anticipation. Never made me dream of them. Four men with boring, safe names, like Gary, a banker, and Henry, an insurance salesman, and Michael, a car mechanic, and Scott, a political science professor.

You could do with a bit of disorder.

You said it, Ellen.

Dillan was honest with me, and that should be what counts.

I decide to pick the gaudiest tie possible because, you know, I can't be too matchy-matchy. When my eyes land on the hot pink tie, I cannot resist it. It's only then that I realize I have no idea of how to tie a tie.

Internet, here I come.

After watching a few videos, I manage to tie it around my neck, knot it, and, with the third try—after nearly choking myself—I affix it properly.

I check myself out in Dillan's full-length mirror. Wow. It's simply impressive, even with the brightness of the tie, how the shirt, jacket, and slacks mold against Dillan's masculine figure.

My roommate is truly a hottie. *And he can be mine...*

I have no idea of what type of shoes to wear. Who looks at men's shoes? A brown pair near his bed seem to be well-worn. He must wear them the most.

Being in the military has its advantages. I'm told what to wear and when to wear it. Simple. Boring. But easy, predictable, and this way, everyone looks the same. If you take all of the guesswork out of the equation, then decisions can be made on important things, like national policies, saving lives, and proudly serving the nation. If I had to worry about what to wear each day, I might not make it out of my apartment on time.

Okay, that's stretching it, obviously. I'm not so clueless that I don't know how to dress myself. Dillan may think I dress like a grandma. And part of me agrees with that statement. I also agree that his number of sexual partners is my problem, not his.

I suppose it's a start, acknowledging that I cannot

control everything. That I cannot, and should not, oversimplify things in order to package them into neat, tidy boxes.

Grabbing Dillan's files on the Joy Fromm case, I lock up and follow his directions to his office. Before I enter his office building, I buy a cup of coffee from a chain cafe, but it isn't nearly as good as Ellen's coffee. I shake my head. Once the dust is settled, I hope to never see that woman again.

The lobby of the Brookshire Mierkle building is a busy one.

My hands itch to clip on a security badge and enter through a turnstile.

I long to direct traffic into a metal detector and inspect purses, briefcases, and other bags. Ellen may have taken me out of my uniform, but she could never remove nearly a decade of military security measures.

Behind the guard, I see a large portrait of a man in his seventies. Below it, I see a golden plaque with Johnson Brookshire's name, etched in an elegant font. So that's Dillan's boss's boss. Beside this portrait is another one, just as stately, of another elderly gentleman by the name of Brian Mierkle.

The guard's newspaper slides down, revealing his face, and I wave. Stupidly. I see no reason why Dillan Pope would wave at a security guard.

"Morning, Mr. Pope," the guard says. His name tag reads Officer Adams, Pinkerton Protective Services.

I'm startled, slightly, at being called Mr. Pope. I mean, how could I forget I'm in Dillan's body?

"Hi," I say back before I slip into the opening elevator. "That's me. Mr. Pope."

I take a big gulp of coffee before I say anything else

idiotic and nearly spit the coffee out. I put *way* too much sugar in the coffee this morning. I'm becoming more like Dillan. I wonder if my tastes will begin to change, too. Like I'll start to lust after busty blondes and video games.

Hopefully not.

The elevator dings and I exit at the fourteenth floor. I consult my notes.

Turn left at the receptionist. Don't say hi. She hates my guts. I don't know why. Make another left at the large windows. My office is second on the right.

Okay, got it. I look up, and the receptionist is staring me down. She's attractive, but not overly so, petite with dirty blonde hair, thick, military-style square glasses, and a disdainful sneer. She can't be more than twenty-five.

"Mr. Brookshire can't wait to fire your ass today, Dillan," she says sweetly, even though her words are loaded with venom. She ignores the ringing phone on her desk. "And that tie is hideous. Please tell me that you were suddenly struck blind over the weekend. I don't normally ridicule the disabled, but I'm willing to make an exception in your case."

This is...*interesting.* Did Dillan throw her dad off a building or something, because unless he rebuffed her advances, I cannot understand a reason for her hatred.

"Trust me, when I look at you—" *I spot her name on the counter* "—Sheila, I wish that I was blind. Have a nice day." I take a few steps, stop, and return my focus to her. Her eyes are totally stabbing me right now. "You might want to get that," I say in reference to the continuously ringing phone. "It's kind of annoying when people don't do their jobs."

I can't hide my smug expression as I walk down the hallway, toward the big windows, which are floor to ceiling in size.

"Ah, there you are, Dillan." A man comes out of a conference room and beckons for me to enter. He holds a presentation clicker in one hand, as if he just finished setting up a projection screen. "I was coming to find you. Mr. Brookshire just arrived, so while technically you're right on time, you're still late." He emphasizes the *late* part.

Then the man shoves the presentation clicker in my free hand. I stare at him as he leaves. Who is that guy?

When I walk through the door, the conference room is full.

Dillan

I have to learn to stop smiling because Keira would not approve of all the appreciative glances she's been receiving since I entered the Metro this morning.

I've been offered everything from a cup of coffee to a date, as well as free tickets to some dude's kid's summer production of William Shakespeare's *Romeo and Juliet.* I said *no* to that one because the dude was wearing a wedding ring, and the first date offer came from a ballsy teenage boy with acne. But I said *hell yeah* to the coffee.

So here's my utterly scientific and foolproof theory on getting free stuff: One, be a woman. Two, smile. Three, wear a military uniform. And holy shit, people can't give me stuff fast enough. If—no—*when* I sell my beer, my number one marketing solution is to use a smiling woman wearing a military uniform.

A sexy military uniform.

I'm sure those exist somewhere. Not in Keira's closet, that's for sure, but somewhere.

Keira is sexy regardless of the uniform.

I get off the Metro and follow the military crowd upstairs.

At the top, I pull out Keira's white security badge, show it to the armed guard, and walk into the Pentagon for the first time in my life. A dozen or more subway-style turnstiles have red or green arrows and I'm intelligent enough—I hope—to know to enter through one of the green-arrowed turnstiles.

After I swipe my badge and go through the turnstile—no intruder alarms go off—I head up another set of escalators and find myself in a large hallway packed with people moving in every direction.

Most keep their heads down and move with a purpose.

Others, like me, stop, and I find that I happen to be standing in line for a Dunkin' Donuts.

Sweet.

Whoever allowed this to happen is a genius. Keira mentioned last night that something like 28,000 people work at the Pentagon. They've got to eat, too. They need their coffee-IV injection.

I'm only halfway through that free cup of coffee, but I order another one when I reach the front of the line, just in case I'm hauled off before I finish the first one.

"Sorry, Sergeant Holtslander, but we've received a disturbing report of body impersonation. While we understand that there are no statutes for this type of crime, and we're not even sure if a crime has been committed, we plan use your situation as a test case. Be a good American and come with us."

Now holding two cups of coffee and Keira's personal notebook—her uniform has, like, twenty pockets—I walk up a moderately steep incline, passing portraits of historic military scenes.

It doesn't take me long to get semi-lost, semi-fascinated with everything.

Once I reach what I suppose is the A-Ring, which is the innermost ring, I take the stairs outside and enter the center courtyard. It reminds me of one of those hotel gardens with trees mixed with chairs, smoking pits, and a small café in the middle.

I have no idea where I'm going, but I walk through the center courtyard, finishing that first cup of coffee, and re-enter the building through another stairwell. I try to stay focused, but there's too much to look at and my eyes are in a constant state of visual orgasm, and when I spot someone riding an adult-size tricycle with big baskets, I swear to God I want one *so* bad.

Consulting my watch, I realize I really don't have much more time to waste—I left early for a reason—I head down about three corridors, and hallways, and whatever else they're called, and find what I hope is 2E801. Because if it's not, I'm staying here anyway. I don't care if they call the Pentagon police.

The office is nicely appointed with dark furniture, several L-shaped desks, closed-off inner office doors, tiled carpets, and a small grouping of chairs that gives me the impression of a mini waiting room.

"Hey Keira," someone says. I look at the far wall. Sitting at the last desk is Sergeant Justin Hauten. I almost don't recognize him in his uniform. He stops short when he sees me, like he can tell something's off. "Not feeling well?" he asks, standing up.

"No, I mean, yes, I mean, something like that," I answer rather quickly, as if I can't get the words out fast enough, confusing both of us in the process. I cough a little even though I don't need to.

Does the military send people home if they are sick, or is there a big room for sick people until they are well again? All I can imagine is a really long line of sick people waiting to see a doctor. Strange, I know, and highly unlikely.

I clear my throat. "I'm just excited to be here and get started on those letters. How are you doing, Justin?"

I've overdone the enthusiasm.

Keira would never say something like that. She'd be like, *"I'm cool, yo, Sarge, how about that new Presidential policy that bans eating ice cream cones while in uniform?"*

Justin's eyes narrow even further, but he answers, "I'm well, thanks. You do realize you're an hour and a half early for duty, right?"

Oh... Think of an answer. "I'm still trying to get used to East Coast time."

Justin nods slowly, his lips flattening. "You transferred from Fort Bragg."

"Yup." I have no idea.

"Fort Bragg, *North Carolina.*"

I nod. "Exactly."

"Keira, North Carolina *is* on the East Coast," he deadpans, tilting his head.

He looks concerned, like maybe I'm truly sick.

How the hell am I supposed to know where Fort Bragg is? It might as well be on Mars for as many times as I've been there. Which is exactly zero times.

"Oh, right," I say, trying to play it off as nothing. "I just didn't sleep well last night. You know, *girl* stuff. Also, I think this might be my fourth cup of coffee."

He observes the thirty-two ounce Styrofoam cup in my hand.

"I'm sending you home, Keira. Obviously, you're not—"

"No!" I interject. Keira will not like it if I get sent home. I have a feeling that that would equal failure in her eyes. "I was just joking with you. I'm fine. I need to wake up, that's all. I'm ready to start the day."

I can tell he doesn't believe a single thing I've said, but he doesn't disagree with me.

"Okay," he says after a few seconds. "I'll open General MacWilliams' secure office for you."

Keira

I recognize Mr. Brookshire from the portrait in the lobby. However, whoever painted the portrait did him a favor because he isn't all that handsome. Stately, yes. Distinguished, absolutely. Handsome, no.

Maybe it's just his expression as he looks at me. At Dillan. With hooded, dark, angry eyes. He doesn't appear all that happy or amused or kind.

It's almost as if he wants me to fall and break my neck.

To be on the safe side, I scan the floor for trip hazards.

The conference room is dimly lit, even with the large windows. All eyes are on me. I clutch the stack of folders in my hands tighter against my chest.

"I'm so glad you could join us, Mr. Pope," Mr. Brookshire says with very little enthusiasm.

To his left, I see Ken Fromm, a slim, handsome man with Asian features. He plays with a pencil and taps it against a blank notepad. When he looks at me, it's piercing, demanding, and charged with something I cannot quite define.

Defiance, maybe?

Ken Fromm does not want to be here, but from what I've read, he has to be or else he forfeits everything to his half-sister.

On Mr. Brookshire's right is Amanda Joy. She is older than Ken by at least twenty years. Men, as they get older, get to be called "distinguished" whereas women, when they age, are often called "tired." Amanda, regardless of her age, is anything but tired.

She sits up straighter than anyone else in the room. She

has taken plenty of notes—she's doing so now as she observes me—and then she does something that changes my perspective: she smiles.

Then I remember that she is a Veteran of the Armed Forces and, in the nineties, she was a truck driver during the first Iraq war, getting supplies in and out of the country for our troops. When she returned stateside, she clawed and fought her way through her father's company, and she is the one responsible for its former success.

The keyword being *former.*

Now she's here at Brookshire Mierkle to fix it, to restore it, to make it whole again. Instantly, I trust her more than I do anyone else in this room, LouAnn Britton included. Earlier, Dillan described what LouAnn looked like, and she's the only one in the conference room to really fit the description of a white woman, short gray hair, smart-ass grin, flawless skin, gray or white suit.

For some reason, LouAnn sits next to Ken Fromm, and gives the appearance she's on *his* side. Within a group, where people sit can be a telling sign. It can suggest power, allegiance, distrust, boredom. In some cases, it means nothing and people just sit down randomly.

But not here. Not at Brookshire Mierkle. Even a child could sense the smothering unease in this room.

I don't know the dynamics here or why she would clearly send the message that she's against Amanda Joy. Perhaps she wants to give the impression—to Johnson Brookshire?—that she's on the side she thinks *he's* on.

I can tell you whose side Mr. Brookshire *isn't* on. Dillan's.

Dillan

Once upon a time, there was this dude who wrote to this girl for like, two years, and it was the most boring shit in the world. The end.

By lunchtime, I've read a hundred letters, the original and its reply, and I have absolutely no idea of what's going on. When I get home tonight, Keira won't have a thing to worry about because there's not one single interesting thing I can tell her about the letters.

Well, I can tell her what the weather was like in Washington, DC, and in Frankfurt, Germany, for all of 1956. I'll be the fucking trivia master if anyone in the world has a weather question for 1956.

What I want to do is find out if either of these two are still alive and just ask them why they wrote such boring letters to each other. That should solve everything. However, now that I understand that these letters were hidden away in a wall in the Pentagon for decades does raise a few questions in my mind. Like, why go through all that trouble to hide something that seems so, I don't know, uninteresting?

People hide stuff for a reason. Affairs. Fraud. Crime. The fact that these letters were hidden suggests something improper. Keira was brought in to see if she could find classified information contained in them.

I, on the other hand, am not trained for that, so I can only observe as an outside source, looking in and analyzing for common sense stuff. You know, like a smart person. I'm good at pretending to be that.

To me, the most logical reason for the letters is an

affair. I'm a human affection expert. Doesn't mean they had to *consummate* that affair. If they loved each other, then these letters might have been some sort of lifeline in an otherwise dreary existence.

But is that a reason to hide the letters? And collect both sets? That would be a lot of work, getting both sets.

It just doesn't make sense to me. I can understand why they would call in someone like Keira for the job. She can comprehend the subtle nuances in the message, in the structure of each sentence, and determine if it is classified or not.

Me? I can only tell you that I'm glad I wasn't in my prime in 1956. Due to my virile, male sexiness, I might have been burned at the stake. If they still did those sorts of things then.

After a couple of hours, it comes as a welcome relief when Justin comes into the general's office and invites me to lunch.

"What about Aaron and Nebraska?" I ask, folding up a letter and shoving it back into its envelope.

"They'll meet us at the Metro entrance. Bring your beret. We're going to the Crystal City Underground for lunch."

CHAPTER TWENTY-EIGHT

Keira

Although less than a minute has gone by since I came in, Johnson Brookshire is clearly agitated. He looks ill at ease in the wide, leather chair at the head of the table. His head is tilted slightly and he wears a scowl like it might be a permanent fixture on his face.

I see my name printed on a tent card on the chair nearest me. I sit down, flip open the topmost folder, and wait for the company president to start the meeting.

"Dillan Pope here—" he points at me with an accusing finger "—is your case manager. He is dedicated to your case and he is also your point of contact if you need anything from Brookshire Mierkle."

"We're not paying you three million dollars to give us an immature babysitter, Brookshire," Ken Fromm says. "For that amount of money, I expect a vice president to handle our case."

"Excuse me," I say, "but I am a—"

"Speak for yourself, Ken," Amanda Joy says, cutting me off, which is a good thing since I was about to say, *I'm a staff sergeant in the United States Army.* "We're happy to have Mr. Pope representing us. Ms. Britton sent over his biography a few days ago. You have an impressive resume, young man."

Ken laughs sardonically. "Us? There is no *us* here. Because last time I checked, everyone quit. I refuse to let you speak for me."

"Currently, Ken, there is no company from which to quit. Because of you, everyone left."

"If we can please get back on topic," Mr. Brookshire interjects. "I have every faith in—" But whatever he was going to say is drowned out as Ken and Amanda start yelling at each other. Johnson Brookshire tries to control the meeting in vain. No one pays attention to him.

Everyone else in the room chimes in, adding their own layers of frustration. Granted, I do not know anyone else and I have no idea if they work for Brookshire Mierkle or Joy Fromm. Everyone on the left side of the table appears to side with Ken Fromm while the right side of the table is in Amanda Joy's corner.

It would appear I am the only neutral party in the room. If this were a formation of soldiers, I would snap them to attention after the first disruption. What would Dillan do in this situation? Sit back and laugh? No. His job depends on his solving this case.

Something flickers on my right. A large white screen comes to life and I realize I accidentally pushed a button on the presentation clicker. Since the guy purposefully gave *me* the presentation clicker, I suppose that at some point, I am meant to get up and brief the room.

Did Dillan create a presentation? He never said anything about that this morning. *I wonder what else he failed to tell me.*

I see a smirk on LouAnn's face. She's watching me. One thing Dillan did mention was the fact that LouAnn was always eager to throw him to the wolves. This tells me that Dillan not only manages to get out alive, but he *thrives.*

I press the clicker again and while something clicks up in the projector, the screen is still white. And blank. Well that answers that question: no, Dillan did not build a presentation for this morning's meeting. But that doesn't mean I can't use a white screen to my advantage.

I stand up more confidently than I sat down and walk to the front of the room. Mentally, I tell myself that I've briefed generals before. I've stood in front of hundreds of soldiers to give security and safety briefs. I've swapped bodies with Dillan Pope.

This should be a piece of cake. I'm not Dillan, so I don't care what happens to him if I fail today. *Liar!* Okay, so I do care.

I've never commanded an audience like this one before —a bickering group ready to cut each other's throats.

So I pretend that I'm briefing a room of naked generals.

I put two fingers in my mouth and whistle loudly. All eyes jerk to me. "Thank you," I say. "Now, will everyone please shut up."

The room goes dead quiet.

Dillan

The Crystal City Metro stop is only two stops away from the Pentagon and it doesn't take us much time to get there.

Everyone is in the mood for burgers—"everyone" meaning "Nebraska"—so we thread through the Crystal City Underground, which consists of businesses, shops, and restaurants linked via an underground tunnel. It also connects to the businesses above ground—hotels, apartments, restaurants—through a series of skylighted staircases.

I've been in the underground twice. Once after a free concert on Crystal Drive that Jon and I attended, and the other time after a night of bar hopping in Crystal City, which is the night Jon and Tanner supposedly met.

Keira said something the other day about how they met even earlier that makes me doubt the memory.

Anyway, I remember the area without needing much direction and I'm in the front, leading the way. However, after remembering that *Keira* wouldn't know where to go, I fall back, and pretend I'm following them. I'm not used to having men tower over me and I have to walk twice as fast to keep up.

Luckily Keira's uniform is extremely comfortable and easy to wear. Justin, Aaron, and Nebraska wear their military uniforms like it's second nature and I admire the confidence they each exhibit without an ounce of effort.

Nebraska's stomach steers us to the Hamburger Shack at the very back of the underground tunnel, near 15th Street.

"This place has nothing on The Itchy Nail," Nebraska says with something like pride.

The Itchy Nail? Oh right, I think, remembering the other night. The tall redhead sort of talked about this the night we went bowling. However, he said it to Dillan. Not Keira.

Aaron looks around, then says, "At least it's pirate-free."

"I'll just sit here and pretend that I know exactly what you're talking about," I say.

"It's a long story," Justin answers.

"I disagree, buddy," Nebraska chimes in energetically. "It's an *interesting* story. Get your facts straight."

"Do we really need argue about this? All of us were there, Nebraska," Aaron says. There's a small bite to his words, like maybe he's tired of hearing about this particular story. I see Aaron eyeing the butter knife and then pointedly looking back at Nebraska, who only laughs at the gesture.

I raise my hand. "I wasn't there." I suppose hoping for an explanation isn't high on their list right now since they ignore me.

I take a good look at Nebraska, who sits next to me. That's when I notice his black eye.

Justin takes pity on me. "Outside Fort Hood, Texas, there's a place called The Itchy Nail. It's part underground bunker, part bar, part covert-interrogation room. It's probably the weirdest place on the planet. It's more or less an urban legend. However, it does exist. Last year, the three of us were kidnapped and brought there to be interrogated by an enemy of the state. A man dressed as a pirate happened to be sitting at one of the tables that night."

I would laugh if he didn't look so serious. What exactly is an *enemy of the state*? Terrorists? Keira would totally know what he meant by that, so I can't freaking ask.

"How'd you get out of it?" I ask.

And was it Halloween night?

Nebraska stretches out, makes some sort of proud sound that is a cross between a happy groan and clearing his throat.

"I totally saved the day."

"You got lucky, is all," Justin says, sighing. He now wears the same type of expression Aaron does: tired to death of this topic.

The night we went bowling, Nebraska boasted about how he singlehandedly solved one of the biggest military conspiracies ever to exist that the public never knew about.

"Luck's got nothing to do with these puppies," Nebraska says, and then kisses his biceps.

An awkward silence ensues after Aaron and Justin both shake their heads. When the burgers come, I can tell the subject has been dropped for good.

"What happened to the eye?" I ask before taking a bite.

I'll never be able to finish this huge burger with Keira's tiny mouth.

"I was hoping you weren't going to ask that question," Aaron says with a groan. He hands over a fifty-dollar bill to Nebraska, who grins like a madman. "I knew I was going to lose that bet. Damn," Aaron says.

He doesn't actually look upset. His smile is lopsided and almost boyish.

Nebraska makes a show of putting the money into his wallet, but Justin snatches it first.

"And I bet *you*—" he cocks at eyebrow at his tall, redheaded friend "—that Keira wouldn't ask in the first ten minutes. So I'll take that."

These three must be the oddest set of friends in the country. The lovers and the best friend. I wonder if Nebraska ever felt like the third wheel. Probably not.

Am I—*is Keira*—becoming the fourth member of this military posse?

"Well?" I ask.

"Well what?" Nebraska asks.

"The eye?"

"I got into a fight with a newspaper stand on Sunday morning," Nebraska answers with a mouth full of food.

"That's literally the dumbest answer I've ever heard," I say.

Aaron laughs.

"Yeah," Justin adds. "But it also happens to be true. We witnessed the entire, ridiculously funny ordeal."

"Oh, well, okay then," I say. "Still doesn't make any sense, though." Then I notice that Nebraska has a rolled-up newspaper between us.

My eyes narrow when he brings it up to the table.

I stand corrected. It's two newspapers.

"Are you telling me you fought someone to get newspapers?" I ask.

"Not someone. Some*thing*," Justin corrects me. "With Nebraska, everything has an equal opportunity of getting into a scuffle with him. Even inanimate objects."

"*Especially* inanimate objects," Aaron says. "He tripped on the curb once he spotted these."

I spread the first newspaper out, which is more or less one of those cheap gossip rags, and nearly choke.

In huge letters, it boldly proclaims, "Alec Huffman Hooks Up With Fan."

Below the words is a picture of Alec and Keira, sitting

in his car, as he leans over. From the angle, it looks like they are kissing.

My face burns. This was from Saturday night. The night I, in Keira's body, went on a date with Alec. I can tell from the outfit in the picture. Plus, he tried to kiss me —Keira—that night.

Keira is not going to like this one bit.

I try to come up with plausible scenarios in which we leave the country tonight so she never finds out, each more insane than the next.

You know that uncle you've never heard of, Keira? He left you a billion dollars, but we have to leave for Europe this instant to claim it. No time to change. Chop chop.

I've completely lost my appetite and I'm afraid to look at the second newspaper. Nebraska proudly does the honors of flattening it out on top of the first one.

This one is worse.

It declares, "My Wild Night With Pitcher-Playboy."

Underneath the headline is a grainy, black-and-white photo of Alec, holding Keira's hand, as they leave Preston's Pub after the Nats game on Friday. Alec drove her home that night. The article appears to be written from the so-called fan's perspective.

In other words, it would seem that Keira wrote to the paper and, in exchange for money, gave an exclusive story.

Which, naturally, is a complete fabrication.

"Oh my God," I say in a panic. My chest hurts. If this isn't a heart attack, I don't know what is. "I...I...need to..."

Punch things.

Hide.

Die.

I look up at Justin. "That's why you asked me if I was feeling okay this morning, wasn't it?"

He nods. "You didn't know about this?"

"No, not at all," I say.

"Strangely," Aaron says cryptically, "both of those newspapers sold out within hours."

"Oh my God," I repeat.

Keira is seriously going to flip out.

I'm not really her, and *I'm* flipping out.

Nebraska flexes his fingers in my face. Aaron and Justin do the same. Their fingers and palms are stained a dull, black color.

"We bought every copy in the region, Keira," Nebraska says with a smile.

"Let me clarify that statement slightly," Justin says. "Once we ran out of money, we *stole* the rest."

I look between the three of them, studying their faces, waiting to see if they are joking.

They aren't.

"You guys did that for me?" They did this for Keira.

No wonder she loves the military. Those in uniform had each other's backs.

"Absolutely," Aaron says, putting his arm around Justin. "What are friends for, Keira?"

"The truth is," Nebraska says with a shit-eating grin, "you'll never be able to get rid of us now."

Keira

"This is what I call a Clean Slate meeting," I say, pointing to the white screen. "I want you to know that I spent an enormous amount of time creating this slide," I joke.

No one laughs except LouAnn. Everyone has turned their anger toward me rather than at each other. I'm not sure if I've made the right decision or not, but I press on.

"In all seriousness, we've got a problem here and not only will I tell you what the problem is, I will work with you to fix it and take Joy Fromm to new heights. Working as a Department of Defense contractor is like working in a quagmire. It's filled with rules and regulations, and there are always bigger companies demanding a bigger share of the pie. Joy Fromm Acquisitions provides a niche product."

I pause for effect. I've read the files and while I'm not quite sure how I plan to spin it, I think I'm on the right track when no one disagrees with me.

I continue, "Let me amend that slightly." I move across the room. All eyes follow me. "Joy Fromm Acquisitions *used* to provide a niche product. And that product was the transportation of federal equipment, supplies, and other logistical services, such as transporting materials for destruction and other waste-management duties.

"Now, during wartime," I continue, "these services are high in demand. The government swells, it surges its military ranks, it needs more equipment and produces more waste. Simple cause and effect. Joy Fromm's mission didn't change, but the circumstances in which you operate did. The war wound down. The need for supplies shrank as a result. Your company didn't necessarily do anything wrong, but during unstable times, it may not be a good time to shuffle leadership. Please accept my condolences on the passing of your father."

"Thank you," Amanda Joy says quietly.

Her half-brother says nothing.

LouAnn cocks an eyebrow that conveys something like, *I don't know what yarn you're spinning, but continue on. I'm curious to see how far the distance is from your face to the floor when you fall.*

"This is the part where I should be politically correct and instruct you to complete about seventeen steps from the Project Management handbook in order to discover your management style and work alongside your peers. That's not going to happen for two reasons: one, both of you can probably recite it verbatim; and two, it won't do either of you a bit of good."

"How dare—" Ken Fromm starts, but I cut him off, smacking the table with my hand.

"I need everyone not named Ken Fromm and Amanda Joy to leave the room." My voice is loud, strong, and my tone is like that of a drill sergeant.

I'm sure that by the end of the day I'll be fired, but at least I'll be able to talk some truth and sense into these two before either LouAnn or Mr. Brookshire kick me out.

I'm prepared to force the issue, but it isn't necessary. Everyone readily leaves, including Mr. Brookshire and LouAnn. She pats me on the back on the way out, but otherwise says nothing. I quietly shut the door when it is just the three of us.

"Was that necessary?" Ken Fromm asks.

"No," I answer simply, sitting at the head of the table and between the half-siblings. "I've been called many things. *Dramatic* being one of them. It gets the message across." I know I've called Dillan *dramatic* a time or two before, so, strictly speaking, I'm still telling the truth. "Listen." I turn to Amanda. "Mrs. Joy, I've read the files, your biography, and the history of your father's company. You've done an amazing job running the company."

Ken tries to say something, but I shush him.

"Mr. Fromm, you are as impressive as your sister. When you two look at each other, you see competition. You see your father's favoritism played out in your mind. You envision a new path for the company. The difference is that each of you see yourself at the helm. This will never work. Ken, you will never work for Amanda. And Amanda, you'll never work for Ken. Now, have I said anything incorrect? I want just a yes or no. No expositions."

"No," Ken answers, begrudgingly.

"No," Amanda concurs.

I nod. "All right. Then there's no need for representation. No matter what Brookshire Mierkle does for you, you'll fight and bicker with each decision and your father's company will never be successful again. Is that what you want?"

Both say *no*.

"I want to meet again tomorrow. I have a few ideas, but I want to think them over before I present them to you in the morning. Give me twenty-four hours. Dismissed, soldiers."

I walk out of the room before either can respond. However, I didn't miss the shocked expressions on their faces.

Dillan

It's exhausting being a soldier. There is no way I can do this for another day. I shuffle into the apartment and take out two beers. I'll be done with the first one within two minutes and I don't want to get up again once I sit on the couch.

After learning about the existence of the stories in the two newspapers, I went back to reading the letters until it was time to leave. A romance has grown between the two letter writers, though their words are passive and muted.

Now that I've cracked into the 1957 letters, they have begun to sign their letters, at the closing, with *Yours Affectionately, Greta*, and, *Ardently Yours, William.* However, they still discuss the weather.

Back in the 1950s, *Yours Affectionately* could equate to *I Want to Jump your Bones the Next Time I See You* in today's slang.

The door opens and closes behind me and I hear Keira come in. She drops something on the counter with a loud slap, opens the fridge, and, after a few seconds, sits next to me on the couch.

With two beers.

Great minds think alike. Wordlessly, she pops the top and drains most of the beer in one shot.

We sit this way for a few minutes.

"How was your day?" I ask finally.

"I didn't get you fired," she says. "Tell me: Why does that receptionist hate you so much?"

Of all the things she could have asked, I wasn't expecting her to ask that.

This tells me two things. One, the meeting with the Joy Fromm half-siblings wasn't the worst part of her day, and two, LouAnn didn't eat her alive.

I take another sip of beer.

"I have no idea. She's been mean to me ever since they hired her. I've never hit on her. Never asked her out. Never dated anyone in her family that I know of."

"She's cute," Keira says. "In a bookish kind of way."

"Hm. I guess so. I can't even tell you what she looks like. For all I know, it's a different woman each day. How'd the meeting go?"

I study her and notice for the first time what she's wearing from my closet.

For a woman who has zero fashion sense, she happened to choose the most expensive blazer in my closet—a four-thousand-dollar Ralph Lauren jacket, and paired it with a pink tie, my light cotton twill shirt, and brown loafers.

It doesn't look all that bad.

Dillan Pope: male fashion model.

If I get fired, it seems like I have another job lined up for me in the fashion industry. It's on the tip of my tongue to tell her she's wearing six thousand dollars worth of clothing. However, I don't think she'd be impressed. She might be horrified, actually.

"I think that if there was a sharp object nearby, like a pair of scissors, that one or both of those half-siblings would have stabbed the other. In fact, I suspect that a sharpened pencil might have been okay in a pinch. Jesus, they hate each other."

"What did you do?" I'm waiting to hear about Johnson Brookshire yelling at her, or LouAnn giving her backhanded compliments for not tripping on her own feet. Stuff like that.

"I kicked everyone out of the meeting except for me and the Joy Fromm siblings."

I sit up straight. "You're kidding, right?"

"Dead serious." She finishes off the second beer and gets up. "Want another?"

"Hell yes."

She hands me my third beer and sits down even closer than before. "I have an idea about them, if you're willing to hear it."

"Okay," I say.

I have my own ideas, but a second brain on the case isn't a bad thing.

"I think they should split up and form their own companies. Amanda is more interested in logistics and transportation, whereas Ken has a knack for finance and contracting. They are only connected because of their father. It wasn't like the elder Mr. Fromm hired them to run his company. They were his children, so his judgment was clouded when he allowed them to co-operate the company."

"That idea certainly has merit," I say. "I suspect that they aren't willing to part with three million dollars for that assessment. They are expecting Brookshire Mierkle—me—to fix them as a whole and get them running again, but with Brookshire's support as the ace in the hole. Our name opens a lot of doors. That's what they are counting on."

"You've had your hand in this game a lot longer than I have. Tell me what you want me to do, and I'll do it. I told them to come back tomorrow and that I'd have the solution packaged for them."

"And they said okay? Did Brookshire threaten to kill you afterward?"

"I avoided him entirely by telling the receptionist that I was having lunch with one of the President's interns. They left me alone after that."

"You mean the President of the United States?"

"Sure, why not," she laughs. "I was vague enough to give them that impression."

"I've rubbed off nicely on you, I think," I say proudly. "What did you do the rest of the day?"

"Surfed online for porn, had a few quickies in the bathroom stall, and antagonized the receptionist. You know, an honest day's work. Now tell me about your day. I've had three beers. I can take it."

I grin. "That place is huge," I say, and tell her about my impressions of the Pentagon, ending with, "It is my dying wish to get one of those adult-sized tricycles."

I don't have the heart to tell her about the newspapers or my lunch with Justin and the gang.

"Yeah, that place is crazy big. You never have to leave it except to go home. What were your impressions of the letters?" She smiles.

The beers have relaxed her.

"Oh, I thought that that was obvious without having to say anything. They are a snooze-fest." I make a loud snoring noise. "Though things picked up once William started discussing Area 51."

"Shut the hell up!" She playfully hits me on the shoulder. "William and Greta. I wonder what happened to them?"

"I think they love each other," I say seriously. "Maybe they are together now, old and married, with a dozen great-grandchildren."

"Doubtful," she says. "They'd have to be close to a hundred. The chances of both of them still being alive are slim to none."

"Yeah, you're probably right. I'm starving," I say, rubbing my stomach like it's a dog's belly. "What about you?"

"You forgot, didn't you?" she asks, her eyes narrowing. Just then, someone knocks on the door. My blank face must answer for me because she says, "You and Alec are going on a date to the exotic location of your kitchen."

Shit. I did forget. I was enjoying Keira's company too much. I was enjoying the fact that even though we are in each other's bodies, we were having a somewhat normal conversation.

That's a rarity for us.

Alec Huffman is the last person I want to see right now. I'd bet anything, including the Ralph Lauren blazer hanging from Keira's shoulders, that Alec knows about the articles.

But more than anything, he has the power to pull Keira away from me, thus ruining our chances of switching back.

CHAPTER TWENTY-NINE

Keira

I open the door and am struck by how handsome Alec Huffman is. Freckles stand out against tan skin. His blue eyes seem even lighter and his reddish-blond hair is just different enough to make me differentiate him from Dillan's brown hair and green eyes.

Both are handsome.

Both are successful.

But only one of them makes my heart beat faster, and it isn't the man standing in the doorway right now.

I let Alec in after giving him a bro hug. He seems tense, like he can't wait to see Keira and tell her something. I pray to God it isn't some sort of love proclamation because I can't deal with that right now.

"Nice jacket," he says to me. "You going out or something?" Alec asks in a manner that suggests he hopes it is true.

"No," I say, getting him a beer. He accepts it without saying anything. "I'll stay out of the way, of course, though I might creep in to grab a bite to eat. Keira never likes to admit these things, but she's a pretty good cook. So I don't plan on missing out. Stacey said she might come over. But, don't worry about us. We plan to keep a low profile, if you know what I mean."

Alec looks at me as if I've sprouted a third eye.

"Uh, okay, Dillan. Thanks for the play-by-play."

I laugh. I might be overdoing the bro-thing by telling him everything.

"Keira just got home. She's getting changed."

He sips the beer, does a double take at the Nine Year Crush label, and takes another long sip.

"This is really good, Dillan. I'm getting a hint of blackberry in the aftertaste. Well done, sir!"

He claps me on the back. I have no idea of what he's talking about, but I just nod like a simpleton and hope it looks convincing.

Dillan—in my body—walks out of my room wearing another outfit that he would classify as "grandma-couture" and warmly embraces Alec.

What. The. Hell.

How many beers has he had? With my smaller frame, he shouldn't have drank more than two. Now I'm worried things will get worse from here.

Also, how many calories are in each bottle? I calculate how many miles I will need Dillan to run in the morning to burn them all off.

Eight. Eight miles.

Strangely, Alec looks uncomfortable after he extricates himself from my body.

Again, what the hell?

"I thought I would bake chicken with portobello mushroom caps and, on the side, asparagus tips wrapped in bacon. I'm not a big bread eater, but I can whip up homemade biscuits if you want. As a starter, however, how does a light house salad with oil and vinegar sound?" Dillan says to Alec as he puts on an apron.

My mouth waters. Bacon. Biscuits. Mushroom caps.

"Sounds great, Keira," Alec says, rubbing Dillan's arms at the same time.

My own arm tingles.

It feels like I can feel it, too. Or maybe I'm imagining things.

"I'll just do a bit of reading," I say stiffly. "In my room." No one is listening to me. I walk toward my true room first, realize I'm heading for the wrong room, squat down to *fake* pick something up. "Food," I say by way of explanation, throw out said fake piece of food, and then head into Dillan's room.

I can tell something's troubling Alec so I plan to listen in on their conversation.

I leave Dillan's door partially open.

Dillan

I shake my head. Three beers is all it took to make Keira's body woozy. Good lord. I gulp down a large glass of water.

As I make food preparations, Alec asks me about my day, and this time I can honestly tell him about working in the Pentagon.

"It's like a maze, I swear," I tell him and he laughs.

The smile doesn't reach his eyes, so I feel it's best to just air out the dirty laundry and get it over with. That way, if he leaves, I won't have to cook all this food.

"Listen," I say. "Someone showed me the newspapers today. I can understand if you're upset, but I'd like you to know that I had nothing to do with them and only found out about them today."

"I believe you," he answers thoughtfully, leaning against the counter, watching me as I make preparations for dinner. "I was worried that you'd be livid at me. I'm used to it, but it's never my intention to hurt those I care about. I thought that once you experienced what it's like, that you'd back out fairly quickly. I should have known you'd take it in stride. You've experienced life-changing events and you've been deployed to war zones. Three newspapers calling you the *Nats' Tramp* won't hurt your feelings."

"Excuse me, but did you say *three* newspapers?"

There's nothing in my mouth, but it feels like I'm choking on something anyway.

He raises an eyebrow.

"How many did you know about?"

"Two," I say.

Crap. Crap. Crap.

Justin, Aaron, and Nebraska missed the third newspaper. Oh, who am I kidding? They would have been well out of money by then anyway. I can't have people stealing things for *me.*

For Keira, I mean. I'd climb to the moon and back to protect her.

"Seriously? *Nats' Tramp?* That's...harsh."

And sexist. I plan to hurt whoever did this to Keira.

"I have a pretty good idea of who's behind it," Alec says.

He finishes the beer.

I start putting food and utensils away. "Who?"

He laughs an uncomfortable laugh, as if he's worried I might do something stupid with the information. And he'd be correct.

"Zoe and her future sister-in-law, Maria. Maria is my ex-girlfriend."

I wash my hands and dry them on a towel.

"Okay, let's go."

"Go? And do what, exactly?" Alec doesn't move an inch.

He must not think I'm serious.

"Oh, I don't know, exchange recipes. Gossip. Dump their bodies in the Potomac. I'm in favor of that last option. What about you?"

"Whoa, hold up, Keira." He holds up his hands. "That's not going to happen. You can't lash out when people call you bad names or when they lie about you. Not in my profession. In yours, in the military, it's different. I get that. But surely you understand that you can't pick a fight with everyone who disagrees with you?"

"This isn't a disagreement. This is libel and I can sue

the newspapers for publishing lies about me."

I can also ruin the lives of those who fuck with the girl I love.

"Listen, Keira, I really like you. I don't want tonight to be about what was said in the newspapers. If you're unsure about dating me, then tell me now. Otherwise, I'd rather get to know you and eat stuff wrapped in bacon. I don't want to dwell on the negative side of my baseball fame. Either way, I promise I'll uphold my end of our bargain and visit the wounded soldiers."

I have every confidence that Keira is listening. I'm rather surprised she hasn't exploded out from my room, demanding answers. I want nothing more than to send Alec Huffman packing.

He's a cool guy and as a dude, I like him a lot.

But here's the thing: I can't speak for Keira on this topic. I just don't know how she feels about him. I suspect she has platonic feelings for Alec, but I cannot be too sure. I'm more confident that she has feelings for me and not Alec.

A knock at the door saves me from having to answer. The amazingly beautiful, long-legged Bernadine Stacey waltzes in before I can even get to the door.

She's poured into into a tiny, red mini-dress that's way too dangerous for mortal men. Stacey's long blonde hair is swept up in a loose bun that gives the illusion that it will suddenly burst free and cascade down her shoulders.

Stacey isn't careless about her appearance, and nothing has actually been left to chance. If her hair looks like it's about to fall down, she's styled it that way on purpose.

She completely ignores me and Alec Huffman, who, to his credit, looks unaffected as Stacey commands the room, and she quietly slips into my bedroom.

"Dillan mentioned Stacey was on her way," Alec mentions slowly. "I kind of feel sorry for him." I look at the ball player oddly. *Why would he think that?* I ask as much. "Women like that aren't real," he says. "Stacey is beautiful. She's more than beautiful, but she's like a painting by a famous artist that everyone loves to look at but no one truly understands." I'm not sure if I agree, but I nod anyway, because I'm supposed to be Keira, not Dillan. "She doesn't make him happy, and he doesn't make her happy. I wonder why they are together," he says more to himself than to me.

Excellent question, I think.

Keira

I'm so angry that I pace Dillan's bedroom. *Nats' Tramp?* Newspapers talking about our dates? I turn on his laptop and search the Web. It takes no time to discover what they're talking about.

While I find a few blogs that discuss, in gossip-like fashion, Alec's new plaything—me!—I can't find the *original* source. Whoever posted the actual story not only deleted the story, but the Internet cache page of it as well. Not just one newspaper, but all three of them. This in itself seems strange, but not perplexing enough for me to forget the knot forming in the pit of my stomach.

Dillan knew.

He knew when he got home tonight and yet he said nothing.

That son of a bitch!

The rational side of me reasons that he didn't say anything because our conversation was a relaxed one. I know that if he brought it up, I would have been livid from the get-go and I wouldn't have been able to learn about his day. I wouldn't have discussed how my day went with him. I would have just been mad.

And that doesn't include the fact that Alec kissed me—Dillan—on their date Saturday night. I've got the proof in a four-by-six color photograph staring back at me on one of the blog's websites.

The knot in my stomach has to be the size of a watermelon by now.

I lean back and spot something red out of the corner of my eye and realize Stacey's standing in Dillan's bedroom.

In a dress that's more or less the size of a Band-Aid.

She looks amazing.

I close the laptop.

"Someone call the fire department," I say.

That's something Dillan would say, right?

Stacey shakes her head. It looks like her hair might tumble down any second, but it stays perfectly pinned up.

"I'm here to break up with you, Dillan," she says pragmatically, as if she were in front of a group of students giving a lecture. "Don't make this harder than it has to be."

Wait, *what?* Okay, what is this *feeling* I'm feeling right now?

Rejection.

"Uh..." I hesitate, unsure of what to say.

My stomach rolls as she looks at me like she needs to comfort me. I'm not even Dillan Pope, but I'm feeling her rejection of him, and it's freaking me out.

What if the longer I'm in Dillan's body, the more his sensations and mannerisms transfer into me?

How else can I explain the fact that it actually hurts that Stacey's breaking up with Dillan?

I don't even know how much he likes her, but it can't be that much if he says he loves me.

I clutch my stomach and sit down on the bed. The watermelon has multiplied.

"Is it about yesterday?" I ask, looking up. She hasn't moved from the doorway. "Because I had too many hot dogs. I wasn't feeling well..."

I can't believe I'm trying to get her to change her mind. I should want her to break up with Dillan. Hell, *I* came up with five damn good reasons yesterday to break up with *her*.

"It was fun while it lasted, Dillan. We both know this wasn't going to be a permanent relationship. And, honestly, you've been acting pretty strange. I know that this may sound weird, but I feel like you're not *you* anymore. You seem...feminine. I feel like we're two cats standing next to one another and all I want to do is hiss at you."

"That does sound weird."

"But...I'll certainly never look at tiramisu the same way again."

"I'm..." I hesitate. *How would Dillan handle this?* "I'm sorry?" It comes out more like a question than a statement.

"You don't need to apologize. Do I—" she waves her hand down her dress "—look heartbroken to you?"

"You look beautiful, actually," I say.

In two steps she's in front of me, and she kisses me on the cheek. "You're a good guy, Dillan. You respect women. But it's time you found the right *one*." She winks. "I've got to go. There's a cab with my name on it and I have VIP Orchestra seats at the Kennedy Center."

"Seats? As in plural? Who's your date?"

I find it ballsy that she hadn't even broken up with me —Dillan—before securing a date for tonight.

"Come out into the living room and find out," she says playfully.

Dillan

Conversation has been a little stilted since Stacey entered my bedroom. I can sense that Alec knows I won't answer in the positive about dating him, but I won't answer in the negative, either, and he must hate the not knowing as much as thinking it's a *no*. Maybe more.

"Where do you think they are going tonight?" Alec asks me. He's flipping through one of Keira's manuals, one of the ones she's allowed to bring home.

Actually, if my gut is correct, Stacey won't be staying long. After yesterday's, uh, sexual-fart incident, Stacey's doing the breakup thing right about now.

Tellingly, this doesn't injure my pride whatsoever.

I feel a little bit freer, like I can finally be myself around Keira without having to worry about hurting someone else. Plus, it saves me from having to end the relationship. It's best if Stacey does it; that way, she's in charge. She's in control, and there's no question about anything.

"Probably a political function. Stacey brings in boatloads of money for her candidates."

She's also incredibly smart and savvy, and knows her way around the Capitol like no one's business.

"She can probably get people to switch political parties," Alec jokes. "I've always been fascinated by U.S. politics."

"Stacey is your go-to for information," I say with a smile on my lips. "She knows everyone in this town. The good. The bad. And the criminal. And she remembers everything anyone has ever said to her."

Stacey exits my bedroom in a calm and collected

manner. Keira brings up the rear, leans against the door, crosses her arms across her chest, and wears an interesting expression that I can't quite decipher.

"Alec Huffman," Stacey announces with her confident *I don't take prisoners* voice. "Get your jacket. You're coming with me tonight."

"Excuse me? I'm sort of on a date right now."

I like how he said *sort of.* Implying he isn't so sure.

Welcome to the *I don't know what the hell is going on* club, buddy.

Stacey laughs, but it isn't malicious. "*They* like each other, not us. It's as clear as day. So...are you coming or what?"

Alec looks between me, whom he thinks is Keira, and Keira, whom he thinks is Dillan, and when neither of us disagree with Stacey's statement, Alec grabs his jacket.

"No hard feelings, right?" he asks.

Keira and I both answer "No" at the same time, and he shuts the door.

"That was..." I trail off.

"Caveman-ish? Barbaric?" Keira finishes for me, laughing. "I know she didn't have room in her dress, but at any second, I expected her to pull out a club, hit Alec over the head with it, and drag him away with her."

"That's pretty much how she won me over," I say.

"Is that all it takes? Hitting men over the head? I've been going about this whole dating thing the wrong way for years."

"Keira, I'm sorry I didn't tell you about the newspapers. I didn't want to hurt you."

"I think I understand. But now the world thinks I've gotten to first base with Alec Huffman. He kissed you, and you didn't tell me."

I lift my hand, which holds tongs for the salad, and say, "He *tried* to kiss me, but I turned away, and he got my cheek instead. The picture is at the *right* angle for the *wrong* image. No kiss."

She spies the tongs in my hand and appears to try and look behind me. I'm not sure how to take her expression. Keira appears to be more or less in a relaxed mood.

"So, can you still make the bacon-wrapped stuff? It sounded pretty good. I can help and get plates down from the cabinet. I don't want you to worry your pretty little lady head about that part. I'll do the hard, manly labor stuff."

She flexes her muscles.

After a few seconds of doing that, she acts like she's carrying a club and pretends to hit me over the head with it. I can get used to this. I haven't actually cooked anything. I've only assembled the salad.

"What would you like wrapped in bacon?" I ask.

"Everything."

Keira

"I have to admit that when I started to read the letters, that I had hoped it would be a romance," I say after demolishing most of the bacon-wrapped food. Dillan could have wrapped bacon around toothpaste and I still would have eaten it.

What we haven't talked about is Stacey, Alec, or what just happened.

I look across the table at Dillan as he puts down his fork. He sensibly has eaten only the salad and a plate full of fresh fruit. I say *sensibly* because I forced him to. There's no way I'm letting him put meat wrapped with other meat in my body.

"Why?" Dillan asks thoughtfully, as if he's actually interested. "Why do you want it to be a romance?"

"I guess it's because I'd hate it if classified information was actually passed back and forth. What was told? What happened because of it? The letters were written during the Cold War."

"What does that have to do with anything?" he asks, genuinely curious.

"For starters, Greta lived in Frankfurt, Germany, which would have been in West Germany at the time. For all we know, she could have been a spy. Maybe *he* was. I don't know how or why they began writing to each other."

"You think it's possible that *Affectionately Yours*, Greta was passing information to *Ardently Yours*, William?" Dillan asks.

"Is that how they are now signing their letters?" I ask. Dillan nods. "Doubtful, but it *might* be possible. I'm not an expert on the Cold War. If all goes well, we've got one more day left of this."

"Yeah, if all goes well," he says with little enthusiasm. I sense he's lost his appetite. He slides his plate away, looks at me seriously, and asks, "Are you thinking what I'm thinking about this ordeal?"

I let out a heavy sigh.

"That our chances of returning to normal are slim-to-none before the deadline?" Ellen's anniversary is tomorrow night. Tomorrow is also the same day Dillan and I met nine years ago. "Yeah. Our best chance is showing up at her party and trying to convince her we've accomplished what she wants us to accomplish."

"It won't work," Dillan says, throwing more rain on our pity-parade.

I put our plates in the sink. I look out the windows. It's dark, and I realize it's nearly eleven. If we're lucky, we'll be back to ourselves in twenty-four hours.

If we're not so lucky… Not only will I be stuck in Dillan's body, there's zero chance I'll have a happy life. I'll be stuck in a job I don't fully understand, in a body I have no interest in actually owning—I want to snuggle up against Dillan, I want to do lots and lots of things to Dillan's body—I don't want to experience my love for him in this…this…twisted way.

"I know it won't work, Dillan," I say, with more anger than I ever intended.

Remember how I used to blame this whole thing on him? Well, I no longer believe that. We're both stubborn. I may be more stubborn than he is. Dillan's challenge is to get me to love him.

What more can he do to make me love him more than I already do? I don't need overly romantic gestures. I don't want him to sing to me or buy me expensive things.

I want to believe that if we are together, that he won't be thinking about someone else or wishing I was more exciting, sophisticated, or exotic. As I think these things, Dillan gets up from the table and stands in front of me. I'm still near the sink. As he stares at me, I wonder what he's thinking.

My own brown eyes watch me intently, a small frown line etches in my forehead, and I resist the urge to fix a thick strand of hair that's come undone.

Those are Dillan's facial features upon my face.

"I understand your anger, Keira."

He takes my hands in his. I'm reminded just how small my hands are compared to his.

I've gotten over the weirdness of watching myself look at me, at my mannerisms played out right in front of me. But I've never really noticed that I'm beautiful. I'm slender, fit, athletic—if a bit on the too-slim side—and I carry my figure confidently. My skin is a lovely caramel hue, and my hair, which is mostly curly and almost always untamable, looks soft and touchable.

Did I need to realize that I'm beautiful?

Or is it that I needed to understand that I am deserving of love, of affection, of someone's time and attention?

I don't need a man to be complete. That's not what I mean. Keira Holtslander is a complete person. She's amazing. She's wonderful. She's smart, funny, and can hold her own in any situation.

If body-swapping into Dillan Pope's body didn't prove that, then I don't know what can.

"Keira," Dillan says, moving his hands up my arms to my shoulders. I have a feeling his next question is going to shatter me. "Why can't you admit it?"

"Admit what?" I ask.

"That you're in love with me." Dillan says it simply, like there's nowhere to hide anymore.

Like he's tired of playing this game.

My heart stops pumping oxygen to my brain. That must be the reason why I'm so light-headed.

"I'm not—" I start as a shadow passes over Dillan's face. He doesn't believe me.

"Be careful, Keira," Dillan cuts in, then pauses, and he appears to be rethinking his statement. He's silent for a very long moment and with each second my heart rate doubles. "Be careful of what you say, tomorrow, to the Joy Fromm siblings. I'd hate for you to lose your job."

"What are you saying?" I pull away from him, away from Dillan's comforting essence. He may be in my body, but it's his pull that attracts me to him.

"I'm saying that none of this is ever going to work. If you cannot be honest with yourself, then I can never count on you being honest with me. Luckily, since I'm you—a soldier—I figure as long as I don't murder anyone, I'll have a job for a few more years. Maybe I'll turn into the base slut or something."

"That is completely uncalled for!" I reach out to slap him, but stop before I ever reach his face.

His hand flies up and grips my wrist, immobilizing me, but it isn't overly forceful. I can get out of it easily.

"Oh, you're offended? How about this one: as you, I have no interest in being lonely or growing old and not being able to tell someone 'I love you' without a petrified look on my face. I mean, it's so unappealing, Keira. I don't know what's happened to you to make you so cold to me, to my touch, to my love."

"Dillan, I..." I what?

I love you.

I need you.

I want you.

He pushes himself away from me, his stare as cold as an ice shower.

"Don't worry about it now. It's too late. Do you know what the worst part is, Keira? I thought we would win. I thought that this might be the most interesting *how-we-met* story for our children and our grandchildren. When I'm near you, I'm short of breath, I get nervous, and I want to impress you to no end." He punches his chest. "I don't know what this feeling is right now, right here—" he pats over his—my—heart "—but I think you've broken my heart."

He moves further away. I have to stop him. I can't let him walk away from me, from us, from *this.*

"Dillan, please, let me explain," I half-yell, half-whisper.

Let me explain my fear of being hurt.

Of rejection.

Of opening up and allowing chaos to enter my life.

Dillan reaches his real bedroom before he turns.

"Explain it to yourself, Keira. You know how I feel. Now it's your turn to figure things out."

Dillan

In the morning, I'm no closer to curbing my anger than I was last night, but at least I was able to destroy things privately. As I look around my bedroom, there's nothing but disaster.

Clothes are everywhere, the bed is in the middle of the room, its sheets torn from the mattress, and the nightstand is not only *not* standing, it's on its side, the contents scattered throughout the room.

It felt good when I did that last night. Looking at it now, however, I'm not so sure it was the right thing to do. Yes, I released a ton of anger, but now I have to live with the fact that my bedroom is an utter wreck.

I don't know how to get Keira to trust me. To love me and *admit* that she loves me. Getting mad at her last night will probably backfire and she'll recede even further into her orderly and neatly squared-off cave.

She needs to realize that love, by its very definition, is chaotic and disorder and not neat. It's messy, it's fun, and sometimes, it's a complete disaster. But you get up, dust off the dirt, and jump back into the sack.

My problem is that I used to equate sex with love. Now I understand the difference.

If Keira and I never have sex but love each other, I think it will be enough for me. No, I don't just *think* it, I *know* it. It would be incredibly difficult not touching her, but if I got to call her mine, I would learn to live that way.

I wonder if I've been giving her the impression that she needs to mold to *me* rather than the other way around. It's my job to get her to fall for me. It's my job to make her realize there's nothing wrong with her, that I adore everything about her, even her crooked baby toes—because they are freakishly crooked.

Now I'm doubting everything I've said and done over the last few days. Did I seem too needy, too controlling, too stupid? Should I march over to Keira's room and apologize until she lets me inside?

I leave my bedroom—I'm not sure what time it is since I yanked the alarm clock's plug from the outlet early on last night—but I feel like she wouldn't have left for work yet. Plus, she would have needed to come into my bedroom and sneak out some clothes.

Her bedroom door is wide open. And it's empty.

Of her.

Of her possessions.

However, her uniforms are still in the closet. I backtrack and spot the duffle bag and two suitcases near the door. But there's no sign of Keira. I even check the bathroom. Nothing.

Then I find a slip of paper on the counter. When I read it, my heart skips a beat and a sense of dread builds up and spreads throughout my body.

"Dillan," it reads, "I'm sorry about last night. Everything is my fault. You've been wonderful throughout this entire ordeal and I hope that one day you'll forgive me. I've loved you since I was an eighteen-year-old girl. I thought I knew everything then. I thought I had it all figured out. I'm sure you can see where this is going.

"I knew nothing of myself, of love, of the world. As a young girl, I planned to join the military, travel the world, and become some sort of romantic heroine. I had it mapped out and everything. Sometimes dreams and reality don't match up and I found myself more and more disillusioned with my choices.

"I thought I would be James Bond, tracking the bad guys and meeting others in secret hangouts. Stupid, yes. Maybe someone out there actually does those things, but not me. When I met you, some of my priorities changed. I wanted to impress you. I was willing to let go of my dreams to be with a man. Desperation clung to me. Do you know how wrong that is? To change everything about yourself to make someone else happy?

"I was disgusted with myself. I saw how happy my parents were—sometimes I didn't know where one parent began and the other ended, they were so similar—but I also knew how conflicted and unhappy Jon was in love. Ever since then, I've always felt that to love someone meant you had to give up a piece of yourself in order to make it work. That wasn't going to happen to me. No way. No how. It took me several years to realize that it wasn't a physical thing that needed to be given up, but that I would need to make room in order to let someone in.

"Even that seemed like too much work. How does one do that? Make room? It didn't even seem possible. Would I have to let go of something in order to gain something? Yes. I have to let go of my fear. My fear of you, of love, of rejection. Of finding out that I've lost myself in you and that one day I'll wake up and not know who I am anymore.

"The joke's on me. A few days ago, I woke up and I didn't know who I was anymore. I *am* lost in you. I am you and I have no idea of how to remedy the situation. Will loving you fix it? I don't think so, because I was in love with you before we swapped, and even as I live in your body, I'm still in love with you. I didn't need to make room to love you. My ability to love grew. Throughout this ordeal, I came to the realization that I *was* worthy of love and that I *wouldn't* lose myself in the process. You see, your Nine Year Crush wasn't one-sided. I felt it, too. I'm too late in telling you this and if we don't change back, it's my fault. I'm sorry, Dillan. I really am. To make up for my stupidity, I have an idea to discuss with you tonight.

"I've already left for work—I snuck in earlier to get clothes out of your bedroom. I have to admit that it was a difficult task since nothing was where it was supposed to be, but I managed, and I'd like to point out that while you may have been snoring, *I* don't actually snore. I plan a kick-ass meeting with the Joy Fromm siblings and I'll meet you at Ellen's tonight at six. I'll fill you in on my crazy idea then. *Ardently Yours*, Keira."

CHAPTER THIRTY

Keira

I step out of the elevator and thrust a small bouquet of yellow and orange flowers at the receptionist, Sheila. The florist assured me that these colors were friendly and not romantic.

Sheila does a double take, drops the phone, and her glasses almost fly off her face. After writing my confession to Dillan this morning, I feel better. Freer. Happier, like I'm finally being who I'm supposed to be, which, all things considered, is sort of odd, given that I'm being myself in someone else's body.

I chuckle when the receptionist refuses to take the flowers.

"Peace offering," I say by way of an explanation. "I'm not sure why we got off on the wrong foot, but I'd like to formally apologize. The fault is surely mine and I could not go one more day without telling you." She takes the flowers from me as if they are about to explode. "Perhaps you can enlighten me as to why I feel like I've been bitten by a snake every time I we come into contact?" I ask as politely as possible. "You know, so I don't repeat the behavior." I give her Dillan's grin, hoping it's enough to convince her, and surprisingly, she smiles.

"My dad warned me about you," she says in a low voice, like maybe she doesn't want others to overhear her.

"Your dad?"

"Yeah, you know, *my dad.* Your boss's boss. I use my mother's maiden name."

No wonder. Dillan had no idea that Sheila was Johnson

Brookshire's daughter. Didn't he date another one of the Brookshire's daughters? Something about an office romance that turned serious, then weird, and then bad when Dillan's boss found out.

Dillan had received the short end of the stick for that one and that was why, according to Dillan, Mr. Brookshire hated him.

"I see," I say, for lack of a better statement. "I'm sorry that it's taken us this long to clear the air. That thing that happened last year, well, that's water under the bridge and all, and there's no need to, ah, repeat history."

Sheila rolls her eyes. "Not interested. I have a serious boyfriend, thank you very much. Listen," she says, a little bit more friendly, "I'm not supposed to say anything, but if you screw up today, and trust me when I say that my dad is really hoping that you do, he's going to fire you. You seem like an all right kind of guy and my sister confided in me not too long ago as to the real story behind *the-summer-that-shall-not-be-mentioned* in our household. Good luck. And," she adds as an afterthought, "thanks for the flowers."

"Mr. Pope," a deep voice behind me says. I turn around. It's Johnson Brookshire. He looks between me, his daughter, the flowers in her hand, and then back at me. "In my office. Now."

Dillan

Finding my way into the Pentagon and to my office is not any easier the second day around. If anything, I must have been so confident in my abilities to navigate the place they called the Puzzle Palace that I got lost. *Loster.* Is that even a word? Probably not, but I'm sticking with it.

I have Keira's letter on my mind and it's difficult to actually pay attention.

When I step inside the big office, the one with the secretary and a multitude of desks, Nebraska's sitting there like he's in trouble for something. The black eye looks darker and I notice that he's favoring his right arm for some reason.

I've decided that if I don't want to get involved, it's best not to ask questions.

So I don't.

"Hey Keira!" Nebraska's face perks up like I'm some sort of salvation for him.

I stop in my tracks and wait.

"Shush, Sergeant Walker," the secretary says. I read the name tag on her desk: Claudette Atkins. She's plump with white-gray hair, light blue eyes, and is about sixty or seventy years old. "Good morning, Staff Sergeant Holtslander," she says to me in a much more pleasant tone. She must like Keira. And I must keep it this way. "The Historical Office of the Office of the Secretary of Defense called about five minutes ago. Seems like you're late for your appointment. I told them that you were already on your way."

Like I know where that is. I might as well go in search

for the lost city of Atlantis.

"Thank you, Mrs. Atkins. I am indeed on my way, as you can tell."

I don't move a muscle. I steal a mint from her desk.

The secretary watches me like a hawk, looking for anything out of the ordinary.

"Oh, that's right. The appointment is *this* morning, Keira?" Nebraska asks with mock confusion. "We better get going, then. I can show her where to go, Mrs. Atkins."

Nebraska stands up, ready to whisk me out of the reception area. I wonder where Justin is. His desk is empty.

"*Sit* down, Sergeant Walker," Mrs. Atkins says in a deathly quiet voice. I have a feeling she could stop a human heart if she wanted to. She also possesses a backbone of steel. "The general has not dismissed you." She turns to me and hands me a slip of paper. "Here's the office number again. Don't forget that you have a zero-nine hundred appointment with General MacWilliams."

Then, without so much as lifting a finger, she kicks me out of the office.

Keira

I follow Mr. Brookshire down the hallway and into a massive corner office that's nothing but floor to ceiling windows. His dark desk is clean and free of most things you might see in a desk, like a monitor, keyboard, and mouse.

He turns as soon as he reaches the desk and leans against the edge. One of his eyes twitches. I'm not surprised when he doesn't offer me a seat in one of the two nicely upholstered leather chairs.

I stand about halfway between his desk and the door.

I'm favoring a quick exit in case he goes bonkers.

"Sheila has a boyfriend," Mr. Brookshire starts, which baffles me as to why he would tell me—Dillan—this. *Doesn't he hate Dillan?* "He's a tattoo artist, and that's what she wants to do with her life as well. I found out *after* I paid for a four-year graphic design and art degree."

"I'm not sure how this is any of my—"

"She has talent. Buckets of it, in fact. But a tattoo artist? Sheila's capable of so much more. I told her that if she worked for me for a year that I'd reconsider helping her buy her own tattoo shop. Of course, my goal was for her to see how prestigious Brookshire Mierkle was and that she'd change her mind about everything. Fucking kids these days. What do you think I should do?"

"Are you seriously asking me?" I don't think I've blinked since I entered his office, and my eyes are starting to water from all the sunlight. Sunlight and shock.

He crosses his arms across his chest.

"You're a hard kid to read, Dillan Pope. Some days,

when I look at you, I see a stupid, lucky-as-shit kid. And other days, like yesterday, I find myself smiling because you've taken charge of a situation like a sergeant at arms. That stunt you pulled yesterday was practically suicidal. It's also something *I* would have done. My youngest daughter; I'm sure you remember Abigail," he says this with one eyebrow expressively higher than the other, "is studying fashion design in New York; my son, Jackson, is a marine biologist; and my oldest, Sheila, wants to be a tattoo artist. It's almost as if my children chose professions that would take them as far away from me as possible. Obviously I don't have a fucking clue. LouAnn swears that you're not as stupid as you look, so, yes, I'm actually asking for your advice."

I feel like this is some sort of twisted job interview.

Answer correctly and move on to the next round.

Answer incorrectly and you get shoved down the garbage shoot and ejected from the building.

How would my own father respond? Or, better yet, how would I answer my dad if he asked me and Jon this question? After a half-minute, I think I might have a good answer.

"What's more important to you, Mr. Brookshire: Happy children doing what *they* love, or miserable children doing what *you* love?"

I see the parallels between the Joy Fromm case and Mr. Brookshire's personal question. Mr. Fromm's children, Amanda and Ken, were eager to work alongside their father, even if that meant the destruction of Fromm's business. Mr. Brookshire's kids wanted nothing to do with their father *or* his industry.

Is this why he passed the case onto Dillan and LouAnn? He didn't want to be reminded of his own failures as a father?

It's a long stretch, but it might be true. It also gives me an idea of how to help Amanda Joy and Ken Fromm while keeping them on the Brookshire Mierkle portfolio.

"You know what they say about fathers, right?" I ask him after it appears he doesn't plan to answer my first question.

"What?"

"A father's job is to give his children wings."

He stares at me for a few seconds.

"Thanks, Dillan," Mr. Brookshire says noncommittally. I can't tell if he means it or not. "The client should be arriving soon. Why don't you go downstairs and meet them in the lobby? I'll ask Sheila to open the conference room."

Dillan

I enter and exit the Historian's office in a matter of minutes. I have no idea why Keira scheduled an appointment with them and they didn't know either, so after a few awkward conversations regarding the weather—remember, I'm now a weather buff—and how the Washington Nationals are doing and whether or not they'll make it to the East Division Series, I leave and start back toward General MacWilliams' office.

On the way, I see someone on an adult-size tricycle. I try to stop them so I can ask where I can buy one, but I suppose running after them and yelling wasn't the best method for achieving the information. But, wow, those things can get up and go.

I can see it now: *Staff Sergeant Keira Holtslander, who happens to be the woman behind the recent scandal regarding Nats pitcher Alec Huffman, was arrested today for harassing a Pentagon mailroom delivery woman for no apparent reason. Find out more tonight during the entertainment portion of the six o'clock news.*

One minute, Keira's a respected soldier, the next she's a walking punch line for entertainment gossips. Let's not let that happen on my watch, especially not after this morning's letter.

I walk through a few more turns, hallways, and corridors and finally arrive at Mrs. Atkins' desk with three minutes to spare for my appointment with the general.

"Mrs. Atkins," I say sweetly. Nebraska's gone and I have yet to see Justin. "Do you know *why* I'm meeting General MacWilliams?"

What I want to ask is if Keira is in trouble. I start moving things on the secretary's desk. The candy tray. A notepad.

She smacks my fingers and puts them back where they were to begin with.

"Sorry," I mutter. Stupid nerves. I'm worried about saying the wrong thing to Keira's boss. What if I screw up the rest of her life?

"The general's just returned from an overseas conference. This is your introductory meeting with him, Sergeant Holtslander." She smiles at me as if she suddenly understands something. "First time meeting a four-star general?"

"Yes, ma'am," I say. It's definitely true in *my* case.

For all I know, Keira routinely hangs out and is on a first name basis with lots of four-star generals.

"Thought so. When you speak to him, speak loudly. He's a bit on the deaf side. Try not to act like you know more than he does, because I can tell you that no one does, and no matter what, don't *ever* try to clean his desk. You keep those three things in mind, you'll do fine, honey."

She hesitates for a second. It doesn't look like she's finished giving me pointers.

"Is there a fourth point, Mrs. Atkins?" I ask.

She smiles knowingly. "You certainly are a smartie. Yes, but I'm afraid it's a point you'll have to discover on your own."

I nod. Someone calls out Keira's name. He's in uniform and the name on his chest says BENSON. I try to find what his rank is, but I don't know what the spread-out bird on his uniform means.

I walk toward him when Mrs. Atkins says, "Colonel Benson, please give this folder to the general. The

President's staff would like him to review it before their thirteen-hundred video teleconference call today."

God, I think, *I can't mess this up for Keira.* If her boss has meetings and video teleconference calls with the President of the United States, then she isn't some regular soldier off the streets.

She's the best of the best.

But then I remember that Nebraska won a bet off the general. If the man's making bets with a goofball like Nebraska, how bad can he be?

Colonel Benson shows me into a busy-looking office. The walls are covered with frames, pictures, plaques, and artwork where a lot of people have signed the matting. The general's desk is just as busy. Multiple piles of folders, books, and stacks of papers sit precariously close to the edge.

A large computer monitor sits smack in the middle. I notice that the base of the monitor sits atop a red dictionary. I suppose this is to elevate the monitor to his eye level.

Pink, yellow, blue, and green Post-it notes are littered everywhere.

How on earth does he find anything?

Some people work well in chaos. I'm sure a four-star general can do more than most. I study the man currently staring at the monitor.

"Would you like something to drink, Sergeant?" General MacWilliams asks me once Colonel Benson walks out and shuts the door. "I've got fresh coffee, soda pop, and those tiny bottles of water." He has a New York accent.

The general is about the same age as his secretary. He's a tall black man with very little hair, a hooked nose, and thin, gray eyebrows above lively eyes. The grin on his face suggests that he always has a joke at the ready.

I laugh a little at the *tiny water bottles* remark and sit down in the chair in front of the cluttered desk.

"Coffee, if you're offering, sir."

Mrs. Atkins was right: I force my fingers *not* to pluck the colorful Post-it notes stuck to the side of the desk. There are a couple near my feet, too.

"I must warn you, Sergeant, that when I make my coffee, it's about as strong as tar. It has the same consistency, too. Still interested?"

"Sounds like a challenge to me. How can I refuse?"

"That's the spirit!" He pours black lava into two Styrofoam cups and hands me one.

I'm slightly worried that the coffee might actually eat through the Styrofoam and attack my hand. Obviously, I've watched way too many old science fiction-horror movies.

With both of his eyebrows at attention, General MacWilliams gives me a pointed look.

He's waiting for me to take a sip.

"Cheers, sir," I say and take a sip. It touches my lips and my body does a little shock-shiver. *The coffee is like a thousand degrees.* "Hmm, good," I say without trying to scream.

I can no longer feel my lips or tongue as I scan the room. I'm hoping to find a place to put the cup, but there's no clear space. The general's desk is way too occupied and the small table next to my chair is more or less a repository for more precariously stacked books.

And of course the trash can is on the *other* side of the room. So I hold onto it like it's the best thing I've ever tasted.

Keira's boss retakes his seat behind the desk, turns his

monitor sideways so he can actually see me, and asks, "So, Staff Sergeant Holtslander, tell me about the letters. What have you discovered so far?"

Leaning forward, I say, "That depends, sir. How fond are you of romance stories?"

"How can I resist such an opening?" the general asks cheerfully.

Keira

After greeting the bickering brother and sister in the lobby, I bring them into the same conference room as yesterday. This time, it's empty—except I notice that a small bouquet of flowers sits at the front-middle of the table. The same flowers I gave Sheila.

I have to admit, it's a nice touch.

"Are you going to show us another blank screen presentation, or do you have another trick up your sleeve?" Ken Fromm asks as we sit down.

"No tricks," I answer. "I want to talk about your father for a moment."

"What about him?" Amanda Joy asks.

"Was he a difficult man to work for?"

"No, he was just the opposite. I think Ken would agree with that," Amanda says.

"So he didn't have a spine or a backbone?" I ask, looking down at Dillan's notes. I'm not really reading anything, I just want to give the impression that I'm asking standard questions.

Ken hisses. "He was not a weak-willed man," he says through clenched teeth.

"I see," I say without much conviction.

"Dad was a master of his domain," Amanda says fiercely. Her face is white, her lips thin and bloodless. "He was firm in his decisions and not easily swayed by others."

She's just as protective of the senior Mr. Fromm as Ken is.

"It would appear that both of you inherited this trait from your father," I say. "It's no wonder you find it difficult to work with each other. Here's what's going to happen. Minus my fee, Brookshire Mierkle will return your retainer. You will not be billed for the remaining three million. I thought I could work with you and turn Joy Fromm into a successful business again, but it cannot be done. Before you storm out of here, I want you to know that this assessment actually comes at the expense of my own job. I can't fix you. Therefore, I'm out of a job. So it's an honest assessment."

"You're giving up on us?" Ken asks me.

It warms my heart that he said the word *us*. So maybe there's something that can be done. I need them to be desperate.

"Brookshire has never lost a client like this before. I mean, you're not even trying, young man," Amanda says. She closes her day planner with a loud snap.

I shrug. "The way I see it, you've already given up on your father's company without any interaction from Brookshire Mierkle. I see little trust or faith between you. You both want to be your father, but you have different leadership styles and different skills. Neither of you is singly qualified to run the company as a whole. I'm sorry, but it has to be said. Now, if the company was uncoupled, so to speak, with one branch concentrating on finance and federal contracts whereas the other specialized in logistics and supplies, then maybe—just maybe—as sister companies, you might stand a chance. Otherwise..." I leave the alternative hanging out there for each of them to imagine the worst-case scenario.

"What role would Brookshire Mierkle take in all of this?" Amanda asks.

"Is Brookshire Mierkle in agreement?" Ken asks at the same time.

Amanda reopens her day planner and appears to be looking at her calendar.

"Mr. Brookshire has given me full authority to do what I will with Joy Fromm. If you want to explore this option, then I'll be with you the entire way. You'll have the full backing of Brookshire Mierkle. If you do not choose this option, then I'll show you to the door, and I'll walk out with you and start my own job search."

The room is silent. It's only a minute, but it feels like it stretches out for an hour.

Am I doing the right thing, or are they going to call my bluff?

In that minute, my self-esteem plummets fourteen floors.

"Ken," Amanda says stiffly. "How does your schedule look for Monday? We can come back in then and work out all the details."

At first, it appears the half-brother might refuse. *Refuse* to answer Amanda. *Refuse* the deal. *Refuse* to breathe, since his face is turning blue.

Finally, he says, "Monday is good. Don't forget that Tanner invited your boys to Thursday's game in Arizona."

"I have it down in my calendar. Jacob and James are looking forward to it."

I feel like I've been thrown a curveball. *There can't be two Tanners in the MLB.*

"Excuse me," I interject, "but are you referring to Tanner Nguyen, Nats shortstop?"

This might be too much of a coincidence.

"Yes," Ken says, his eyes narrowing slightly. "Tanner is my cousin on my mother's side. I don't see how it's relevant."

I feel like celebrating from here to Sunday. I wish we

had established this early on. It would have saved us a lot of time.

"You're probably not going to believe me, but Tanner is one of my best friends."

Dillan

I sit, stunned, with the molten lava still between my hands—even after ten minutes, it's still steaming—as General MacWilliams finishes his own love story, which is to say how he and his wife met forty years ago.

It wasn't something typical, like they met in college or she was his high school sweetheart. No, at eighteen, he had gotten into a fight with one of the boys down the street, both were arrested, and she—his future wife—was one of the precinct's secretaries. Love at first sight, but only on his side.

"I tried to find ways of getting arrested just to see her, Staff Sergeant Holtslander," General MacWilliams says with a hearty laugh. "I got arrested so many times that summer that the judge said it was prison or the Army. I think you know which I chose. It took a couple of years of wearing her down, but I'm a persistent chap, and thirty-five years ago, she made me the happiest man alive." He pulls out an ancient wallet and shows me pictures of his kids from when they were in grade school. "She gave me five kids. Most of them were rotten—they were just like me—but they grew out of it. All but one joined up. I may have the stars on my chest, but my wife wears the pants. So if she ever calls and you answer the phone, it's best if you tread carefully. In fact, it's probably best if you don't answer the phones. Leave that to Mrs. Atkins. She knows how to handle Mrs. MacWilliams. The secretary out there is probably the reason I'm still married," he laughs. "So, now tell me about the letters."

I look down at the coffee. It's bubbling. *How is that*

even possible? I'm still hoping to find a place to put it, but I've given up on that quest, and I'm sure as hell not going to drink it now.

Not with the bubbling.

I inform the general of my basic assessment, about how William and Greta are more or less pen pals, and how, once it reaches 1957, their communication is more affectionate and headed in a romantic direction.

"While I have many more letters to sort through, I'm of the opinion, at this point, that there is no classified information contained in the letters. This may change in the future letters. I can only give you my current assessment. William and Greta have graduated into emotional topics, such as feelings, family, and opinions on events of the day, whereas before, their text centered on the weather, more weather, the 1956 Summer Olympics, and non-opinionated cultural events. If the progression continues, I fully suspect that by the end of the letters, they will have declared their love for one another. I'm curious to know what became of them."

"What do you mean, *became of them?*" General MacWilliams asks.

Someone knocks on his door and Mrs. Atkins pops in. "I have the CENTCOM Commander on the phone, sir. Says it's urgent."

I stand up. It's obviously my cue to leave.

"Where are you going, Holtslander?" he asks me gruffly.

"Apologies, sir, I thought you would need privacy before taking the call," I say.

"You do not leave until I dismiss you." He turns to Mrs. Atkins. "Tell General Zimmerman I'll be with him in one minute."

My face turns red as Mrs. Atkins, who was pointedly

staring at my cup of coffee, closes the door.

"I was caught up in the story, General," I say. "Please accept my apologies."

"Sergeant, nothing can top a good love story in my mind. Now tell me: *became of them...* What do you mean by the question?"

"I wonder if they end up together or if something bad happened. You must admit that it is strange, and perhaps tragic, that both sets of letters are together."

"Strange, yes. Tragic, no. I see that Colonel Benson did not convey everything to you. William and Greta married in 1957 and had nine children. Unfortunately, William died in 2003. Greta lives in a nursing home in Silver Spring, Maryland. However, your mission has not changed. I still need to know why the letters were hidden away in a wall of the Pentagon, why they were together, and if they passed classified information back and forth."

"Will do."

"Dismissed." He picks up the phone just as I leave his office. I close the door behind me.

I can't wait to tell Keira everything about William and Greta. She still has work to do. I don't care how we fix this thing with Ellen, but come hell or high water, we have to swap tonight or live in each other's bodies for the rest of our lives. I, for one, have no interest in being in the Army. I'm not cut out for this shit. Every muscle in my body hurts from sitting stiffly in the general's office.

Mrs. Atkins offers me a kind smile. Her gaze shifts to the cup of coffee I'm cradling carefully. She pulls something out from under her desk. A trash can.

"You're an angel, Mrs. Atkins," I say with immense relief. I'm sure I would have found a place to discard the coffee, but there's something reassuring about her pulling it out from under her desk for me. "I'm guessing the fourth point was don't accept the coffee?"

"You got it. He's proud of that stuff. I have to line this sucker with ten heavy-duty trash bags because he's the only one that can drink that goop. Go and put a little ice on your lips. The bottom one's looking a bit puffy."

CHAPTER THIRTY-ONE

Keira

Somehow I manage to make it through the day without getting fired by Johnson Brookshire. After my meeting with Amanda Joy and Ken Fromm, LouAnn took me to Old Ebbitt Grill for lunch, and she celebrated by drinking two glasses of wine.

I had water. While she talked, I tried to look like I was listening, but my mind was mostly focused on tonight. On my conversation with Dillan. Several of the waitresses acted like they knew Dillan, but with my success with the Joy Fromm siblings and my optimistic feelings about tonight, I wasn't about to let jealousy dampen my mood.

"I already know how I'm going to decorate his office once he resigns," LouAnn boasts after the second glass. "And you're coming with me, kiddo. I don't know how you did it, Dillan. I even had an empty box waiting for you in my office in case everything went to shit." She stops what she's doing and looks at me closely. "It may be the wine talking right now, but when I look at you, it's almost like I'm looking at someone else. I thought you had green eyes, Dillan."

LouAnn shakes her head, takes another bite of her salad, and moves our one-sided conversation in another direction. Something about how she plans to fire half of the fourteenth floor.

I thought you had green eyes, Dillan. He does, and his eyes are brilliant and deep, and all I want, more than anything else, is to see his eyes look at me. The real me.

I watch LouAnn eat, I see the wine glass go back and

forth to her lips, and I hear the muted sounds of the restaurant around me, and I know something's different.

Whatever it is, it isn't earth shattering. It feels more like a gentle shift in balance, like a small part of me—of Keira—is fading out. I don't know how else to explain it. Is this part of Ellen's plan? Is something of Dillan's true nature coming back into his body?

I wonder if my letter has anything to do with this? For all I know, in five minutes my mind will travel outside of Dillan's body and jump back into mine. What will my body be doing right now? I'm pretty sure my appointment with General MacWilliams has already happened. I think I was supposed to meet with the Historian's office. Internally, I sigh. I forgot to tell Dillan about that.

Checking the watch at my wrist, I groan. I have hours to go before I see Dillan tonight.

Dillan

The waiting is killing me. I keep checking the clock on the wall, but it sure as hell isn't moving any faster. In fact, I'm pretty sure the ticking hands are moving slower on purpose.

"If you keep looking at it, Keira, I have a feeling the clock will develop a complex." It's Justin. I didn't hear him come inside the secure office. He's sporting a bruised jaw and his uniform looks extremely wrinkled, like he just came back from a wrestling match. With a bear.

I don't know how soldiers are supposed to look, or act, or what most of them do day in and day out, but most of the military in the Pentagon, from what I've seen over the last two days, do not look like how Justin looks right now.

"I guess I'm a little on edge," I say. I place the letter I was reading down on the desk.

It's the last letter, and I can positively answer one of General MacWilliams' questions. However, now that I know the outcome, that William and Greta got married but that William died in 2003, it turns on some sort of emotional switch within me. I'm happy *and* sad.

Mixed in with all of this is my lack of patience. I want it to be six o'clock already.

Justin looks at the empty box. I've stacked the letters I've read in another set of containers next to the desk.

"You're a fast reader. What are your initial thoughts?"

"I know why the letters are together. And, to be honest, I don't think I've ever read anything this romantic. Like, *real* romance, Justin. An ocean couldn't keep these two souls apart, though it took something of a misunderstanding to bring them together. In one of the last letters, Greta talks about her past. She was orphaned during World War II and lived a nomadic, almost gypsy-style life before finding work at a German canteen when she turned eighteen. She confesses that, in late 1952, when she met an American soldier—William—stationed at the time at the new United States European Command in Frankfurt, she found an opportunity to better her life."

I look up at Justin, who's still standing near the door but takes a step closer to the desk. I ask if he understands what I mean.

"Her intentions were self-serving at first? She wanted to marry an American soldier to leave her home country?" Justin asks. He looks at the letter on the desk with interest.

"Exactly, and *Ardently Yours,* William, who wasn't exactly a *wet-behind-the-ears* kid, but a soldier with ten years of service, probably wasn't thrilled about that. But..." I pause for effect. "There's a twist."

"I'm all ears," Justin says with a smile.

I pick up the last letter and read it aloud, *"My dearest William, my last letter must have been unhappy in your hands since I have yet to receive your reply. I will not, I cannot, take back my words. I must seem deceitful in your eyes. Please know that it was only because, when I first met you, that I knew I was destined to be with you. It was during our exchanges that I fell in love with your warmth, your kindness, and I cherished every word you wrote to me. It is because of my love for you that I can admit my actions were, at first, less than honorable. I regret that this will be my last letter to you. No doubt you have noticed that I have returned your letters to you as well. I cannot bear to look upon them without another part of my soul breaking. As I close this letter, please know that I will always be Affectionately Yours, Greta."*

"Ouch," Justin cringes.

From the letter's envelope, I pull out an aged, yellowing card and place it facing away from me so that Justin can see it clearly.

He picks it up and grins. "It's an airline ticket from New York to Frankfurt, Germany."

"He didn't write back because he was on his way to her."

Then something else falls out of the envelope that changes everything.

Keira

LouAnn forces me to return to the office with her. Even though it looks like it will rain any second now, we still walk the entire way. The wind picks up.

Her Blackberry has buzzed twenty-three times since we left the restaurant. I know this because she gave the phone to me and I had to read her e-mails out loud to her.

Twenty-two of the messages are congrats messages. Apparently, five minutes ago, Johnson Brookshire announced his retirement and confirmed that LouAnn Britton would take over the company. Mr. Brookshire was taking a much-needed vacation with his family. I smile, wondering if my words had any affect on the man.

The twenty-third message was from a guy named Terry Richmond. It only read BITCH in bold letters.

"Serves him right," LouAnn says, laughing her head off. "After his hair transplant last year, it looked like a pubic mound had attacked him. Can't have that disaster running the company. It is a family company, after all."

I need to remind Dillan to never cross his boss.

"You're still coming with me, right, kiddo?" LouAnn asks. Even with the wine and the bold laughter and her joyous mood, I sense the doubt in her expression. It's brief, though.

"Up to the office? Yes, I'm coming up with you." *If only to at least carry the Blackberry.* I can't have her firing half of the fourteenth floor five minutes into her new position.

"Don't be dense, Dillan." She punches the elevator's up button. We're alone as it goes up. "With me. As in, you get promoted, too. It comes with a twenty-thousand-dollar pay increase."

At first, I'm shocked. Just how much money does Dillan earn in a year? LouAnn's Blackberry continues to buzz and she takes my silence as a lack of affirmation.

"Thirty thousand," she states as we pass the tenth floor.

That's almost my entire yearly salary as a staff sergeant in the Army. I shake my head in disbelief, but there must be something of Dillan left in his own body because I blurt out, "Fifty thousand."

"That's my boy," LouAnn says wickedly as we exit the elevator. She sneers at Sheila, who sneers back, and I follow LouAnn to her office. That's when I notice that *she* has her Blackberry. I don't remember giving it back to her.

It's *my* phone that's been vibrating since we entered the elevator. Checking the missed calls, I see that Dillan has called me repeatedly. I call him back.

"What's up, Dillan?" I ask, and realize too late that I said that in front of LouAnn. She stops just short of her office, turns, and studies me as if she's never seen this version of Dillan before.

"I found something you need to see," Dillan says. Through the phone, he sounds out of breath. "Can you meet me at Ellen's in fifteen minutes?"

My heart does a little flip. He must have found something that will change us back.

"Yes. I'll see you then," I say, and end the call. "Got to run, LouAnn. Congrats on the promotion. I'll see you in the morning."

Her expression never changes as she closes the gap between us. "You've been acting very strange lately, Dillan." Her statement comes out calmly, casually, but I feel undercurrents of electricity beneath her words. She inspects every inch of my face, my eyes, my nose, everything.

After a silent, tense moment—for me, at least—she takes a step back. She knows something's different. *But who on earth would guess correctly?*

"Must be the wine and the fact that you're looking at the most powerful woman in the building. Get out of here. I have a feeling there's a girl mixed up in whatever's going on with you. In fact, take the rest of the week off."

Dillan

After the photo fell out of the envelope, I knew that I had seen it before. At Ellen's. I get to the Corner Bakery before Keira does and when the door opens easily, I'm a little dumbfounded and walk in.

I thought for sure I would have to pound on the door for her to let me in.

Strangely, not much looks different from how it did before. Ellen was remodeling the bakery, right? I see the same chairs and tables in the front of the store, the same decorative elements on the wall, and the same counter displays. Movement from behind the chilled glass display counter catches my attention.

Someone's loading food onto white shelves.

"You're early," a small voice says. "The celebration doesn't begin until six."

I try to see who is talking, but it sounds like it belongs to a small girl. Ellen's granddaughter, maybe. A blonde head pops up from behind the glass display counter. She looks about ten.

"Is Ellen here?" I ask.

"Oma's in the back."

"Oma?"

"Ellen is my grandmother. My *oma.* That's the German word for grandmother."

I'm happy to hear that. I smile and advance toward the counter. It has something that interests me. From my notebook, I pull out the photo that fell from the envelope, the photo that made me pick up the phone and call Keira a dozen times.

On the counter sits a black-and-white photo of an American soldier and his young bride. I place my photo beside it. A small laugh escapes. It's the same photo.

Now, why would Ellen have this exact photo? And on her counter, no less?

Behind me, the front door dings open and Keira rushes in, but stops. She chose my second-most expensive blazer, a plaid shirt, no tie, and black trousers. My eyes hurt after looking at her. She wasn't kidding, in her letter, that she had to sneak out clothes.

She snuck the *wrong* clothes. It's a testament of my love for her that I do not immediately make fun of her.

Keira stays near the door. She wants to know how I feel about *her* letter.

"Stay there, Keira," I say gently.

She looks terrified of showing me how she feels. All I know is that I'm tired of running from her instead of running toward her. It takes me longer to get to her than I thought it would—Keira has shorter legs—but when I'm in front of her, I'm happy.

I'm happier than I've been in a long time.

I don't care what form I'm in. We both could be slug worms for all I care and as long as I am with her, I'd be the happiest slug worm in the world.

"Do you hate me?" she asks quietly.

"Never," I say.

"I'm sorry for everything."

"There's nothing to be sorry for," I say. "Here." I hand her the photo, but she looks confused.

Her expression says, *Why are you showing me a photo and how can it change us back?*

I bring her up to speed on the letters, including how and why the letters ended up together, and then, once we get to the counter, I point out the framed photo at the counter.

"Oh, my God," Keira says. She looks back and forth between the photo in her hand and the one on the counter. "This can't be true..." She trails off.

"Hello Keira. Hello Dillan," Ellen says as she comes out from the back of the bakery. She looks at the object in Keira's hand. "I see that you found the photo of my parents, William and Greta Hall."

Keira

Ellen unties her apron and comes around to our side of the bakery. I notice a small girl standing behind the counter.

"Oma," the girl says, slowly. "Please tell me that you haven't gone and done *it* again?"

Ellen chuckles. "My granddaughter is something else. For some reason, she thinks her *oma* is a witch." She turns to the girl and says something in German. The girl storms away in a huff.

Ellen directs us to a purple table outfitted with turquoise chairs. As we take our seats, Ellen's granddaughter returns and loads food into the chilled glass display counter. The scent of baked apple pie hangs in the air.

"Coffee?" Ellen asks us.

We both answer *no* so fast that I think we gave the speed of light a run for its money.

Ellen laughs again. "They had quite a love story, didn't they? He married her the same day he landed in Frankfurt. He didn't even change out of his uniform before he left his job, signed out on leave with the base commander, bought a ticket at the airport, and boarded the plane." She takes the photo from my hand and stares at the image. "My mother, in her earlier years, was a Gypsy. She is something of a witch, or, if not that, then she has a touch of enchantment in her. She has always been a romantic and she passed that on to me, too. It's tough to resist a good love story."

She looks between me and Dillan, as if to illustrate her point.

"Is that why you swapped us?" I ask. "You wanted to see another happily ever after, or something like that?"

"Well," she says, slightly more seriously. "From the look of things, the fact that you haven't changed back yet, I don't know if this story ends up a happy one. Dillan, you've been on my radar for several years. I've been waiting to find your match, and she didn't show up until you, Keira, stormed into his life and turned it completely upside down. The electricity between the two of you was so charged that morning that I couldn't ignore it." She observes us quietly for a few seconds, then she touches our hands. "Nothing's changed on that front. The electricity is still there."

"How much more time do we have?" Dillan asks.

Ellen removes her hands, but Dillan moves in and takes mine. A smile spreads on Ellen's face.

"It varies. It isn't a precise charm. I had hoped you would have changed back by now. You two..." She clicks her tongue. "You two are probably my most stubborn pair. I sense there are a few loose ends that you first need to tidy up. While you're early, I'll get some food in your bellies. I hope you'll stay for my little get-together, but, if you don't..." She winks.

Ellen stands up. There's no way I'm letting her off this easy.

"That doesn't explain the letters or the photo or how all of it ended up hidden away in a wall for years."

"Oh, about that." She chuckles as if it's of no consequence. "My dad, after he had been promoted to colonel, worked for the Secretary of Defense many, *many* years ago. He brought the letters to show a friend who was something of a historian. As the story goes, this friend was going to catalogue the letters and include the story in a book he was writing about American soldiers marrying German girls. Well, my mother, the little minx that she was, wasn't having any of that. He might have gotten the letters out of the house and into his office at the Pentagon, but my mother wasn't about to let anyone *read* them. Her last letter to him still mortifies her to this day." Ellen smiles. "I was fifteen years old when she created some sort of charm to hide the box. She said it worked, but I always wondered what became of them. Now, I know."

I take a deep breath.

Her explanation would sound ridiculous if she hadn't already displayed her knack for creating her own charms. As it stands, I can't challenge her answer. On the other hand, I certainly cannot use it in my report to my boss.

So now I know *why* the letters were grouped together and *how* they ended up in a wall of the Pentagon.

I'm fairly optimistic that nothing classified was revealed in the letters. But I still owe an answer to General MacWilliams on that front and I won't be able to fulfill that obligation until I can read the letters myself.

I should be upset that Dillan removed the photo from the general's secure office, but, interestingly enough, I'm not.

"It's a strange coincidence that your parents' letters turn up in the course of my military duties," I tell Ellen before she can get too far. "In fact, it's the only reason I'm even up here in Washington, DC."

"A strange coincidence, indeed," she says with a coy smile.

I really don't like being played with, and that's how I feel right now.

"Were you somehow involved in *that*?"

Ellen returns to the table. "I can only do so much,

Keira. Something like *that* is beyond my abilities. If you want to know my opinion, I'd call it *fate.* If I were you, I wouldn't get in fate's way."

Dillan

I'm still holding her hand. Keira hasn't pulled away, even as Ellen retreats to the back of her bakery. Someone—probably Ellen—turns on some music, and the sounds of cleaning, cooking, baking, and other innocuous noises waft in and out after the granddaughter brings us a plate loaded with pastries, cookies, and a lone piece of apple pie.

"I don't see what the problem is," the girl says emphatically. Her hands are on her hips and she looks at us like we are a pair of idiots. "Oma doesn't do the swap thing unless she's sure about it. She's never failed. Which one of you is the dimwit?" She squints and looks at Keira. "Interesting."

"What's interesting?" Keira asks defensively. The look on her face tells me that she's annoyed with herself for being annoyed at a ten-year-old.

"Normally it's the guy who screws up everything. You'll have company soon. Anyone who's ever received one of Oma's charms shows up for the anniversary party."

The girl skips away and I turn to Keira. "I don't know if things can get any weirder."

I'm still holding her hand. For some reason, I'm scared that she will pull away. I don't know if I can handle her rejection right now.

"Yeah, I know." She nibbles on one of the plainer pastries. If she's feeling anything like I am, then she won't have much of an appetite.

"About your letter," I say. She stops chewing. "You said you had a crazy idea..."

She looks relieved, like she's glad I didn't bring up what

the rest of the letter said.

Keira turns to me. "After I wrote the letter, I honestly thought we would change back. Nothing happened. I felt a few things throughout the day. Little *odd* things that told me maybe we were in the process of changing back. Probably wishful thinking on my part. Okay...here's my idea. Take it or leave it." She takes a fortifying breath. "We have to acknowledge that we may not swap back. And if it doesn't happen, then neither of us will ever be happy. But I think we can be happy...together. Like this. As the other. We'll get used to being this way and if we're together, then we won't have to worry about slipping up. I guess what I'm saying is that I...*I want to be with you.* I'll love you from *this* body."

Something inside of me soars. Keira wants to be with me. *Can we make it work?* We'll have to.

"Will we be together in *every* sense of the word?" I croak out this question.

I'm actually afraid of both answers. If *yes*, then I've lost every bit of skill I've gained over the years. We might as well be virgins. If *no*, then I know it will kill me to live with her, be with her, but not be *with* her. *But Keira is worth it.* She clears her throat and tightens her hand in mine.

"Yes, Dillan. In every way. I'm yours. You're mine. I'm in love with you, no matter what."

Everything inside of me warms. I feel feverish, hot, excited. Heat spreads down lower and I want nothing more than to lie naked with her.

"Do you think Ellen will mind if we leave?" I ask. I need to be with Keira, and I need us to be alone.

I watch as she swallows hard. She's affected, too.

"Let's get out of here," she says.

CHAPTER THIRTY-TWO

Keira

Things are very uncomfortable *downstairs*. The stiff and erect sort of uncomfortable.

I grab Dillan's hand and we run back to the apartment, laughing all the way. The gray sky opens and it begins to rain like crazy. The faster we get to our apartment, the better.

Dillan, in my body, still runs faster than I do, but I don't care. We dash into the lobby of the apartment building and gain the attention of every eyeball presently available. I laugh harder. I wonder if I'll regret any of this tomorrow. God, I hope not. I don't want to regret anything from this point forward.

Inside the elevator, our wet bodies collide into each other, but we don't do more than that. I have a feeling once we start, we won't stop, and I don't want our first time to be in an elevator.

The hallway to the apartment seems to stretch out and double in length. It's like a math equation: wanting *something* plus the time it takes to get *that* something is always *twice* as long as previously expected.

Then the key is in the lock and the door is thrust open by both our hands, and it slams behind us, and Dillan, on tiptoes, presses me against the door, and his lips crash on mine. My body digs into his and my erection throbs and my ears ring and my hands pull him harder into me.

His fingers scramble at the jacket, the shirt, and I help him. Buttons fly, the wet jacket is flung, and we stumble over to his room, kissing, moaning, begging for more.

"I want you so much, I might burst," he says once we reach his bedroom door. We look inside and remember that his room is a mess. We'd kill ourselves trying to get in there. "Your room?" he asks.

"Yes."

then we are going to go all the way.

"Oh, my God," she whispers, kissing me harder. Her fingers rake my back. She pulls at my wet hair. "That feels incredible."

Keira

Dillan's hands are scorching hot. When he touches me *there*, I know there's no going back. It feels intense, incredible, and erotic. Honestly, I have no idea how we are going to manage this. I feel like a fumbling teenager again, learning the ropes of sex.

I find it interesting—and fitting—that at eighteen, I wanted to lose my virginity to Dillan. Now, at twenty-seven, I get to experience a different sort of *first time* with him.

"I apologize for this in advance," he says mischievously.

"Whaaaaa..." I ask, just as he pushes me down on the bed, straddles me, and locks his lips on mine. Our bodies fit together perfectly. "You are so evil," I say, laughing.

I feel his heat touching me, touching the core of him, and instinctively I thrust up.

The tip of this throbbing erection, maybe an inch, I'm not sure, slips in and then back out, and cascades of pleasure ripple through me so fast that I can barely breathe.

Dillan moans in my ear and I swear it's the sexiest thing I've ever heard. Some other emotion builds up in me. Power. Lust. Control. Possessiveness.

"And I apologize in advance for this," I say heatedly. I clasp my arms around Dillan and roll us over so that I'm now on top. His hair has come undone and wet strands splay every which way on the pillow. His legs are wide open, his hips reaching, thrusting—I know my own body's signs—and I say, "It's about time I admit that I'm in love with you, Dillan."

I hear his quick intake of breath.

"I'm in with love you, too, Keira."

It shatters my insides when he says it.

Dillan's body knows what to do, but I'm the wrong person to drive it. I think I'm in the right spot when I push.

"A little more to the left, Keira," he says with a chuckle.

"Sorry." I try again, laughing. I reposition my arms.

"Uh, now you're too low." Dillan shifts. "*Way* too low." He makes an odd face and I laugh-snort. "You're a terrible aim, Keira."

I can't stop laughing. He reaches between us and moves Dillan's package into the correct position. Suddenly everything fits and my laughter abruptly stops.

I suck in air.

The tip of me slides in.

Slowly.

Wickedly.

Sinfully.

Everything there is hot, wet, and tight, and it's like he's pulling me in.

When I'm all the way in, it feels like I'm already sweating. I'm on my elbows, above Dillan, and my muscles are contracted to keep me from crushing him. But Jesus, it's the sweetest feeling I've ever experienced.

"I had no idea it could be like this, Dillan." And I'm not just talking about the sex.

He swallows hard. "Me, neither."

Dillan

Heat builds and I moan as she slides in. Our bodies fit perfectly, and when her lips lock on mine and she thrusts in and out a little bit, I feel like I'm on fire.

The problem is that we have zero rhythm.

"I have no idea of what I'm doing," Keira says, her voice a combination of humor and lust.

"It still feels good, though," I say, sucking on her neck. "Do a slow rocking movement." When she goes in deep during the next thrust, I actually do a scream-moan. I clap a hand over my mouth. "I can't believe I just did that. That's so porno."

She thrusts like that again, and again, and again, and each time, I scream in pleasure.

"I've never been a screamer before," Keira says. "I don't care who hears us, Dillan." She molds her body to mine and seems to find a good rhythm. The bed rocks, I moan into her ears. She moans into mine. I've never experienced pleasure like this. I never knew the full feeling, the emotional closeness of this before. I've had sex, lots of it, but I've never made love.

Not until Keira.

Something builds, it spreads, it's hot, it's intense, and without warning, an earth-shattering climax crashes through me. Keira's lips find mine when it happens.

Keira

Dillan shakes beneath me, climaxing, and it sets me over the edge. There's no way I can hold anything back. I have no experience. He holds me tightly as he comes down from his high.

I thrust again. He moans.

"I'm afraid I'm going to hurt you if I keep going," I say.

"And I'll hurt you if you stop," he jokes.

I press myself as close as possible to Dillan and kiss him, and I move. It's deep, it's shallow, it's fast, and it's slow, and hearing his moans combined with mine and knowing that he loves me and that I return his love fills me so soundly, so completely.

It starts slow, the pressure, the build-up, and it ramps up with each thrust. I don't know where the pleasure begins or ends. All I know is that an overpowering feeling explodes inside me. I yell out something incoherent—gibberish, probably—as the pleasure washes over me. In equal parts, I'm sure I'm either dying or hallucinating, because I've never felt anything like this before.

It takes me a second to realize I've crashed on top of Dillan.

"You're crushing me," he says with a laugh. I move and lay beside him, panting.

"That...was...amazing," I say. "Man want woman," I say in a caveman voice as I pull in him into me. I reach in for a kiss and I'm promptly rewarded. "On a scale of one to ten, I'd say my performance was easily a ten."

He thumps me on the chest and I laugh out loud.

"I loved every second of it, Keira," Dillan says. "I love

you. I have loved you for so long."

I smile into his kiss. "It took us long enough, didn't it? I meant what I said in the letter. I had to learn that loving you didn't *also* mean giving myself up. There's more of me because I love you. I'm not different, but I'm not the same. I feel happier than I've felt in, oh, forever. Thank you for being patient with me. We can work through this, can't we? I mean, we'll figure it out as we go."

"We have all night to practice," he says, kissing me. I feel breasts against my arm.

"You know what I mean." I feel the stirrings of another erection.

"Yes, I did. But your body knew what *I* meant," he laughs as he crawls on top of me and proceeds to blow my mind.

Dillan

I don't know if I'll ever the hang of being a female after our third round of sex. Things are *sore.* My inner thighs refuse to obey even the simplest of commands, like moving or walking to the bathroom.

Even shifting in bed hurts.

"Does it ever quit?" Keira asks me, pointing down to her fourth erection. She's pushing it with her finger.

"It's never been with the girl he loves. Cut him a little slack," I say sleepily. "It will go down after a few minutes." I snuggle in close and in a matter of minutes, I'm fast sleep.

I'm not sure what wakes me. It's dark outside, I feel Keira's warm body pressed next to mine, and I smile contently. I nearly fall back asleep.

Then I realize Keira isn't just lying next to me, she's on her side, propped up on her elbow, and, with the fingers of her free hand, it feels like she's writing words into my chest.

I stay still for a moment, trying to figure out what she's writing.

Wake. Up. Dillan.

"I'm awake," I say groggily. I pull her in close. She seems...smaller.

Curvier.

I think I feel her long hair tickling my chest.

She flattens her hand, moves it across my chest—my flat chest—and then walks her fingers down.

Down.

Down.

Her hand wraps around me, around an erection attached to me.

The real me.

To Dillan Pope.

I'm over the moon. And the fact that Keira is next to me means I'm double over the moon.

"Guess what?" she asks. She starts to move her hand in a coordinating manner. It's hard to concentrate.

I pretend to play along. My smile is so big, my mouth nearly refuses to obey me when I say, "What?"

"It worked."

"What worked?"

She growls at me, grabs my hand, and places it against her breast. I chuckle, lean up, and kiss her. I remember that before I fell asleep, every part of *my female anatomy* was sore, so I don't press for more than kissing.

"I certainly did a number on myself," she says. "I can barely move."

"Keira, I love you," I say seriously. I want to say it over and over again but I have a feeling she'd kick me out of bed. "I want you to promise me one thing."

"Hm, what's that?" She nuzzles into me.

"Don't ever let me eat four hot dogs, okay? The results aren't pretty."

Keira laughs and hits me with the pillow. If she still loves me after bringing up *that* embarrassing moment, I'm golden.

CHAPTER THIRTY-THREE

Keira

In the morning, as Dillan sleeps in—I informed him that LouAnn gave him the rest of the week off—I dress and head into work. Surprisingly, there isn't much for me to fix over the last two days.

The general's already off on another official trip, the secretary says a few jokes about the general's coffee that I don't quite understand and how my lips still look swollen.

I'd say they're swollen from kissing Dillan for about four hours total since last night, but I'm understanding the gist of the meaning to be that the general's coffee is somehow responsible.

I'm not about to disillusion her of this thought even though it makes zero sense.

I make it through the day by reading as many of the letters as possible and I skip ahead. The last letter breaks my heart, but now that I know the outcome, I'll be happy to report to the general that there was no classified information passed in the letters.

During lunch, I see Justin and Aaron, their heads close together as they discuss something only the two of them can hear, and I'm reminded of Jon and Tanner.

I write myself a note to call Tanner and to e-mail Jon later. Only they really know the details of their relationship, but if part of their argument was about me and Dillan, I feel like it's only right to inform them of the new development.

Later in the day, Colonel Benson pulls me aside.

"I wanted to let you know that a full-time billet has

opened up in the Army G2 staff. Lieutenant General Patricia Martin, the Army's top intelligence officer, is interested in having you join her team when you've completed General MacWilliams' investigation. Human Resources Command is cutting your orders this week. Luckily, you won't have to move far, since the Army G2 is one floor above us. Congratulations, Staff Sergeant."

As the colonel moves away, I notice that Justin, Aaron, and Nebraska are within listening distance.

"You know what this means, right?" Nebraska asks.

I do a double take.

Nebraska has a black eye and his arm is in a sling. I look at Justin. He has a bruise on his jaw. Aaron, who I gather is more or less the sensible person in the group, looks normal. Gorgeous, yes. But normal.

I know that Justin is highly trusted by the Chief of Staff of the Army. So he and his friends must not be doing anything illegal. My mind goes to James Bond and spy stuff.

Do *they* do that kind of stuff?

Do I know what this means? "You get to ask me to Tuesday Night Trouble?" I ask.

"Man you're good," Nebraska says and hands a twenty-dollar bill to Aaron.

I laugh as we leave the suite. I spot someone riding one of those adult-size tricycles.

"Let me ask you guys a question." Three sets of eyes look at me. "How do I get my hands on one of those?"

I point at the receding figure.

Dillan will look utterly ridiculous riding a gigantic tricycle, but my love for him has opened up all sorts of ridiculous possibilities. Looking up at my friends, I seem to be in the right company.

Nebraska puts his heavy arm around my shoulders.

"I think that this calls for another bet with General MacWilliams," he says cheerfully.

Behind us, Justin and Aaron just groan.

Dillan

The walk from *my* bedroom door to *her* bedroom door is like three light years away. We can't get there fast enough, and it doesn't help that we trip over the coffee table.

Keira's room seems smaller with both of us in it. Or maybe it's because I feel bigger around her. She smells like rain and sex.

Her hair is wet. She's wearing my pants and not much else. I'm still wearing *everything.*

"This is a problem," I say, before crashing right back into her. I feel her smile beneath my lips. Yes, technically I'm kissing myself. Screw it. I don't give a shit anymore.

I've never wanted someone as much as I want Keira. Every second I'm not touching her is agony for me.

I pull off my shirt, the bra—which doesn't come off fast enough, so I rip it off—the pants, everything, and I watch as Keira removes her pants, and within a few seconds, we're naked in front of each other.

And we don't know where to begin or what to do. From this point, it feels like things move in slow motion.

Her—my—erection is evident. Her eyes are dark and heavy with arousal. I'm feeling heavy down *there.*

"We'll figure this out together, all right?" I say.

I feel like a virgin. Clumsy and all knees and elbows.

"Okay," she says.

I lean into her, our clammy, wet skin touching, and I reach up to kiss her while I let my hand lightly travel down her chest, her stomach, and then, with an intake of breath, I gently palm the erection. I won't do much more than that, but I need her to know that if we're going to do this,

Dillan

I wake up a man. I shower like a man. I finally get to take a dump like a man. It feels good being back in my body.

Keira wrote another note this morning. "P.S. I'm not moving out. Deal with it. Love, Keira."

She could have written *eat shit, love, Keira*, and I probably would have been okay with it because it had *love, Keira* at the end.

I put Keira's suitcases and duffle bag back in the guest bedroom even though I don't actually plan to let her sleep in that room ever again.

But first, I have to put my room back together. Thank God we didn't come in here last night. We would have broken our necks just trying to make it to the bed.

I chuckle as I think about last night, our fumbling, our excitement.

We had no idea going in that we'd swap back. Well, I think Keira hoped for it.

I was just happy being near her.

Later, I try to play *NFL Pro*, only to realize everything I've saved and built up over the last year was somehow lost. Odd. Oh well. I doubt I'll have time to play video games anyway. I get a few texts from people at work congratulating me on LouAnn's and my promotions.

Then, after lunch, LouAnn calls me and asks me what I'm going to spend my raise on.

"I'm taking Keira out for dinner," I say, not thinking that the raise is anything significant.

"That must be some dinner, kiddo. I hope you're not spending the fifty grand on a private jet to Paris for that dinner. As long as your happy ass is back to work on Monday, you can do whatever you want. Cheers."

Fifty grand?

There's no way LouAnn would have just offered up fifty grand. I'm not sure how she did it, but I know that Keira is behind it somehow.

I start dinner a few hours later, and when Keira comes home in her frumpy uniform with a scowl on her face, I don't do what I did the first time she did that. I don't hit her with the fridge door and I don't offer her a beer.

I dry my hands on the dish towel, move to the door, and kiss the scowl off her face.

If I had done that move a week ago, it's possible none of this would have happened.

"I got put back on orders," she says seriously.

That's not good, right?

I think being *put back on orders* means the Army's moving her somewhere else.

"Okay," I say slowly. "What does that mean?"

Dear heart: please start beating again.

"Well, for one, it means I'll have to learn a new system of getting around the Pentagon. I'll be working on the *third* floor, not the second floor. And two, I'm hoping it's sort of, kind of, maybe okay that I live here with you. Unless you don't want Jon's bratty little sister hanging all over you."

She begins to remove her clothing. "Sometimes in various stages of undress." She backs me into the corner in the kitchen. "And being bossy." She orders me to remove my clothing. "While eating all of your food." She sneaks a piece of chicken from a plate on the counter.

"You little thief," I say, smacking her on the rear.

My God, she's gorgeous naked.

"You can afford it," she says, a smile tugging at her lips.

"Apparently," I say. "Sergeant Brunette neglected to mention that I got a raise."

"Well," she says coyly, "the raise I'm going for today is the different kind."

And when her hands unbutton my pants, she gets the raise she was looking for.

I turn off the stove as she walks to the bedroom.

She looks back.

What else can I say? I follow her.

Keira

Dillan stands over my shoulder as I type out the e-mail addressed to Jon and Tanner. "You can't begin it with the words, *Don't have a heart attack, but...*" Dillan says.

I laugh. "What do you suggest, then?"

He kisses my neck—a total stalling move as he thinks of an answer—and finally says, "Write, *We now understand what all the fuss is about.* They'll understand."

I type it out and press *send.*

"What is this fuss you speak of?" I ask. "I demand a demonstration."

"Your wish is my command, Sergeant Brunette," Dillan says with a gleam in his eyes as he hops onto the bed.

A wicked thought comes to mind.

"Hold that thought," I say, dodging his outstretched arms, and head to the bathroom.

Opening my makeup satchel, I grab a tube of lipstick and write a note for Dillan on the mirror.

It's nothing elaborate, like what Stacey wrote, but something else.

Last week, he asked me a question that I never answered. I refused to. In fact, we'd made a bet on it and I won, so I technically don't have to answer.

So, with my mauve lipstick, I write 0/0/4 on the mirror. It may take him a few minutes to remember the bet. And when he does, I know he'll ask if *he's* number four, or if four would have been how I answered *last week.*

Obviously, I couldn't predict the future when we made that bet, but I'll leave him guessing.

Sure, I've lived in a man's body, I've dodged an

aggressive woman as she tried to seduce me, and my well-ordered life might have crashed around me, but a girl's got to keep a little mystery in her relationship.

Sometimes, a girl needs a little disorder in her life.

And, as I exit the bathroom and stare at the gorgeous man I've been in love with for the last nine years, I realize I got it.

I got it in spades.

Author Note

Writing can be a solitary profession. However, I am surrounded by amazingly talented women who made this book shine. My editor, Susan Helene Gottfried, who happens to be a gifted writer in her own right and a rock-goddess, loves grammar and editing about as much as I don't. Opposites and all that jazz. It is a relationship made in heaven and I am delighted that I get to work with her.

I'd also like to thank Anita B. Carroll, my cover artist. I mean: look at that gorgeous cover. And the totally cute couple on the front. Her design exceeded my expectations and I can't wait to knock on her door when it's time to design the next book in this series. (Yes, there will be at least three stand-alone books in this series... maybe four.)

I would be remise if I didn't acknowledge Dayle Dermatis. She's a wickedly good proofreader (among other things) who understands widows and orphans and kerning and other bookish-things that make books Look Good. Trust me when I say that this book looks a helluva lot better because of her.

To my sister, Samantha, who is my biggest cheerleader, beta reader, idea sounding board, best friend, and confidant. Thank you for encouraging me.

To Mary and Becky, my initial beta readers, thank you for taking a chance on me. You're my girls.

Finally, and most importantly, to my readers. Holy cow, thank you. Thank you beyond my wildest dreams. I ask that if you enjoyed Collide Into You, please tell a friend. Your mom, or sister, or neighbor, or daughter. Loan them your copy or buy a copy for them. Go onto GoodReads and/or Amazon and leave a review. Readers look to other readers for recommendations, and reviews help discoverability. I would be honored if you helped me spread the word about Collide Into You.

Until the next book... Happy reading!

About the Author

Kelly Washington is a former soldier who now writes in the military romance genre. Past lives include flutist, soldier, trainer, security assistant, intelligence analyst, and senior executive assistant. She and her family call Washington, DC home. Contact her anytime at kellywashwrites@gmail.com or at her website, www.kellywashington.com. Sign up for her "reading room" at www.kellywashington.com/newsletter to receive notices of upcoming releases, previews, and the occasional free short story.

Novels

Falling For Him (The Complete Series)
Falling For You (Vol 1)
Hungry For You (Vol 2)
Ready For You (Vol 3)
The Pale Waters
The Queen of Scarred Heart
The Daughter of Lava
The Priestess of Reclaimed Souls

Short Stories

"Smolder"
"Captive"
"Ignite"
"A Sinful Wife"
"Homecoming"
"Prism of the Crab Gods"
"The Christmas Journey"
"The American Flag of Sergeant Hale Schofield"
"Flowers in Winter"
"Breaking Kayfabe"
"The Wrong Side of the Tracks"

Bonus Material

Long before Keira and Dillan fell in love, Sergeant Justin Hauten and Lieutenant Aaron Parris fell in love. It wasn't love at first sight and it didn't begin easily. You see, crazy, zany, ridiculous things happen around Justin, his buddy Nebraska, and Justin's love interest—Aaron.

Turn the page for an excerpt for **FALLING FOR HIM: A M/M Military Love Story (The Complete Series)**.

Chapter One

The handwritten letter was folded up in his Kevlar pocket. The day was hot, windy, and Staff Sergeant Justin Hauten —a machine gunner, career Army sergeant, built like the Terminator but still a small-town-Texas boy—had a few minutes to kill.

Justin never put things in his pockets, least of all letters, and he figured it was some sort of mistake, or a joke one of the other Sergeants was trying to pull. For the record, Justin had never once fallen for one of their stupid jokes.

He jumped back into the idling Humvee (the driver, Specialist Walker, was taking a piss), pushed his M4 and a camera to his side, and opened up the carefully folded piece of paper. It quickly became apparent what it was.

Justin, it began, *you make me weak. Every time you walk near me, my heart beats double-time. Can you hear it or feel its pulse? My body radiates heat for you and my body, voice, refuse to obey when we talk. Everything about you turns me on. From your muscular body, your green eyes, to how strong and long your fingers are. Are your lips as soft as I imagine them to be? Will your heat match my own should we ever touch? I long to reach out to you, to skim my fingers along your arm, or back, or leg. And more. I want so much more that my hand is shaking as I write this. I've watched you from afar, desired you at a distance, for all these longs months, and I'm taking a chance now. I have to let you know how I feel. I will burst otherwise. I'll stay hidden for now. But soon, very soon, I will confide in you. I hope you will not be disappointed. All Yours, T.*

He read the letter three times and with each reading, his opinion changed. First, he was pretty sure it was a joke. All of his buddies, even his company commander, called him Hotten, based on his physique and his last name. But this letter, the deep confiding, with its secret longing written in each word, told him that it probably wasn't a joke and that one of his buddies had the hots for him.

He looked at the top of the letter. It was dated four months ago.

Justin refolded the letter and placed it back in his pocket. He wasn't sure how to feel.

He looked out over the Afghanistan landscape, pondering. The red dirt, the mud-hut homes, the deep craters left by some roadside bombs, the Afghani peoples' mixed expressions as they passed by, the eager faces of the children wanting chocolate bars or to practice their broken English. And those were the good days. He didn't like thinking about the bad days around here.

"You ready, Hotten?" Specialist Sean "Nebraska" Walker adjusted his sunglasses and inspected himself in the mirror as he got back into the driver's seat. Nebraska was as tall as a lumberjack and built like one, too. Throw on a plaid shirt and he'd be a dead ringer for the old Brawny Paper Towels man, minus the creepy mustache.

"Yeah, Nebraska, let's go."

As the desolate, yet hopeful, scenery went past, Justin wondered who T was and if there were other letters. Did T place the letter in his pocket four months ago, or did he write the letter then but just now put it in his pocket? Nebraska spoke into the two-way radio, informing the command that they were done for the day and en route. A static reply came back.

"You heard that, Hotten?"

"What?"

"The camera. Captain Phillips wants it first thing."

"Right, yeah, I heard." Justin shook his head.

"You alright, man? You look, I dunno, confused about something. You're not getting cold feet, are you?"

His mind went straight to the letter, but Nebraska wouldn't be talking about that, would he?

"What?"

"Seriously, man," the driver whistled. "Something's stuck in your head, but that's your business. I'm talking about the camera. The mission."

"Oh, right. No cold feet. I'm still game." Justin patted the camera sitting in his lap. *As long as it doesn't get us killed.*

The showers were deserted, thank God. Justin stripped down quickly and let the hot water cascade over him. He checked his wrist for the hundredth time, but the white outline of a missing watch made him laugh. He figured it was about midnight.

He had spent the entire day with Nebraska, as usual, taking pictures of the landscape and other landmarks for the commander. So far, the commander was happy with their progress, but he hadn't gotten exactly what was needed just yet. Their mission had begun a month ago. One month left, he thought to himself as he soaped up.

He rubbed the back of his neck, and the muscles screamed at him. Justin turned the water knob all the way to the left and let the scalding water hit the aching muscles and then cascade down his back.

Earlier in the day, another letter had turned up in a notebook he used day in and day out... a letter that wasn't there yesterday. Same handwriting, but dated two months ago. He could remember some of the words.

This is more than a crush. I want to taste you, feel you, kiss you. I love it when you smile.

Justin was beyond flattered. Unlike how civilians thought the military thought about gay men and women, he had never encountered hatred or the lesser treatment of those living under the Don't Ask Don't Tell rules before that rule was recently abolished. One of his former commanders was gay, and everyone knew it. *And he was one of the coolest guys I've ever known,* Justin thought.

He just didn't know how he was supposed to feel toward

the person writing these words to him. He reread the letters as many times as he could get away with—privacy was difficult to come by around here—just to make sure the notes were indeed for him and not for someone else. Justin was pretty easy going and not the type to play things out to the hilt in his mind, but something about the situation combined with this mission set him on edge. He didn't see the scenario ending favorably if he found out who the letter writer was. Did he want to find out?

The shower water was a little less hot now, and it was only a matter of time before his skin pruned up. Plus, any minute now, someone else would come in and steal his solitude.

He wondered more about T. T didn't have to be from his company, though it was more than likely he was. T could be from Kabul at ISAF headquarters, but it was doubtful. His admirer had to have access to his equipment that those at Kabul wouldn't have.

Sergeant Terry Ingram, maybe? God, he hoped not. The man was a sexist jerk and his personality was, well, beyond offensive at all times. What about Lieutenant Tom Ackers, the executive officer? No, he was married with a couple of kids.

Perhaps T was the last name...

Then his mind went in another direction. *Be honest with yourself!* The idea sort of turned him on. It was taboo, new, and intriguing...

A surge went through him.

What would it feel like? To kiss a man, to have his skin covered completely by T? He'd never once thought of this. In his thirty-one years, twelve of which he'd been in the military, he never let the thoughts of another man, let alone a mystery man, enter his thoughts sexually. But had it been there, under the surface?

He tried to think about the girl back home, Julia. His cock swelled a little more, but if he were honest with himself, he would have to admit that he was already slightly hard. He lathered some bar soap and lowered a hand, sliding his palm over himself, then wrapped the hand around his hardness.

He pleasured himself and climaxed rather quickly and intensely, just as the water turned ice cold.

Justin wasn't sure which of the two images—Julia, or T—heightened the experience.

Chapter Three

It was near dusk when he had what he needed. Red and pink streaks ribboned the sky as the sun sunk lower. It was a gorgeous image and one that he would have loved to capture on the camera, but he needed the last bit of sunlight as he dug out his notebook. He motioned for Nebraska to take the camera back to the vehicle as he made a few notes.

Three weeks had gone by, and the commander was beginning to lose patience with him. Three weeks, and three letters—which were getting to him. Justin was both annoyed and aroused by them. The last letter was dated one week ago.

In my dreams, when I touch you, you shiver and beg for more. I'm rubbing your back, hard, digging into your sore neck muscles, when you turn around, push me down, and kiss me like you've never tasted anything so sweet.

But he couldn't discern any odd behavior by any of his friends. The only person showing any behavior beyond the normal was his commander, and Captain Phillips was showing the "I'm pissed at you" kind. At times, the Captain would have an "I'm going to kill you after all of this is over if you don't get what we need" mentality, too.

Suddenly, someone was yelling.

Nebraska.

Justin hauled up to the top of the hill behind him and spotted two M4's and one handgun pointed at Nebraska. Shit!

"Give us the camera," one was shouting at Nebraska. Justin couldn't tell who they were, but they weren't military men. He sprinted down the steep hill, tripped, and fell down the rest. Everything that could have possibly hit him or poke him did. Rocks. His M4. The holstered M9 firearm at his side. Even the pens in his side arm pocket. He counted himself lucky that none of his weapons discharged.

He did his best to stand up, but his right knee wouldn't cooperate and he quickly collapsed. He pulled out his M9 just as one of the three pointed an M4 at him.

"Hello, Hotten," the man said sarcastically. Captain Phillips? "I understand you got what I need?"

Justin's mind whirled. What was the point of this? He was going to give the camera to Captain Phillips tonight. Why go to all these lengths?

"You okay, Nebraska?" Justin asked.

"Think I just crapped in my pants, but, yeah, doing pretty good. You?"

"Not too excited about the turn of events," he said to his friend, then addressed the commander. "You're a son of a bitch, you know that?"

"Insubordination, Staff Sergeant?"

"Figure that's the least of my worries at the moment."

"Instruct your little friend here to hand over the camera and no one gets hurt."

"First, there's nothing little about Nebraska, and second, you're not in a position to make any demands. The way I see it, we have the camera and I have a gun pointed at your head. I'm pretty sure I know which of us is the better shot, Captain."

"Yeah, but what about Nebraska here? He's not exactly a sniper. He's more like a lumbering oaf, tucked into Kevlar like a stuffed sausage."

"Cute," Nebraska muttered. "But he does have a point,

Justin. Not the sausage part, but the shooting part. And really, the other two fellas here, let's not forget about them. I know I haven't. The good captain failed to make introductions."

Justin desperately wanted to look at the two men focused on Nebraska, but he didn't trust that Captain Phillips wouldn't shoot the second he did. The two other men were not in his company, of that he was certain, but other than that, he was at a loss as to who they were.

"Who are your friends, sir?" His knee was beginning to throb and, if he wasn't mistaken, a small amount of blood was trickling down his temple. His whole mouth had a metallic taste. A tooth was loose.

Great, just great.

"I like to call them Mr. A and Mr. B."

Clever. These two were either from the State Department or the CIA. Did they really have to be wearing sunglasses? So cliché. It was practically dark now.

"Back down, Captain Phillips," one of them said as he pointed his weapon down to the ground. "You too, Sergeant Hauten. No one is getting shot today." The other man, probably Mr. B, followed suit and lowered his M4. "Do we have an understanding, gentlemen?"

Justin laughed out loud. "The only reason I have my weapon pointed at Captain Phillips is because he has his pointed at me. Perhaps the reason is obvious to everyone else, but why is Captain Phillips pointing his weapon at me?"

"Captain Phillips, I am ordering you to lower your weapon."

"I want the camera first," the captain said, slightly stuttering. Justin could barely make out the sweat pouring down the man's face.

Justin knew what he had recorded over the last two months on the camera currently hanging around Nebraska's neck, and none of it warranted this type of behavior from the company commander.

"Listen, guys," Justin began. "I don't know what's going on, but this son of a bitch doesn't look like he's going to back down, so perhaps you can do someth—"

A shot rang out and Justin's ears began to buzz. It took a couple of seconds before he realized the captain had just shot him. He actually shot him.

"What the fuck?" Justin screamed at the man. Mr. A, or B, quickly wrestled Captain Phillips to the ground and even handcuffed him. Nebraska was at Justin's side, inspecting him.

His shoulder seared and while he knew he wasn't going to die from a gunshot wound to his shoulder, he was so pissed off that he might black out from a sudden stroke. Justin noticed strange things that he probably wouldn't have noticed otherwise.

Nebraska had thick eyebrows, which were now tightly knit in concentration as he tried to stop the blood flow. Nebraska also had a lot of freckles.

"Jesus Christ, Nebraska. You should wear sunscreen."

"Sure, whatever you say, buddy."

Something banged against his other shoulder: the camera. It was still around Nebraska's neck. A bird screeched in the background. Footsteps, and then he was being carried.

The drive back to the base was the longest and the roughest possible. And not because his shoulder hurt. It hurt like a bitch. It was because Captain Phillips was sitting right beside him, handcuffed, cursing up a storm at the injustice of it all. What an asshole.

It was hell being shot, but the nurses were cute and the drugs felt nice. Justin found out later, after his surgery, that Mr. B confiscated the camera from Nebraska. But not before Nebraska punched him soundly on the jaw.

"My knuckles feel like crap, but that dude deserved it," Nebraska said. He had parked himself in the chair beside Justin's bed two nights ago, after the incident, and refused to leave.

Justin chuckled. "Did Mr. B punch you back?" His friend was sporting a fresh black eye.

"Nope," he smiled, his crooked teeth showing. "It was Mr. A once he realized Mr. B wasn't going to be able to get up on his own."

"Did you find out who they were?"

"I haven't left your side, man, except to take a piss. But I asked around..."

"And..."

"Word is that they are CIA, investigating Captain Phillips on corruption charges or something or another."

"Doesn't sound like a CIA type of operation. We both know what's on that camera. Did it seem like something to shoot one of us over?"

Nebraska laughed and then cupped his face, muttering an ouch. "I dunno, man. Perhaps the man is deranged, or maybe he just hates your guts and needed a small reason to shoot you. Not everyone loves you, man."

"Yeah, yeah." Secretly, Justin hoped that wasn't true.

"Speaking of," Nebraska said and reached into his pocket. "This was dropped off for you." He handed over an envelope, sealed, with his name scrawled on the outside.

Justin recognized the handwriting immediately.

"Whoa," Nebraska whistled. "What's that look for?"

"What look?"

"That look, when you saw the envelope. It was a combination of dread and eagerness. Odd."

Justin shook his head. "It's been an odd few days."

"True that, my friend. So, are you going to read it?"

"Right now?"

"Yes, right now."

"No."

"No?"

"No."

"Holy shit on toast! You know who it's from. You're holding out on me. For months, all I hear about is Julia from back home and now you get this letter and you aren't going to read it in front of me."

Nebraska snatched the letter away from Justin and ripped it open.

"Hey! You gave me a paper cut, you dork." He tried to reach up, but his bandaged shoulder and sore body prevented him from doing so.

"Let me read it for you, my goodly injured friend." Nebraska cleared his throat and began to read. "It's dated yesterday, by the way," he casually mentioned.

"Shhhhh. Keep it down," Justin begged.

"Ohhh. Maybe it is a love letter. One of the nurses, perhaps. There are a few pretty ones around here." He paused and then focused on the letter. "*'Justin, my love, my wounded soul mate.'* Okay, it has to be said," Nebraska said roughly. "This chick has horrible handwriting, and that opening is just corny. But, anyway, back to the letter. *'I desperately long to see you, to ensure that you are safe and in the care of skilled doctors. If I could be at your side, at this moment, as your friend Nebraska is.'* Wait a minute," Nebraska looked closely at Justin. "This is just creepy. It's like you have a stalker."

"I suppose you do, too. You are mentioned, after all," Justin pointed out as he tried to steal the paper back. Anything to keep him from reading the rest of the letter. Nebraska dodged it smoothly. "Just give me the letter. It's, ah, private."

"You, private? My ass is more private than you are."

"I'd prefer it if you didn't read the letter," Justin said through clenched teeth.

"This is too funny. Your face is turning a deep shade of red. It isn't becoming. Calm down or the nurse is going to inject you with insulin or something."

"Fuck!" he muttered under his breath. What he needed was morphine. "Fine. Go ahead."

Nebraska cleared his throat again. "*'Soon I will tell you who I am. I will look into your green eyes and hope to see acceptance, perhaps—if I am lucky—the same feelings in return. Until then, Justin, be well. Yours, T.*'"

Nebraska refolded the letter, his eyes narrowing, and stuffed it back into the envelope. Justin could tell he was thinking, trying to figure out who the letter was from.

"The letter makes it sound like you've received others."

"Yeah. I think this one is number four or five. I've been getting them for about two months now."

"So... not a nurse?"

"I don't think so."

"Someone in the unit?"

Justin nodded.

Nebraska jumped up, clearly excited. "This is completely awesome!"

Justin was stunned that Nebraska wasn't ribbing him about the whole thing.

"Why?"

"Crazy Julia has competition."

"What does that have to do with anything? And don't call her crazy."

"I can't wait to see how this whole thing unfolds. And I plan to be there when it does."

"Interested in taking my spot for me?"

Nebraska just laughed and turned to leave.

"Wait, where you going?"

"*'My dearest Justin,'*" Nebraska mimicked, laughing, but then turned somewhat serious. "I'm hungry as shit, man. See you later."

Everyone deserved a great friend like Nebraska. Before his friend closed the door, he could hear him talking to himself about guys whose name began with T.